Agent in Peril

Alex Gerlis was born in Lincolnshire and worked as a BBC journalist for nearly thirty years. His first novel, *The Best of Our Spies* (2012), has been an Amazon number 1 bestseller and is currently being developed for television serialisation by a major production company. The other books in the Spy Masters series of Second World War espionage novels are: *The Swiss Spy* (2015), *Vienna Spies* (2017) and *The Berlin Spies* (2018). *Prince of Spies* – the first novel in the Prince series, commissioned by Canelo – was published in March 2020, followed by *Sea of Spies*, *Ring of Spies* and *End of Spies*. *Agent in Peril* is the second in the Wolf Pack series and follows the publication of *Agent in Berlin* in November 2021. Alex Gerlis lives in London, is married with two daughters, and is represented by Gordon Wise at the Curtis Brown Literary Agency.

www.alexgerlis.com

Facebook: Alex Gerlis Author

Twitter: @alex_gerlis

www.canelo.co/authors/alex-gerlis/

Also by Alex Gerlis

Spy Masters

The Best of Our Spies
The Swiss Spy
Vienna Spies
The Berlin Spies

The Richard Prince Thrillers

Prince of Spies
Sea of Spies
Ring of Spies
End of Spies

The Wolf Pack Spies

Agent in Berlin
Agent in Peril

ALEX GERLIS
AGENT IN PERIL

CANELO

First published in the United Kingdom in 2022 by

Canelo
Unit 9, 5th Floor
Cargo Works, 1–2 Hatfields
London, SE1 9PG
United Kingdom

A CIP catalogue record for this book is available from the British Library.

Print ISBN 978 1 80436 048 4
Ebook ISBN 978 1 80032 157 1

Look for more great books at www.canelo.co

Printed and bound in Great Britain by Clays Ltd, Elcograf S.p.A.

1

Main Characters

Principal Characters

Jack Miller American journalist & British agent

Sophia von Naundorf British agent

Barnaby Allen (Barney) MI6 officer

Piers Devereux Barney's boss at MI6

Sir Roly Pearson British Intelligence Chief

Basil Remington-Barber MI6 officer, Berne

Noel Moore MI6 officer, Berne

British Characters

Tom Gilbey MI6 officer

Lord Swalcliffe Government scientific adviser

Air Vice-Marshal Frank Hamilton Head of RAF Intelligence Branch

Group Captain Martin Marlow RAF Bomber Command

Flying Officer Lawrence Reed RAF officer shot down over Ruhr

Wing Commander Andrew Allen 'A. A.' – Barney's cousin

Philippe Moreau British agent in France

Squadron Leader Harry Wright 617 Squadron, RAF

Reg British security officer, Geneva

Bert British security officer, Geneva

Flight Sergeant Graham Crown Wireless operator, RAF

Polish Characters

Roman Loszynski (Dawid Fiszer) Scientist from Poznań

Lea Loszynski wife of Roman

Max Loszynski son of Roman and Lea

Raisa Loszynski daughter of Roman and Lea

Piotr Drobiński Polish diplomat, London

Henryk Kamiński agent of The Poznań Group

Bolesław Piotrowski Poznań Group agent in Poland

Kapitan Stanisław Makowski RAF 303 Squadron

Major Witold Szymański friend of Roman, Poznań

General Brygady Stanisław Wiśniewski Air Vice Marshal, Polish Air Force

Marek Weiss ZOB contact Warsaw ghetto

Zhenia Krakowski (Helena Kamińska) ZOB agent

Konrad Lubnauer airport manager, Poznań

Aleksander Ładoś Polish Legation, Berne

Juliusz Kühl Polish Legation, Berne

Zofia Żegota, Warsaw

Andrzej Żegota, Krakow

German Characters

SS Brigadeführer Karl-Heinrich von Naundorf late husband of Sophia

Harald Fuchs (Rudi) SS officer, Berlin

Professor Hans-Peter Schmid prisoner at Steinwache, Dortmund

Gisela Haussmann sister of Hans-Peter Schmid

Father Albrecht Priest near Tübingen

Dr Otto Kurz Gestapo officer, Poznań

Bruno skipper of the *Elfriede*

Dora wife of Bruno

Paul *Elfriede* crew

Emil *Elfriede* crew

Axel chandler, Duisburg

Kriminaldirektor Klaus Braun Kripo, Duisburg

Kriminalinspektor Franz Lindner Gestapo, Düsseldorf

Irma contact of Jack's in Dortmund

'Arthur' doctor in Dortmund

Lotte agent in Gelsenkirchen

Rainer Kühn hotel manager, Duisburg

Siegfried Schroth actor in Düsseldorf

Swiss Characters

Johann Burch banker in Zürich

Harald Mettler clerk at Swiss Embassy, Berlin

Felix agent in Düsseldorf

Christoph train guard

Fritz plumber, Berne

Russian Characters

A. I. Stepanov (Arkady) NKVD Commissar, Berne

Leytenant Mikhail Danielovich Marshak Red Army officer, Krakow

Polkovnik Krupkin NKGB officer, Krakow

Nikolai Soviet Legation, Berne

Svetlana Soviet Legation Berne

Others

Pavol Slovakian resistance

The Wolf

The wolf makes a perfect spy because it is such an adaptable creature, able to function equally effectively within a pack or on its own.

It isn't uncommon for a wolf to travel long distances away from the pack, often as far as five hundred miles. It may have to do this to find a partner or a new territory.

Sometimes the wolf will travel long distances through hostile territory to escape danger, but on other occasions it will make such a journey in the full knowledge that it is walking towards extreme peril.

But whether in its home territory or having travelled, whether in a pack or alone, the wolf remains a formidable creature, its intelligence and resourcefulness easily underestimated.

The wolf will operate from the shadows, its glowing eyes seeing everything.

And its ability to spy undiminished.

Part One

Prologue

Poznań, Poland
June 1938

'That little man over there… you mean to say that's *him*?'

Professor Roman Loszynski did his best to ensure the group of men talking about him didn't realise he could hear them. He was far enough away for them to assume that. But he objected to being described as 'little'. Certainly, another two or three more inches would do no harm, but he'd always assumed he was near enough average height.

'Yes, General Brygady, sir, that is him.'

'Good Lord, I wasn't expecting him to be one of… *them*. He looks like a tailor!'

'I can assure you, sir, Loszynski is one of the finest…'

Loszynski missed the last few words and turned briefly to look towards the men, an innocent smile playing across his face. The fact he could hear them from so far away was due in part to the fact that the wind on the apron at Poznań–Ławica airport was blowing strongly in his direction, carrying their words an unlikely distance. The wind and his mother: she'd died when he was seven and he'd only ever known her speak in little more than a whisper. Her legacy to him was that from an early age his hearing had become unnaturally acute. His childhood nickname had been *nietoperz*.

The bat.

The group was walking slowly towards him now. His friend Major Witold Szymański was in front with the General Brygady, the man Witold warned him about, the one who'd just described him as 'one of them'.

3

He recalled Witold's warning. 'He's one of the most important men in the Polish Air Force, Roman – please don't be put off by his… manner. You'll find he's blunt – and he has… old-fashioned views.'

'You mean he doesn't like Jews, Witold?'

'Don't worry, Roman, as soon as he hears about our project and your role in it, he'll be fine. You just need to be calm and not rise to his bait.'

The group came closer: Major Szymański, the air force marshal Roman had already taken a disliking to, Roman's good friend Lieutenant Stanisław Makowski, two men from PZL, the leading aircraft manufacturer in Poland, and Roman's colleague from the university, Bolesław Piotrowski, doing his best to keep in the background as usual.

'Sir, may I have the pleasure of introducing you to Professor Roman Loszynski from Poznań University? Roman, this is General Brygady Stanisław Wiśniewski, Air Vice Marshall of the Polish Air Force.'

Wiśniewski nodded at the professor, who reached out to shake hands.

'Professor Roman Loszynski is one of our most brilliant Polish academics in the field of electronics, sir.'

The Air Vice Marshal huffed. 'Do you mean one of the most brilliant Polish academics or one of the most brilliant academics in Poland? There is a difference, you know.'

'That may well be the case, sir, but Professor Loszynski is proving to be of enormous help in critical aspects relating to the development of the PZL.37. More specifically, sir, he is responsible for some of the most important work relating to the bombing capability and effectiveness of the new plane.'

Major Szymański paused as another aircraft taxied near to them and the group huddled closer to shield themselves from the noise and the draught. General Brygady Wiśniewski nodded, not taking his eyes off the professor, trying to work out how much he trusted him.

'It's too noisy out here,' he said eventually, as if annoyed that should be the case on an airfield.

And the wind, said someone else and Szymański remarked it was an ill wind and the group laughed in a knowing manner, because that was all people talked about these days – the ill wind buffeting Europe, particularly from Germany and coming towards Poland. The country had only been independent since 1919 and a constant topic of nervous conversation was how long it would remain so: how long would Hitler allow it to remain so.

They adjourned to the boardroom, where the walls were covered with diagrams of the PZL.37 in various stages of development.

General Brygady Wiśnicwski settled himself in the leather chair reserved for him and lit a large cigar and accepted a glass of vodka from a tray being passed round the room. He made a joke about not drinking and flying and everyone laughed, some rather too enthusiastically.

As they settled down, Roman Loszynski noticed the group had been joined by the airport manager, a rotund man called Konrad Lubnauer, who had a habit of appearing where he was least welcome, like this meeting. He was a member of Poznań's sizeable German minority and spoke with that distinctive accent. Lubnauer sat at the end of the table, next to Lieutenant Makowski. The tray of vodka glasses was alongside him and he leaned over to help himself to first one drink and then another.

Szymański asked one of the men from PZL to give a brief update of where they were and repeated the word 'brief' as the man pushed his chair back noisily and stood in a formal position, an officer addressing his troops.

He spoke of how the PZL.37 had been in development since late 1934 and early prototypes had been made during 1935: progress had been good, if one took into account the inevitable ups and downs of aircraft development, and in June 1936 the first flight of the PZL.37 prototype had taken place successfully.

'You mean, it didn't crash!' The Air Vice Marshall laughed and asked for another vodka to be passed to him, and the man from

PZL looked put out that his carefully prepared presentation had been disrupted.

'Indeed, sir. Production of the PZL.37 commenced soon after that, though we continue to modify and improve the aircraft. As you can see from the diagrams and photographs, sir, the PZL.37 is a twin-engined aeroplane, designed as a medium bomber, constructed from metal. It has a four-man crew. We now feel—'

'Perhaps, General Brygady, if I may—' said Major Szymański.

'What you want, Szymański, is for me to commit the air force to ordering God knows how many of these planes, which look nice enough, without us being sure of exactly what benefit they'll be to us.'

Major Szymański indicated to Lieutenant Makowski to pass another vodka to the air vice marshal. 'We are extremely impressed with the PZL.37, sir. We believe it has the potential to be one of the most outstanding bombers in the world: we are of the view that it is far in advance of any comparable aircraft. In the current difficult situation, sir, we would all agree that it is vital that Poland has every means at its disposal to defend and protect itself, and this aircraft would give us a significant advantage. Its standard bomb load is twenty bombs, totalling 4850 pounds, though we're hoping this load can be increased to around 5700 pounds. Even with such a payload the PZL.37 will have a speed of around two hundred and fifty miles per hour and a range approaching sixteen hundred miles with...'

Major Szymański paused to catch his breath and everyone round the table watched General Brygady Wiśniewski. He nodded his head and Roman Loszynski thought he heard him mutter, 'Impressive.'

'And the purpose of today is to fill me with vodka so that I agree to the Polish Air Force buying hundreds of these wonderful aircraft, the most marvellous plane in the world?'

'The purpose of today, sir, is to appraise you of an important development in connection with the PZL.37, which we think can help ensure it is the most effective bomber in the world.'

'That's quite a claim, Szymański.'

'I know, sir. An important feature of the development of military aircraft since the end of the Great War has been the way aircraft have been designed with specific roles in mind: broadly speaking, this means fighters and bombers. By their nature, bombers tend to be slow and lack manoeuvrability but perhaps their biggest drawback is that dropping bombs from an aircraft isn't a very accurate business.'

'You can say that again.'

'However, we believe that we may well have the prospect of going a long way to solve this issue with the PZL.37. This is where Professor Loszynski comes in. Roman, perhaps if you'd care to explain?'

Loszynski remained seated as he spoke, leaning forward to address his remarks directly to the senior officer, who was sitting across the table from him.

'As Witold says, sir, ensuring bombs hit their target has long been a problem. It's not surprising really: if you imagine an aircraft flying at twenty thousand feet and at two hundred and fifty miles an hour dropping a bomb weighing the best part of two hundred and fifty pounds – well, it's asking an awful lot for that to be accurate. If I may give an example: imagine a house in the middle of a large field. Even if a bomber flies very low – below ten thousand feet – the chances of it hitting the house are remote. The bomb landing in the right field would be some achievement.

'The Department of Advanced and Applied Electronics at Poznań University was asked to see if we could develop a solution to this and my colleague, Mr Bolesław Piotrowski here, and I have been working on this.'

Professor Loszynski asked Lieutenant Makowski to pass a case to him. From it he removed two boxes: one the size of a biscuit tin, the other smaller.

As he sorted them, he noticed the airport manager, Lubnauer, making extensive notes, which seemed odd, though perhaps no odder than him being there in the first place. Loszynski placed the two boxes in front of him and laid out a long electrical lead and an antenna alongside them.

'We call these the Tatra boxes, sir, it was Bolesław's idea.'

'If I may explain?' said Bolesław. 'You may be aware that in the Tatra Mountains they have a tradition of making highly intricate wooden boxes. They are beautiful to look at, but more to the point, the boxes are also a puzzle: they can only be opened by working out the very clever mechanics – such as twisting one leg of a box one way and another leg in the opposite direction. We felt the secretive nature of these boxes would provide a good name for this secret project, sir.'

'This is very much a prototype, but...' Roman Loszynski prised the top open to reveal an array of wires soldered to various electronic parts. 'The idea is to place the larger box as close as possible to the target. If you look here, there's an opening to connect the lead which then runs from the box and connects to an antenna, like the one here. The idea is for the box to send out a signal that is transmitted via the antenna. The smaller box here is to be placed in the PZL.37. This box receives the signal from the Tatra box on the ground: when that signal is of a specified strength, the bombardier knows that is the optimum time to release the bombs.'

General Brygady Wiśniewski indicated the box should be passed to him. He looked at it carefully and lifted it up as if to weigh it. 'It's big, isn't it?'

'Yes, sir.'

'Surely something like this would need to be much smaller, much less obtrusive? If it's to be hidden in a place that is intended to be bombed, then something this size will stand out.'

'It would indeed, sir, and we are currently working on scaling it down. And that's not the only problem: the antenna we are currently working with is five feet high, which is clearly too much. We need to get that down to two feet at the most. But there's another issue, sir.'

'Another one?'

'The maximum height at which the PZL.37 flies is twenty-three thousand feet. However, currently the signal from the main Tatra box extends no higher than twelve thousand feet. That is very low for a bomber to be expected to fly over a target, which is when it is most vulnerable to anti-aircraft fire. We are working on extending the range of the signal to be much closer to twenty thousand feet, though that is proving to be problematic.'

'And how long will all this take you?'

Roman Loszynski looked at Bolesław Piotrowski who spoke next. 'It's hard to say, sir, because this is a matter of trial and error – making adjustments, testing them and then going on to the next adjustment. I need to put Professor Loszynski on this full time and also employ a team of technicians to work with him and, ideally, we need our own dedicated workshop for the project.'

'So how long, Piotrowski?'

'Perhaps a year, sir, before we are certain that every aspect of this works.'

'A year? Can Poland really afford the luxury of waiting a year? Look at the way that madman in Berlin behaves: I doubt we have that long.'

Piotrowski coughed and said he quite understood but with the right funding it would...

To everyone's surprise the air vice marshal nodded and said he quite understood: this would be ground-breaking if it came off and it was important not to rush it. 'Please send me a detailed budget by the end of the week. And I'll require monthly updates.'

As the meeting ended, he called Loszynski over. 'I'm very encouraged by this.'

'Thank you, sir.' Loszynski noticed that Lubnauer the airport manager had appeared next to him.

'You're going to be around to see this through, I hope, Loszynski?'

The professor was confused by the question, but replied that he would be.

'Good: I hope you're not planning on going anywhere, eh?'

Chapter 1

'I need to see your papers, please, Frau von Naundorf.'

The train had only just pulled out of the station in Stuttgart and the man who'd introduced himself as a Gestapo officer said it was a routine check, but Sophia had noticed she was the only one of the four passengers in her first-class compartment being checked. Her name had clearly been passed on to him by the *Bahnschutzpolizei* officer standing behind him. The railway policeman had first questioned her just before the train arrived in Nuremberg and she thought he looked suspicious at the time, but she'd put it down to her being understandably nervous and, in any case, nothing had happened.

Until now.

She smiled sweetly as if this was an inconvenience but said of course she understood and opened her handbag, removing the folder containing all her papers, handing them one by one to the Gestapo. Her identity card – the *Kennkarte*; her passport – the *Reisepass*, and then the all-important travel documents: the permit allowing her to leave the Reich, the one allowing her to re-enter it on the return journey and the letter signed by SS Brigadeführer Konrad Busch saying that Frau von Naundorf was travelling to Zürich on official business and all assistance should be accorded to her. The letter carried an impressive array of official stamps, though seemingly not quite enough to impress the Gestapo officer.

'May I ask the nature of your business in Zürich, Frau von Naundorf?'

She tried not to look too uncomfortable. The compartment was overheated and as she'd decided it would be safer to travel with just one suitcase, she was wearing her fur coat, which she was reluctant to remove because of the amount of jewellery she wore underneath it.

'It is confidential business.'

The Gestapo officer said nothing, appearing to wait for her to elaborate.

'It should be enough for you that this business is on behalf of the SS.' The other passengers in the compartment all shifted uncomfortably. 'But if you remain unsatisfied then I suggest you contact SS Brigadeführer Konrad Busch at Prinz Albrecht Strasse. I'm sure he'll be able to put your mind at rest.'

Another smile, this one not so sweet.

The Gestapo officer said very well, he was only doing his job and he wished her a pleasant journey, but for the remainder of it Sophia von Naundorf felt like a fugitive.

And as they got closer to the Swiss border, she began to realise that was indeed what she now was: a fugitive.

It had been pitch dark when Sophia von Naundorf first woke three days earlier, on the morning of Tuesday 9 March. She'd glanced across the empty side of the bed to the large clock with a pale green luminous dial on the bedside table.

It was two o'clock.

Although the night was silent, she had a Berliner's first thought on waking at such an hour: air raids. She left the bed, pulled back the curtain and lifted the blackout blind just enough to see a vast, dark sky, hardly lit by a new moon and undisturbed by searchlight beams or enemy aircraft. The last major air raid had been exactly two weeks earlier. Although she'd been out of the city that night, it was still the main topic of conversation, though one only conducted in hushed tones and with those they trusted.

A neighbour confided in her that according to her brother, the city had been attacked by nearly three hundred British aircraft. The wife of one of her husband's SS colleagues – who thought of her as a friend – told her she'd heard that more than seven hundred civilians had been killed and Sophia had heard that same figure from other people.

What if they bring a thousand bombers, Sophia? Heinrich says that could happen any day – or night!

She poured herself a glass of water and plumped her pillow but couldn't get back to sleep. She dozed a bit between four and five and at five-thirty wondered about getting up to make herself some tea, but her maid was a light sleeper and the last thing she wanted over the next few days was to give her maid any grounds for suspicion.

It was hardly a surprise she couldn't sleep. She'd lived dangerously enough over the past few months, since the Englishman had arrived in Berlin. But that was nothing compared to the risk she was about to take. First, she needed to arrange the meeting and then handle it with great care, so as not to arouse any undue suspicion.

It was no surprise she'd hardly slept.

–

She waited until ten o'clock: Konrad's secretary answered the telephone in a tone that suggested no phone call from a woman could possibly be important.

'I'm afraid Brigadeführer Busch is busy all day: he's in Potsdam tomorrow, Thursday is booked up and Friday is his physiotherapy day so—'

'Please inform Brigadeführer Busch that my name is Sophia von Naundorf. My husband is SS Brigadeführer Karl-Heinrich von Naundorf. We are personal friends. I'm sure Konrad can spare me half an hour today, preferably this morning.'

During the brief silence that followed she could picture the secretary, the thin smile on her stern face vanishing once she realised she was dealing with the wife an SS general. Sophia asked the secretary for her name and the woman didn't give it but did say it just so happened she'd spotted a gap in Brigadeführer Busch's diary and would she be able to make a meeting at half past eleven?

–

'Sophia – Sophia, how marvellous to see you! You look as wonderful as ever.'

She smiled the sweetest smile she could manage, which took some effort. Konrad Busch had joined the SS at the same time as her husband, ten years previously, and the two men had become good friends. Karl Heinrich assumed they were family friends too, though Sophia was surprised how well she managed to conceal her distaste for Busch and his wife. While her own husband was undoubtedly handsome and cut an imposing figure, Konrad Busch was an unattractive man: his head was disproportionately large in relation to his body and his face was pale and pockmarked and his nose looked as if it were broken. He was a brute and a bully and Sophia had long thought his behaviour was a conscious attempt to compensate for his repulsive looks. She'd noticed a lot of that.

'But please, Sophia, do sit down. You'll understand if I don't get up.'

He held up a walking stick with a silver handle by way of an explanation and Sophia nodded that of course she understood. Konrad Busch had been serving with her husband in the 6th Army during the Battle of Stalingrad. He'd been evacuated in January after being shot in the leg. He seemed to recover soon enough and now served behind a desk at the SS headquarters on Prinz Albrecht Strasse.

Sophia paused before sitting down, just long enough to unbutton her best coat, the one that tapered sharply at the waist to accentuate her figure. The fur-trim collar shielded some of her face and removing the coat felt like a magician's revelation. She handed the coat to the secretary and brushed her dress as she sat down. She'd taken care with how she dressed, fully aware of how Busch leered at her. Her low-cut dress showed more cleavage than she would normally allow on a March morning and certainly in front of Busch. She was wearing expensive Vol de Nuit perfume by Guerlain and she could sense that Busch had already caught the scent.

'And how are dear Hannelore and your wonderful children?'

'They are very well, thank you, Sophia.'

Hannelore Busch was his equally fanatical wife, an unpleasant woman with five children, who never missed an opportunity to pointedly ask Sophia when she was planning to start her own family.

Busch asked if there was any news of Karl-Heinrich and she said she'd heard nothing and feared the worse. Busch looked awkward, in the manner of someone uncomfortable in dealing with bad news. He muttered something about Karl-Heinrich being so smart that if anyone could get out of there he could and Sophia replied this seemed unlikely seeing the surrender was over a month ago and... She paused, shook her head and bit her lip and Busch told her not to be defeatist and she did her best not to glare at him. Was there anything he could do to help, he asked?

Actually, there was, said Sophia, and edged her chair closer to the Brigadeführer's desk. She noticed his bulbous nose twitch as he caught her scent again and his lips looked moist as the tip of his tongue poked through them. She lowered her voice and spoke in a calm but urgent manner.

'Karl-Heinrich always regarded you as his most loyal and trustworthy friend. Over the past few years Karl-Heinrich had collected gold, jewellery and money from Jews – as I'm sure you're aware. He deposited this in a bank in Zürich.

'Karl -Heinrich told me if anything ever happened to him, I was to go to Zürich to collect everything he's deposited in a bank there and bring it back here. I think I should do that now, but I'll need papers to allow me to leave the Reich to get into Switzerland.'

She added that she needed Konrad's help in obtaining the right papers: ideally papers that would enable her to leave the Reich and return to it and if the papers could indicate she was travelling on official business – maybe for the SS, who knew – that would be a great help and very much appreciated. She edged a bit closer, her hand on his desk and noticed he was doing everything he could to avoid staring too obviously at her breasts.

Busch hesitated as he rearranged the pens on his desktop and turned a lamp on and off. It was quite something she was asking, he said.

'I realise that, but here's a lot of gold, Konrad, he got it from Jews before he sent them on their holidays in the East! I know he would wish you to have some of it, as a small token of his respect for you.'

'Do you know how much is in the bank?'

'I'm not too sure, Konrad, but the last time we spoke Karl-Heinrich estimated it could be worth as much as twenty thousand Reichsmarks. I have no doubt Karl-Heinrich would wish me to give you something in the region of five thousand Reichsmarks… as a mark of gratitude.'

Fat beads of perspiration had gathered on Busch's forehead and he made a panting sound. His tongue ran across his lips and he gave the appearance of a child being let loose in a toy shop and told to take what he wanted. He bent down to retrieve something from a desk drawer and she undid one button on her blouse, hating herself as she did so.

'This will take me a few days to organise, Sophia. It's what… Tuesday today… maybe if you return here on Friday, I can have the papers then?'

'Your secretary said you're not here that day, it's your physiotherapy day.'

'Of course, I quite forgot. Perhaps next week?'

'I think the sooner I withdraw everything the better, don't you agree?'

Konrad said he did, though he gave the impression that this was all an inconvenience, too much like hard work and not without an element of risk and for a moment or two tapped a pencil on his desk and then seemed to remember Sophia's promise about him receiving something. He smiled, revealing a set of yellow teeth with a couple of gaps, and said very well, Thursday then – but in the afternoon, please.

–

As she left Prinz Albrecht Strasse she compiled a mental list of what she needed to do between now and Friday. Normally she'd have written everything down in her small leather-bound notebook, but this was not a list to be committed to paper.

From Prinz Albrecht Strasse she turned into Saarland Strasse and then walked the short distance to Anhalter Bahnhof where there was only a short queue at the first-class ticket counter.

'There is a train to Zürich which departs at eight o'clock on Friday morning.'

'And it arrives at what time?'

The ticket clerk looked slightly uncomfortable as he explained that the train was scheduled to arrive at seven that evening. But…

'But what?'

'But there are often… disruptions these days.'

Sophia said she quite understood, and yes, please, could she book a first-class ticket to Zürich for the Friday morning, returning the following Tuesday morning.

Back in her apartment in Charlottenburg she told her maid that, as she was going to be away, she could have a few days off, from the Thursday afternoon to Tuesday morning.

She started to sort what she was going to take with her. As she was only supposed to be in Switzerland for five days, she knew it could look suspicious if she took too much, so she decided to take one medium-sized suitcase along with a large handbag.

On Wednesday morning she managed to get a message to Berne telling them they may not hear from her for a while. She didn't want to risk saying more than that.

She returned to Prinz Albrecht Strasse on the Thursday afternoon to collect her permits and suggested to Konrad that perhaps he'd like to come to her apartment the following Wednesday to collect his share. The SS man could barely contain his excitement. When she returned home, the maid had already left. Sophia packed the suitcase. Karl-Heinrich's diary – perhaps the most important item she was taking – would go in the handbag.

–

It was still light when the train approached Singen on the German side of the border. Apart from the constant fear of being pulled aside and asked to leave the train and the sense of being a fugitive, the journey had been long but unremarkable and the disruptions the ticket clerk had referred to – a euphemism for the damage caused by Allied bombing – had not happened.

The train was held outside the station for a good twenty minutes before the Border Police – the *Grenzpolizei* – slowly worked their way through the carriages for one final check.

Reisepass... permits... Kennkarten...

When they reached her compartment, the policemen asked each of the four passengers to open their bags and the two men searched each one, though Sophia was sure they paid more attention to her suitcase. An officer put on a pair of leather gloves before checking her suitcase: within a matter of seconds, he held up the silver candlesticks her friend Esther had entrusted to her for safekeeping before her family fled Germany.

'What are these?'

'My husband wishes me to sell them in Zürich. He obtained them as part of his duties in the SS.'

The *Bahnschutzpolizei* officer appeared unsure how to press the matter. Sophia smiled politely throughout and spoke in a calm voice, resisting any temptation to pull her husband's rank on them.

The Border policeman asked to look at her papers once more and had just got out his notebook when the train jolted sharply as its brakes were released and from the corridor came a shout that they were to get a move on.

A quarter of an hour later the train was in Schaffhausen on the Swiss side of the border and the officials there were markedly more polite.

She relaxed slightly as the train hurried south to Zürich.

She allowed herself a few minutes of silent joy at leaving Germany, but it was short lived.

She still felt like a fugitive.

And she realised she would probably remain one for the remainder of her life.

Chapter 2

Switzerland
March 1943

Three nights in Zürich, three different hotels.

Sophia von Naundorf hadn't planned her stay like that: in truth she'd not given much thought to where she'd stay, other than she felt it would be safer not to book a hotel in advance. She wanted all trace of her to vanish once she entered Switzerland.

When you're a lone wolf your trail should be unpredictable: follow nature's course, leave no trace.

The train had pulled into Zürich Hauptbahnhof just before half past seven that Friday evening and she followed the crowd to the main exit. Even on the station concourse the contrast with Berlin was striking. People seemed calm and healthy, no one looked edgy or suspicious and some people even smiled, with a brief nod of the head as they passed each other by. It reminded her of Berlin a dozen years before. It all felt so civilised and what was most noticeable was the almost complete absence of uniforms.

Outside the station she spotted a large hotel on Bahnhof Strasse and decided it looked fine – how could a hotel in the centre of Zürich not be fine? The hotel was the St Gotthard and inside it didn't feel as refined as she'd expected and the receptionist was less than welcoming.

'Do you have a reservation?'

'No, I've travelled today from Berlin and I was hoping...'

The receptionist's face hardened at the word 'Berlin' and she sighed as she looked at a chart on the desk. 'I have a room at eleven francs a night, including breakfast. If you wish to book dinner now that is a further five francs.'

The receptionist pushed a registration card towards Sophia.

'And the room has a bathroom?'

'No, all those rooms are booked.'

Sophia was too exhausted after the journey to look elsewhere and she realised the sheer size of the hotel at least offered a reassuring anonymity. She used the *Kennkarte* she had with her in the name of Bertha Schmitt to register. Bertha had been with them as a maid for a few weeks the previous year but it had not quite worked out. She was a nice enough girl but rather too absent-minded. A few weeks after she left, Sophia had found her identity card with her old address in Schönefeld and had kept it as she didn't have a forwarding address.

She checked out of the St Gotthard on the Saturday morning and decided to try and find somewhere to stay by the lake. She hoped the water would have a calming effect. Hotel Eden au Lac on Uto-Quai seemed ideal: she booked a room overlooking the Zürichsee for fourteen francs. That afternoon she went for a long walk by the lake, her mood as reflective as the sun catching every movement on the surface of the water.

The sense of being a fugitive was still there but now she began to feel an overwhelming calmness about what she'd done and what she was planning to do. She was absolutely certain she'd chosen the right path. It was to her eternal regret that she remembered so little of her mother, who'd died more than twenty years ago when Sophia was just ten. She could never be certain which of the few memories she had of her were accurate and which were down to the imagination of a grieving daughter.

One memory she did retain in sharp relief was of them going for a walk in the park, not long before her mother went into hospital. It may have been their last walk together and although Sophia had had no idea whatsoever of what was to come, she somehow must have caught her mother's portentous mood.

'Always be a good girl, Sophia: always do what Papa tells you and obey your teachers.' She had a clear recollection of her mother gripping her gloved hand very tightly at that point and they'd walked on in silence for quite a while. 'And... always do the right thing, Sophia. Don't be swayed by people you don't trust or who you know are in the wrong: be modest and grateful. Try not to complain or worry unduly about small matters.'

Her mother had said nothing for some time and, looking back, Sophia realised she must have been too upset to talk. When she had continued, she'd looked directly at Sophia, who'd noticed her mother's eyes were heavy with tears. 'If you can't be honest with yourself, my darling, you cannot expect other people to be honest to you.'

She thought of the photograph of her mother, the first item she'd put aside to pack earlier that week. It was a poignant photograph: taken just a few months before her mother's death, when she must have been aware of her impending fate. Her mother was sitting in an armchair in their lounge, staring out of the window, the diffuse light from the window catching her face. When Sophia packed the photograph the previous day, she decided to remove it from its heavy frame – she needed the space – and for the first time saw her mother's writing on the reverse.

As soon as you trust yourself, you will know how to live.

It was a quote from Goethe and it afforded her some comfort, particularly written in her mother's hand.

She trusted herself.

She'd come to realise that remaining in Berlin was no longer an option. She had to flee Germany. She knew her work as a British agent operating in the heart of the Reich exposed her to the most extreme danger: a clandestine life was one measured in weeks and months rather than years. She'd been operating as a British agent for nearly two and a half years and she'd been riding her luck for most of that time.

And she knew too that she must do the right thing, as her mother had urged her all those years ago. The right thing was not just leaving the Reich. It was also continuing to work against it by remaining a British agent. But before that, the right thing also entailed that she did what she could to ensure her husband was brought to justice. She wasn't even sure if Karl-Heinrich was still alive. Tens of thousands of the German soldiers defending Stalingrad had perished, but hundreds of thousands had been taken prisoner and her sense was that her husband would have been cunning enough to make sure he was one of those.

Doing the right thing would mean getting hold of everything Karl-Heinrich had stolen. It would mean helping to hunt him down. It would mean behaving like a hungry wolf.

And then she would know how to live.

–

She checked out of the Hotel Eden au Lac the following morning and took a taxi to the centre of the city. She asked the driver to go through Paradeplatz so she could see where she'd be going the following day and noticed a smart-looking hotel across the road from the bank and asked the driver to drop her there.

A plan was forming in her mind.

The Savoy Baur en Ville was a smart hotel, set in the heart of the Swiss banking industry and very much a place where bankers would feel comfortable, which was to say that the place was as quiet as a monastery, any conversations that did take place were conducted *sotto voce* and eye contact was clearly regarded as a faux pas. The other guests – the few she saw – were so discreet it was hard to tell their nationality.

Bertha Schmitt paid fifteen francs for a room at the front of the building, overlooking Paradeplatz.

The following morning, she took breakfast in her room and sat at the window, from where she spent the next hour observing the bank. She watched as the staff entered, all so smartly dressed, all so polite. Most importantly, she spotted nothing suspicious. After the last couple of years she felt qualified to notice anything out of the ordinary, the subtle and almost invisible warning signs that all was not as it should be: her every sense attuned to pick up the person hanging around to no purpose, spending too much time observing passers-by, to spot the cars parked nearby with the driver waiting and watching, to notice whether the entrance of that building somehow seemed different – it was hard for her to put her finger on it – than that of nearby buildings. She was the lone wolf once more, its eyes darting to spot any sign of danger, every sense strained to spot the right opportunity.

Everything seemed normal, so she left the room, leaving a 'Do Not Disturb' sign on the door. Following the receptionist's directions, she walked up Bahnhofstrasse to the Jelmoli department store, which was full of items that were simply unavailable in Berlin, and all so beautifully presented. She soon found exactly what she had in mind.

She returned to the hotel and prepared for her visit to the bank. At eleven o'clock she found herself at the entrance of Bank Leu, the building she'd been so carefully observing that morning. One of the doormen greeted her politely and escorted her to an upper floor office, the room wood-panelled and heavily carpeted, lit only by a lamp on the desk of a man perhaps in his fifties who looked very much as she imagined a Swiss banker would appear, though a similarity to a funeral director also came to mind.

Johann Burch was formality personified, though perfectly polite. He said nothing as he carefully studied all the documents she'd passed to him.

She was Sophia von Naundorf now and he looked intently at her identity papers: the *kennkarte*; her *Reisepass*; three further documents proving that Sophia von Naundorf lived at the address in Potsdammer Strasse in Berlin.

A brief nod of the head indicated he was indeed satisfied she was who she said she was.

'And the other papers, please, Frau von Naundorf.'

She handed over the document with all the details of account held in the name of Karl-Heinrich von Naundorf, along with another document signed by her husband giving his wife full access to the account upon provision of the correct code.

Herr Burch nodded once more and opened a folder on his desk and spent a few minutes studying its contents, evidently comparing them to the documents she'd presented. The room was utterly silent apart from the sounds coming from an ornate gold carriage clock on the mantelpiece and Herr Burch's breathing and occasional coughing. He picked up his telephone and muttered something about coming in and as they waited – for a good three or four minutes – he said nothing, looking first at her and then at his folder before taking out a cigar, which he twirled in his fingers before placing it unlit in a large glass ashtray.

You know how much I trust you, my dearest? The only circumstances in which you can access this account is if something has happened to me and you need the funds. I know you will not take advantage of my trust in you.

The man who'd been summoned entered. From the way the two men acknowledged each other she imagined the other person was Herr Burch's superior. At no stage did he acknowledge Sophia, but instead concentrated on the paperwork, nodding frequently before saying that everything was indeed in order and Herr Burch could proceed.

'The final stage, Frau von Naundorf, is the code. Please write it on this blank sheet of paper and fold it before returning it to me.'

He handed her a blank sheet of paper and a pen. She hesitated, recalling her husband's careful instructions.

Memorise this code, Sophia. Never write it down.

She wrote down nine numbers: 2-1-8-4-0-3-5-8-4

She slid the folded paper to Herr Burch who opened it and then showed it to the other man. Neither said a word but looked intently at her.

There's a further code, my dearest: they will not ask for it, you must volunteer it. If you don't, you won't be allowed access to the account.

'My understanding is that I have to provide you with one further code?'

Both men nodded. There was a faintest trace of a smile on Herr Burch's face. He passed her another sheet of blank paper.

1-8-7-8

The two men looked at it together, comparing it to something written in the file.

'I wish to withdraw all the money in the account, along with the gold and jewellery being held in the deposit box. In other words, everything. I want to close my dear husband's account here.'

'May I ask the reason, Frau von Naundorf?'

'Do I need to give a reason?'

The other man, the one she assumed was Herr Burch's superior, stiffened before replying. 'Not as such, no – but I thought that maybe you were being—'

'Being what?'

'Being hasty perhaps: a matter like this does require due consideration and—'

'Did you ask my husband for a reason when he opened the account?'

The two bankers glanced at each other and Herr Busch said that wasn't the way Swiss banks tended to operate. 'We don't ask those kind of questions, Frau von Naundorf.'

'Yet you asked me for a reason as to why I wish to close the account?'

'There have been occasions when the wife of a client is sometimes understandably confused as to the most advisable course of action.'

'I can assure you I'm not at all confused. May we proceed with my withdrawing everything associated with my husband's account?'

The shoulders of both men sagged at the same moment, as if defeated. Herr Busch said very well, this would take perhaps an hour to arrange and perhaps Frau von Naundorf would care to return to the bank at – he glanced at his wristwatch – half past two?

'But it's now just after half past eleven. You said this would take around one hour, not three hours.'

'I wondered if you wished to take lunch and return after that?'

Sophia said she wasn't hungry and was more than happy to wait for the hour it would take. She sat in the reception area outside Herr Burch's office, during which time a succession of men in dark suits walked past, all pausing slightly to glance in the direction of the woman who had dared ask to withdraw all her funds. She could imagine it had scandalised the officials of Bank Leu.

After she'd been waiting for an hour she did ask Herr Burch's secretary how much longer it would take, and the reply was not too long and would she like some coffee, maybe?

Over the course of the next half hour Sophia decided that something was wrong: that perhaps enquiries were being made in Germany, or at least of the German consulate and who knew what the response would be, but was it possible she could be asked to leave Switzerland – that she could be escorted to the border and handed over to German police? Had her past caught up with her; was she already a wanted a person? She worried she'd been too rash, that her decision to come to Zürich first had been an ill-advised one.

She heard a commotion outside the door, different voices, a door being closed, another opened and this, she decided, was what she had feared. Maybe Konrad had suspected her after all and made a complaint about her, maybe—

At that moment the door swung open and Herr Burch entered, followed by a tall man, a younger version of Burch, carrying a box, which he placed on a table in front of her. Together they took everything out – the cash, the gold, the jewellery – and handed it to Sophia who carefully placed everything in the leather briefcase-style overnight bag she'd bought earlier that morning.

After various forms had been signed, Herr Burch insisted on escorting her to the entrance. How long did she plan to remain in Zürich and where was she staying, he wondered?

She replied that she was returning to Berlin the following morning and showed him her ticket for the return journey, and said she was staying at Hotel Eden au Lac and he nodded approvingly.

Herr Burch waited as the doorman called a taxi and instructed the driver to take her to Hotel Eden au Lac on Uto-Quai. Sophia waited until the taxi was about to cross the Limmat before telling the driver she realised she had one further appointment and please could he head back and drop her in Frau Münster Strasse and of course she'd pay him the full fare.

She waited until the taxi had driven off before entering the Savoy Baur en Ville through its rear entrance. She told the receptionist she'd be checking out very soon and would be most grateful if they could prepare her bill and what time was the next train to Geneva?

–

She arrived in Geneva at a quarter to eight that Monday evening. Throughout the journey from Zürich, she'd fought the urge to sleep, a feeling exacerbated by the comfort of her seat and the gentle motion of the train. She kept the leather bag containing the cash and the gold wedged under her feet, determining not to lose touch with it and certainly not to let it out of her sight.

Soon after they'd left Zürich a thought occurred to her, one which kept her amused as she concentrated on staying awake. Today was 15 March – the Ides of March. And she recalled this was the date when the ancient Romans traditionally settled their debts.

She couldn't think of a more appropriate date on which to have taken her husband's money from Bank Leu.

She spoke no more than a few words in French – nothing that would amount to a sentence – so on her arrival in Geneva she looked for a hotel close to the station. She booked a room for two nights at the Hotel des Familles on Rue Lausanne where the receptionist spoke German, though only with a good deal of reluctance. The concierge proved to be more helpful, happy to provide her with a street map of the city and happy too to mark on it the two places she intended to visit the next day.

The following morning, she took a taxi to Quai des Bergues and arrived just as the branch of Credit Suisse was opening. She explained she needed to open an account and make a large deposit and she was directed to a Madame Ladnier who spoke good German.

'How much to intend to open your account with, please?'

When Sophia explained it was around four thousand in francs – Swiss francs of course – and Madame Ladnier said 'of course' too and Sophia then said she had some jewellery and larger items as well and Madame Ladnier asked for some identity and when she showed her the *Reisepass* Madame Ladnier looked not so much worried as serious and said perhaps it would be better if they went into a private room.

They counted out the cash – of which there was just over four and a half thousand Swiss francs, the equivalent of around two thousand eight hundred Reichsmarks and Sophia thought of Konrad and what he was missing out on. Madame Ladnier itemised all the gold, jewellery and the candlesticks and placed it all in a safety deposit box and then went through the various forms needed to open the account. The whole business took around one hour. Sophia kept five hundred francs and thanked Madame Ladnier very much. It had been agreed that Madame von Naundorf's address in Berlin would not appear anywhere on the account details.

'You don't need to explain, Madame von Naundorf, I quite understand. We have a number of customers from Germany and indeed elsewhere in Europe in similar circumstances. The way the Nazis are treating you people...'

She stopped and nodded as if Sophia would understand, and she did: Madame Ladnier was assuming she was Jewish. The Swiss woman briefly placed a hand on her shoulder and told her not to worry. 'You have been registered as an "in bank" customer, which effectively means your address is this branch. As long as you bring your identity with you, you will have full access to your money.'

From Quai des Bergues she took a taxi to Avenue de la Paix and the headquarters of the International Committee of the Red Cross, where her plan was to present them with her husband's diary and its admissions of the atrocities he'd committed in occupied Poland.

She would be doing the right thing, as her mother had urged her. She was sure the evidence against her husband could not be more damning. The Red Cross was bound to be grateful. She'd give them all the details necessary to identify him including the letter from him in which he'd confided to her that he'd be using a false identity, that of Oberleutnant Karl Naundorf of the Wehrmacht.

Except they couldn't have been less interested. She explained to a man at the front desk the purpose of her visit and he told her to come back the following day and she insisted this was urgent and she must see an official today and the man said to wait and an hour later two officials – a man and a woman, both Swiss German – arrived and took her to an office accompanied by a secretary who sat at the back of the room taking notes. They listened as Sophia explained in great detail why she'd come, constantly referring to the diary and her husband's letters.

'I am afraid that this matter does not come under the jurisdiction of the International Committee of the Red Cross.' The woman who'd spoken held out her hands as if to indicate the matter was closed.

'But surely, this is tantamount to an admission of a crime committed against civilians... I thought the Red Cross was meant to protect civilians?'

The man laughed briefly and said this was a very complicated matter, one for legal experts indeed and he didn't expect her to understand the complexities of the ICRC's role, though normally the word of a wife against her husband was not something they'd—

'And in any case,' said the woman, 'your husband – if he is still alive – will be a prisoner of the Soviet Union, which is not party to the Geneva Convention that governs matters relating to prisoners. There is nothing we can do to help you.' She closed her notebook and the pair of them stood up.

'Madame Marinova will show you out.'

Madame Marinova – who'd been at the back of the room taking notes – said nothing as they walked briskly through a series of corridors and into the reception area where Sophia thanked her very much and said she'd see herself out, but Madame Marinova said she'd walk with her as far as the road.

'I am not surprised by the reaction of those two officials. I've worked here for a number of years and I continue to be shocked at their lack of interest in crimes committed by German soldiers. My advice...'

Madame Marinova turned round to check no one was nearby. 'My advice is to go Berne and take the information you have to the Soviet Legation there. Take this... I've written the address down for you.'

Chapter 3

Warsaw
January 1943

In the early hours of the Tuesday morning Roman Loszynski risked leaving the cellar to go to the room they'd been living in on the top floor.

At first Lea had pleaded with him not to go: they were the only ones remaining in the house who knew about the cellar and she was convinced that as long as they remained there, they were safe. But he insisted it could just as easily turn into a trap and, in any case, the children were cold, they'd run out of water and young Raisa had cut her knee when they'd hurried down and he wanted to get some antiseptic because in the ghetto, small cuts had a habit of becoming lethal ones very quickly.

The children fell asleep in the early hours of the morning and when he whispered that it sounded quiet outside, Lea replied in the abrupt manner he'd become used to recently that this wasn't necessarily good news and why was he being so foolish? An hour later she apologised and said maybe he ought to go up after all, so long as he was careful. He slowly climbed the stairs from the cellar to the ground floor, pausing for a while by the door to make sure there were no strange noises on the other side. He crept through the filth and then up the first flight of stairs, taking care to avoid broken steps and testing the others to check they didn't creak too much.

All five floors of the tenement house appeared to be abandoned, though he wouldn't be surprised if there were others in the house: the ghetto was like that, the people who'd survived that long seemed to have developed an ability to disappear into thin air, to vanish for a few crucial moments.

He pushed open the door to the room which now passed as their home: the bare floorboards, the empty walls covered in damp, the two or three bits of furniture, the small pile of their belongings next to the thin mattress on the floor the children shared and their most precious possession, an ancient stove which it took all of his skills as an engineer to coax into life for a few hours at a time, just enough to take the worst of the chill off the room and warm some food up so the children didn't have to eat raw potatoes or whatever else they'd managed to scavenge.

He prised open the floorboard under the window to check if there was any food hidden there, but wasn't surprised to see the space was empty. The Germans allowed even fewer rations into the ghetto these days. It was only a matter of time before they starved, which he suspected was part of a German plan – to let the hunger get them, along with the typhus.

He stood by the cracked window and pulled aside the large sheet of cardboard. To his surprise, the ghetto below him looked much as it did before they'd heard the Germans were on their way. It was still a version of hell, a bleak, defeated and packed urban landscape, but not much different from a couple of days ago.

They were on Nowolipie, at what was now the southern end of the ghetto. To the north – beyond Pawiak prison – he could see smoke drifting across the rooftops, seemingly around the Umschlagplatz. The streets below appeared deserted at first but as he watched he noticed figures darting around, moving furtively between buildings. They were clearly Jewish fighters and some seemed to be armed: there was no sign of the Germans.

To the west he could just make out the Gestapo headquarters close to the junction with Smocza, its looming presence still watching over the ghetto.

He returned to the cellar to bring Lea and the children up. He still thought of her as Lea, of course, though for the past three years they'd been Bronka and Dawid Fiszer, the children Max and Raisa.

Until very recently he'd thought of Professor Roman Loszynski – his previous identity – as a burden: he was desperate no one should know who he really was.

But now, he realised, the time had come when his real identity could save their lives and the key to this was hidden in the cellar: two metal boxes wrapped in oilskin and two notebooks, both bound in soft black leather, both also bound in oilskin.

After he brought Lea and the children back to the room on the top floor he waited until night time. He and Lea were sat on the floor, their backs against the damp wall, watching the children, asleep in front of them. Until a week ago they'd had a chair, which they took turns to sit on, but that had now been used as firewood. To his surprise Lea was amenable to the plan he'd been telling her about.

'I thought you'd be against it, Lea.'

'Why?'

'Because it's not without risk.'

She laughed. 'And living here like this, that's without risk? We don't have any alternative, do we, Roman? We ought to have left Poznań when we had the chance.'

'And go where, Lea? It's no use going over all that again, I've told you how much I regret hesitating but—'

'I agree this is our only chance of escaping the ghetto, Roman. If we stay here, it's only a matter of time, isn't it?'

Roman agreed and there was no point in delaying things. Everyone knew the Germans would be back any day to finish off the ghetto. He'd go and contact them now.

'I'll go.'

'Are you mad, Lea?'

'I'm more likely to be trusted than you.'

Bronka Fiszer slipped out of the tenement house on Nowolipie at two in the morning and waited for a couple of minutes in the entrance of the abandoned building next door. She needed time to acclimatise herself, to get her eyes used to the dark and to sense any movement around her.

It was also an opportunity to get some fresh air after all those days in the house and the time spent in the cellar. Calling it fresh air was stretching matters: there was a pervasive smell of burning and a fetid atmosphere, though that had been the case for years. The fact there were now so few people in the ghetto made little difference. At one stage there'd been half a million people crammed into less than one and a half square miles. Now there were no more than fifty thousand.

She headed east along Nowolipie before cutting through a series of tenements, skirting along the dark edges of their empty courtyards and then over piles of rubble before emerging on Nowolipki, which is where she encountered the boy and girl, still in their teens and crouched behind a wall, demanding she tell them where she was going.

She replied in Yiddish, though it wasn't her first language and she worried she may sound too hesitant. 'I'm on my way to see Sowa.'

The boy's eyes widened and he started to speak but the girl stopped him.

'Who?'

'Sowa: he commands a Jewish Fighting Organisation unit in this area. I've met him before.'

'And where do you think you're going to find this Sowa?'

Lea stepped back as she heard the safety catch on a gun being released. 'The last I heard they were on Zamenhofa – at forty-two, I think, close to the junction with Kupiecka. I'll know the building when I see it.'

To her surprise they said she could carry on, though each time she turned around she was aware of being followed by them, shadows darting in the dark like bats.

She found the building on Zamenhofa: in its day it would have been an imposing property, its handsome stonework suggesting it was an important place, a bank maybe. She moved into a boarded-up doorway and within moments someone appeared at a window alongside it.

Who was she... what did she want...?

Moments later she was pulled into the building, searched and then hurried in the dark to a staircase and down two flights to a basement. She was taken to a small room, searched once more and told to wait. Two minutes later the man she knew as Sowa entered.

He nodded at her and walked round the room, all the while his eyes watching her intently, even in the gloom. She could see why his codename was Sowa. The owl.

'We've met before, Mr Weiss.' She knew it was a risk using his real surname but she was anxious to prove she was genuine. He nodded and asked her to remind him and she said a few months ago, perhaps October... after the mass deportations of the summer... she'd found a pistol under the floorboards of a room where another family had been arrested and had handed it over to the Jewish Fighting Organisation. He'd been very grateful.

He said indeed they had been. They had so few weapons they were thankful for whatever they could get their hands on. Even starting pistols!

He switched from Yiddish to Polish, obviously recognising that was her first language.

What do you want?

She told him that her husband needed to see him and please could he come to where they were living on Nowolipie, and he asked what was it about and she said her husband would explain but it was very important and it was something that could benefit the ghetto and certainly help the Jewish Fighting Organisation.

'He's got an army that could come and rescue us? That would be a help!'

'He has information... he'll explain.'

35

'And why can't he come here with it.'

It must have been her tone of voice, because she pleaded with him: it was something they'd kept secret for years, and as unlikely as it sounded, it could help defeat the Germans, and Sowa asked where she lived.

'I'll send a fighter back with you. If she's happy with everything then I'll come tomorrow night.'

–

Marek Weiss – Sowa – appeared the following night, a gentle tap at their door just after two in the morning, even though neither Lea nor Roman had heard anyone climbing the stairs.

He was a good-looking man, perhaps in his late twenties, clean-shaven and neat in appearance, which was almost unheard of in the ghetto these days. He commanded the Jewish Fighting Organisation unit in that part of the ghetto. The JFO had been formed as the resistance to the Nazis and had around seven hundred members, most of them members of the left-wing Zionist Hashomer Hatzair group or the secular and socialist Bund. It said something about the unity of the JFO that neither of them was sure which group Sowa belonged to.

Sowa and Dawid – that was how he'd introduced himself – shook hands and Dawid suggested they go down to the cellar. Dawid removed the panel that concealed the entrance to the cellar and then unlocked it, leading Sowa down the steep steps.

They sat opposite each other, two candles casting the small space in a yellow, flickering light. Dawid leaned forward to speak, as if other people could overhear them.

'I'm registered as Dawid Fiszer, but that's not my true identity. I obtained the Fiszer identity for myself and my family soon after the Nazis invaded.

'My real name is Roman Loszynski. Before the war I was a professor in the Department of Advanced and Applied Electronics at Poznań University. As part of my job there I'd been working on a top-secret project with the Polish Air Force to develop a special device to… Are you familiar with military aircraft at all? I don't want this to sound too complicated.'

Sowa said not really but perhaps the professor should carry on.

'The Polish Air Force had commissioned a new bomber called the PZL 37 – development began in 1935 and it went into production in late 1938. It was proving to be a quite outstanding aircraft, but I was asked to devise some equipment to improve the accuracy of its bombing. Here, look…'

He indicated to Sowa that he should move, and lifted an old carpet to reveal a wooden panel and when he removed that he used a chisel to prise apart two wooden planks. He reached down into a hole and picked up two boxes along with a package. He opened the boxes and explained to Sowa that although they'd just look like a jumble of wires to him, these were actually very advanced prototypes of the two devices. He opened the other package: two notebooks and a sheaf of blueprints.

'These are all the calculations and notes on this equipment. No one else has this kind of detail and there were quite a number of issues still to be resolved when we stopped working on it. Since then, I've done a lot more theoretical work. It's all in these books and this here – this is my Roman Loszynski identity.'

'What happened to the project?'

'We'd reached quite an advanced stage of development in May 1939 – after the PZL 37 was already in production – and were ready to undergo the final trials, with the receiver on the plane and using real bombs on the targets. However, the senior officer in the Polish Air Force responsible for this – a man called General Brygady Stanisław Wiśniewski – was replaced, and the man who took over didn't see it as a priority at first. By the time he did – in August – the crisis with Germany was such that it would have been impossible to go ahead with it. There was the threat of war and the very last thing I wanted to do was let something like this fall into the hands of the Germans.'

Sowa gingerly poked his forefinger in one of the tins.

'With another two or three months of development in a well-equipped workshop this could change the outcome of the war,

37

Sowa. Whoever has it would gain a significant advantage over their opponents. And we don't want the Germans to get it.'

'Obviously. But they don't know about it, do they?'

The professor shrugged. 'The problem is, they do. A new head of the local Gestapo – a man called Kurz – arrived in the city in the October, a month after the occupation. One of the first things he did was turn up at the university asking questions about the project. They were searching for me, but we'd gone into hiding by then.'

'How did they know about it?'

'I don't know, but fortunately once war was declared we'd destroyed all of our work, apart from what you see here. We were deported to Warsaw as the Fiszer family. If the Germans know where I am they'll come after me: they'll want me to develop these devices for them, and no doubt they'll use my family and—'

'Why didn't you destroy all of this?'

'I've always hoped there'd be a time when I may be able to get this to the Allies – and enable me to escape Poland, with my family.'

'And you want us to help you escape with these boxes? Professor, our job is to defend the ghetto. The Germans came on Monday, as you know. A thousand of them including their Lithuanian and Latvian friends with orders to deport eight thousand Jews through the *Umschlagplatz*. We were waiting for them and managed to drive them away, but we all know they'll be back. It's hard enough for our fighters to get in and out of the ghetto, but to get your family and all this out...'

'I could get you more weapons, Sowa. There is someone in Poznań who knows about me and all this – and he has links with the resistance. If I can get a message to him, I can ask them to get me and my family to the Allies, they'll be desperate to do that.'

'Who is this person?'

'Someone who completely understands the importance of the project and someone I trust completely. Is there any way you could contact him in Poznań?'

Chapter 4

'Start from the beginning, please, Larry.'

'It's Lawrence.'

Jack Miller mumbled an apology and took out another packet of cigarettes. The young RAF pilot opposite him had been smoking continuously since their session began two hours earlier and the fug in the room had turned the atmosphere quite unpleasant.

'Then please start from the beginning, Lawrence.'

Flying Officer Lawrence Reed helped himself to a cigarette and kept the packet next to him. He took a while to light the cigarette, longer than necessary. Jack Miller still hadn't worked out whether he was doing this to annoy him.

'I've told you a dozen times already, sir.'

'You've told me twice, actually, and I've told you that's how these debriefs work: we need all the information you can give us. Each time someone gives a new account subtly different facts emerge... something you may have forgotten or thought of as unimportant... and these may actually turn out to be very important to us. So, if you don't mind...'

'It feels more like an interrogation than a debrief.'

Jack Miller said he was sure that if Lawrence was ever interrogated, he'd take a very different view. He was to regard this as more of a friendly chat.

'Are you American?'

Jack Miller said he'd already told him that any personal details relating to him were immaterial. What mattered was that he was working for British Intelligence and if Lawrence would be so good as to answer the questions then... well, the sooner he did, the sooner they'd finish. So perhaps if Lawrence could tell him once more.

The RAF officer looked at him as if he still wanted to know more and Jack Miller smiled, because if Lawrence only knew half of it then he'd be astonished. Miller found himself wondering if he'd ever be able to tell anyone about his role as a British agent and, more to the point, he wondered if anyone would ever believe a word he said.

Lawrence seemed to get the point because he shifted from his slouching position and sat up straight. Jack Miller opened his notebook and told the young pilot he should start at the beginning, as before.

Reed spoke softly. Jack Miller was attuned enough now to English accents to have a sense of their backgrounds: the upper-class boys, the middle-class ones – though some of them regarded themselves as more upper class – and the working-class boys, not too many of them among escaping aircrew, certainly not among the officers. He'd describe Lawrence Reed as one of those upper-middle-class ones: a slightly condescending tone, sounding much older than he was.

'Monday the first of February, thirty minutes past midnight, took off from our base at RAF Rufforth, which is near York – in England.'

Miller didn't rise to the bait, but reminded Reed to not omit any detail, so when he said 'our base' please could he...

'158 squadron. Nine Halifax bombers led by Wing Commander Buffy Yates. I think I've already spelt Yates for you. Johnny West had to turn back after half an hour because his number two engine was playing up, so there were eight of us crossing the Channel, which we did just after one-thirty. We were flying Mark Ones, which aren't quite as quick as the Mark

Two but have a better range, around eighteen-fifty miles. We reckoned the round trip would be around fourteen hundred miles, possibly slightly more, but perfectly doable, not least with the option of landing in Kent on the way home if needs be.

'Double target, as we call it: first the Peugeot factory at Sochaux, which is two-fifty miles south east of Paris: do you want me to spell it?'

'I know how to spell Paris, thank you.'

'I meant Sochaux, actually. After Sochaux the boss would make the call: plan was to send at least four of us fifty miles south-west to a town called Besançon, if I've pronounced that correctly.'

Miller said it would do and to carry on and Reed asked how come he was able to write so fast and Miller explained he was using shorthand and no, he hadn't been a secretary.

Do carry on.

'It was a newish moon and there was more cloud than we were expecting so visibility was poor, which is a bad thing as far as finding our target is concerned, but a good thing as far as avoiding the enemy goes. Their anti-aircraft fire was way off and I don't think their night fighters could spot us. So, the boss said to let go of half our bombs over what we took to be Sochaux: truth is dropping bombs is always like that. Near bloody impossible to pick out a small target like a factory from twenty thousand feet. The best you can hope for is to hit the right part of the town. The boss then said five of us – my plane included – would head to the second target while the other three were to split up and head home by separate routes: he hoped that way the enemy would be confused. I say, would it be possible to have another cup of tea, plenty of milk, three sugars?'

While they waited, Miller watched Reed grow increasingly nervous. The cockiness seemed to be a veneer, beneath which Flying Officer Lawrence Reed was clearly a bag of nerves. Given that he was just twenty-two and what he'd been through it was hardly surprising. Reed sipped gingerly at the scalding drink – such an English habit – and then continued.

'Squadron Leader Sinton – we call him Fixer – led the five of us heading to Besançon. Target there was the railway station and the marshalling yard. Fixer said we should drop to fifteen thousand as we approached Besançon but once we'd done so we flew straight into a sky full of anti-aircraft fire. Fixer was hit pretty soon after that and the last I heard from him was to drop all our bombs and get the hell out of the place.'

Reed paused to finish his tea and then take another cigarette. His hands were trembling now, so Miller lit it for him. His firm jaw quivered slightly and he nervously ran a hand through his hair.

'I dropped another four thousand feet and spotted the railway line to my right so banked towards it, called the drop and then turned north and home sweet home, which was when… my own bloody fault, climbed far too fast and the Halifax doesn't awfully like that so there was a bit of a stall and as we were busy sorting that out a night-fighter got us. There was just this bloody explosion at the rear of the aircraft and you could sense it moving down the fuselage, like a train coming towards us. I gave the order to bail out and Harry – my co-pilot – managed to get the cockpit open and we jumped but, in truth, I'm not sure how many of the others made it, no question that the three at the back of the plane were killed. I saw another parachute as I was coming down, but didn't see anyone else once I landed.'

'And you destroyed all the confidential stuff… logbook, flight maps and—'

'Of course! I'm not stupid, you know.'

Jack Miller said he wasn't suggesting he was but had to check and took out a map and asked Reed to show him roughly where he came down and what happened next and for the following three hours – including a short break for sandwiches and of course more scalding, sweet tea – Reed described what had happened after he landed, Miller stopping him frequently to check on a location or a name or to look at the map.

Reed spent most of the time concentrating on the large map spread out of the table between them. He reckoned he must have landed just south of the village of L'Écouvotte, though he stayed well clear of it. He found a wood to hide in, buried his parachute and decided to remain there until the following night when he headed south and—

'Why south?'

'Not sure: had to head in one direction or the other, eh?'

He described how he crossed the canal at a point where there was a tiny island, so it was easy enough to swim across, then into another wood about two miles south, where he found a woodsman's hut and was able to dry off and there was a lamp and he was able to study the silk map from the lining of his jacket and realised it was only around forty miles to the Swiss border to the south-east and if he was bloody lucky and just attempted six or seven miles a night then he could reach the Alps within a week.

'Didn't you come across anyone?'

The young pilot shook his head.

'You see, Larry – Lawrence, sorry – the way you're describing it, it's as if you'd landed in a barren wilderness, one totally devoid of any other human beings. But you were in Occupied France: did you really not encounter any Germans – or local people?'

He said he had, of course, but only from a distance. 'I've shown you my route. I was very careful. I was fortunate enough not to bump into anyone.'

Miller said fair enough but even at a distance was relevant and they needed to go through that, not least because it was important to know where German patrols operated.

And so another hour, followed by the account of approaching a farmer just east of the village of Le Barboux and taking the risk of asking the best route over the mountains and the farmer clearly knew who he was and handed him over to a guide who he said was connected with the Maquis and they crossed the Jura mountains and here he was.

Jack Miller closed his notebook and said that was enough for today. They'd have another session tomorrow and soon after that

Larry – Lawrence, sorry – could be on his way: Spain, then back to England, and back flying planes and Lawrence said yes, absolutely, they need every pilot they can get their hands on.

Once the pilot left the room Jack Miller began to write his report. Actually, Reed was a very brave and resourceful young man. He'd worked out where he was, devised a plan, stuck to it and hadn't panicked. And above all else, he'd been lucky. Of course, it was all catching up on him now, but at least he wasn't dead or in a German prisoner of war camp.

But as with all the escapees – the prisoners of war and the RAF aircrew – they had to be properly debriefed once they reached Switzerland and this is what Jack Miller had been doing for the best part of a year.

There was always the remote possibility the Germans could infiltrate a spy into Switzerland, someone who'd be able to inform on the British operation and reveal the escape routes to Spain. It was unlikely, but something they had to be alert to. And all the escapees needed to be thoroughly questioned to ensure they'd not be compromised in any way, plus there was the possibility that something they said would be of real intelligence value. The farmer outside Le Barboux, for instance: that would need to be checked out.

But the ones Jack Miller was most interested in debriefing were the Germans: three or four times a month a German would turn up at the British Embassy on Thunstrasse seeking refuge and offering to help and they needed very careful vetting. Miller would spend days with them, fully aware they could be a plant. He very much enjoyed the drama this entailed.

But there was another reason why he so relished these jobs. Some of the Germans came from Berlin and he'd pay them special attention, looking for any hint they may have come across her, even if they just knew Charlottenburg. He was desperate to find out if they had any possible connection to the woman who'd given him a purpose for living, and who was the reason he'd remained in Switzerland after escaping himself from Germany.

Sophia.

She was his first thought in the morning and his last one at night and in the few hours of disturbed sleep she was a constant companion, as she was during the day.

It was just over a year since his own escape from Germany – getting on for fifteen months, actually – and after the immediate trauma of the escape, he now had time to reflect. It had taken him that long to recover, that long to be able to consider his situation with some degree of equanimity.

He'd arrived in Germany from Philadelphia in 1936 to cover the Berlin Olympics: a bright young American journalist, not long divorced, a bit down and a bit lost, not that he'd have ever admitted it. Looking back, he was seeking excitement. He certainly found it. He'd been instantly seduced by the drama of Berlin, appalled and fascinated at the same time; conscious he was an eyewitness to a dreadful history unfolding before him. Berlin was a city that constantly occupied every one of his senses, an unremitting mix of sounds, sights, smells and even taste, which meant he had little opportunity to think about himself, other than to be alert to danger – and there was plenty of that.

Berlin felt like an utterly inappropriate love affair, the longer it went on the harder it was to disentangle oneself from it.

A chance meeting with an Englishman called Edward during the Olympics meant he was able to remain in Berlin as a freelance journalist. And then, in November 1937, came an invitation from Edward to visit London, a few agreeable meals and then a suggestion Jack may like to meet some friends of Edward's to discuss work, a drive to a country house and before he realised what on earth was going on, he found himself being interrogated – was he a Nazi, for Christ's sake! Had the room not been guarded he'd have walked out, but then Edward came in and it turned out he was being recruited as a British agent.

In Berlin.

And that's what he'd been after that, an agent in Berlin.

The work had been exhilarating and terrifying. It was also exhausting: to maintain his cover he had to work full time as a journalist and the British were demanding masters. Being one of their agents was no part-time occupation. He knew he was a successful agent, but he also knew he was lucky. If his time in Berlin had taught him one thing it was never to underestimate the role luck plays in one's life. There were enough times when he feared he was about to be caught, but somehow the encroaching shadow of the Gestapo remained just that, a shadow: just distant enough, for the time being.

And looking back on it now his biggest stroke of luck had come in Berlin, in his role as a British agent. It was October 1940 when he'd met Sophia von Naundorf. As the wife of a senior SS officer, she was an even more unlikely British agent than him.

It was, he now reflected, the most profound stroke of luck he'd ever experienced. Sophia had proven to be brave and effective and without him quite realising it at the time, she became the most important person in his life. It was a few months after he'd escaped to Switzerland that he began to appreciate how the intense and constant pressure he'd been under in Germany had prevented him from admitting to himself the depths of his feelings for Sophia.

These feelings only began to emerge in the frantic few days before his escape from Berlin, with the Gestapo closing in on him. Sophia had risked her life to protect him and arrange his escape. And in that time, alone in her apartment, there was what he could only describe as a shared affection between the two of them, a closeness and an intimacy and, on his part certainly, love. He sometimes wondered whether it was his imagination playing tricks, but he was quite sure it was a feeling she shared. He could still feel her hands gently brushing the tears from his cheeks, the way they sat quietly together, holding hands and with no need to say a word because what was unsaid was so much more profound.

And then the escape into Switzerland and his arrival in Berne and the dreadful news of the death of his younger brother, Tom, at Pearl Harbour. Looking back on it, all of his pent-up emotions exploded and he must have had what they called a nervous break-down. He was angry with the British, who he believed had used him, he somehow felt responsible for Tom's death and this was combined with the tension he'd been controlling these past four years and the fact that he was utterly exhausted.

What was worse – far worse – was the fear he'd never see Sophia again. He knew enough about life in Berlin – far more than anyone in Berne – to realise the chances of Sophia surviving were remote and the chances of her escaping to Switzerland even more so.

But while there was even a distant chance she'd get out or that he could return to rescue her, he was prepared to wait in Switzerland. That's what he'd told Basil Remington-Barber, the British spy chief in Berne: as long as Sophia was in Germany, he was staying in Switzerland.

And so, he'd remained. It had taken a month in a sanatorium for him to recover his health and Basil and Noel Moore – espe cially Noel – had been patient with him. He'd spent time in an isolated cottage in Emmental with an elderly couple from Frankfurt who'd escaped the Nazis and who didn't speak a word of English and by the end of his stay his complete immersion in the language meant his German began to sound like that of a native speaker, to the extent that he now spoke it with the hint of the Hessian dialect common around Frankfurt.

And then he'd been put to work. Noel Moore's respons-ibilities in Berne included looking after escaped prisoners of war and aircrew and monitoring others who turned up at the British Embassy, seeking help or offering their services or both. Jack Miller's job was to de-brief these people, his knowledge of Germany being crucial.

–

In the middle of March, he met Noel Moore for a catch-up. Jack had spent three days with a German woman who turned up at the embassy and claimed to have escaped and was offering her services: she said she was from Cologne and her father had been Jewish and it was only a matter of time before the authorities worked that out and could she maybe work for the British?

Jack's instincts had been not to trust her, and this was vindicated: there was a large Jewish community in Basel and through them they found a Jewish lawyer from Cologne who met the woman and saw through her in five minutes.

Nothing she says is true: she's a Nazi.

Once they'd discussed this, Noel said jolly well done and actually, he didn't know if he'd mentioned it but Basil was going to join them and, as if on cue, Basil knocked on the door and entered.

Basil Remington-Barber was more serious-looking than normal. The relaxed – even casual – manner was absent and he and Noel Moore exchanged looks as if to see which of them was going to speak first.

'This is about Sophia, isn't it?'

Noel Moore coughed and said yes it was, but he wasn't to—

'If something bad has happened to her I want to you to tell me immediately: none of your English euphemisms and hand-wringing and—'

'It is about Sophia, but it's not necessarily bad news, you see...'

'What Basil is trying to say, Jack, is that Sophia has gone missing... Please let me finish, Jack. Last Wednesday – the tenth – she sent us a message through the kiosk on Budapester Strasse. The message said we may not hear from her for a while, that's all, but crucially there were no code words in the message to indicate she'd been caught, which is positive. But since then, nothing. We have a chap in Berlin and he's seeing what he can find out, but it was what... less than a week ago. I'd say that no news is good news.'

'Really, Noel?'

'I think Noel means that it's not necessarily bad news. My hunch is that she's gone to ground, may even be on her way out of Germany, who knows?'

Chapter 5

Poznań
February 1943

Zhenia Krakowski arrived in Poznań just before three o'clock on the first Tuesday in February.

After Sowa told her she was going to Poznań, she was sent to see Tadek who lived on Franciszkańska, on what was now the eastern boundary of the ghetto. The crumbling tenement building he lived in overlooked the ghetto wall with views of the Krasiński Palace to the south. Like most buildings in the ghetto, it was more of a shell than anything else, dust and filth everywhere, the walls covered in mould. Most of the floorboards had been removed: they made decent firewood. She was taken down to the basement.

Sowa told me about your journey, Zhenia, but I want to hear it from you. And, please, speak in Polish.

She explained how she had to travel to Poznań to find a man called— Tadek interrupted and said don't tell me his name, it's too dangerous, and she said she had an address though they weren't certain he'd be there. And if she did find him he wouldn't be expecting her, so she'd have to persuade him to read the letter she'd be carrying then he was sure to help and if he did so then that ought to also mean the Jewish Fighting Organisation would receive a much-needed supply of weapons.

Tadek listened carefully, fidgeting with his beard and nodding as he did so. 'Very well, very well... your Polish is excellent. Is it your first language?'

She explained not really, they'd spoken Yiddish at home, of course, but her father had insisted she speak proper Polish, not just Polish with a Yiddish accent. It had helped her get a job before the war and now...

'And now it is standing you in good stead. And you look the part too, Zhenia: fair hair and green eyes. No one would suspect you're Jewish. They must have sent you out of the ghetto before?'

'A few times, just within Warsaw though.'

'Day trips.'

'That's what they call them, yes.'

'And they went well I assume... Were you nervous?'

She replied they must have gone well because... because here she was. Of course she was nervous, but she'd followed all the instructions she'd been given and felt she could now manage a mission like this one.

'As long as my papers are good... I'm reasonably confident. And if they search us, well, it's not like with the boys.'

Tadek nodded. It had been a year or so now since they'd risked sending one of the men on a mission like this. The danger of them being strip-searched and seeing they were circumcised was too great. He asked her a few questions about herself – her age, jobs, interests – and then said very well, follow me, and took her to another room where an elderly man was hunched over a large desk, surrounded by papers, photographs, pens and bottles of inks.

Tadek introduced him as Leyb and when Leyb turned around, Zhenia's first reaction was to think that he looked just like a religious scribe, right down to his long beard and head covering. Tadek announced that Leyb would be responsible for making her false *kennkarte* and other paperwork. They discussed how she should look for her photograph – *maybe brush your hair this way, some lipstick perhaps*.

When she returned the following day, she found she was now Helena Kamińska. They'd made her two years older – twenty-three – and from Praga, a suburb on the right bank of the Vistula, which she'd said she was familiar with as an aunt lived there before the war. Leyb seemed particularly pleased with a letter he flourished in front of her: it was from the hospital of the Holy Spirit in Elektoralna Street in Warsaw, transferring her for a period of up to two weeks to the City Hospital in Poznań.

Miss Kamińska has made an excellent job of re-organising our pharmacy, despite the current situation… We hope she will be able to do likewise with you… Look forward to her return…

Leyb also handed over a travel pass, permitting her to travel by train from Warsaw to Poznań on Tuesday 2 February and to return any time before 16 February.

–

She took the quarter past nine train from Warsaw. It was scheduled to arrive just after one but to no one's surprise it was approaching three o'clock when the train pulled into the central station in Poznań. Until then all her paperwork had seemed fine: not even a raised eyebrow. There was a checkpoint at the station though, a long queue and just three Gestapo officers with Polish policemen beside them. Even though she spoke German, Tadek had instructed her not to use it or let on that she understood.

That will mean they have to translate… it will give you time to think… and be polite, of course, but not too polite the Germans aren't stupid: they know full well how much most Poles despise them… if someone is too friendly, that could make them suspicious.

'Where are you staying?'

The Polish policeman was translating and appeared hostile. She sensed he was an ethnic German with a dislike of anyone from Warsaw.

'At the City Hospital.'

'And the name of your boss?' The Gestapo officer was studying the letter.

'I beg your pardon?' She began to feel her throat tighten and her heart race. She couldn't recall his name, despite having re read the letter on the train.

'It's not a difficult question: the name of your boss. The man who signed this letter. Come on, I haven't got all day.'

'Wójcik, Tadek Wójcik.'

'That's not what it says here.'

'Are you sure?'

'Of course I'm sure: it's signed by Ryszard Zieliński!'

'Mr Zieliński? Well, yes – he signs these letters, but he's more of an administrator. My actual boss is Tadek Wójcik.' She allowed herself to smile at the Gestapo officer, surprised he'd made such a basic error. He scowled at her and asked her date of birth and she replied without hesitation.

'I've been to Praga, you know.'

She smiled, her throat tightening once more.

'The big church – the main one there – what's it called again?'

'You mean St Florian's Cathedral?'

The Gestapo officer looked at the Polish policeman who nodded.

They allowed her through.

It was now close to three-thirty. Outside the station she caught a tram to the Old Town, walking through the Old Market Square to a tram stop opposite a small park. After a short while the number 18 arrived. Twenty minutes later it arrived in the district of Jeżyce in the north-west of the city. Once she spotted the botanic gardens, she left the tram at the next stop.

Opposite the botanic gardens... the third road after the tram stop... halfway down on the right, number 24. It's a green door – and if he's still there the name will be on a brass plate next to the letterbox.

Her instructions were that if they'd moved, she was to say she was from the university and had a letter for him and please could they be so kind as to let her have his new address?

She was petrified as she approached the gate of number 24, she felt as if her legs were no longer capable of proper movement. She hesitated and at that moment a pleasant-looking woman emerged from the side of the house and smiled at her, before walking down the path and asking if she could help.

'Is this the house of Bolesław Piotrowski?'

'I hope so – I'm Lilka Piotrowski. How can I help?'

She introduced herself as Helena Kamińska and said she had an important message for Mr Piotrowski and there was nothing to worry about but if she could come in to deliver it in person then she'd be grateful.

'You'd better come in.'

–

Bolesław Piotrowski was older than the professor had described him – three and a half years of German occupation had evidently taken their toll. His hair was thinning and flecked with grey, his fingers stained yellow from tobacco, his appearance gaunt and worried-looking. He led Zhenia into a dusty and untidy study at the rear of the house.

'I have a message for you from a very old friend.'

Piotrowski looked at her suspiciously and indicated she should continue.

'Professor Roman Loszynski – from the Department of Advanced and Applied Electronics at Poznań University. He says you know him very well.'

Bolesław Piotrowski nervously ran his fingers along the side of his head and narrowed his eyes as he studied her. He frowned, as if struggling to place the name.

'Loszynski, Loszynski... ah yes... Loszynski: we were more colleagues than friends, you understand. But it's a long while since I last saw him or heard from him – it would have been August '39. I'm no longer at the university... I now work as an engineer at the lorry factory. I'm no longer involved in... anything. I just work and come home.'

He held out his hands to indicate 'that's it' and placed an unlit cigarette between his lips, his hands trembling. From the lining of her handbag, she carefully removed an envelope and held it towards Piotrowski. He seemed reluctant to take it.

'What is that?'

'A letter to you from Roman Loszynski.'

His arms remained folded. 'Have you met him?'

She nodded.

'And is he here, in Poznań?'

'He's in Warsaw.'

'Where in Warsaw?'

'The ghetto.'

He nodded, taking in the news. 'At least he's alive... I wondered... tell me, if you've met him – what's his wife's name?'

'Lea. The children are Max and Raisa.'

'And they're alive too?'

'As much as anyone who's left in the ghetto.'

His shoulders appeared to sag as he held a hand out for the letter.

> *My dear friend,*
>
> *I trust you'll know this letter is from me. At the very least you ought to recognise my writing, but in case you have any doubts, think back to the New Year party at J's house in 1937 – and what happened after it. And the following summer, when we all went on that picnic and ended up swimming in the river. Who knew the Warta could be so cold in August! And do you recall the trouble you and I had with our expenses after the Białystok trip in 1938!*
>
> *I'm now in Warsaw and have been here for three years. But I am not alone. I have the Tatra boxes with me, along with the notebooks and all the diagrams. I would like to pass them on to people who can make good use of them against the people who aren't our friends, if you follow my meaning.*
>
> *But I need help: I need someone to get the four of us out of here and to safety. Then I will hand everything over to the people who will help us.*
>
> *The person who has delivered this letter to you – you can trust her: she and her friends will get the boxes to you*

if you can then arrange for us to escape the city. In return,
I ask you provide them with what she is going to ask for.
      R

He read the letter once more and said nothing as he folded it up and placed it under a book on his desk.

'I am satisfied this is from Roman. The friends he refers to – you and your friends – are you the resistance in the ghetto?'

She nodded.

'And what is it you're asking for?'

'My instructions are that we need some weapons; groups outside the ghetto have more access to them than we do. We will smuggle the professor and his family and the equipment out of the ghetto to a safe house in the non-Jewish part of Warsaw, and then hand him over to you. In return you give us the weapons.'

Bolesław Piotrowski leaned back in his chair and finally lit his cigarette. 'I leave home at four o'clock in the morning for work. When I return, I'll bring someone with me. You'd better stay here until then. We can't risk you wandering around Poznań, can we?'

–

She'd been in the attic for around twenty-four hours. Bolesław Piotrowski's wife, Lilka, had brought her food and escorted her to the bathroom on the floor below, but she said little, other than urging her to keep quiet.

Just after three on the Wednesday afternoon, Lilka returned and took her down to the study, where Bolesław Piotrowski was sitting next to another man. Piotrowski didn't introduce him but asked her to repeat her story. When she finished, the man spoke: he seemed calmer than Piotrowski

Please tell me about these boxes you saw… How is Roman's health… and that of his family… How can you smuggle them out of the ghetto… Please tell me a bit about the ghetto – which streets are still in it… Who commands the Bund these days… and the other groups in the Jewish Fighting Organisation?

He spoke softly, frequently smiling, and his questions were phrased in a subtle manner, clearly designed to be absolutely sure she could be trusted. She replied in detail, taking care to drop in as many facts as possible to help vouch for her authenticity.

When she finished, he nodded as if she'd passed an exam and told her his name was Henryk. 'You will return to Warsaw tomorrow. I'll follow next week – we'll need to agree a way we can communicate when I'm in Warsaw. I'll want to come into the ghetto first to see Roman. Do you know what weapons they're expecting?'

'Sub-machine guns and grenades, I'm told. As much as you can let us have: we're desperate.'

'Everyone wants sub-machine guns, but I'll see what we can do. We're a small group here, but well-connected.'

'Are you AK?'

Henryk and Bolesław looked at each other before the latter replied. 'I'm sure you know how complicated it is here in Poland. Allegiances in Poland were complex before the war: now, well… I can't imagine there's anywhere in Europe where it's more complicated. But then, nowhere else in Europe is occupied in such a brutal fashion as Poland. In most other countries, if people do what the Nazis say then they can just get on with their lives. Here, they hate us. That makes everything so complicated.

'We're a group independent of the Armia Krajowa. We call ourselves the Poznań Group and our origins go back to around 1938, before the war. We were a group of what you might call intellectuals – and democrats. The core of the group was at the university – which is how we know Roman – and there were also a number of air force officers based at Ławica airport. There were others too: some lawyers and other professionals. Then, we were a group of like-minded people coming together, now, our role is different. Those of us who remain do our best to help oppose the Germans. We keep away from the Home Army because the Armia Krajowa has some very right-wing elements in it. At the same time, nor are we socialists or communists. We see ourselves as democrats.'

'And the Germans – they don't suspect you of anything?'

'The Poznań Group has always been very careful: someone would only be invited if at least two other members vouched for them. Unfortunately, many of our members are no longer here: either they've been arrested or have left the city or just avoid being involved.'

Henryk shifted in his chair before continuing. 'I was a lecturer in the mathematics department at the university: I've never been political so I was able to carry on working when the university re-opened. It's different for Bolesław though.'

'I lost my job: one of the first things the Germans did was close down the Department of Advanced and Applied Electronics at the university. In the weeks before the invasion, we'd destroyed much of our sensitive work – anything that could assist the Germans, including the PZL bombing project. Roman Loszynski went into hiding in August, before the Germans arrived, and I know he took the latest Tatra boxes with him, along with some diagrams and his notebooks. His plan was to get out of the city, but the last I heard was that the family were deported. But this is why Roman is so important: he has details of the project and the boxes. We thought everything was lost. The Gestapo turned up, you know, around a month or so after the invasion.'

'It was October, wasn't it, Bolesław?'

'It must have been, Henryk. They were clearly looking for the equipment and anything to do with the PZL.37 project. They asked for Roman specifically but fortunately they didn't seem to realise I'd been involved in the project, they seemed to think I was too junior. As far as we could tell they gave up the search, though they did keep looking for Roman. Soon after, they closed the university and I was assigned to the lorry factory. Thank God Roman is alive and still has those boxes with him. We must do everything we can to help.'

–

On the Friday morning – the day after Zhenia Krakowski returned to Warsaw – there was an air of excitement in the office of Dr Otto Kurz, the head of the Gestapo in Poznań.

Kurz's office was on the top floor of the Dom Żołnierza building on Niezłomnych, the Gestapo's headquarters in the centre of the city. The reason for his excitement was a telephone call he'd just received from the Gestapo office at the university. The university had been closed soon after the invasion, but Kurz had actually been responsible for the university reopening in 1941, this time as a German university. A number of the Polish academics were kept on: some because they were harmless, others because they were ethnic Germans and therefore trusted, and a smaller number who weren't trusted but who Kurz preferred to have where he could see them, as he put it.

By 1941 Kurz realised that the resistance in the city was complicated. It wasn't just the Home Army they needed to watch out for, there were also at least a dozen smaller groups. He'd even tried to draw a diagram showing all the different groups, but soon gave up. He'd heard rumours there was a group based around the university, though they couldn't be sure.

Henryk Kamiński was one of those on Kurz's watchlist: as with a number of others at the university, there was no evidence against him, otherwise he'd have soon been dispatched to the dungeons on Niezłomnych. But Kamiński was one of those whose record seemed to be a bit too good to be true, his file was too clean, too devoid of any signs of political involvement or activity. The very fact that there was nothing against him gave Kurz grounds for suspicion.

And now he'd just been told that Henryk Kamiński had applied for a week's leave: he wished to visit a relation in Warsaw and had requested a travel permit allowing him to make that journey. According to his file, it would be the first time Kamiński would have left Poznań since 1939.

Kurz smiled: if Kamiński was up to something, it would be a real feather in Kurz's cap, but he didn't want the Gestapo in

Warsaw to get wind of it: they'd take it over and he couldn't risk that. He'd have to have Kamiński followed.

There was a knock at the door and his secretary showed in a plump and anxious-looking man. He was clutching his trilby against his chest and walked uneasily to the chair Kurz pointed to. The man hesitated before sitting gingerly on its edge, still gripping his hat.

'Thank you for coming so soon, Herr Lubnauer. How are things at the airport?'

Konrad Lubnauer replied that the airport was busy, thank you very much for asking, sir.

'And the matter you raised with us, back in 1939 – the project to improve the bombing accuracy of the PZL.37: have you any more information?'

Lubnauer replied that he'd told him everything he knew.

'And the people involved?'

'The airforce and PZL people, all of whom have gone, as you know – and the Jew from the university – Loszynski.'

'And you can't think of anyone else?'

Lubnauer shook his head. 'Sometimes Loszynski was accompanied by others from the university, but I can't recall any names or faces, I've told you.'

Kurz watched Lubnauer: the man was worried. They'd noticed this in the past few weeks among the ethnic Germans in the city. They'd been full of swagger and enthusiasm in September 1939. Now, with setbacks in Stalingrad and elsewhere, it was as if they were no longer so sure. 'How about this man?' He handed Lubnauer a photograph of Henryk Kamiński.

'I may have seen him, sir, but I cannot be sure, it would have been five years ago. People change and—'

'Look, Lubnauer, you came to us with very interesting information. Our colleagues at the Air Ministry in Berlin were intrigued by it. They said, if it is true that the Poles were making progress with a device to improve the bombing accuracy of their planes then we would very much like to get our hands on it. And more to the point, it would be a disaster if the British got hold of it. But you've given us no evidence, Lubnauer, nothing… just gossip and speculation and…'

'I promise you, sir, they were carrying out trials and had all the—'

'Maybe you're deliberately sending us on a wild goose chase, Lubnauer?'

Lubnauer leaned so far forward he almost toppled over. He pleaded with the Gestapo officer. *Nothing*, sir, could be further from the truth. He was more German than Polish, his loyalties lay unquestionably with the Reich and if there was anything… *anything*… he could do to demonstrate that then he'd be—

'Anything, Lubnauer, really?'

'Of course, sir.'

'In that case, Lubnauer, I'm sending you on a mission. The man in this photograph is called Henryk Kamiński and I want to know if he's anything to do with the PZL.37 project. Kamiński's planning a trip to Warsaw and we think he's up to no good. You, Lubnauer, will follow him there.'

Chapter 6

England
February 1943

Barney Allen could be forgiven for assuming that every large country home within an hours' radius of London had been requisitioned by one branch or another of the government.

It was the same with iron railings, notably the ones that used to enclose parks and public spaces. They'd all been hurriedly removed in the first year of the war, apparently to be used for the construction of aircraft and tanks. His brother-in-law had confided to him at the weekend that he'd heard there were dozens of warehouses filled to their ceilings with unused railings. The wrong type of metal, apparently.

And likewise with the country homes: owners for whom these large, often run-down houses had long been a burden had been quick to hand them over to the government in acts of apparent patriotism. Now it seemed they had more than they knew what to do with, different branches of government finding themselves lumbered with draughty homes that were costly to maintain and usually came with an owner or two living somewhere in the grounds.

MI6 had taken on around a dozen of these houses: they were invaluable as safe houses or training centres for agents. The Service had been given the pick of the locations, selecting ones that were well protected and isolated and were able to ensure they came without annoying owners on the premises.

It was the first time he'd been to this one. A Service car with a driver had picked them up early in the afternoon from St

James's and Barney was relieved the only other passenger was his colleague, Tom Gilbey. He and Tom had been at school together – Tom a year above him – but they'd become close friends and in fact Tom had been responsible for helping to recruit Barney to the Service in 1936, seven years previously.

He and Tom were a rare pair in the Service: colleagues who trusted each other. Both men were now reasonably senior in the Service, running agents and operations in Nazi-occupied Europe.

The journey would give them an opportunity to catch up, though in fact much of the journey was taken up with gossip about school friends: who'd been promoted, who'd been killed, who was having a good war, who wasn't.

Their boss – Piers Devereux – had planned to travel with them but had been prevailed upon to accompany another attendee at the meeting, Sir Roland Pearson. It was agreed that his ample figure couldn't have been comfortably accommodated in the same car as the rest of them. Roly, as he was known, had also been at school with Tom and Barney, though some years above them. Now he worked for Winston Churchill, based in Downing Street, acting as the prime minister's eyes and ears on all matters to do with intelligence.

They took the Great North Road as far as Hatfield and then a series of increasingly bumpy B roads. They drove through the village of Essendon and then on to what could best be described as a pothole-strewn country lane. After a mile or so a high brick wall emerged on their left and soon after that they turned into a gated drive which led to a large house set behind a row of swaying conifers.

–

Barney Allen – Barnaby to the less familiar – had grown used to these meetings. One only had a vague idea about the agenda beforehand and even less of a notion as to who would be present. In this case Piers had told him and Tom that the meeting was one 'the RAF had requested'.

Barney and Tom Gilbey were shown into a large lounge at the back of the house. Behind the large bay windows was a terrace, with a long lawn beyond that. The man who'd shown them into the room drew the blackout blinds and then the heavy curtains: despite the time of year, there was still an hour or two of daylight remaining. The yellowing lights of the chandelier had little impact on the all-pervading gloom.

No sooner had they sat down than they heard the crunch of another car arriving on the gravel and then muted conversation in the hall. Within five minutes the room was full.

Piers Devereux was there with Roly Pearson, of course. No sooner had they entered the room than they were followed by Lord Swalcliffe, who Barney had met on occasion. Swalcliffe occupied a similar role in Downing Street to Roly Pearson. His brief was to be the prime minister's scientific advisor. He was regarded as a difficult man with a brilliant mind, the latter apparently excusing the former. Churchill relied on him for all matters scientific, as with Roly on intelligence. But this didn't mean the two men got on. There was an undeniable tension between Roly and Lord Swalcliffe, marked by a rancour and pettiness that did not become their roles. More than once Roly had told Barney that Swalcliffe's background was 'Continental', as he put it, only given a peerage to mask a Germanic-sounding surname, Roly assured him.

Last to enter the room were two RAF officers: Barney Allen recognised Air Vice-Marshal Frank Hamilton, the head of RAF Intelligence Branch.

With all seven men seated there was an awkward period of shifting in their chairs, followed by bouts of coughing, the lighting of cigarettes and pipes and a degree of uncertainty as to who should start the proceedings. The RAF had requested the meeting, but it was taking place on Service premises. Barney sensed Frank Hamilton was trying to work out the protocol. Roly Pearson came to his rescue.

'Frank, you requested we meet, so why don't you kick off, eh?'

Frank said he was very grateful and indeed was very grateful they could all attend at such short notice and very grateful too for the use of this venue, and Roly Pearson said perhaps he should get to the point and Hamilton said yes, of course and perhaps if he could introduce his colleague?

'Group Captain Martin Marlow is based with Bomber Command at their HQ in High Wycombe. You'll recall, Lord Swalcliffe, that in August 1941 you commissioned a report on the effectiveness or otherwise of Bomber Command's raids on occupied Europe?'

'Of course, Frank.'

'I know the report had a very restricted circulation, so perhaps if I summarise? In essence, it said our bombing performance over Europe was pretty bloody awful. The report analysed around six hundred and fifty raids, that is where our bombers that actually got anywhere near their intended target without being hit by the enemy or having to abort through mechanical failure. Of those aircraft that got through, only one in three got within five miles – five miles, gentlemen – of their target.'

Frank Hamilton paused for the others to absorb this. *Five miles.*

'And as bad as that is, it hides regional variations. Over the French ports, two in three of our aircraft got within five miles of their target, which is not too bad. Over Germany, just one in four got within five miles of their target. And over the Ruhr...'

He looked up and around the room, as if someone was bold enough to venture a guess.

'Over the Ruhr it was one in ten.' He shook his head. 'Our bombs are landing in fields or woods or rivers... anywhere but their intended target. We're making life uncomfortable for a lot of cows in occupied Europe, but not so much for the Nazis!'

'If I may, Frank?' Lord Swalcliffe leaned forward. 'The purpose of the report was to inform the prime minister's thinking on our strategy. He was as shocked as I was by its findings. As a consequence, I was able to look afresh at what our strategy should be. Essentially one can either pursue a policy of precision bombing – as is favoured by the Americans – or of area bombing. Given that precision bombing had clearly not worked, I advocated a policy of the strategic area bombing of German cities. I'm pleased to say this was accepted by the prime minister and, last February, I believe it was, Arthur Harris was put in charge of Bomber Command with instructions to implement this strategy, known as the Area Bombing Directive. I hope that helps, Frank.'

'It does indeed, sir. Over the past year Arthur's been working towards a full-scale bombing campaign. We've had to wait for the production of new bombers – the Lancaster only came into service last year – and much of the year has been spent seeing how we can improve our bomb navigation system – you'll be aware we're using the new Oboe system, which is a technology based on radio transponders. Now Arthur is ready to start the main phase of this campaign and perhaps, Martin, if you don't mind picking up the baton?'

Group Captain Marlow smiled pleasantly.

'The area we are here to discuss today is the Ruhr valley. Air Marshal Harris had intended to launch a major area bombing offensive against it before now, but the bombing of the German ports and the U-boat bases in France were seen as a priority. However, on the twenty-first of January the combined chiefs of staff authorised a Combined Bombing Offensive in the Ruhr valley. The order was issued to Bomber Command on fourth February. Its objective, if I may quote, is "the progressive destruction and dislocation of the German military, industrial and economic system, and the undermining of the morale of the German people to a point where their capacity for armed resistance is fatally weakened". Bomber Command intend to commence this offensive at the beginning of March.'

There was a good deal of nodding of heads and Roly Pearson said that was jolly good to hear and of course one wished the operation every success but… but what precisely was the purpose of bringing us out here?

Frank Hamilton said thank you, Roly, he was about to come to that. 'Notwithstanding the fact that we are undertaking an area bombing offensive, the need for accuracy is still paramount. Area bombing is based on the premise that if you send enough aircraft over a target the odds are that one or two of them will actually hit the intended target.'

'Hopefully the odds are better than ten to one!'

'Indeed, Sir Roland. But this is where we need your help. Even with aerial reconnaissance it is still not easy to get an accurate picture of the impact of the bombings. What we really need is what I believe our American colleagues refer to as "eyes on the ground". And this is why we're here. To see if you chaps can help us with eyes on the ground.'

Lord Swalcliffe shot a 'well then' look at Roly Pearson who turned immediately to Piers Devereux.

'Piers? Very much your area, is it not?'

Piers said it most probably was but he'd be very grateful if the colleagues from the RAF could be more precise as to what it was they wanted.

'Let me give you an example,' said Frank Hamilton. 'Let's say we launch a raid over Essen, target being the main Krupp factory. What would be of enormous assistance to us is if on the day after the raid – remember, our raids take place at night – your agents in the area could get as close as possible to the site and assess what the damage is and, if possible, take photographs. If an agent on the ground can say yes, this section was obliterated, or they're still fighting fires here or that section is unscathed – well, all that would be of enormous benefit to us. It will give us a better idea of how we're doing and it will also help us plan future raids.'

A silence followed.

Roly Pearson looked at Barney Allen and Tom Gilbey and raised his eyebrows and they both looked at Piers Devereux, unsure quite how to respond.

'Clearly we are in a tricky position here, gentlemen, because anything we say could endanger our covert operations inside Germany.' Devereux smiled, not wanting to give the impression he didn't trust everyone in the room. 'But I think it would be a mistake to assume that the Ruhr or indeed anywhere else in Nazi Germany is awash with Allied agents. Would you not agree, Tom?'

Tom Gilbey said if one was quite honest, one would say the cupboard was pretty bloody bare. One tried these days to send agents in on specific missions. Perhaps that could be something worth considering.

'Barnaby?'

'The cupboard's not completely bare.' He was aware everyone had suddenly leaned forward in his direction. 'As Piers says, one doesn't want to say anything that could in any way compromise our agents and I wouldn't want to raise your hopes unnecessarily but... we do have... let me put this another way... not all agents are the same. Some are trusted, full-time agents who effectively run networks of other agents. These other agents can be a real mixture: some may simply be sources who occasionally provide intelligence, others may not even realise they're assisting this country, others are more committed.

'We do have some of these people – the sources, if you like, people sympathetic to us – in the Ruhr. But we've not been able to use them for over a year. The senior agent who ran them escaped from Germany at the end of 1941. That agent is the only person who could contact and activate these other agents.'

'And how feasible is it that he could do that?'

'I'll look into it. That's as much as I'll commit to.'

Frank Hamilton said that was fair enough and perhaps if they reconvened in what... a month?

Barney Allen said that may be too soon, it would depend on a lot. 'It means I have to get my agent back into Germany and—'

'Perhaps it would be best to wait until the raids start, Barney? That way your agent can also make an assessment while he's there.'

'Fair enough. But remember, even if we pull that off, who knows what's left of our network. They may all be dead.'

The room fell quiet and then Roly said on that cheerful note they should all go through to the dining room where supper was being served and he understood there was a rather decent cellar here, which the owners had generously given the Service access to.

—

They waited until the two RAF officers and Lord Swalcliffe left. It was a pleasant night, dry and not too chilly, none of the dampness that seemed so prevalent in the countryside. Roly Pearson had produced a box of very good cigars and suggested they adjourn to the terrace.

'They say a good cigar is at its best when smoked outside.'

'Really, Roly? Never heard that! I say, these are H. Upmann. Where on earth did you get them from?'

'Don't ask me to reveal my sources, Tom! Didn't want to waste one on Swalcliffe though. You know Upmann were suspected of being German spies in Cuba during the Great War? Ironic, eh?'

They agreed it was and took a few minutes to light and then savour their cigars.

'I presume, Barney, it's that American chap Miller you're talking about?'

'Indeed: he had a small network in the Ruhr. Not sure whether they're still around, but we'll need to send him back in.'

'Will he go?'

'He will if he's instructed, Piers.'

'Really? I thought he'd cut up rough about Sophia being kept in Berlin?'

'Indeed, but he's a first-class agent: if any of his Ruhr network are around then it would be quite something to get them back to work, don't you think?'

'You used Sophia on the Peenemünde bombing, didn't you, Tom?'

'Yes, Barney's been very generous with her.'

'The problem is,' said Barney, 'that may have been a mission too far. I'm not sure how much longer we can keep her going. In the normal course of events, we could send her over to the

Ruhr, though we'd struggle to get a plausible cover story. Pretty Berliner wife of a senior SS officer wondering around the bomb sites of the Ruhr in her fur coat and high-heeled shoes... but let's see, eh?'

Chapter 7

'Do you know this man? Here, look carefully.'

Marek Weiss passed a photograph to Henryk Kamiński who peered at it for a while and then stood up to hold it closer to the flickering lightbulb hanging from the ceiling, the only source of light in the room. They were in the basement of the Jewish Fighting Organisation's base on Zamenhofa: Marek Weiss – the man known as Sowa – Zhenia Krakowski who Kamiński had met in Poznań and his old friend and colleague, Roman Loszynski.

'I don't think so, it's a bit blurred.'

'I told you, Kamiński, we took it on the street with a hidden camera. If we'd taken it in a studio with nice lighting and—'

'Can I have a look?'

Roman Loszynski walked over to look at the photograph his friend was holding.

'I know who that is.'

'Really?'

'Absolutely. It's Konrad Lubnauer: he was a manager at Ławica airport in Poznań, maybe he's still there, I've no idea. When we used to meet at the airport to work on the PZL.37 project with air force officers he was always hanging around. He'd even come into our briefings.'

'Are you're sure?'

'It's obviously been a few years since I've seen him but... yes... it's Lubnauer all right.'

'And was he a Nazi?'

'I've no idea,' said Loszynski, 'but he was hardly going to advertise it in 1938, was he? But he's an ethnic German, so who knows?'

'Why do you ask?'

'I was watching when you arrived at Główna station.' Zhenia angled her chair and turned to face Henryk Kamiński. 'I was there because I would recognise you. The idea was after I'd followed you for a while, I'd signal to the next person who you were. But as soon as you left the train, I spotted this man also leaving it, clearly hurrying to keep up with you. I managed to let one of my back-ups know and we were able to separate him from you. Another team followed him and took this photo.'

'Before we do anything else,' said Sowa, 'we need to deal with him. And we're going to need your help, Kamiński.'

—

Zhenia – the woman calling herself Helena Kamińska – had left Poznań early the previous Thursday morning. Late that night – it must have been close to midnight – Henryk Kamiński was woken by the pinging sound of small stones striking his bedroom window. He sat upright for a moment or two, just to be sure his ears hadn't deceived him. The dog next door barked once.

A minute later he heard tapping at the back door. He told his wife it was nothing, but she should remain in bed. He removed his pistol from its hiding place behind the upstairs sink and went down to the kitchen. When he opened the back door, a man stepped forward. In the darkness of the kitchen, it was hard to make out the man's features, but he was short and appeared to be well built and in his fifties.

'I have five minutes, Kamiński, so listen carefully to my instructions.'

The man sat at the kitchen table and Kamiński joined him. The man leaned close, speaking just inches from his ear. It was hard to place his accent, it sounded as if it could be Silesian.

Tomorrow, you must apply for permission to travel to Warsaw next Tuesday. When you arrive, you should leave Główna station and head north, towards Krolewska and then into Saski Park. A smartly dressed woman with a small dog will approach you and ask for the time... give it to her and then ask her the dog's name... if her reply is Wilk then you're to follow her, she'll pass you on to someone else...

Kamiński laughed at the idea of a small dog being called 'wolf' and the man asked if he understood everything because he didn't have long and Kamiński said yes, please carry on.

'If someone approaches you and asks for directions to the Brühl Palace you'll know there's an emergency. You must do what they say. Got that?'

Kamiński said he did, and the man was already standing, buttoning his jacket and heading to the door. He paused for a moment, looked at Kamiński as if checking whether he was up to it and wished him a good journey.

The dog next door barked one more time.

–

The train journey was as uneventful as a train journey in occupied Poland could be and Główna station felt very different to the last time he was there. Then it had been full of families and had a busy but jolly atmosphere, people excited at the prospect of a journey or pleased to have reached their destination. Now it seemed more like a military camp, German troops everywhere. He left the station by the north exit and as instructed headed across Krolewska and towards Saski Park where he'd be looking out for a small dog named wolf. He heard some shouting in German behind him but knew better than to turn round. At that moment a large man pushed past him and then fell in step with him.

'Can you tell me the way to the Brühl Palace?'

The man's voice urgent. Kamiński was unsure how to respond and the man repeated his question and then hissed, 'Follow me.' He wheeled to his right and led Kamiński down a narrow alley.

'We'll wait here,' he told him, struggling to catch his breath. 'Let's share a cigarette,' he said, 'and then we'll move on.'

They ended up in a building on Bielanska, which as far as he could tell was north of Saski Park, the wall of the ghetto a hundred yards or so to the west. The man hurried him to the top floor of what appeared to be an abandoned office building and showed him into a small internal office.

'Wait here: there's water and a little food in that cupboard. Someone will come and get you tonight. Whatever you do, stay here. Don't make a sound.'

It was midnight when he became aware of soft footsteps slowly approaching his room. He wondered whether he should try and hide but there was a tap at the door and the woman who had come to Poznań the previous week entered.

'There was a change of plan today, we had to create a diversion, but you're safe here for the time being. Tomorrow morning we'll move a few blocks and hide somewhere else and then move into the ghetto.'

The following morning a boy no more than sixteen brought him some workman's clothes and boots and said to come with him. They made their way to the top of Bielanska and then along the rear of Dluga, through the narrow alleys and in and out of backyards. They came to a tenement building and the boy scrambled over the rubble and dropped into what appeared to be a hole at the edge of the building. When Henryk caught up, the boy beckoned him into a cellar. They crawled along it for a while and then into a narrow space, no more than three feet high, which meant Henryk had to lay flat.

'Wait here,' the boy said. 'A man will be here soon.'

Henryk asked how long and the boy shrugged before disappearing.

–

Henryk had got it in his mind that the man wouldn't arrive until nightfall and he tried to make himself as comfortable as possible, which was actually near impossible given the circumstances. He felt something scuttling by his feet and then caught a pair of tiny eyes staring at him, as if offended he was occupying their space.

But the man arrived less than an hour later, crouching down to introduce himself – Jarosław – before explaining the plan, using his forefinger to sketch a route in the dust on the ground.

'We're here – on Dluga. We'll move up to Miodowa – here – and enter the sewers there. We'll then move in this direction under the ghetto walls and through the sewer canals to the bunker on Mila. I'll leave you there and someone else will meet you. You must be an important person?'

Henryk said not really, no more so than anyone else and why did he ask?

'I'm a sewer engineer. No one knows these sewers better than me. The Germans are always on the lookout for people using the sewers to get in and out of the ghetto. The Jews only use me for someone important.'

'Are you Home Army?'

Jarosław shook his head and looked offended, spitting in the dust. 'Absolutely not. Gwardia Ludowa.'

The People's Guard. The communist resistance.

Jarosław said they'd better get a move on.

The journey was a perilous one: at times the filthy water reached to their chests and then it would drop away almost entirely, but the curved surface was always slippery. Jarosław kept a few yards in front of him, his whistling sometimes audible above the babbling water, turning round frequently, the torch he carried lighting up a reassuring grin on his face, although Henryk was unsure who it was meant to reassure.

He only realised they'd reached their destination when he became aware that Jarosław had moved further ahead of him and was talking with someone. He heard Helena's voice say to come here and as he did so Jarosław brushed past, on his way back out of the ghetto, muttering, 'Good luck.'

He stayed in the bunker on Mila for an hour or so, washing as much of the filth off him as he could manage and changing clothes.

Helena then took him to the basement on Zamenhofa and an emotional reunion with Roman. Marek Weiss then said they really needed to get to business, so they went into another room where on a table the Tatra boxes were on display, as if in a museum. Spread out next to them were the blueprints and the two notebooks, along with a collection of leads.

Henryk whistled in appreciation and said this was remarkable, they'd given up hope all this still existed and then turned to Weiss and said he probably had no idea how important this was, and Weiss said actually he did and he wanted to know how Henryk and his friends were going to meet their side of the deal.

'If you get Roman, his family and all this out of the ghetto then we'll take over from there.'

'And the weapons, Karmiński?'

'You know how hard it is to get anything, but we can get you half a dozen Błyskawica sub-machine guns and a dozen Vis semi-automatic pistols, Polish Army stock.'

'Is that all?'

'We have Sidolówka hand grenades, maybe two dozen.'

Sowa nodded approvingly. 'Sidolówka? I thought they were Home Army?'

'They are: we borrowed them.'

The laughter briefly lifted the tension. A few minutes of negotiation followed: any more sub-machine guns? Impossible, but maybe another three pistols... and another half dozen grenades?

They shook hands. Henryk Kamiński said he needed a day and access to a telephone but hopefully the weapons could be in Warsaw within two days. Weiss nodded and said when they had them, they'd get Roman and his family out of the ghetto and to a safe house near Wschodnia station on the other side of the Vistula.

Zhenia said Henryk would be taken to a bunker on Franciszkańska and from there out of the ghetto through a different sewer in the morning. Someone would take him to the safe house where he'd wait for the family – and have an opportunity to use a telephone.

And it was then, just as he was preparing to go, that Weiss told him to wait and produced a photograph and asked him if he knew this man.

–

Marek Weiss was adamant. Konrad Lubnauer – the man who'd followed Henryk Kamiński from Główna station – had to be dealt with.

'Our people were watching you, Henryk: they're sure Lubnauer was on his own, but that's not unusual. The Gestapo often use Polish collaborators. They think they're less conspicuous – and more dispensable. We can help them in that respect. As you were approaching Krolewska, one of our team posed as a Gestapo officer and demanded to see his identity card. That delayed him enough for us to get you clear.'

'And you want me to go back there and act as bait?' Henryk Kamiński looked surprised.

'Exactly. He's been spotted hanging around the Krolewska area all day. Our plan is to get you out of the ghetto and changed back into your own clothes. Then you're to walk round the area. Hopefully, he'll spot you.'

'And what do I do?'

'Nothing, Kamiński, I told you. Just walk around, don't look behind you and we'll take care of things. The man who approached you yesterday – the one who asked for directions to Brühl Palace – will then come up to you and take you to the safe house near Wschodnia.'

'And you're able to operate like that outside the ghetto?'

Marek Weiss allowed a tight smile. 'We have friends.'

Henryk Kamiński did as he'd been instructed. After leaving the ghetto through another sewer he'd emerged into the cellar of a house on Nalewki where he was able to wash and change into his own clothes. He then followed a woman pushing a pram, eventually finding himself on Krolewska and soon walking past the place where Lubnauer had been stopped and he'd been hurried into the alley. He'd been told to walk purposefully and not too quick or too slow and he was beginning to wonder how long he could keep this up when he noticed the woman with the pram who had removed her hat, which was the signal that Lubnauer had been spotted and he was to leave the area now.

He crossed the road and as he did so heard a commotion some fifty yards behind him. Despite his orders, he couldn't resist looking back.

Lubnauer's body lay motionless in the middle of the road, a pool of blood quickly spreading around it. Next to him was a motorbike, its front wheel alongside his head, its engine revving. He heard a woman say, 'It went straight into him,' and a man shout, 'It didn't even stop!' At that moment the motorbike spun round and sped away.

Kamiński felt a tug at his sleeve and when he looked up the man who'd led him into the alley the previous day told him to come with him.

–

Dr Otto Kurz found out about Konrad Lubnauer's death the following day. When Lubnauer had called him on the Tuesday to say he'd lost Kamiński he'd begun to wonder whether his plan was quite as clever as it had first seemed. Lubnauer sounded panicked and out of his depth. Kurz did his best to reassure him, telling him to calm down.

'These things happen, Konrad. Stay around the area, the chances are Kamiński will return to it. Which direction was he heading in when you managed to lose him?'

Lubnauer replied he hadn't managed to lose him, he'd been stopped by a Gestapo officer and asked to show his identity but as far as he could tell he'd been walking in the direction of Saski

Park: he knew that because he must have walked round it a dozen times since.

But since telling Lubnauer to stay in the area and to keep in touch, he'd heard nothing. Reluctantly he decided to send one of his most trusted officers to Warsaw. *Don't let on, though, but ask around, see if there's any news on a Konrad Lubnauer.*

The officer rang him a few hours after arriving in Warsaw to tell him he'd found Lubnauer – on a slab in the central morgue in Warsaw.

'He was crossing Krolewska when a motorbike hit him full on.'

Kurz didn't like his officer's tone but decided to deal with that another time. 'And the motorcyclist: was he arrested?'

'Apparently not, seems he got away. But the local Gestapo are letting the police handle this one, they're treating it as an accident.'

Dr Otto Kurz told his officer to return to Poznań and to remember not to say anything to anyone. He walked over to his window, overlooking Niezłomnych, and thought about 1939 when he first knew he had to find the Jew Loszynski. With the benefit of hindsight, he ought to have stopped the deportations or asked for help, but this had been something he thought he could manage on his own.

Now he realised what a dreadful mistake he'd made. He looked down at the pedestrians hurrying by with their hunched shoulders and no responsibilities and for a brief moment envied them.

He'd carry on looking, of course. He'd question Kamiński when he returned to Poznań. But he knew the chances of him finding Loszynski were slim.

The one consolation was that at least his superiors were unaware of his failure.

Chapter 8

It was by far the hardest task the British had given him. For the first time Harald Mettler felt his life was in danger.

When he'd first arrived in Berlin five years previously – he couldn't believe he'd been there that long – he'd been little more than a messenger. But very gradually his role was enhanced, becoming increasingly dangerous. It evolved into what the Englishman had described as that of an odd-job man, a fixer.

Now he realised that he was a secret agent.

A British secret agent in Berlin.

He had to admire the skilful way he'd been manipulated by Basil Remington–Barber, the elderly British spy chief in Berne. This mildly eccentric Englishman gave the appearance of being slightly absent-minded and far too trusting, but Harald Mettler soon realised this was a well-crafted front. The Englishman was actually patient, intuitive, very clever and had a habit of making young Harald – as he called him – feel important.

They'd first met in 1936, an apparently chance encounter on the train from to Berne when Mettler was returning from an anti-fascist meeting in Geneva. He'd been appalled at what he'd seen earlier that year in Germany and felt he ought to do something about it, but on the journey back to Berne he was reflecting on what a waste of time it had been. And not just a waste of time: he was worried he'd taken far too much of a risk. He was, after all, an official of the Federal Political Department, the Swiss

Foreign Ministry. Even as a very junior official he wasn't supposed to become involved in political activities and it was while he was regretting his rash behaviour that the Englishman introduced himself.

He introduced himself as Basil – he'd made a joke about not confusing it with Basel – and it soon became apparent Basil knew exactly who he was. Over the next two years Basil patiently nurtured Harald Mettler, persuading him that working for the British most certainly did not mean working against the interests of Switzerland. Far from it, indeed: surely it was not in the interests of Switzerland to have such a powerful neighbour in the hands of the Nazis, who he knew Harald despised? Harald was to see it as working to undermine the Nazis: if anything, it was his patriotic duty.

But in the meantime, they had to be patient. Harald Mettler applied for a transfer to Berlin and that eventually came about in April 1938: a posting as a junior official – a clerk really – in the consular department of the Swiss Embassy in the German capital.

Part of his job was to be one of a small number of messengers, trusted to deliver the diplomatic bag from the embassy on Corneliusstrasse to Berne and back again.

And for a few years that was the extent of his work for the British: picking up messages and packages in Berlin and delivering them to Berne and sometimes taking letters back with him. His postbox, as the Englishman called it, was a news kiosk on Budapester Strasse, where a one-armed war veteran called Reinhard was the point of contact between Berne and British agents in the city.

But as the war progressed, it became clear there were fewer British agents in the city. His debriefings in Berne were now, more often than not, carried out by a man called Noel, who he'd known from the British Passport Control Office on Tiergartenstrasse when he'd come across him on official business.

He'd meet with Noel Moore whenever he was back in Berne, calling a number as soon as he arrived and asking the person answering to tell Maria he was in the city and the person would reply and say Maria was out until a particular time and Harald would know that was when the rendezvous would be. He'd walk the short distance from his apartment on Zähringerstrasse, near the university, to the rear of a small, shabby office building on Schützenmattstrasse. The meetings would usually be in the evening when the area was quiet. He'd approach the office building from the other side of the road and if he saw a black bicycle with a red saddle propped up on the side wall, he'd cross the road and know it was safe to enter.

The meetings tended to be quite quick.

Is everything in order?

You have no worries?

And then he'd hand over whatever he'd brought with him from Berlin and Noel would do likewise with whatever was to be taken back to Germany and then he'd slip him some money – sometimes as much as a hundred Swiss francs, sometimes fifty. Harald would insist that wasn't necessary and he wasn't doing this for the money, but Noel would smile conspiratorially and place the money inside Mettler's jacket pocket nevertheless, patting it to ensure it was safe. They'd then each smoke a cigarette or two and Noel would ask him about Berlin – the mood, food shortages, fuel, any gossip he'd picked up, what were people saying at the embassy...

Harald would leave first, Noel passing him by on his bike a few minutes later, always whistling a jolly tune.

But that evening in March 1943 it was very different. When he entered the building on Schützenmattstrasse Noel Moore wasn't alone. Sitting at a table in the damp room was Basil Remington-Barber, his overcoat drawn tightly round him and a cigarette held horizontally in front of his face, meaning he sat behind a veil of blue-grey smoke.

Good to see you, Harald, you look well – please, please do sit down.

Harald said thank you very much and was going to say he may look well but he didn't feel it – actually he was exhausted and living a clandestine life in Berlin was taking its toll, especially after all these years. But he didn't bother: this was clearly no welfare meeting. If Basil Remington-Barber was there it was about something far more important than how he was feeling.

'Have you heard of cricket Harald?'

'It's an English game, isn't it, Basil?'

'Well, yes – others play it too – Indians et cetera – but that's not the point. Do you know anything about it?'

Harald shook his head and said not really, though he thought it may be something like hockey and Noel Moore laughed while Basil made a play of looking appalled.

'Never mind: I'm using cricket as a way of describing its team structure. Don't look quite so confused, Harald, you'll soon catch my drift. There are eleven men in a cricket team and when batting the best batsmen bat first and so on, with the least competent batsmen batting towards the end. Got that?'

Harald said he had, though he wasn't sure he had and if he didn't know Basil better, he'd have thought he'd been drinking.

'Now, every so often a batsman – say he's been coming in at number six or seven – does frightfully well, so in the next game he's moved up to bat at – say – four or five. We call that being promoted up the batting order.'

Harald nodded and said he got it, hoping Basil would now start to make sense. He was used to the Englishman being discursive, but he was struggling to see the point of this.

'It's quite an honour to be moved up the batting order. Happened to me a few times. Did you play much cricket, Noel?'

Noel looked as if his mind was elsewhere and said 'pardon' and when he did reply said he preferred tennis and Basil made a disapproving noise.

'Point is, the higher one is in the batting order, the more responsibility one has. It's more dangerous too, faster bowling and the like. All of this is by way of telling you you're being promoted up the batting order, Harald.'

He paused and lit another cigarette and watched the young Swiss for a response, but Mettler said nothing at first and then asked if Basil would mind being a bit clearer.

'You've done jolly well for us in Berlin, Harald. We trust you. You do what we ask you to do and you've avoided being caught, which is no mean achievement after all this time. But up until now you've been batting lower down the order for us: you've been a messenger, an odd-job man as I call it, a fixer as London have taken to describing chaps like you. But now I need you higher up the batting order. When you return to Berlin, we want you to be an agent – gathering information for us.'

Harald found himself saying that was indeed an honour, though in truth he'd felt a wave of fear sweep over him. He wanted to say he'd prefer to be asked if he wanted to be a British agent rather than being told he was one, but Basil was looking at him as if he'd done him an enormous favour.

'Is there any particular mission?'

Basil said absolutely, of course, and perhaps Noel would be so good as to take the new ball, which must have been an English joke because both Basil and Noel laughed while he didn't have the faintest idea what they meant.

Noel Moore pulled his chair closer to table and produced a flask, which he passed round. Basil drank from it first and when it was handed to Harald the whisky tasted of tobacco.

'You recall how at the end of 1941 we asked you to keep an eye on that woman in Charlottenburg, Sophia von Naundorf?'

'You mean the one with the SS officer husband?'

'Correct. Your job was simply to pass by every month or so, make sure she was still around and be there in case there was ever a problem.'

'Which I have been doing. Is there a problem?'

Both Noel Moore and Basil Remington-Barber nodded.

'We last heard from her just over a fortnight ago, on Wednesday the tenth when she sent a short message through the kiosk on Budapester Strasse saying we may not hear from her for a while. Importantly, there was no coded warning embedded in the message, which there would have been had she been caught or was about to be caught.'

'And that's it, old chap,' said Basil. 'Since then, nothing. Now London's jumping up and down wanting to know where the hell is she – as if it's our fault, dammit – and when I reply saying we'd quite like to know too, that doesn't seem to ameliorate matters. So, we need to know where she is.'

'The last we heard of her husband,' said Noel, 'was that he was taking part in the defence of Stalingrad and, as you know, that didn't end terribly well for them, so he's either dead or a prisoner, though I suppose there's a very remote chance he made it back to Berlin. We'd quite like to know what happened to him. That could give us a clue as to where Sophia is.'

For the next hour they briefed Harald, suggesting ways he could find out what had happened to Sophia, advice on how to ask about her in the least obtrusive or obvious manner, other places she could be and…

'What we really do need to know though is whether she's been captured. If she's in the hands of the Gestapo, we need to know – and it so happens we have a contact inside Prinz Albrecht Strasse, though he doesn't know he's a contact of ours, if you see what I mean. He's someone who if approached in the right way will know it's in his interests to help you. You need to listen carefully, Harald.'

Chapter 9

Berne, Switzerland
March 1943

'Is this all?'

The man was pointing at the documents she'd shown him as if they were of little consequence. Sophia started to respond, and then stopped herself. She was tempted to ask the man opposite her what more he wanted, but thought better of it. She was beginning to get used to people in Switzerland being so dismissive of her.

It was the Wednesday 17 March and she'd travelled from Geneva to Berne the previous day, staying at a *pension* on Kramgasse overnight and presenting herself at the Soviet Legation soon after it opened the following morning. They'd been quite pleasant at first: when she showed them her *Kennkarte* and *Reisepass* and said she had information to help the Soviet Union and they'd taken her to a side room and said someone would be with her soon.

Half an hour later a man more or less her age entered and explained he worked for the legation – he gave no name, no job title – and perhaps she'd like to start from the beginning. Which she did: she told him her husband was a senior SS officer – a Brigadeführer, and there was a delay as she had to spell it, twice. She told of how she disagreed strongly with him because she was opposed to the Nazis, though he was unaware of that – she'd married him before he'd become a Nazi. She explained how she'd discovered this diary – she pushed it towards him – in which her husband wrote in detail about the murder of Jews in Kielce and

85

elsewhere in the diary were details of other atrocities committed in Poland. He was last heard of at the headquarters of the 6th Army at Gumrak Airbase – near Stalingrad – and she assumed he'd be captured and—

'How do you know he wasn't killed? Many thousands of your soldiers were killed at Stalingrad.' A thin smile revealed a row of yellow teeth.

'I agree it's quite possible he was killed, but if anyone could avoid being killed it would be him. In any case, he'd arranged a disguise, as a Wehrmacht officer called Oberleutnant Karl Naundorf. He was gambling on a junior army officer being treated very differently to a senior SS one. Here, look at this letter…'

This was when he asked if this was all and Sophia replied it was and she hoped the Soviet Union would be able to use it to apprehend her husband.

The man said to wait please, which she did. For over an hour. The next person to come into the room was much older, perhaps in his sixties and he moved stiffly, in the manner of someone with a bad back. He sat down slowly, wincing as he did so. He looked at Sophia for a few moments, nodded and handed her a card:

A. I. Stepanov

Soviet Legation to Switzerland

Berne

'What is it you want from the Soviet Union, Frau von Naundorf?'

She was beginning to think very much the same. It had never been her intention to have anything to do with the Soviet Union. Her original plan had been to escape from the Reich, withdraw everything from the bank in Zürich, travel to Geneva to inform the Red Cross about her husband and then present herself here in Berne at the British Embassy and resume her career as a British agent.

But it had gone wrong in Geneva when the Red Cross didn't want to know about her husband. They weren't interested, but the woman who'd shown her out of the building had suggested she contact the Soviet Legation in Berne and here she was.

She now regretted doing so. She ought to have considered the matter more carefully because she now realised that, had she done so, she'd have realised that turning up at the Soviet Legation like this was too rash and impulsive. She ought to have taken precautions, maybe gone to the British first to see what they said. Maybe they could have passed the information about Karl-Heinrich to the Soviets – they were meant to be allies, after all.

But she had to admit that she was too preoccupied with ensuring her husband was brought to justice and, if she was honest, she also had to admit that she was motivated in good part by a desire to see him punished.

She looked at the man sitting opposite her – A. I. Stepanov, according to his card – and he seemed pleasant enough, and although he smiled at her in quite a pleasant manner and wasn't leering at her in the way so many men did, she still wondered if she shouldn't gather up everything laid out on the table and leave.

She explained to A. I. Stepanov that she didn't really want anything as such, but she felt her husband deserved to be punished for his crimes and expected the Soviet Union would feel the same way.

'And you say you have money and gold from his account in Zürich?'

She hesitated, worried the man would see through her reply.

'I told you, I left Berlin last Friday and travelled to Zürich. I visited the bank on Monday, but it turned out there was very little in the account, just some cash.'

'How much?'

'Just three hundred Swiss francs.'

'Is that all?'

'I'm afraid so: it's typical of my husband to exaggerate like that, to make himself sound important. He was all bluster.'

'It hardly seems worthwhile – going to all the trouble of opening a Swiss bank account with so little in it.'

'I know: maybe he withdrew some funds without me knowing.'

'And where's the money now?'

She pointed to her handbag and he asked to see it. She'd concealed the other two hundred she'd kept in her bra.

'And what do you intend to do, Frau von Naundorf?' He placed a sarcastic emphasis on the 'von'.

She said she wasn't sure what he meant, and he shifted awkwardly in his seat and asked what were her plans: would she be returning to Germany, for instance, and she said she doubted it, she was just looking for justice and—

'Would you be prepared to be of assistance to the Soviet Union?'

'I'd rather hoped that providing this information would be of assistance to the Soviet Union.'

'But after this matter has been dealt with. Would you be prepared to be of further assistance?'

She knew better than to say 'no', so she said she was prepared to do anything to help defeat the Nazis. She was now beginning to feel hot and uneasy and was worried her discomfort showed. There was no question now in her mind that she'd made a big mistake coming here. She would leave now and go straight to the British Embassy. She leaned forward to collect the diary and the other papers but the man opposite her held up a hand to indicate she should stop and moved everything towards him.

'First things first, Frau von Naundorf. It will take us a few days to investigate the matters you have raised regarding your husband. In the meantime, you will be a guest of the Soviet Union.'

'Thank you very much, but I'm fine, thank you, I have a room at a very pleasant *pension* on Kramgasse and—'

A. I. Stepanov put up a hand to stop her and said there would be no need to return there. 'We have a very comfortable and secure place where you will stay.'

–

The very comfortable place turned out to be on the outskirts of Münsingen, a small town that followed the River Aare on its course south-east from Berne, with the Bernese Oberland and the High Alps in the distance.

She'd been driven there straight from the Soviet Legation that morning, soon after her encounter with A. I. Stepanov. She didn't exactly feel like a prisoner, but she had little doubt that if she had done anything other than what they'd suggested, matters would have been very different.

She was accompanied on the journey by the first man she'd met at the legation, who sat in the front of the car next to the driver. A woman sat next to her in the back. The journey took less than half an hour and was conducted largely in silence. They drove through Münsingen, at which point the man in the front turned round and spoke sharply in Russian with the woman sitting next to her, who looked contrite as she leaned across her and drew the blinds on the windows.

Sophia could just about make out where they were going through the front window: they turned off the main road, along a narrow road with farmland on either side, and then slowed down to turn onto a track that took them alongside a wood until they came to a house, the grounds of which were enclosed by a high wall.

And this was where Sophia von Naundorf remained for the next few weeks. The house was rather elegant: the design reminded her of Bauhaus, with stunning views of mountains through the picture windows, and parquet wood flooring and walls covered in landscapes. Her bedroom was on the first floor, with its own bathroom, and this was where she spent most of the day, coming downstairs only for her meals and to walk in the grounds twice a day, always accompanied by the woman who'd sat next to her on the journey from Berne, the man who'd first interviewed her constantly lurking in the background.

Very little was said – the woman spoke little German – and while the door to her room wasn't locked, whenever she opened it, someone appeared in a matter of moments. The external doors were certainly locked the whole time.

She had begun to think about how she could escape and get to the British Embassy in Berne, but her situation was hopeless. Even if she got out of the house, the walls were some ten feet high, their tops studded with broken glass.

The Tuesday after she arrived there – she reckoned it was 23 March – she heard a car pull up at the front and she was soon summoned downstairs and into the lounge overlooking the garden. A. I. Stepanov was sitting in the sofa and indicated she should sit opposite him.

'We are making progress.'

'Have you found my husband?'

He shrugged as if to indicate not that kind of progress. 'There are hundreds of thousands of German prisoners in and around Stalingrad. What I require you to do is write a letter to your husband now. Tell him everything and if we find him, we'll make sure he sees that letter and the extracts from his diary. You'll write the letter now – everything you need is on that table. I'll wait for you to write it. If I'm satisfied with it the letter will go in tonight's diplomatic bag to Moscow. With some luck it should be with our comrades in Stalingrad by the end of the week.'

Sophia spent the next hour and a half writing the letter. More than once, she found herself overwhelmed by an emotion she couldn't quite put her finger on. It felt as if she was writing her husband's death warrant and she couldn't decide whether she was relieved or appalled at doing so. Stepanov constantly peered over her shoulder and made the occasional suggestion or asked her to start the page again.

When she'd finished and he was finally satisfied he said she was to remain there for the time being and he'd be back with news.

'Is it not possible for me to return to Berne?'

He laughed and said that was out of the question. He hoped to return soon with news. In the meantime, Frau von Naundorf should enjoy the views.

A. I. Stepanov returned exactly one week later, on 30 March. He stood formally in front of her as he delivered the news.

'This morning I received a cable from Moscow: it contained the text of a communication from one of my colleagues in the Beketova prisoner of war camp in Stalingrad Oblast. The communication informed me that thanks to the information provided by you, your husband was identified as one of the prisoners there. Comrade Commissar Semyon Mikhailovich Chernyakhovsky investigated the matter and is satisfied the prisoner arrested is indeed a senior SS officer. He was executed yesterday morning.'

Sophia was shocked by the abruptness of Stepanov. He sat down, watching her carefully and asked if she was shocked.

'Yes, but...'

'But what did you expect, Frau von Naundorf? According to my colleague, your letter to your husband was read to him just before his execution. Comrade Chernyakhovsky said he'd never seen any prisoner so angry and distressed. Apparently despite being handcuffed your husband had to be strapped to a chair before he was hung and as a result, he took ten minutes to die.'

Sophia was aware she was sitting very still and must have looked calm, so she said nothing for a few moments, looking out over the garden and the Alps beyond. It could not have been a more tranquil scene, but she felt her blood turn cold and her body shake from the inside. She heard herself telling the Russian this was what she expected, and certainly no more than her husband deserved, and she was pleased justice had been served.

They let her into the garden and she walked around for a while, trying to deal with all the different emotions: the shock at the news of her husband's death but also the overwhelming sense of relief.

After a few minutes Stepanov joined her, walking stiffly alongside. 'Have you thought of the other matter which we discussed, Frau von Naundorf?'

'What other matter is that?'

'The matter of whether you would be willing to be of further assistance to the Soviet Union.'

She walked towards the wall and then stopped to admire a flower bed. Saying 'yes' would be a way out of this place, but it could mean her being taken to the Soviet Union or sent back into Germany. If she said 'no'... she had a notion of what would happen if she said 'no'.

'I need time to think: after all, I've only just been informed of my husband's death.'

'Your husband was a Nazi: his death was as a result of information you gave us!'

'Yes, I know that, but nonetheless, I need some time to think – to consider matters.'

'It would be in your interests to work for us. It's Tuesday today. I expect your response by the weekend.'

She said if he could allow her a week, she'd definitely have an answer by then and Stepanov grunted his approval.

When she returned to her room, she discovered most of her papers, including her passport and the 300 francs, had disappeared from her handbag. When she tried to go down to ask about it, she discovered the door to her room was locked.

She'd entered Switzerland feeling like a fugitive.

Now she realised she was a prisoner.

Chapter 10

The Berlin office of Swiss Intelligence – known as Bureau Ha – was based inside the military attachés department on the third floor of the country's embassy on Corneliusstrasse.

Harald Mettler was a frequent visitor there, usually to sort out something to do with passports or identity cards. He was always fascinated by the clandestine nature of the office. The door would always be locked and to enter he had to pick up a telephone just by the door and then he'd be let in.

The man in charge was a Major Widmer, a serious but studiously polite man who like him was from Fribourg and would always make a remark or two to acknowledge the connection and agree how different Fribourg was to Berlin!

Harald Mettler returned to Berlin at the end of March, after the Englishman had promoted him to British agent and Noel Moore had briefed him on his mission: to find out what had happened to Sophia von Naundorf and her SS officer husband.

Within days of his return to Berlin he had a breakthrough. He was called up to the Bureau Ha office where one of the major's assistants handed him a sealed package. It contained *kennkarten*, she said, German identity cards.

We no longer require them, but even so, Major Widmer wants them to be stored securely, but not in our safe: he worries someone may use them by mistake. Please lock them in a safe in the consul-general's office.

Mettler waited until he was the last one in the office that evening before opening the sealed package. It contained two dozen envelopes, each holding one *kennkarte*. On the front of each envelope was a handwritten note giving the dates when the card inside had been used. Each card appeared to have been used three or four times before apparently being retired.

He opened every envelope before choosing one, in the name of Wilhelm Linderbach, born in Erfurt in 1903, making him three years older than Mettler, working in Berlin as an accounts clerk.

He placed the remaining cards back in the consul-general's safe and studied Wilhelm Linderbach's card. He realised he didn't look much like the photograph, but the man was wearing heavy black spectacles and Mettler reckoned if he wore a similar pair and combed his hair differently that would make a notable difference. He knew he couldn't do anything about the fingerprints, but Linderbach was from Erfurt, which was helpful. He wasn't too sure what the Thuringian accent sounded like, but it was close to Bavaria and people often remarked how the Swiss accent was similar to the Bavarian one.

One week later, and wearing the heavy black spectacles, he set out as Wilhelm Linderbach. His first visit was to the *stadtbad*, the swimming pool on Krumme Strasse, close to where Sophia lived, which she visited regularly on most weekday mornings. He booked a day's pass to the members club where the steward seemed to be approachable so Mettler asked him about a friend of his he hadn't seen for a while.

We always used to have such good chats… Frau von Naundorf, Sophia. I think she had one of those lockers. I've not seen her for a while and I was wondering…

The steward said come to think of it, he hadn't seen her for a while either – she used to be such a regular customer. The following day Mettler went to Potsdamer Strasse in Charlottenburg, where the von Naundorfs lived.

Watch the place first then follow someone in – always appear business-like and in a hurry. It's a good idea to try and deliver a parcel, say it came to you by mistake, something like that.

He followed Noel Moore's advice, walking past the apartment block after work over a couple of evenings. There were no lights on in the apartment and no sign of anyone guarding the block or watching it. On the Saturday morning he passed by the block twice and on the second occasion he spotted a woman leaving and hurried to hold the door open for her, slightly doffing his new trilby, which he hoped concealed much of his face.

He hurried up to the von Naundorfs' floor and knocked on the door of their apartment. There was no reply. He was aware of a door opening behind him and when he turned round an elderly lady was standing there, alongside a brass plaque with the name 'Schmidt' on it.

She asked if she could help and he explained how he lived in an apartment block nearby – on Richard Wagner Strasse actually – and this package had come through his door earlier in the week and he was going to return it to the sender and then someone suggested there was a Frau von Naundorf who lived on Potsdamer Strasse.

'I understand she may live on this floor?'

'She lives in that apartment.'

'I see, thank you. And do you know if she's in?'

Frau Schmidt looked Mettler up and down and took half a step back, in an attempt to get a clearer view of his face.

'What did you say your name is?'

'Linderbach, Wilhelm Linderbach. Would you know if Frau von Naundorf is in? If so, I'll leave the package with her.'

He held the envelope so she could see it clearly. It only said 'Frau von Naundorf, Charlottenburg' on the front. Inside was a copy of *Frauen-Warte*, the magazine of the *Frauenschaft*, the Nazi women's organisation.

'Frau von Naundorf is away. I have no idea where she is.'

'Perhaps if I could leave this with you?'

Frau Schmidt was already holding out her hand to take the envelope.

'When was she last here?'

'You ask a lot of questions, don't you? Just like the others. She's been away for the best part of a month now and every few days they come to see if she's back. Maybe I should take your name and address – in case she returns?'

It was clearly time for him to leave and he could only risk one more question. He dared not ask who the 'they' was who came to see her every few days.

'And her husband, is he around?'

'I don't know how you know she has a husband, but in any case—' Frau Schmidt leaned forward in the direction of Mettler's ear '—he's out east. Who knows what the hell's happened to him!'

–

He moved quickly after that, worried he'd pushed his luck as far as it could go – though before leaving the block, he did go down to the basement where he saw the von Naundorfs' Mercedes was still there.

He hurried away, catching a tram on Schloss Strasse and vowing never to return to Potsdamer Strasse. He'd be able to tell Berne that Sophia hadn't been seen at her apartment for a month and the place appeared to be empty and the car was there, but he knew they'd press him on the Gestapo connection.

Harald Mettler put off contacting Harald Fuchs for a couple more days, knowing just how dangerous approaching the SS officer would be. Noel Moore had told him not to worry as the man would be even more terrified than he was and for perhaps the first time Harald had snapped and said it was easy enough for him to say that from the safety of Berne, but he was the one who was being asked to approach an SS officer and he could think of a thousand ways in which this would end with him as a long-term guest in the bowels of Prinz Albrecht Strasse and Basil had said as long as he was careful it all ought to be fine.

Just remember to mention the photographs.

Harald went to Neukölln and was able to establish that Harald Fuchs still lived at the address Noel had given him. He returned the following evening, arriving early enough to be waiting opposite the building where Fuchs lived and spot him entering.

He followed him in, the SS officer holding the front door for him but ignoring him until he realised Mettler had followed him up the stairs and was behind him as he unlocked him door.

'Can I help you?'

'I wish to talk with you in your room.'

'Who the hell do you think you—'

'I'm a friend of the late Werner Lustenberger. I believe you knew him as Joe, back in 1939: he knew you as Rudi.'

The SS officer looked horrified and hurried them both into his room.

'You'd better have a very good explanation for this because I can assure you the authorities will—'

The Swiss told him to listen very carefully because after that he doubted he'd want the authorities to know what he was about to say. He told the now-terrified man that he knew all about him – Untersturmführer Harald Fuchs, nickname Rudi. He knew about his homosexual relationship with Werner, nickname Joe. He didn't tell him that Lustenberger – Joe – was also a British agent. There was only so much information he needed to share with the German.

Fuchs began to protest but Mettler insisted he could prove it.

'What do you mean prove it?'

'I mean there are photographs of you naked on this very bed, taken in this room in February 1939 when Joe drugged you and photographed a number of secret documents you'd brought home with you from Prinz Albrecht Strasse.'

Fuchs was speechless at first, his head slowly moving round the room as if checking he wasn't in some kind of dream. He muttered this was nonsense when Harald produced an envelope from inside his jacket and handed it to the German.

'It was four years ago, Rudi, so let me jog your memory. The first four photographs are copies from dozens that Werner took of documents you'd brought home from work. One has lists of different military units, the other is for General von Brauchitsch. The documents were passed on to the British, for whom Werner worked. You'll notice both of these documents show your name: Untersturmführer Harald Fuchs. And if that isn't bad enough, Rudi, this last photograph of you, well we don't know if Werner intended the British to see it or why he took it, but it is rather handy, don't you think?'

Fuchs stared at the photographs in disbelief, as if reading his own death warrant. It showed him asleep, sprawled naked on the bed, the bed covers and wallpaper identical to those in the room they were standing in.

He stepped back and told Mettler the photographs were all fake and he'd have him arrested and in fact... His hand moved towards his revolver.

'I told you, these photographs are copies and there are far more of them. Should anything happen to me or should you fail to do what I ask then copies of the photographs will be sent to your superiors in Prinz Albrecht Strasse.'

'Ask me to do what?'

'Can we sit down, Rudi, perhaps? If you give me the information I require I promise you'll never see or hear from me or indeed anyone associated with me ever again. You'll have to take my word for it, but I can assure you I don't find this particularly easy either. I'm taking an enormous risk.'

Harald Mettler explained what he was after. He wanted Rudi to find out what he could about two people: a Sophia von Naundorf living on Potsdamer Strasse in Charlottenburg, and her husband, an SS Brigadeführer called Karl-Heinrich von Naundorf.

'I don't want you to do anything other than get me the information: see if there's a Gestapo file on the woman. With the husband it ought to be easier as I assume the SS has records. He was last heard of in Stalingrad, if that's any help. And if I suspect anything at all, Rudi... remember, the photographs.'

–

They met a few days later in the Schöneberg, in a small park between Pallas Strasse and Grunewald Strasse.

It was a Sunday and he'd arranged to meet the SS man at eleven o'clock, but Harald had taken up position on the top floor of a café overlooking the park a good hour before that. As far as he could tell nothing was untoward. At five to eleven he saw Fuchs enter the park, thankfully in civilian dress but striding into it with a swagger, marching to the centre of the park before stopping to look around.

Just stroll around and act normally, I'll find you.

He waited until ten past eleven: there was no sign of anyone else acting suspiciously. Five minutes later he was alongside the German.

'I was wondering where the fuck you were.'

'You have the information?'

'I give it to you and that's it, agreed?'

'That's the deal, Rudi.'

'According to a note on his file, the Brigadeführer was executed by the Red Army on the twenty-ninth of March. That's all I know about him.'

'And his wife?'

'A Gestapo file on her was opened on the nineteenth of March at the request of SS Brigadeführer Konrad Busch who reported her missing and asked for any information on her to be passed to him. There was a further note on the file that Sophia von Naundorf had crossed the border into Switzerland on the evening of Friday twelfth of March on a train to Zürich. They say they have no record of her returning back, although she had purchased a return ticket for Tuesday sixteenth. She never made that journey. The file says Gestapo officers have visited her apartment on a number of occasions but there's no sign of her and the maid insists she has no idea where she is.'

'And no one would know you've seen the file?'

'Do you think I'm stupid?'

Mettler didn't answer the question. He had the information Berne wanted. Whether they'd be pleased with it was another matter.

–

He was debriefed by the two Englishmen when he was back in Berne a few days later. They listened to him in silence in the damp room at the rear of the office building on Schützenmattstrasse, the only sound other than his voice being the rain lashing against the window. Basil Remington-Barber chewed at the end of a cigarette.

'So, it would appear she's been in Switzerland since the twelfth of March? Almost a month.'

'Do we believe the SS man, Basil?'

'I think we have to, Noel. It all fits, in any case. She's just vanished. Intriguing she appears to be in Switzerland but hasn't bothered to contact us. You'd have thought she'd want to know about Jack at the very least.'

'And you don't think approaching this Rudi chap like that – you don't think we've possibly shot ourselves in the foot, do you, Basil?'

'In what way Noel?'

'Alerting the Germans to our interest in her?'

'If I may say, sir, I very much doubt he's going to tell anyone about this. He was absolutely terrified when I met him.'

Basil nodded and said he thought as much and at least he had something to tell London and maybe this Rudi character would be useful to use again and Harald Mettler said under no circumstances would he ever go near him again.

Chapter 11

Basil Remington-Barber's summons to London at the end of March was a good example of how complicated and tedious life had become. Prior to September 1939 this would have been a straightforward and most agreeable business: a journey via Paris and all the pleasures that entailed.

Now it was a far more complicated matter, certainly devoid of any pleasures. A Swissair flight from Geneva to Barcelona, then Iberia to Lisbon and from there the seven-thirty BOAC morning flight to Whitchurch airport just outside Bristol.

He had rather hoped this visit wouldn't be as rushed as the previous one had been: he'd hoped to stay overnight with his ailing brother in Wiltshire, but he was met by a Service car and taken straight to London and St Ermin's hotel.

He was permitted half an hour in his room: Barney Allen would be waiting for him in the Caxton Bar.

–

Barney Allen had come straight to the point. Presumably Basil had heard the Ruhr offensive had begun?

Basil nodded as he felt an overwhelming tiredness sweep over him.

Barney said it was the first concerted use of the RAF's area bombing strategy and the idea was to send hundreds of aircraft over at a time and concentrate the bombing on particular targets.

It had started with a raid on Essen on 5 March. He asked whether Basil had heard anything, and Basil said not to be ridiculous, the Ruhr was more than three hundred miles north of Berne and Barney said no, not heard the actual bombing, but heard anything about its impact?

Both men laughed and ordered another drink and the atmosphere was quickly more relaxed, so for a while they gossiped about people in the Service and the war generally and then Barney asked what agents Basil might have in the Ruhr and the older man shook his head.

'None, I'm afraid, Barney. Struggling to keep together the few we've got in Germany as it is. Why do you ask?'

Barney explained at some length: area bombing was by its very nature imprecise and the RAF needed better intelligence on the results of their raids. Aerial reconnaissance was all well and good, he said, but what they wanted was what they termed 'eyes on the ground'.

'Eyes on the ground?'

'A phrase they've picked it up from the Americans: that's quite the thing now, trying to sound clever by using these asinine American phrases. The RAF want us to see if we can find people who can visit the sites of these air raids and report back. Even take photographs.'

'Good Lord: that's a tall order.'

'What about Sophia?'

'Still not heard anything since her last message, when she was still in Berlin. Where are we now, I lose track these days – it's Wednesday thirty-first today, isn't it? Last heard from her exactly three weeks ago. Doing our best to find out what's happened to her.'

'And Jack Miller?'

'Jack's behaving himself in Berne. Very helpful to have around and does a decent job of debriefing escaped aircrew and PoWs. But I've no doubt that as far as he's concerned his real purpose of being in Berne is to be as near as possible to Sophia, so to speak.'

'Earlier in the war – indeed even before it – Jack had a nice little network in the Ruhr: Dortmund, Essen, Gelsenkirchen. His cover was damned good, as you know, Basil, covering football matches. I'm wondering what the chances are of getting them back in the game. Waking them up, as we call it.'

'Without Jack, near impossible I'd say.'

There was a long pause during which both men studied their whiskies – Basil's had ice; Barney's was neat.

'I take it you know what I'm about to ask, don't you, Basil?'

The older man nodded and asked when he thought he should send him in.

'As soon as possible, Barney.'

'Let's hope Jack's decent about it.'

—

'Germany?'

Jack Miller said 'Jesus Christ', which he knew annoyed Basil Remington-Barber intensely. Basil had told him more than once that although he wasn't religious he regarded that as 'uncouth'. Such an English word, uncouth.

'Yes, Jack, Germany. London wants you to know just how important this mission is. Indeed, it's their top priority at the moment.'

They were in Basil's office in the British Embassy on Thunstrasse. Noel Moore was there too and the atmosphere was every bit as awkward as Basil had feared it would be.

'You mean to say, you want me to go back into Germany, clandestinely?'

'Well, you can hardly go openly, can you, Jack?'

The American paused, taking it all in and looking at Basil in that annoying way he had when Basil had said something he didn't like, as if he thought the Englishman was mad.

'We'll make sure you have a decent cover, Jack, you can be assured of that.' Noel Moore was adopting his usual calm and reassuring tone.

'Decent?'

'Watertight then: the best cover money can buy, so to speak.'

'You're buying it?'

'Not as such, no... turn of phrase.'

'But I'm a wanted man there.'

'You won't be going anywhere near Berlin.'

'Shame, I could have had a good look for Sophia while I was there.' Then he paused, reflecting on what he'd just said. It had been a quip but now he was thinking about it and maybe it wasn't such a bad idea after all. If he was in Berlin, he was bound to be able to find out what had happened to her.

'You'll be much further to the west, Jack – that's the plan. Of course, if you're saying you don't feel you're up to it then...'

'I didn't say that Basil.'

'You didn't seem awfully keen and I—'

'"Awfully keen"? Christ, Basil, you spring this on me and act then act as if I'm being ungrateful. I need to know everything about this mission. You know as well as I do that my chances of pulling it off and returning alive are slim, so I have to know just what you have in mind.'

'All in good time, Jack, all in good time.'

'You have to at least give me some idea of why you're sending me in, Basil.'

'Very well: you'll get a more thorough briefing in due course but I imagine you've heard the phrase "eyes on the ground"?'

'Why would you imagine?'

Basil Remington-Barber sighed in the manner of an adult dealing with an awkward child. 'Because I'm told it's one of your American phrases, which is imposing itself on our language. Having said that, it does rather neatly sum up the purpose of your mission. The RAF has launched a large-scale bombing campaign in the Ruhr. We need to gather more intelligence on likely targets and also – perhaps even more importantly – on how effective the bombing has been. *Ex post facto*, as we say.'

'Meaning?'

'Meaning after the event. We need you to see which of your agents are still around and wake them up, so to speak. Get them working for us again. First things first though. We need to sort out your cover story. I've asked Noel to look after that.'

'We're working on a German identity for you,' said Noel. 'Thank heavens your German is now excellent.'

The following morning Noel Moore shared his thoughts on creating Jack's identity. 'I don't like to talk about problems, Jack, but the problem is that you're of an age whereby you ought to have been conscripted by now in Germany – anyone between the ages of eighteen and forty should have been called up. We could give you papers that show you're either medically exempt or have been invalided out of the forces, but the Germans are rather strict in that respect – you have to be very unwell or seriously injured and that's hard to fake.

'Having you as a member of the armed forces, home on leave – that's also risky, as is putting you in one of the occupations that's exempt from conscription, that's not nearly as straightforward as it may seem: we can never be entirely sure what occupations are on that list and we're told it constantly changes.'

'So, what are you proposing?'

'You're what, Jack, thirty-five? Chap we use to make the documents thinks it's feasible to age you a bit, say to forty-two. We can make your hair grey and give you some spectacles and hope that works. He also had the idea of giving you call-up papers. We have copies of these and we'll come up with one ordering you to report to the *Kriegsmarine*'s training base at Kiel on the first of May. You'll be a sailor!'

'And my name and occupation and where I'm from – all of that?'

'I'm working on it, Jack. Give me a couple of days.'

–

'Have you ever been to Mainz?'

'No.'

'Pity, because it's now your hometown. Here we are...'

Noel Moore stood up and pointed to a large map to his office wall. 'All rather conveniently set around the Rhine. Here on the southern tip is Mainz: it's just some twenty-five miles south west of Frankfurt, on the other side of the Rhine. If you follow the river north you come to the area we're interested in, the Ruhr Valley. In particular, these major industrial centres from Cologne here to Düsseldorf, Duisburg, Essen, Gelsenkirchen, Dortmund... you know the area?'

'Some of it.'

'But at least you know your way around, Jack. Come over to the desk.'

Noel Moore opened a folder and carefully removed some papers from it.

'This is a *kennkarte* for Hans Schumacher: it's not finished yet because we need to sort out the photograph, but all the other papers verify your identity. Hans is a travelling salesman from Mainz. In February last year the RAF raided Mainz on two consecutive nights and dropped around four hundred tons of bombs. The city was extensively damaged, especially the centre and your family lived here... just off Hindenburg Strasse, on Colmar Strasse. According to our information, most of the apartment blocks there were obliterated with dozens of casualties, your family included: Schumacher is a particularly common name in those parts. Should anyone try and check into your background they'll be unable to verify anything. You now live in a lodging house in the south of the city, here in Langenbeck Strasse, not terribly far from the crematorium, as it happens.'

Noel Moore pointed out the ephemera of everyday life: bus tickets, cinema tickets, a bill for dry cleaning.

'This is Hans Schumacher's *Mitgliedskarte*, his Nazi Party membership card. Basil wasn't too sure about whether to make you a member, but I think it helps. You joined in March 1942, just a few weeks after your family would have been killed by the RAF, so remember you're a bitter man. And here's the Nazi Party lapel badge.

'You represent a ship's chandler based on Rheinallee, which is here... see it? Just by the port. By all accounts there are dozens of them round there and some were destroyed in the air raids. Gives you a reason for pottering around the Rhine though, trying to sell your wares. Let's put all this away and you and I need to go and see Basil.'

—

Basil Remington-Barber stood in front of a large calendar, pointing a pencil at various days as if wondering whether they were in the correct order.

'Tuesday sixth today... when do you think all of Jack's paper-work will be ready, Noel?'

'We'll get the photograph done this afternoon. Tomorrow we'll have all the clothing, everything from Germany. Wednesday it's the woman...'

'Get him over the border on Thursday night, Noel: Friday's a better day to travel inside Germany though — busier day on trains and buses, more crowded.'

Jack never found out her name. She was Jewish and had fled Mainz in 1939 and now lived in Basel. She'd agreed to come to a safe house on the outskirts of Berne. She wasn't to ask any questions and she certainly wasn't to mention it to anyone.

The woman sat opposite Noel Moore in the middle of a large lounge, formally dressed as if at a job interview. The two were lit by a single overhead light, but the rest of the room was cast in darkness. Noel explained to her that she was to relax and simply answer his questions. He told her a colleague would enter the room and sit behind her and take notes. He hoped she understood if he asked her not to turn round, and she said of course, she quite understood.

It took the best part of six hours altogether, with a brief break for lunch. Prompted by Noel's questions, the woman described Mainz in detail: the school she went to, the parks she walked in, the shops, the different areas, the cinemas, the famous

Rhine promenade, the cathedral, of course, though she under-stood it had since been destroyed by the bombs, the Guttenberg Museum...

Noel asked her to describe different areas, dropping in Colmar Strasse among dozens of other streets he named. She'd had a friend there... before the Nazis of course... a nice area, lots of families, maybe a bit crowded... the number seven tram went there, if she remembered correctly...

She was less familiar with the port area – her father had been an optician on Schiller Platz, you understand... but yes, she knew of Rheinallee, not the most pleasant part of Mainz...

Noel thanked the woman very much and nodded at Jack, who slipped out of the room. He now felt he had a reasonable sense of Mainz.

The final briefing took place on the Thursday morning, before his departure that night. Basil assured him he was as well prepared as any agent he'd ever sent into Germany.

'Your identity is solid; your German is excellent. Remember what I said: stay for no more than a week. As I've told you, the purpose of your trip is to find out which of your old contacts are still around and which of those you can get working for us again. Be very circumspect though, Jack: it's possible people have changed their minds. They may be terrified and feel the safest thing to do is turn you in. If you can't find anyone then so be it, but I'd hope that from the sources you had in that area before, one or two... maybe... and there's something else...'

He paused to light a cigarette. 'A pal of mine in the Swiss police let me read the debriefing notes of a policeman who escaped from Germany. Usual self-serving stuff really, but what stood out was something he said about how they were trained to spot suspects – Allied agents, fugitives, escaping prisoners and the like. He said that in the first year or so of the war they concen-trated too much on paperwork and not enough on how people behaved. And he said something very interesting: that the reason people got caught was invariably because they were too friendly and eager to please, their stories were often too fluent and they didn't seem wary enough of the authorities. This chap said not to forget how oppressive the Gestapo and that lot are – I'm sure you don't need reminding – and people are frightened of them. He said they tended to be alerted when someone appeared to be trying too hard not to be nervous when they're being questioned.'

–

As Jack received his final briefing on Thursday 8, A. I. Stepanov finally returned to the house near Münsingen.

Sophia had been expecting him for most of that week. She'd last seen him the previous Tuesday when he'd come to inform her of her husband's death. It was also when he'd told her it would be in her interests to work for the Soviet Union.

That week was up on the Tuesday, but there was no sign of him then, nor the following day, and Thursday came and the morning was silent and lunch consumed on her own in the dining room watched over by the woman who spoke little German and the man who'd first interviewed her. The man – she learned his name was Nikolai – was less hostile than the woman, once in a while even smiling at her. When she was allowed into the walled garden there was always a guard watching her and she was also aware of at least one more guard at the front of the house.

That afternoon she paced around the bedroom: five steps from the edge of the bed to the small dressing table, three steps from there to the door, turning around and four steps to the window followed by a while staring out of it. In the three weeks since she'd been confined in the house some of the lower slopes on the High Alps in the distance had begun to lose some of their covering of snow. There were few trees other than those in the garden: seven of which she could see from the window, three to the right, four to the left, their branches bowed as if in conversation.

She had little doubt that if she refused outright to assist the Russians then they'd dispose of her with as little compunction as they had her husband. But volunteering to help them could be almost as dangerous. If there was any way to escape, she'd be prepared to take the risk, but the house had been well chosen: remote and well guarded.

She knew she needed to be clever and she wasn't sure how. At the moment, it felt as if A. I. Stepanov was the one being clever. The waiting was driving her mad.

The light in the Bernese Oberland was beginning to drop when she heard activity at the front of the house, beyond the locked door of her bedroom. There was the sound of car doors slamming, the front door opening and conversation in Russian followed by laughter. Sophia rinsed her face in cold water and brushed her hair before putting on her lipstick. She had just put on the smarter of her two pairs of shoes – which made her an inch taller – when there was a knock at the door, moments before it was unlocked. The woman nodded at her.

A. I. Stepanov was sitting in the lounge and greeted her politely. *Please do sit down... Would you like tea? I hope you are well...*

He was smoking a strong Russian cigarette, its aroma pungent, the smoke from it quite dark and she soon felt it at the back of her throat. She was grateful when the tea arrived.

'You've now had plenty of opportunity to consider my suggestion that it would be in your interest to work for us.'

It was a statement rather than a question but A. I. Stepanov peered at her through his cigarette smoke and raised his eyebrows in expectation of an answer.

'After all, we met last Tuesday, was it not? You asked for a week to consider my proposal. You've now had over a week. The Soviet Union is not usually quite so patient.'

'I understand that, sir, and I appreciate you giving me the time to think things over. May I just say that my husband did dreadful things and deserved his fate, but nonetheless the news of his death came as a shock. I needed time to clear my mind.'

'And your answer, Frau von Naundorf?'

She shifted on the sofa, not wanting to appear too relaxed. She edged forward, smoothing her skirt as far as it reached over her knees. She spotted his eyes widen as they concentrated on her legs and she waited until he eventually looked up.

'I'd be happy to work for the Soviet Union, sir: I think it is important that all patriotic Germans do what they can to save their country by getting rid of the Nazi menace. I'm aware of the considerable sacrifices made by the Soviet Union and I would like to think that I could play a small part... as indeed I already have.'

She'd rehearsed the little speech countless times and had delivered it in a way that she hoped sounded sincere.

'And I've been thinking about the best way I could assist the Soviet Union. I realise that as the wife of a senior SS officer I've been living at the heart of the regime. I know the names of people, where they work, the structure of the different organisations... which units colleagues of my husband have been with, where they're based... I've no doubt all this information would be invaluable to the Soviet Union. If I had an opportunity to write all of this in some detail—'

'I'm sure that would be useful, yes, Frau von Naundorf – but we actually have in mind a more active and clandestine role for you. However, that will take a few more days to plan. In the meantime, I am happy for you to do as you propose. I will arrange for you to have a typewriter. You will produce a report along the lines you outline. It will be a way of occupying your time usefully until we are ready for your mission.'

'And do you know when that will be, sir?'

'No more than one week, Frau von Naundorf.'

–

She'd bought herself one week and she was determined she'd use every moment of that time to find a way to escape. At first it seemed not so hopeless: she discovered the window in the bathroom was not nearly as secure as it seemed, and she thought if she could prise it open with a knife she'd stolen during a meal then she could just fit through it. During one of her walks in the garden she spotted a pipe leading from that bathroom window to a ledge not too far below it. If she could find a way from there over the wall… maybe using a towel to cover the broken glass on top of the wall…

But on the Saturday evening she discovered the bathroom window was now firmly bolted. Someone else had spotted it. For two days she sank into a deep depression, angry with herself for having approached the Soviets at all.

On the Tuesday morning she was busy typing away – a mixture of real names and plenty of made-up ones, tedious lists of where different offices were – when she heard a commotion downstairs and soon after that Nikolai unlocked her door and said she was to come down immediately to help.

At the foot of the stairs, she saw why: a torrent of water was gushing from the kitchen, the whole of the ground floor flooded by three or four inches of water and rising. The woman thrust a mop at her and indicated she should get to work.

The flood was to be her salvation.

Chapter 12

Switzerland and Germany
April 1943

Jack Miller arrived in Basel on the Thursday afternoon, the train from Berne pulling into the Bundes-Bahnhof exactly on time, as Swiss trains tended to do, far more so than German trains – his experience was their efficiency was something of a myth. The station was on the left bank of the Rhine and as soon as he'd cleared the ticket barrier, he entered the branch of the General Post Office at the station and waited until the middle of the three telephone booths was free.

Call this number when you arrive... say it's Franz, sending best wishes to his aunt... then pretend to make another call, for at least five minutes... after that, leave the station, turn left and walk up Garten-strasse: that will take you to St Jacobsstrasse, we're at number twenty-one.

Noel Moore hadn't said as much but Jack assumed the wait in the Post Office was to ensure whoever was watching him was ready. He didn't turn round once on Gartenstrasse, at the end of which he turned onto St Jacobsstrasse and headed for number twenty-one.

...three doors before it there's a bookshop: pause to look in the window and if a woman wearing a blue coat and a beret stops beside you and wishes you pleasant reading then you know it's safe to enter the consulate.

Like Swiss trains and clocks and in his experience with pretty much everything else Swiss, it had gone exactly as planned. The woman in the blue coat and beret had actually followed him into number twenty-one St Jacobsstrasse and led him to an office on the third floor where Noel Moore was waiting and asked him how he was.

'I'm fine, thank you, Noel, but this all seems rather excessive? It's not as if I'm in Germany yet!'

'I do realise that, Jack, and I apologise for all the fuss, but you know how it is: one has to be so careful being so close to Germany and it helps to get you in the right frame of mind, eases you back into your clandestine life.'

'I don't think I ever left it: doubt I ever will.'

'That's the price one pays, Jack. We did have a rather splendid safe house in the Altstadt but for some reason Basil convinced himself it was compromised and then we found another one by the Wettstein bridge but the landlord turned out to be terribly German, if you know what I mean, and this place is, well... secure and not overlooked and in any case one can leave very much incognito through the back door so – here we are: welcome to Basel!'

For the next few hours Noel went through everything in meticulous detail. He took Jack into another room: its curtains drawn and laid out on a table the clothes Jack would be taking to Germany – the ones he'd be wearing, the ones he'd pack, the suitcase, the toiletries, the other ephemera of a traveller – everything German, down to their faded labels. And not one but five tiny Minox Riga cameras, all expertly concealed in the false base of the case along with dozens of strips of film.

One for you of course, and give the others to any agents you find: pity we couldn't spare more.

They went through his identity and all the documents that went with it. Hans Schumacher: the travelling salesman from Mainz, employed by a ship's chandler based on Rheinallee, last address at a lodging house on Langenbeck Strasse, though he'd just moved out of it hence the letter from the landlady confirming his final payment and return of his deposit. Then various tickets and receipts, all from Mainz, none terribly interesting, and the photographs of his family, tragically killed by British bombs in February 1942 at their home on Colmar Strasse.

'And here's the letter, Jack, announcing your career as a sailor and ordering you to report to the *Kriegsmarine*'s training base at Kiel on the first of May. It's terribly convincing, don't you think?'

Jack read it through carefully and then grinned and said it was ironic because he was very prone to seasickness and Noel said that was exactly what he wanted to talk about.

'What, seasickness?'

'Not as such, Jack, but about casual conversation. This letter would be an example: if you come to show it to anyone then that remark about always being seasick, well that is a good way of defusing any tension there may be – it's mildly amusing and conveys the impression of you being relaxed. Another example would be Colmar Strasse, where your family lived.'

'And where they died: that's hardly amusing is it?'

'True, but what I was going to say is you should make up some stories about the area and specifically about your neighbours. Nothing too detailed or elaborate, but the kind of anecdotes one would inevitably have – the old woman who lived next door, her cats... one surviving the bombing... the man across the corridor who owed you money, killed on the same night... these kinds of stories. Just remember what Basil said about acting naturally. Now we need to talk about your journey, don't we?'

After that Noel left Jack alone to get changed. There was a small suite – bedroom and bathroom – and he had a bath but avoided shaving on Noel's instructions and applied the hair dye again, so by the time he was finished Hans Schumacher certainly looked closer to forty-two than his own thirty-five years. He spent a while studying himself in the mirror: there was no question he'd aged in the last few years, more so than would be expected. It was hardly a surprise.

There was a meal waiting for him along with a bottle of beer, which Noel said he wasn't to say a word to Basil about. 'It's hardly going to get you drunk, eh?' And then Noel said he should go back to the bedroom and try and get a rest for a couple of hours.

He'd not expected to fall asleep. Instead, he lay clothed on top of the bed – Noel said it would be good if they looked more creased – and allowed himself a few moments of fear about what lay ahead and then his thoughts turned, as they always did, to Sophia and he wondered whether she really was in Switzerland or still in Berlin.

He must have dozed off then because he woke up with someone shaking him by the shoulder and for a moment he assumed he was in Berlin and under arrest and sat up with a start, but then Noel said there's a cup of coffee for you here, please don't knock it over, and then we must really get a move on.

It was four-thirty in the morning – still pitch dark – when Noel led him into the area at the rear of twenty-one St Jacobsstrasse and into the back of a bread van and told him it wouldn't be long. Noel sat in the front next to the driver and kept up a quiet commentary: *we've just crossed the river on the Wettstein, all rather pretty round here, shame you can't see it, Jack... the minster's over to our left, beautiful red sandstone, you ought to try and visit it one day... we're on Riehen Strasse now, not long to go... here we are, Schwarzwald Allee: you remember what to do?*

It was all very quick after that: the van stopped and moments later the rear doors opened and Noel hurried him out and gripped his hand and wished all the luck in the world.

He was on his own now in a silent city and on the edge of another world.

He was in the north-east of Basel and he could sense Reichs Bahnhof in the distance, though he couldn't see it: maybe it was the smell or just his imagination. He crossed Schwarzwald Allee and found the entrance to the marshalling yard just as Noel had described it. Beyond the gate was a hut with a dim yellow light seeping through the door and standing very still next to it was a man in dungarees and a cloth cap with a lit cigarette in his mouth and when Jack said it was warm for the time of year the man replied it would be summer soon and the two briefly shook hands and the man said to follow him.

Christoph: he's a guard on the train from Reichs Bahnhof to Lörrach in Germany. He was a secret Swiss Communist Party member, fell out with the comrades when the Soviet Union signed that pact with the Nazis in 1939. He approached us and we use him sparingly but he's utterly reliable. Do what he says.

Christoph said to follow him and once they were in the guard van of the next train to Lörrach, Christoph spoke in a distinctive Basel German dialect.

'We're scheduled to depart at seven-fifty. The journey should only take forty minutes and we cross the border into Germany after thirty minutes: the German check can take place at any point on the journey. In my experience, it's best not to hide: those bastards could find a baby mouse. Sometimes I have an assistant guard: that's what you'll be today. This your identity card: it belongs to another guard.'

'Is he in on this?'

Christoph said the other guard didn't know about it and would be none too pleased if he found out.

Chapter 13

Switzerland
April 1943

The flood in the house near Münsingen took most of that afternoon to clear up that Tuesday, 13 April.

It was unpleasant work – the water was filthy – but at least it got her out of her room and it was something different to do and after an hour a certain camaraderie developed between the small group of them: Nikolai, the woman whose name she now discovered was Svetlana, one of the two guards, the cook and the gardener.

A plumber appeared later in the afternoon: a short, portly German-speaking Swiss brought in from Berne. He spent two hours in the basement, making a lot of noise and fuss and by the time he emerged he said the problem was solved and maybe he could now have a drink.

A damp smell pervaded the whole house. All the windows and doors were kept open and by the following morning the electricity was working again and it felt they were back to normal and Sophia returned to worrying about how A. I. Stepanov was due to return any day now with news of what he described as her more active and clandestine role.

She was in the garden on the Wednesday afternoon when she heard shouting from inside the house. This time the water flooding out of the basement was considerably worse than the previous day. The water now emerged as a torrent from under the floorboards in the hall and moved so fast it was hard to keep a balance. She was sent to her room and then brought down again to help clear up, but it was a thankless task. By the time the hapless plumber arrived from Berne the whole of the ground floor was under water.

They all gathered on the top floor landing and waited there for an hour. When the plumber emerged, he was drenched through and talked quickly and nervously: the sewer below the house had burst and its contents had merged with the spring which supplied the water and the pressure was too great and all he'd been able to do was stop the water from the spring but the solution was temporary and he had no idea how to get rid of the water and...

The Russians argued and there was much shouting. Nikolai told the plumber he was useless and the plumber replied that he was a good communist and Nikolai said that didn't make him a good plumber, which was the cue for more shouting. The plumber said he knew another plumber, one who wasn't a comrade, and Nikolai said he didn't care, as long as they could sort this mess out.

The plumber who wasn't a comrade arrived first thing the following morning and after an hour told them this would take at least a day to fix, probably two. Ideally, he'd like more help, people to pass him equipment and maybe he could bring in some help from Berne?

Nikolai said that was out of the question. He'd have to make do with people in the house and he replied that it had to be a German-speaker, otherwise it would be a disaster. Which was how Sophia became a plumber's assistant. She spent the best part of two days perched at the top of the steps leading down to the basement. Alongside her was the plumber's bags and tools. He'd carefully explained what they were all called and within an hour it was all working rather smoothly.

Now pass the larger wrench, please... thank you... next I'll need the big spanner... the pipe bender please, that's the one... I'll need the pliers with the red handle next...

When Nikolai was out of earshot the communication became more conversational. 'So you work for the Russians then?'

'Not exactly!' She laughed and he asked how come she was there.

'It's best not to ask.'

'Are you a communist then?'

She said she wasn't and he said she didn't sound Swiss, unless she was from Zürich maybe and she thought about going along with that but then found herself saying actually she was German, from Berlin.

'And how come you're here.'

'It's a long story.'

'We have all day. Can you pass me that tin with the grease in it, please? Maybe you're a prisoner?'

She passed the tin but didn't answer his question and he nodded and said he understood. 'I got the impression you're not here voluntarily.'

They finished at ten that evening, with a plan to start first thing in the morning. As the plumber hauled himself up from the basement he came alongside Sophia. One of the guards was near them but seemed more bothered with checking the tools.

'If you need any help, make sure you let me know tomorrow. I'll have this job finished by lunchtime. Think about it.'

–

Sophia did think about it that night. She thought that the plumber seemed a straightforward person, intuitive enough to realise she was in trouble and needed help. She thought about how Stepanov would be returning any day now and she'd then be sent on what he described as a clandestine mission.

Her absolute fear was that she'd be sent back into Germany on a spying mission. She'd be a wanted person in the Reich. The Russians would have no qualms about her being disposable.

She wrote a letter that night and folded the paper as tightly as she could manage and put it inside a sock.

The following morning, she slipped the sock into the tray at the bottom of the plumber's toolbox. When he asked her to pass a spanner, she moved down the steps with it and whispered that there was a letter inside a sock hidden in his toolbox and could he deliver it for her?

Where to?

When she told him, he said he knew where that was and yes, he'd do that, though he wasn't sure when. She said the sooner the better because she may be in danger and he said, of course – he understood.

'And you'll be able to tell them exactly where I am?'

'Of course.'

Chapter 14

The Gestapo searched the train when it pulled into a siding some five minutes after it crossed the border into Germany. Lörrach Hauptbahnhof was in sight down the track. The check was surprisingly quick, though as Noel had pointed out, there wasn't exactly a long queue of people in Switzerland desperate to get into Germany.

When the Gestapo entered the guards' van, Jack was busying himself with the wiring in a control box and grunted '*grüezi*' and just nodded when they replied with a '*Heil Hitler*'. They didn't even ask to see his card – they were far more interested in the smoked sausages presented to them by Christoph.

A speciality of Basel, for you!

As soon as they left the guards' van Jack moved fast. He had five minutes to get changed into his civilian clothes and then enter the main part of the train. By the time it pulled alongside the platform Hans Schumacher was just another passenger, joining the throng leaving the train, showing his ticket and *kennkarte* at the barrier.

He took a tram from outside the station to the centre of Lörrach and then walked slowly in the direction of the bus stop. He paused at a kiosk to buy a copy of the *Völkischer Beobachter* and three packets of *Neue Front* cigarettes. The newspaper – along with his Nazi Party lapel badge – would help his image as a loyal Nazi. The *Neue Front* cigarettes were the most expensive brand and he'd learnt from his time in Germany how well people responded to cigarettes: *please, take the pack, there's only a couple left in it!*

The ten o'clock service to Freiburg was already waiting when he reached the bus stop, the bus's noisy engine causing the entire chassis to shake. He bought his ticket and found a seat towards the rear, but not right at the back because if they checked passengers, somehow those sitting there seemed to get more attention. And he sat on the left-hand side, by the window but with a good view of the door, so he could keep an eye on who came on the bus.

The bus left five minutes late, heading north out of Lörrach and up the Wiesental Valley, the Rhine River to the west, the Black Forest in the distance to the east and surprisingly little evidence of a country at war in between.

A large woman joined the bus at Müllheim and even though there were plenty of spare seats chose to sit next to him, her thick coat, which smelt of fried oil, pressed against him. He closed his eyes and woke when the bus pulled into Bad Krozingen and a police officer came on board to check their tickets and *kennkarten*. His nose shrivelled as Jack's companion rooted in her handbag for her ticket and he seemed only too eager to glance briefly at their tickets before moving on.

They arrived in Freiburg at midday: the next service to Frankfurt was at twenty past twelve, so he had just enough time to buy a ticket and a cheese roll.

The bus finally stopped outside the Schumann theatre on Moselstrasse in Frankfurt just after five o'clock. Jack was surprised the city showed no sign of bomb damage: the industrial suburbs to the south of the city were busy and unscathed. There was no question this was a city at war though, the streets teaming with military vehicles and men in grey uniforms.

He was grateful the city centre was so busy, large numbers of people shuffling along, no one keen on paying much attention to anyone else and if he was pushed to describe the mood of people, he'd have said they looked tired, more so than in Berlin when he'd fled from there at the end of 1941. There seemed to be a general air of resignation and many of the women in particular appeared to be exhausted, their faces as grey as the uniforms around them.

He crossed Bahnhofs Platz into the main station and patiently waited in a long queue at the ticket office. It took twenty minutes for him to reach the glass window with a gap at the bottom and an elderly clerk with an enormous moustache behind it.

'A ticket for tomorrow to Düsseldorf, please.'

'Not for today, then?' The moustache looked offended he was buying a ticket so far in advance and made a point of moving to look up at the queue and people waiting to travel now.

Jack said yes, tomorrow, please, and placed Hans Schumacher's *kennkarte* on the ledge by the gap under the window, making sure his Nazi Party membership card was just visible under it. The moustache must have got the point because he asked what train did he want to take and Jack said he'd go for the eleven o'clock train, second class, please.

It was a short walk from the station to the hotel, the Vier Jahreszeiten on Scharnhorst Strasse. It took longer to check in, it always did for guests who'd not booked in advance, and the clerk called over the security officer who studied his papers.

'Purpose of your stay in Frankfurt?'

'I'm on business: tomorrow I travel to Düsseldorf.'

The security officer looked bored and was grateful when Jack took out his cigarettes and offered him one. He nodded to the clerk. *No problem.*

–

The train journey to Düsseldorf the next morning was uneventful. Apart from at the station in Frankfurt, his papers were checked twice during the journey and on both occasions the check was quick and straightforward: each time Jack made sure his Nazi Party membership card was with his *kennkarte* and each time he noticed a quick glance at his lapel to check out the Party badge.

He'd been to Düsseldorf a few times before. In his previous life as a sports correspondent, travelling around Germany to report on the country's football teams had turned out to be an excellent cover for his espionage activities. Fortuna Düsseldorf played in the Gauliga Niederrhein regional league. They didn't just play in it, they dominated it, ending as champions for five years in a row up to 1940. It was always a pleasure to visit Fortunaplatz, the club's ground on Flinger Broich, to the east of the city centre. He liked the people there – less suspicious of him than they were at some clubs – and he also liked the team's style of play: more attacking than most German teams, apparently more interested in scoring goals than stopping them.

The city had been an important intelligence target too – hence his visits. It was a major industrial city and Jack had compiled detailed lists of the factories and photographs of many of them too.

The one disappointment about the city though was his difficulty in finding people inside it to help him. That was no great surprise. The Gestapo office in the city was reputed to be the largest in the Reich outside Berlin, nearly four hundred people working out of the building on Prinz Georg Strasse. There was a noticeably oppressive atmosphere in the city, as if any form of opposition had been strangled at birth.

The communist party had been quite powerful at one stage in Düsseldorf but that had been more or less eliminated and as far as he could gather, the few members who'd survived had either joined the Nazi Party or owed their allegiance to Moscow.

But the last time Jack had visited the city had been in 1941, maybe six months before he'd escaped to Switzerland. And it was then that he'd finally found someone. At the time he felt it was too hasty: he'd not had enough time to nurture them. Recruiting an agent was like a romance: they had to be wooed.

He only hoped they were still there.

He arrived in Düsseldorf just after four that Saturday afternoon. That morning he'd sent a telegram from Frankfurt to book a room at the Monopol–Metropol on Kaiser Wilhelm Strasse, just across the road from the station. He had a bath, changed and waited until six o'clock before heading out.

From the hotel he headed west towards the Rhine, dropping down to Graf Adolf Strasse before turning into Königs Allee, always his preferred destination in the city. It seemed to specialise in welcoming cafés, ones which felt less tense than other places in the city, places where he somehow wouldn't stand out. He walked past the Hemesath and the Mainz and eventually came to the Cornelius, which faced Schlageter Platz.

He realised the chances of the man he was looking for still being there were remote: it was more than two years since he'd been there and since the man had responded so well to Jack's suggestion that maybe he'd be interested in helping people who were on the same side.

He pushed the door open and entered the café. It was quieter than he remembered it and there was a chill to place, as if the lack of people and the lack of coal were having an effect. Out of the corner of his eye he caught sight of the man. It was as if in the intervening two years he'd not shifted from his position behind the bar. He was as large as Jack remembered, the black eye patch still giving him the appearance of a pirate, the white shirt still straining against his bulk and dotted with stains and patches of sweat. Round his neck was the same red silk scarf and behind him the portrait of Adolf Hitler was still at a very slightly rakish angle: no one over the past two years had thought to give the Fuhrer a bit more dignity. That was a good sign.

He wondered whether Felix had spotted him, but he was serving another customer so Jack waited until there was a space at one end of the bar and it was evident that when he came over, Felix didn't recognise him. Another good sign.

What can I get you?

Felix looked tired and his thick fingers, stained with tobacco, were drumming the top of the bar, splashing in the pool of beer another customer had left behind.

Jack asked for a glass of Altbier, the local rust-coloured beer. Felix placed the glass in front of him and made to move off.

'Do you remember me, Felix?'

He stopped and looked Jack up and down, frowning and moving his head to get a clearer view.

'You remember I used to come here – a few years ago, when I was covering Fortuna?'

Felix opened his mouth in shock for a second or two before composing himself and moved closer, leaning over the bar, his elbows in the remains of the beer.

'You're the American: Jack?'

Jack said he was, but not any longer, if Felix understood what he meant.

Felix nodded, still awed to be in the presence of a ghost.

'You remember that when we met a couple of years ago we had a discussion about the war and you confided in me that you hated the Nazis and would do anything to destroy them? That was the phrase you used?'

Felix nodded and said it was two years ago. 'And you never returned.'

'I'm here now.'

'Two years later? What took you so long?'

Jack said it was a long story but there was a war on and Felix laughed and said he'd never have recognised Jack and surely America was now at war with Germany so how come he was still here?

'I'm not: I'm now Hans Schumacher. Look.'

He took out his papers, taking care they didn't get wet from the bar's surface. Felix shook his head in amazement and said he'd be back in a moment as he had another customer and there weren't too many of them these days.

Jack didn't hang around the Cornelius for much longer that night. He stayed for another half an hour but it began to get busier and in any case the kind of business he wanted to discuss with Felix wasn't done in a bar.

The following morning – the Sunday – he went for a long walk round the Hofgarten on the banks of the Rhine and at exactly half past eleven knocked on the back door of the Cornelius and moments later was sitting in Felix's cosy but tiny apartment above the bar. For the next hour he listened patiently as Felix unburdened himself.

In the past two years, I've not been able to speak with anyone like this… I've despaired… they've taken all the Jews from the city… God knows what's happened to them… I lost my eye in the Great War, I always thought that was why no woman was interested in me… now I thank God I have no family… if there's anything I can do…

Jack told him there was. 'I'm going to give you a tiny camera and show you how to use it. There are things that we will want you to do, but for the time being get as many pictures as you can of factories and other important industrial targets.'

'There's the Rhenania Ossag refinery in Reisholz, not far from here. Hit that and… boom!' Felix threw up his hands to indicate an explosion, a broad grin creasing his face.

Jack explained how Felix was to take the photographs and store them somewhere safe.

'One day someone will come into the bar and ask if the botanical gardens are nearby and you'll tell them—'

'The Floragarten, on Kronen Strasse—'

'Indeed, but let me finish. They will then ask if there is a café there where they can buy good food. You should respond they'd be better off eating at the café by the entrance on Bilker Allee. You'll both then know to trust each other. Have you got all that?'

Felix said of course, but Jack made him repeat it and the rest of the afternoon was spent practising with the Minox Riga. Felix wasn't the best student, clearly not technically minded and his thick fingers made operating the tiny camera tricky.

As Jack prepared to leave Felix became emotional. 'I felt as if I'd been a coward: I've done nothing to stop the Nazis. I've just… watched…'

Jack said he wasn't to worry because now was his chance and he really must leave because he had an early start in the morning and when Felix asked him where he was heading, he hesitated. He should have known better.

Only tell an agent just as much as they need to know.

Bonn, he replied.

Duisburg was always a likely target for the Allied bombers.

It was one of the largest industrial centres in the Reich and its position at the confluence of the Rhine and the Ruhr rivers made it the largest river port in the world and supposedly an easy target from twenty thousand feet.

By the time Jack arrived in the city on Monday 12 April Duisburg had already been hit hard by four major air raids, though Basil had confided in him it wasn't enough.

'Lots of damage and disruption and whatever, but the place still functions... that's the case throughout the Ruhr, Jack: the bombing is obviously unpleasant and something they could do without, but it's hardly bringing the place to a standstill. Here, look at this.'

The older man had a map of the city opened on his desk and a pad of paper next to it. 'Rivers, canals, docks, factories – everywhere: quite concentrated. You'd have thought that just dropping bombs anywhere over Duisburg would cause mayhem, but seemingly not. Four hundred and fifty of our aircraft attacked the city at the end of March – just a week or so ago – and we want to see what state the place is in. And we need some agents in the bloody place. You used to visit Duisburg, Jack, didn't you?'

Jack said he did: Turn-Borussia Duisburg had been one of the top teams in the Gauliga Niederrhein and that had given him a good excuse to visit the city. But he'd never found it easy to recruit agents there: there was a young journalist on the local newspaper who'd been a good source but he'd disappeared sometime in the middle of 1940 and there was a manager at the Prinzregent Hotel who'd been an excellent source for a while but when he'd last been in the city – it must have been in January or February '41 – the man didn't want to know him.

'Was he hostile?'

Jack shrugged. 'More that he totally ignored me: wouldn't look at me, turned away when I approached him.'

'What's his name?'

'Rainer Kühn.'

'Could he have been scared, rather than hostile?'

'Possibly, Basil: seems Herr Kühn didn't live up to his name: Kühn is German for brave, you know?'

'Thank you, Jack – I did know that. Do you think he informed on you?'

'No, I'd have soon known if he had, wouldn't I?'

Basil said that was what he thought. 'So maybe he's worth approaching again?'

'Maybe.'

Basil turned a sheet of paper towards Jack. 'This is from London: they've come up with a list of likely targets in Duisburg. The steelworks here – in the Ruhrort and Wannheim areas – and the Thyssen factory, which we think is here... they're also interested in the Homberg synthetic oil plant... and the rail network of course, especially the marshalling yard at Wedau, here. Find out what you can, get plenty of holiday snaps and recruit an agent or two and London will be delighted.'

But the city seemed surprisingly intact. The train from Düsseldorf happily took an age to travel the final three or four miles into the city, giving Jack ample opportunity to observe the industrial heartland through his carriage's grimy window and even take a few photos when he was sure no one was watching. There was evidence of bomb damage, but as far as he could see it had all been tidied up and neatly arranged in small mountains. All around were factories busy at work, people and vehicles moving around, smoke spiralling from their chimneys.

There was a Gestapo control at the ticket barrier and the man who questioned him didn't even smile when he made the seasick joke and asked him which companies he'd be visiting in the port to sell his wares. Jack explained it was more a matter of knocking on doors than having an appointment.

'Do you have samples on you, please?'

'I don't carry samples: if a company is interested then we send them on.' He had the catalogue Basil's forger had come up with. He doubted it would stand up to more than a very cursory inspection.

The Gestapo officer looked set for more questions but was then called over by a colleague. He reluctantly allowed Jack through.

He decided to stay at the Berliner Hof on König Strasse, across the road from the station. He checked into the hotel and decided to eat at the Palast nearby on the corner of Kuh-Tor and Sonnenwall. Before the war it had a reputation as a relaxed place; now it felt very military: half the customers were in uniform and Hitler gazed down from every wall. He allowed himself a glass of beer and a schnapps to give him enough courage to approach the Prinzregent, just round the corner on Universitäts Strasse.

A person walking into a hotel where they weren't a guest could be suspicious, so Jack had his story ready. He needed it as soon as he'd stepped into the lobby, where a man in a pitch-black suit stepped into his path and asked if he was a guest and Jack said no, he wasn't, and before he could continue the man asked to see his *kennkarte*. He looked at it carefully, checked Jack's date of birth and nodded when Jack showed his Nazi Party membership card.

'I'm in Duisburg on business and if I can be honest with you then, well…' He looked slightly embarrassed and moved closer to the man, apparently taking him into his confidence, which always seemed to do the trick.

'I'm staying at the Berliner Hof. I used to stay here before but it's more expensive, but the Berliner Hof is nowhere near the standard of this place.'

The man smiled appreciatively and nodded his head. *Thank you.*

'I became rather friendly with a manager here – I think his name was Kühn. Is he still here, by any chance? I was hoping maybe I could negotiate a rate more acceptable to my employers: they're very mean, I sometimes wonder how Aryan they really are, if you get my meaning!'

The man laughed and said he did and yes, Herr Kühn was indeed still a manager here, in fact he was now *the* manager here. All the others had been conscripted. In fact, he was still on duty and if Herr...?

'Schumacher, Hans Schumacher – from Mainz.'

Five minutes later Jack Miller was sitting in Rainer Kühn's office, the hotel manager looking quite hostile.

'Get the hell out of here and don't you dare come back. I'm very tempted to call security and tell them to let the Gestapo know—'

'Please, please, Rainer... obviously you're not going to do that, are you?'

The hotel manager shifted uncomfortably behind his oversized desk and leaned over it to pick up a lit cigar from its ashtray. Jack noticed the man's hand was shaking.

'You were very helpful when I used to come here.'

'You were an American then!'

'I still am. I'd like to continue our friendship. I still have evidence of how co-operative you were before, the details you gave me of all the companies in this city who used the hotel, the lists of their senior managers, the maps... the—'

'Nonsense: you're talking nonsense. You were a guest and liked to have a chat. I never told you anything that was sensitive and even then, I regretted confiding in you, in fact I—'

'You're prepared to take the risk, are you, Rainer? Do you honestly think I'd have come here like this if I didn't have something on you, something I'd be able to use to persuade you to help me again?'

The hotel manager looked terrified. He was a large man wearing a well-cut pin-striped suit – the kind designed to hide his bulk – but in the past few moments he appeared to have shrunk and looked defeated: he seemed to lack both the energy and courage to call Jack's bluff.

'What do you want me to do?'

Jack explained carefully: some information on the factories, on the damage caused to them, some photographs. Then he should be ready to be approached by someone who'd book in as a guest and would ask to see him privately and complain about the towels and Rainer would apologise and offer to change them and if the guest asked if they could they have an extra bath towel, then he'd know to trust them and should do what they asked. Rainer had fallen silent, studying the end of his cigar and Jack worried how plausible all this sounded. Maybe he should have come up with something more sophisticated, but Rainer said very well, on the understanding he'd help the person just once and he wouldn't do anything that would put him in danger and Jack said of course not.

Rainer stood up and said he still had a bottle of Scotch, which he kept in his safe. Would Jack like a glass?

The drink relaxed him. 'You heard about Stalingrad?'

Jack nodded.

'It's the reason I'm helping you now. When we first met and I helped you… it was because I thought this war would be bad for Germany. Now, it's far worse than I could have imagined then. Stalingrad was a disaster. My nephew was there, we've heard nothing of him… my neighbour's son was killed there… I could name a dozen other men I know of – all under the age of thirty – who were there and who've been killed or are missing. If this war carries on there'll be a Stalingrad every month.'

–

Hans Schumacher left Duisburg on the Tuesday morning. The short journey east to Essen took less than an hour on a bus that was surprisingly empty, allowing him to sit on his own at the back and even grab a few photographs of the factories that lined the road between the two cities.

Essen was a company town, dominated by dozens of Krupps factories, all at the heart of the German war effort. The main

Krupps factory was the size of a not-so-small town, dominating the city between the two railway lines. The journey bisected the main factory complex and although another two or three passengers had joined at Altendorf, he still felt able to take more photographs. There was some evidence of bomb damage, but the enormous complex was clearly operating at full capacity.

He left the bus at Adolf Hitler Platz and walked down Adolf Hitler Strasse to the main station. He had no intention of staying in Essen any longer than he had to. He'd visited it a few times before – both Schwarz-Weiss and Rot-Weiss were successful teams in the Gauliga Niederrhein – but he'd singularly failed to find any agents in the city. He wasn't sure what to put this down to, though he'd be the first to admit that finding agents required a lot of luck and he'd never had any in Essen.

He hoped London would be satisfied with a few blurred photos and there was another reason for leaving the city so quickly. He wanted to put anyone interested in him off his scent. When he checked out of the Berliner-Hof they'd made a point of asking where he was going next and he told them he'd be staying a few days in Essen before returning to Mainz. All the more reason to move on.

–

He was in Gelsenkirchen by lunchtime, the short journey north on the branch line from Essen providing him with more opportunities to take illicit photographs.

Gelsenkirchen was the coal capital of the Ruhr and, like an alchemist's den, the town specialised in turning the coal into fuel. He hadn't needed Basil to tell him what the targets were in the city: the Nordstern, Wanne-Eickel and Buer synthetic oil plants, the giant marshalling yards at Schalke and Herne.

He'd visited Gelsenkirchen plenty of times because it was the home of Schalke, the football team that dominated Gauliga Westfalen and which he'd covered winning the German Championship in 1939 and 1940.

Gelsenkirchen was also the place where one of his best agents had lived. He hoped she still did. He'd recruited Lotte fairly early on in his career as a British agent and she was utterly reliable, very smart, with a perfect temperament and impeccable judgement, allied with a considerable amount of courage. Nothing was too much trouble for Lotte. Nothing was a problem. Everything was a way to help defeat the Nazis.

Lotte was a finance manager at the Buer synthetic oil plant, the largest in the city. Before that she'd worked at Nordstern and seemed to have contacts at other plants elsewhere in the city. The quality of her intelligence was first rate: it allowed the British to gain a considerable insight into how good the Germans were at turning coal into fuel.

His method with Lotte was always the same: he'd telephone the apartment she shared with her elderly mother the night before and ask for Gudrun.

The following day he'd meet Lotte at the station cafeteria at lunchtime, always a busy place where people paid little attention to others. They would appear to be two strangers sharing a table and a cigarette and their brief conversation was polite and about the weather. After a short while – never more than ten minutes – Lotte would get up and politely wish him a good journey and he'd wait another three or four minutes or as long as it took him to finish a cigarette and then leave.

And without fail, inside the zipped bag between his feet on the floor Lotte would have somehow placed an envelope full of photographs, maps, diagrams and notes. At no stage did he notice her bend down and unzip his bag or do it up again.

A magician in the city of alchemy.

He waited until seven that evening before he called. He'd last been in Gelsenkirchen in the late summer of 1941, but he still remembered her telephone number.

Jack said he was looking for Gudrun and he heard a slight intake of breath: there was no Gudrun here, she replied, her voice clear and slightly put out.

The following lunchtime he was studying the arrivals and departures board in the station, well positioned to watch the cafeteria. He spotted Lotte going in and waited to see if anyone was following her. She sat on her own, sipping a drink, smoking and not looking around. She didn't look in the slightest bit perturbed, but after ten minutes – exactly the period of time they'd agreed all those years ago – she left, walking across the concourse to leave the station by the opposite entrance.

He followed her as far as the post office where for the first time they made eye contact, the briefest nodding of heads to tell each other they thought it was safe and then he left first, walking to the small alley at the rear where she joined him a few moments later. They waited in silence, a few yards apart, long enough to be certain they were on their own and only then did they speak.

Lotte asked him how he was and said it had been a long time and Jack said he was fine: now his name was Hans, Hans Schumacher, and he was a travelling salesman from Mainz, and she said his accent was excellent.

'Maybe we should walk for a while? I have to be back at work in half an hour. I'm combining my lunchbreak with a visit to the bank, company business.'

Jack told her as much as he could as they walked through a small park just to the north of the station. He explained how he'd had to leave Germany at the end of 1941 and he was sorry he'd not been in touch but had thought that was safer. He explained how he was now looking to make contact again with some of his agents and obviously she—

'What is it you want? I don't have long.'

'You're not under suspicion?'

'Of course not. Once the United States joined the war, I wasn't surprised not to hear from you, so I stopped gathering intelligence. It was very fortuitous because last June the Gestapo and our company security officers carried out a major investigation into our department. Whether they suspected anything, I have no idea, but they searched all of our offices and our homes. Of course, they found nothing, I'd even got rid of my camera. I don't have anything to give you. If I'd known you were coming…'

Jack said there was no need to explain, he was just glad she was safe and said he was going to give her a new camera if she was happy to resume her work and she said of course: would he be her contact?

He explained it may be someone else, but then told her how she'd be contacted and how she'd know to trust them.

She glanced at her watch and said she was worried she was running late, but just wanted to say one thing. 'When I first started working for you it felt hopeless: the Nazis seemed to be invincible. I just felt I had to do something. Now it is very different. The atmosphere here in Gelsenkirchen is very different: before it was quite triumphalist. Now it is one of despair. Everyone knows this city is a major target and people are terrified of the bombing. Everyone seems to know families who've lost soldiers in the east and although people don't talk about it much, you can see fear in people's eyes. Starting to work for you again, it gives me hope.'

–

He left Gelsenkirchen later that Wednesday afternoon. It was April 14 and he'd been in Germany since the previous Friday. He was worried about the timing: Basil said he should aim to stay for a week and ideally travel back to Switzerland over the weekend. He'd made it sound like a holiday.

Jack knew Dortmund would be his most important stop and so he made the decision to skip Bochum, one of the places on the list Basil had from London. He hadn't operated an agent in Bochum since 1940, but it wasn't as if the town was a mystery: Bochumer Verein had four large steel plants in the centre, grouped between and either side of the two main rail lines. There were enormous marshalling yards at Dahlhausen and Langendreer and a slightly smaller one at Weitmar. He'd already provided all this intelligence to the British.

He travelled to Dortmund by bus, taking a longer route, which meant changing at Castrop. It was getting dark when the bus stopped on Königswall, just south of the main station.

Jack was rather pleased with himself.

The mission had gone well so far: he'd never felt threatened or in danger, which he put down to a watertight identity and his own ability.

And luck. Never underestimate the part that luck plays, as Basil always reminded him.

But his luck would run out in Dortmund.

Chapter 15

Switzerland
April 1943

'You do realise it's six-thirty in the morning.'

The duty officer at the British Embassy in Berne said he did realise that and repeated how terribly sorry he was to have woken Mr Remington-Barber up but as he'd just said, the man was most insistent and it all seemed rather urgent. 'This gentleman arrived at the embassy a quarter of an hour ago and insisted he needed to see you in person. He says he has an urgent message for you.'

'And you don't know who he is?'

'Only that he seems to be local, sir.'

'Christ, this is all I need. I presume security have searched him?'

'Of course, sir.'

'Very well. I'll be with you by seven. Lock him in a room if necessary.' Basil Remington-Barber chuckled at his little joke.

'I've done that already, sir.'

—

Fritz had arrived back at his home in Brückfeld in the north-west of Berne late on the Thursday night. He couldn't get Sophia out of his mind, this well-spoken German woman with the most beautiful dark eyes which melted his heart but were also full of fear and urgency. He'd little doubt she was held against her will at the Russians' place near Münsingen.

139

He left home at six the following morning and the man at the British Embassy said no, he wasn't Herr Basil Barber but if Fritz cared to leave a message, he'd make sure he got it when he came in. Fritz had asked when that would be and the man said around nine o'clock, and that was when Fritz had made a fuss: this was urgent, a matter of life and death, and he insisted that the man call Herr Barber immediately.

He'd been taken to a side room and at seven o'clock a short, smartly dressed older man came in and introduced himself as Basil Remington-Barber and he understood Fritz had a message and how could he help?

Fritz pushed the letter towards the Englishman who took his time to put on his reading spectacles before carefully reading it.

Dear Herr Basil,

I was told by Jack that you were the only person I should contact if I ever found myself in Switzerland.

I escaped from Germany and entered Switzerland on Friday 12 March. For reasons I will not explain here, I have been held by the Soviets against my will for the past month.

I am now desperate: I have no desire whatsoever to work for the Soviet Union, but I fear that is what they want me to do. I'm being held as a prisoner in the countryside near Berne. The kind man who I hope will have given you this letter will be able to tell you exactly where I am.

I implore you to rescue me as a matter of extreme urgency, and I do hope you are able to tell dear Jack that I am safe and am counting the minutes until I see him again.

If you are able to come to my aid, I can assure you it is my intention to continue the work I have been doing on behalf of your country.

Sophia von Naundorf

Basil Remington-Barber read the letter once more and asked the Swiss man to explain the circumstances in which he'd met Sophia and describe exactly where she was being held. He asked him to wait and went to reception and told them to ask Mr Moore to come to the embassy immediately.

Despite the man's protests about needing to be elsewhere at eight, Basil and Noel interrogated him for another hour before they were satisfied: he was genuine and this was no trap. He'd been very precise pointing out just where the house was on a map and his description of Sophia was very accurate.

—

Sophia had woken with the sun that Friday morning. She trusted Fritz the plumber and had no doubt he'd deliver her note to the British Embassy and she likewise had no doubt that once the man Jack had told her she could trust had read it, he'd come along to rescue her.

She'd sat patiently by the window, looking out over the fields of the Bernese Oberland. She could just make out a bend in the track that led to the house and kept her eyes on that, imagining a British convoy majestically sweeping to her rescue.

But by late morning she was still staring out of the window. She also fully expected Stepanov to turn up, and she imagined a race between the two diplomats: who'd get to her first, the British or the Russians.

—

The ambassador had been characteristically cautious in his very Foreign Office way. 'I don't think this is an appropriate request to make of the Swiss authorities, Basil.'

'It's perfectly appropriate, Sir Clifford. In the past year we've provided the Swiss police with the intelligence to break up three communist cells in the Berne area alone. They owe us a favour. Isn't that how diplomacy works?'

Sir Clifford said it was a good deal more complicated than that and, ideally, he'd like the opportunity to run this past London, perhaps sending an urgent cable and hopefully by Monday they'd—

'She could be dead by Monday. We cannot afford to wait. She's an outstanding agent and Lord knows we have few enough of those. I'm sure London would take a very dim view of matters were the opportunity to rescue her be wasted.'

'And how would you propose to rescue her, Basil?'

'Captain Gerber is a great friend of the British. He is more than prepared to bring a dozen of his men with us to this house near Münsingen and help rescue Frau von Naundorf. And of course—' he looked the ambassador in a pointed manner '—Winston himself has taken a particular interest in the work of this agent, Sir Clifford. Surely, we wouldn't want to disappoint him, eh?'

–

Just after lunch the sun shone brightly over the fields. Beyond the bend in the track Sophia watched what looked like a mist hovering over a field, eventually realising it was the dust thrown up by a tractor turning in a distant corner. For a while she was captivated by the tractor, twisting and turning and transforming the landscape.

Then she spotted movement in the foreground, three cars on the road, approaching the house. Very calmly, as if she was expecting them, she checked that her handbag was nearby and decided to put on her shoes. Soon there was shouting downstairs followed by loud knocking on the front door.

She put on her coat and pressed her ear against her door. A man was talking loudly in a Swiss German accent, demanding to be let in.

She heard Nikolai respond that this was not possible as this was a Soviet diplomatic property and therefore out of the jurisdiction of anyone else.

The voice replied that this property was not registered as a diplomatic one and therefore as a Swiss police officer he had every right to enter and if the gentleman standing behind him would mind putting away his gun, he'd be very grateful.

There was much shouting in Russian downstairs and then she heard Nikolai ask if they could come back later that afternoon. Through her window Sophia saw two Swiss policemen had made their way into the garden and were watching the house.

At that moment there was more knocking on the front door. The Swiss voice again. 'We understand a German woman is in the house. We want to check if she's here and give her the opportunity to come with us. Then we'll leave.'

She heard footsteps running up the stairs and her door was opened. It was Svetlana, indicating she should follow her. Sophia moved back into the room, shaking her head. That was when the front door crashed open and amid the general commotion, she was sure she heard someone shouting in English. Svetlana slammed the door shut, but as she did so it was pushed open.

Along with a Swiss police officer were two other men in suits and the older of the two came towards her, a broad smile on his face and a hand held out in greeting.

'Sophia von Naundorf? I can't tell you how delighted I am to meet you. My name's Basil Remington-Barber, by the way.'

Chapter 16

Dortmund, Germany
April 1943

Jack Miller must have visited Dortmund a dozen times in his previous life as a sport reporter-cum-British spy based in Berlin.

It was a convenient staging post for his espionage missions into the Ruhr: easily reached from Berlin and well connected to the other industrial cities in the region.

The city was home to Borussia Dortmund, a team with the habit of giving FC Schalke a good run for their money in the Gauliga Westphalia and Jack always enjoyed his visits to Stadion Rote Erde in the south of the city.

More to the point, Dortmund was a centre of the German steel and mining industries and it came as no surprise that Basil had shown him a long list of targets in the city: the Vereinigte and Hosch Eisen steelworks, the enormous marshalling yard at Verschiebahnhof, the Dortmund-Ems canal terminus.

Dortmund was also the home of some five hundred thousand souls, two of whom were of particular interest to him. If both were still around, then he could end his mission in triumph.

–

Jack knew he needed to move fast. He left his case at the left-luggage office by the bus station and hurried to the ironmongery on Johannes Strasse, arriving just minutes before it was due to close.

He realised he was taking a risk, but he desperately needed to contact the doctor he knew as Arthur. The ironmongery was the place where they always met. The owner was a contact of Arthur's: a short man called Walter, with broad, square shoulders, his spectacles permanently perched on the top of his head. Jack had little to do with Walter other than a brief exchange when he entered the small, gloomy store. A mutual nodding of heads and Walter would say the nails he'd ordered had arrived, which would indicate all was well and Arthur was waiting for him in the small storeroom behind the counter.

But his visits were always arranged. It had been nearly two years since he'd been there, and he'd never turned up when Arthur wasn't there. Walter didn't recognise him at first and Jack stood with his back to the counter as Walter finished serving another customer.

When he left, Jack turned round and slowly a horrified look of recognition crept over Walter. He shook his head in disbelief and said he was to leave now.

'I promise you, I'm not planning on hanging around, but I need to make contact with Arthur.'

Walter frowned as if he wasn't sure who Jack was talking about.

'Arthur — the doctor from the main hospital on Beurnhaus Strasse. I used to meet him here — you remember? I need to get a message to him. I tried phoning him, but the number didn't work.'

'I've not seen him for over a year and I hope I never see the bastard again. He owes me money. I was risking my neck letting you two meet here: I'd been a patient of Arthur's; he'd saved my life and I reckoned I owed him a favour. But I thought it was just one meeting. After that, he paid me, and I only did it because of the money. You must go.'

'How much does he owe you?'

Walter shrugged and Jack noticed he'd moved along the counter and his hand was now close to the telephone on it.

'Here, take this.' Jack placed two five-Reichsmark notes on the counter, away from the telephone.

Walter couldn't help looking surprised and grateful. He grasped the money and put it in the top pocket of his overalls.

'And you have no idea where Arthur is?'

'Maybe at the hospital still, I don't know and I don't want to know. I just don't want any trouble. I can't believe you've come back here after all this time. You're not German, are you?'

'In case you have any clever ideas—' Jack looked at the telephone '—then remember, you allowed us to meet here. You'd be in as much trouble as me. Understand?'

Walter said he did, and if he didn't mind, it was time to close the shop. It would look odd if it was open past its closing time.

Jack left the shop and headed back to the centre, angry with himself for the way the visit to the ironmongery had turned out. It was the first time he'd had a conversation with Walter and he felt uneasy. He decided to go back to the shop, which was taking another big risk, but perhaps he could persuade Walter he had something against him, a letter maybe.

He turned back and reached the top of Johannes Strasse just as a black sedan pulled up outside the ironmongery and three men climbed out, all in the unmistakable attire of the Gestapo.

–

On his previous visits to Dortmund, he'd stayed at neat and tidy guest house on Kessel Strasse, close to the station and run by a pleasant woman whose husband had been killed in the Great War. Her daughter, Irma, helped her run the place.

Irma was one of the most beautiful girls he'd ever come across, although she was desperately shy and seemingly oblivious to her looks. Her mother was a devout woman, leaving early in the morning for Mass and making the return trip in the early evening. After a few visits, Irma became more relaxed in Jack's company, and by late 1940 she would slip into his room as soon as her mother departed for church.

He'd be hard pressed to describe it as a romance, but he knew Irma had become obsessed with him and he believed she'd do anything he asked but after his close shave with Walter, he determined to be even more careful. He returned to Königswall, collected his case and walked to Brück Strasse where he checked into the Römischer Kaiser Hotel.

He left his case in the room, hid the Minox cameras and films between the bed frame and the mattress and headed to the market place where he spent ten minutes in the Ratskeller and then hurried towards Kessel Strasse.

He'd only just left the market place when three black sedans pulled up about fifty yards in front of him on Viktoria Strasse and around a dozen plainclothes men got out and quickly spread out on either side of the road. This was a common sight in Berlin: setting up a random checkpoint was one of the Gestapo's ways of catching people unawares. Jack turned round: a group of uniformed policemen were blocking the other end of the street. Another group assembled ahead of him.

He carried on walking, making sure not to slow down or speed up.

The Gestapo man who stopped him looked bored and ignored his 'good evening' as he held his hand out impatiently for Jack's papers.

When Hans Schumacher showed his Nazi Party membership card he waved it away, saying he'd not asked to see that, and Jack started to get worried, because a Gestapo officer who could be so dismissive of his *Mitgliedskarte* clearly meant business. Nor was he interested in his *Neue Front* cigarettes, but he did want to know why Herr Schumacher wasn't serving the Reich.

Jack showed him the *Kriegsmarine* conscription letter and made the joke about being seasick, which the officer ignored.

'Wait here.' Jack waited by the side of the road, a few yards from an older woman in the same situation: both looked at each other. The woman seemed to be terrified.

Another officer came over. Something about the Hans Schumacher papers wasn't right, he said. Jack asked what he meant.

'You tell me: what are you doing here?'

He told him about the ship's chandlers on Rheinallee and then began a story, which he wasn't sure how he was going to end, about how the offices had avoided being bombed and the owner thought that was thanks to him because on the night of the raid he…

At that moment there was a commotion behind him and the Gestapo officer looked up. There was more shouting and someone must have called the officer's name because he thrust Hans Schumacher's papers into Jack's hands and told him to wait there, before pushing past him and rushing down the street.

For a moment Jack stared at the papers. It was an inexplicable error of the Gestapo man to have returned his papers, but Jack didn't plan to hang around to ask him why. To his left was an alley and within seconds he'd darted into it, hurrying through the dark web of narrow streets spinning off it before emerging onto Nikolai Strasse and then Kessel Strasse. As the guesthouse came into view he stopped dead in his tracks, taking two or three steps backwards, bumping into a man who told him to be careful.

It took up the whole of the small window on the ground floor, behind which was the neat lounge with its paintings of holy scenes and small potteries of Jesus and the display unit with the Dresden china tea set.

It was a black swastika flag set against a white circle and the scarlet red background. He crossed the road to find a safer position from which to observe the house, just in case there was some mistake, though for the life of him he couldn't imagine what that could be.

He was in the doorway of the bread shop diagonally opposite the house when the two women walked past him. Unmistakably, it was Irma and her mother, both dressed in the uniform of the *Frauenschaft*, the Nazi women's organisation: white tops, black ties, voluminous black skirts. Irma's beautiful long hair was pulled back into a severe bun. They were laughing as they crossed the road, neither so much as glancing in his direction.

He hurried back to the hotel, where he lay on the bed and wondered how much longer his luck would hold. He'd managed to slip away from the Gestapo checkpoint on Viktoria Strasse and he'd avoided the guesthouse. It was Thursday tomorrow: he'd seek out the doctor and then make his way back to Switzerland. He may even be in Berne for the weekend. He felt his eyes getting heavy when there was a knock at the door and a woman's voice announced it was the maid: she had brought more towels.

His hand was on the door-handle when it burst open. He felt a sharp pain to his head and everything went black and when he came to, he was pinned face down on the bed, a knee digging into his back and his wrists being forced into handcuffs.

When he was hauled up, he found himself facing the two Gestapo officers who'd questioned him on Viktoria Strasse. Around them, men were searching the room. One of the men demanding he give his real name and he said 'Hans Schumacher' before he was punched in the face and dragged out of the room.

—

Willkommen in der Hölle.

He didn't need to be told where he was.

He knew of the Gestapo prison next to Steinwache police station by reputation, which was about as bad as it got in the Reich.

Steinwache wasn't carefully tucked away in a suburb or isolated in the countryside. It was in the centre of Dortmund, just north of the main station, the goods yard visible from between the bars on the cell windows for those lucky enough – if lucky was the right word – to be in a cell with a view.

Willkommen in der Hölle was scrawled on parts of the walls where prisoners hoped the guards wouldn't spot the slogan, though Jack reckoned the Gestapo were quite happy to encourage that image.

Willkommen in der Hölle was the greeting the other inmates muttered as he was dragged past them to his cell.

Willkommen in der Hölle: welcome to hell.

To his surprise they left him alone for a few hours after he was taken to the cell. He was also surprised to be given food: a bowl of thin stew, mostly carrots and gristle but it was warm and there was a piece of bread with it, which was more or less edible if he dunked it in the stew. He was given a chipped metal mug half full of tepid water and a narrow bed to sit on and he had enough time to take stock of his situation.

He was an optimist by nature – his prison metal mug was half full of water rather than half empty. Notwithstanding that, it was hard to see his predicament as anything other than dire. It could only be a matter of time before they discovered he wasn't employed by the ship's chandlers on Rheinallee and that the lodging house on Langenbeck Strasse didn't know who he was. The identity Basil and Noel had given him wasn't designed for close examination.

And then the Minox Riga cameras: he couldn't remember how many he had left but they were bound to find them and the film he'd already taken. He was doomed and wondered if the best course of action was to confess now, to give them something, a name maybe, send them on a wild goose chase, anything to buy time – though even then it was pointless because he was in Dortmund, at the heart of the Reich, and there was no one to rescue him.

The next thing he knew, Sophia was at the door of his cell explaining there'd been a terrible misunderstanding and he was to come with her and behind her was a group of Gestapo officers, all acting very deferentially towards her and nodding at him in a shame-faced manner.

'Get up, didn't you hear me!'

He was woken from his sleep by a guard shaking him by the shoulder, the dream broken.

The interrogation was rough and unpleasant that night, but it seemed this was just the start, that far worse was to come.

They asked him to give his proper name and where he was from and what he was up to. He remembered the training he'd been given years ago in England, a wet and very unpleasant weekend where he'd been quite badly roughed up and by the end of it, he wondered whether it was an exercise at all, but it had been brutal enough for him to take notice of what they told him and now he realised it had been quite useful.

Most important of all, he remembered the advice of a sadistic little man with greasy hair and a leather jacket who'd actually slapped him very hard across the face and then sat him down and explained that under interrogation one should always listen to the questions he was being asked, because these would reveal how much they knew.

If you gave a package to a woman in a red coat the main post office then you'd expect them to ask about it – what was in the package, who was the woman... if they don't ask, they don't know. And never reply straight away: allow yourself enough time to give a considered answer.

They told him there was no Hans Schumacher from Mainz, certainly not one who matched his description, nor anyone of that name who was a member of the Nazi Party there. Or who worked for a ship's chandler on Rheinallee or anywhere else in the city, for that matter.

And why had he escaped from Viktoria Strasse if he had nothing to hide?

Where had he got the false papers from?

They were still checking with the Kriegsmarine in Kiel, but they doubted that conscription letter was genuine.

Jack listened carefully to the questions. They didn't seem to suspect he wasn't German, and they hadn't asked him about the cameras or the film, but he knew it was just a matter of time.

He was taken from the interrogation room to another cell, this one a damp, windowless room, which seemed to be below ground level. A single bulb in a metal grill cast a pool of weak, yellow light over the room.

He was pushed into it, his shins hitting a wooden plank chained to the wall that passed as a bed. It was only when he lay down that he became aware he wasn't alone in the room.

He made out a dark shape on a bed on the other wall and then the shape coughed, a rasping, unhealthy noise, which only ceased when the shape sat up and stared at him for a while.

Eventually Jack said good evening and his name was Hans and the shape said nothing, though it nodded its head.

The cell was silent other than for the rasping breathing of the shape alongside him. In the disconcertingly long gaps between breaths, he could just make out muffled screams further down the corridor. He was now aware of the nasty bruise behind his ear and waves of nausea sweeping over him.

'Are you from Dortmund?'

The shape had sat up and addressed him in a cultured voice.

'No, I'm from Mainz.'

'Mainz? I often wonder what Johannes Gutenberg would think of Germany now: the man responsible for the miracle of printed books and now the country is run by people who burn them. What do you think?'

Jack replied that he wasn't really very political, and he was only here because of a misunderstanding and he hoped that in the morning he'd—

'You don't sound German?'

Jack was so shocked he didn't reply and thought about how the sadistic little man in England with the greasy hair and a leather jacket had told him about the Germans' habit of using stooges.

Don't underestimate how fearful and vulnerable you'll be as a prisoner of the Gestapo: if you find your cellmate is being friendly it's surprising how easily you'll find yourself confiding in him.

Jack said of course he was German and said maybe he was confused by his Hessian accent, and the man said nonsense, he actually spoke the Hessian dialect and he doubted Hans was anything other than a fluent German speaker and he should know.

'I was a professor of modern languages at the University of Tübingen. I'm an expert in accents. If you were to push me, I'd say you weren't French or Italian or Slavic, for that matter, most probably a native speaker of another Germanic language – maybe

English or Dutch. But don't worry, I'm certainly not going to tell anyone.'

He said that last sentence in English and Jack didn't reply, listening instead to the man's breathing and the distant screams.

'How come you're here?'

The man hauled himself up before answering. 'The usual story: thrown out of my job at the university in '37 – it took them until then to realise I wasn't a Nazi. I ended up being sent up here to work at the Hosch Eisen steelworks and that's when I fell in with a communist cell there and I suppose I became a Marxist and now I'm here and imagine I'll be dead by the end of April, and somehow I've come to terms with that and—'

'But why are you in here?'

'I was a fool: I believed another colleague was sympathetic and he even mentioned he'd been a communist earlier in the thirties and like an idiot I tried to recruit him, which is when they arrested me. They've been trying to get me to give them the names of other members of my cell, but of course I refuse. Not betraying my comrades is the one dignity I manage to retain.'

He said nothing for a while, contemplating his fate and then leaned closer to Jack.

'Marxism provides all the answers to the state of society, you know that? You realise where you are, don't you?'

'Steinwache.'

'It's a perfect location to explain capitalism: we're surrounded by steelworks, ahead of us the Stock Exchange and the cattle market and abattoir. I've mentally composed many a compelling essay about our situation. A perfect illustration of the excesses of capitalism and in it lies the truth of how it will destroy itself. Do you agree?'

Jack said he wasn't political and needed to rest, but the man wasn't finished.

'My name is Hans-Peter Schmid. I don't want you to tell me anything about yourself, I'm happy for you to pretend you're who you say you are, but can I ask that if you ever get out of here, you to do me a favour?'

The man spoke for half an hour, occasionally checking Jack was listening, and when he finished the laboured breathing filled the room and the only thought that occupied Jack's mind was that his chances of leaving Steinwache weren't much better than those of Hans-Peter Schmid.

–

Sometime on what he assumed was the Thursday morning the interrogation resumed. They were now pleased to tell him they'd established that the *Kriegsmarine* conscription letter was a fake, as were all of his papers – clever forgeries indeed and perhaps he could start by explaining who had provided these to him?

An interrogation is like a journey, Miller. If you can find a better route, take it. Otherwise, stick resolutely to the one you know.

Which was the sadistic little man's way of telling him to stick to his story. He stayed with it for a few hours, filling his answers with long and inconsequential stories about imaginary characters who plagued his life and perhaps who'd be able to help him and then the main interrogator seemed to lose his patience and the last thing he remembered was being kneed very hard in the stomach and vomiting so violently it sprayed across the room.

When he came round, he was face down on the stone floor, its surface damp, sticky and foul-smelling. His vision was blurred and when he wiped his mouth he saw his hand was covered with his own blood and a voice was saying that this man needed to be in the infirmary immediately otherwise he'd be dead within hours.

The voice was familiar, though for the life of him Jack couldn't place it, and he assumed it was his delirium. He felt his sleeve being yanked up and a needle jabbed into his arm.

It was dark when he came to: he was on a bed in a high-ceilinged, narrow room, the only light coming through a mottled glass panel above the closed door. He lay very still as he recalled the events of what he assumed was earlier that day; the interrogation, the physical assault, collapsing and vomiting and someone talking about blood and then the injection. There was a glass of water next to him and when he sat up to reach for it he felt surprisingly well: a slightly sore stomach but nothing broken and even his head was not as painful as the previous day.

He must have dozed off again because he was woken by the door being opened and then closed quietly and a figure in a white coat pulled up a chair alongside him. The man leaned very close and as he did so Jack was able to place the familiar voice he thought he'd heard in the interrogation room.

The man he knew as Arthur had been his best agent in Dortmund. He was a surgeon at the main hospital on Beurnhaus Strasse and he was the person he'd met in the back room of Walter's ironmongery on Johannes Strasse. Arthur would give a verbal summary of first-class intelligence before handing over a package of documents. He'd never say how he'd got hold of the information, but he didn't need to: London was always delighted.

Now Arthur looked drawn and tired. He'd aged ten years.

'I'm off-duty in a few minutes so I don't have long, you understand? What the hell are you doing here?'

Jack briefly recounted his story. He told him how he'd been desperate to contact him, but his telephone number didn't work and he'd made what turned out to be the mistake of going to the ironmongery and—

'I don't trust Walter. He was always after more money.'

'I think he must have contacted the Gestapo when I left.'

'All the more reason to get you out of here. Do they know your real identity?'

'Not yet.'

'Have you said anything about me?'

'No: I get the impression the Gestapo are just warming up. They've not mentioned the ironmongery either. I've no idea of what I could say then – you have to help me, Arthur, I beg you I—'

'I was so shocked when I saw you. You weren't nearly as badly hurt as I made out, but I had to get you away from them, which is why I gave you that injection. It's now eight o'clock on Thursday evening. I'm back on duty at seven tomorrow morning. I'm not sure I can keep you in the infirmary much longer after that.'

'How come you're working here?'

'You think I have a choice? Last March I was called to the medical director's office at the hospital where a Gestapo officer was present. I thought that was the end of me. I'd not heard from you for a while and I assumed they'd caught up with me, which I always feared they would. In fact, he said they were looking for doctors to work at the infirmary here and would I like to volunteer. It was impossible for me to say no, apart from anything else, it would have drawn attention to myself.'

'Can you help me escape?'

Arthur didn't respond, instead standing up and pacing the room, deep in thought. 'I certainly can't risk letting you stay here. But helping you escape will be an enormous risk too. Let me see what I can do.'

–

Jack Miller was woken early the following morning by a hand gently shaking him by the shoulder. Arthur was leaning over him, his face just inches away. When he spoke, Jack caught a sweet smell of alcohol.

'It's a quarter to six. I can only stay with you for a minute or two – then I need to go and hide somewhere until my shift starts at seven. There are clothes and boots for you here and a rucksack with some food and water and a bit of money. Put the prison uniform in it too and get rid of that when you can. Once you're dressed tap on the door: if I respond with two taps, you'll know it's safe to come out. Opposite this room is a fire exit, which I've unlocked. Go down to the lower ground floor and then use this key to get to the outside and—

'Hang on: this is a Gestapo prison; you mean to say it's as easy to get out of as that?'

'This is the infirmary section and I managed to get you into the ward for prisoners who are too ill to get out of bed, let alone escape. But we don't have time to discuss the matter: the door from the fire exit opens onto Mühlen Strasse. Turn right and after fifty yards or so you'll see a men's clothes shop and alongside it an alley. Halfway down the alley you'll find a motorbike propped against the wall: it's an old one I got hold of when my neighbour died and it's not registered to me. It has a full tank of fuel. The keys are in this rucksack. You're on your own then. You need to get the hell out of Dortmund. You need to move. Quick!'

Just as he'd assumed the professor in the cell had been a stooge, Jack Miller thought this must be a trap. Escaping from Steinwache prison sounded too simple.

But in the event, everything was just as Arthur had described it. The door on the lower ground floor from the fire exit opened onto Mühlen Strasse. He turned right, but moments later spotted two policemen approaching him. He knew if they stopped him he'd be totally exposed without any papers, but they nodded and wished him a good morning and Jack smiled too and nodded. This was an unlikely extension of his luck, which he assumed had expired on the Wednesday night.

The motorbike was in the alley off Mühlen Strasse and he was pleased to see it was a DWK, a popular bike in Germany, highly regarded for its performance. He wheeled it to the end of the alley and then along the backstreets into Münsterstrasse. He remembered this was not an uncommon sight in Germany, bikers often wheeled their machines for a good part of their journey, such was the scarcity of fuel.

He headed north, in the direction of Münster, but then turned east towards Hamm, keeping south of the town before dropping onto a side road and pulling into a wood to take stock of his situation and hide the prison clothes. He knew the DKWs had a reputation for over-heating, yet this one didn't seem to be in any danger of that. But an overheating motorbike was the very least of his problems. His mental map of Germany gave him a good sense of where he was, and his priority now was to get as far away as possible from Dortmund.

He'd head to Bavaria.

–

He had to drive through Thuringia first. Keeping to side roads and avoiding towns he managed to average forty miles an hour. By noon he was on the outskirts of Eisenach, beyond that the Rhön Mountains. He'd made good progress, but he knew he couldn't go on much longer: he was virtually out of fuel.

He found a garage on a remote road south of Eisenach and continued his journey south. He stayed to the east of the Rhön mountains but the roads became more precarious and his progress slowed. It took two hours to get to Meiningen and the light was beginning to fade and he was feeling exhausted. South of the town he headed into the Thuringian Forest, driving deep into it until he found an area that felt safe. He laid the bike on the ground and opened the rucksack. It contained a few rolls of dry bread, a sausage, some cheese and a couple of apples. He covered himself and the bike in bracken and fell asleep.

He woke at dawn on the Saturday morning, the forest sounding as busy as a city. It took him a moment or two to orientate himself. He ate half a roll of bread and the remainder of the cheese and walked through the forest until he found a small stream, which meant he could top up the cooling tank on the bike and his own drinking bottle.

He headed south after that, but this time into Bavaria: Bad Kissingen, Würzburg, Stuttgart and then he'd be less than an hour from his destination.

His estimate was that it was no more than two hundred miles.

Chapter 17

Switzerland and Germany
April 1943

'If you feel ready to talk now, we're all ears.'

Sophia von Naundorf blinked and remained silent. She was disconcerted by the two men sitting looking at her in something approaching wonderment, as if she were an exotic creature from far away. The older of the two men was smiling in the way her grandfather used to, his head tilted slightly to one side.

'Perhaps you'd like another cup of tea, or maybe coffee?'

She thought about the events of the previous day: the Swiss police raiding the house near Münsingen, the Russians trying to stop them and then a group of men bursting into her room and one of the men – sitting opposite her now – introducing himself as Basil Remington-Barber.

She'd been a British agent for two and a half years and every minute of that time had been laced with tension and fear. Now she was in the presence of the one person in Switzerland Jack had told her she could trust. For a moment or two she'd stood in silence, but when he said, 'It's all right, my dear, you're safe now,' her emotions overwhelmed her. She'd burst in to tears and was still sobbing when they brought her to the house where she was now.

She remembered the man called Basil asking her lots of questions and the other man – taller and younger – introducing himself as Noel and telling Basil to leave her alone. A doctor had examined her, and he told them she was suffering from nervous exhaustion and she needed a good night's sleep and he was going to give her something to help with that.

An ornate carriage clock on the mantelpiece showed it was just before one o'clock. She estimated she must have slept for something like twenty hours.

'What day is it, please?'

Basil told her it was Saturday – 17 April – and made a joke about working weekends and then asked if she felt up to answering a few questions and she replied that she had a few of her own first.

'Where am I?'

'This is a house we use not too far from Berne: it's perfectly safe and we want to assure you you're no longer under any threat from the Russians. The Swiss authorities are rather cross with them, what with one thing and another.'

'And the Germans?'

'What about them, my dear?'

She bristled each time Basil called her 'my dear' and Noel must have spotted this because he addressed her as Sophia and assured her that no one knew she was here: not the Soviets, not the Germans and not even the Swiss authorities.

'What we need to know, my dear, is everything about your escape from Germany: how you got to Switzerland and what you've been up to since then. By my reckoning it's been five weeks since we last heard from you and we need to—'

'You're not in any form of trouble, Sophia, please understand that.' Noel shot a sideways glance at Basil. 'You were a first-class agent in Germany and we want you to know how much we appreciate that and we're going to look after you. Should you wish to continue working for us in some way or—'

'Where's Jack?'

'I beg your pardon?'

'Jack: Jack Miller. He left Germany in December 1941 and I've not heard from him since. I must know what's happened to him and I must see him.'

Neither man responded: Noel looked at Basil, making it clear it was the more senior man's responsibility to reply. Basil smiled at the patterned rug between them, interlocking his fingers in an awkward manner, his hands then joining together in prayer.

'Jack has indeed been with us since he left Germany.'

'And is he still here?'

Basil shrugged and began to wring his hands. 'Not in so many words, my dear, not exactly.'

'I'm afraid I don't know what you mean, Herr Basil.'

Basil spread out his hands as if to indicate that he didn't either.

'What Basil is trying to say, Sophia, is that Jack *has* been in Switzerland and is indeed based here but at the moment is on a—'

'It's an operational matter, my dear, and the less one says the better it is all round, not least for Jack.'

Sophia's eyes filled with tears and for a minute or so she let them flow freely down her cheeks. She turned round to gaze of out the window and when she faced them again, she dabbed her eyes.

'He's not in Switzerland then?'

'Not at the moment, no.'

'When will he return?'

Noel said they really weren't sure but hopefully very soon and she wasn't to worry and then she snapped, saying it was not for them to tell her not to worry. They couldn't possibly understand everything she'd been through and the depths of her feelings for Jack.

'The thought of seeing him again, of being with him… that is what has kept me going during the year and a half since he left Germany. Until I'm with him again…'

She stood up and stormed out of the room.

'Good Lord, Noel, whatever have we done to deserve this? It was bad enough Jack falling in love with her, but now having her declare her undying love for him… maybe I'm getting far too old for this but it does rather complicate the business of espionage, don't you think? I'm sure there must be a Shakespeare quote about not mixing business with pleasure, eh?'

Noel nodded.

'Let's just hope Jack gets back soon.'

'Let's just hope he gets back, Basil.'

–

'I've been estranged from my family for many years.'

It was just three nights previously in their windowless cell in Steinwache that Hans-Peter Schmid had asked him to listen carefully because he wanted to ask him to do a favour if he was ever released.

That had seemed unlikely at the time. Now Stuttgart was behind him and the Schönbuch forest emerged to the west. He was just a few miles from his destination.

'My family were – are – all devout Roman Catholics. After university I was conscripted and fought in the Great War and my experience there soon put paid to any faith I had in God. It caused a major rift with my parents: neither of them really forgave me and they both died in 1928.

'I have a younger sister called Gisela: we were very close when we were younger and remained so despite the rift with my parents. However, in 1932 Gisela married a teacher called Ernst Haussmann who was ten years older than her. Haussmann and I strongly disliked each other, not least because he was an ardent Nazi. Under his influence Gisela had less and less to do with me, to the point where I'm afraid we became estranged.'

There was a pause as Schmid coughed violently.

'Haussmann died suddenly in 1937. Gisela contacted me after his death and asked me to forgive her and tried to assure me how much she hated her husband's support of the Nazis. To my shame, I rebuffed her. I wrote a formal letter of condolence and I visited her once, but we never resumed our relationship. Now, of course, I bitterly regret that, but I have no intention of writing to her

162

because the Gestapo would find out and that would inevitably make her life difficult.'

Hans–Peter Schmid crawled out of his bed and knelt beside Jack, his clammy hand gripping Jack's arm.

'Gisela lives just north of Tübingen. Many years ago, there was a Cistercian monastery at Bebenhausen. It's closed now, but nearby there's a religious house for retired Catholic priests and Gisela is their housekeeper. I would like you to visit her and explain my situation. Tell her how much I regret what happened between us and please assure her I hold no grudge against her and indeed I wish her to forgive me. You could ask her to pray for me, that will appeal to her. She may help you too.'

'How will she believe a stranger turning up on her doorstep?'

'We had secret nicknames for each other when we were younger: she called me Petri and I called her Liggi: no one else will be aware of that.'

—

The last few miles of the journey were the most perilous. With the end in sight, he'd made a mistake when leaving Stuttgart. Instead of taking a longer route down country lanes, he'd stuck to the main road. It was full of military traffic, heading in both directions. At one point two police motorbikes passed him, heading towards Stuttgart. In his side mirrors he saw them slow down and then turn around to head back towards him. He was stuck between two Wehrmacht lorries and when two tank carriers approached in the northbound lane, he quickly overtook the lorry in front of him before turning a sharp left into a narrow farm entrance, braking hard and pulling the bike onto the grass verge even before it had stopped. He waited there for a while, his breathing heavy as he worked out what he'd say if they caught up with him.

By his reckoning he was just a few minutes from his destination. He resolved to abandon the motorbike before then.

—

He'd driven through the village as the professor had instructed before turning right up a steep hill, the woods growing increasingly dense. He managed to haul the bike into the woods and wheeled it as far as he could. He was well away from the road when he found a dip in the ground where he laid the bike down and spent a few minutes covering it with branches and bracken. He carried on walking up through the woods, crawling through the undergrowth as the trees became less dense.

The house was as Hans-Peter had described it: some parts handsome and castle-like, other parts plain and crumbling. A drive stretched to the front door from the road and a large, overgrown lawn surrounded the house.

He stayed within the cover of the woods for a while, watching the house and keeping an eye on any comings and goings. It seemed very quiet: occasionally elderly priests would wander out and walk on the lawn for a short time. He headed around the perimeter and at the back of the house found a kitchen with its door open.

He was just yards from the door when a woman came out.

'Can I help you?'

'I'm looking for Frau Gisela Haussmann.'

She nodded and moved closer to him, wiping her hands on her apron. 'I'm Frau Haussmann. I've already told them in Tübingen that we're not taking on anyone else here. I'm sorry. Try the farms, they always need help.'

'I'm not here looking for work. I have a message for you from Petri. He says that Liggi would want to hear from him.'

Her eyes opened wide in shock and she gasped. 'Hans-Peter – where is he, is he in trouble?'

'He's in Dortmund, but is there somewhere we can talk in private?'

She pointed to a small building just yards from the back of the house and told him to follow her. She unlocked the door: it appeared to be a storeroom for discarded furniture. She checked the shutters were closed and told him to stay here and she'd return in an hour. When she left, she locked the door.

When she returned, she had bread and cheese wrapped in a cloth and a flask of soup. *Now tell me about my brother.*

He told her he was a friend of Hans-Peter's and had been able to visit him in prison and Hans-Peter had begged him to visit his sister. He gave her Hans-Peter's message. She took the news of her brother's fate calmly, sitting very still as her eyes filled with tears.

'My brother was very outspoken against the Nazis: I take it you share his views?'

Jack allowed the slightest of nods.

'My biggest regret was not taking notice of what Petri said. My husband was a very dominant and overpowering man and he despised my brother. I felt I had to choose between them and took the view that I'd made a commitment to Ernst when we married. I bitterly regret not being more tolerant of Petri's views on politics and religion. I wish I'd not been so judgemental: now it sounds too late, but maybe I can take some comfort from his message.'

She toyed with the strap of her wristwatch, looking far from convinced that what Jack had told her was going to bring any comfort.

'Would it be possible for me to stay here overnight? I'll leave tomorrow.'

'Where are you heading?'

'South.'

'You're on the run, aren't you?'

Jack said nothing.

'I can see it in your eyes, in the way you hold yourself. We've had others here: a couple of Polish slave labourers who we sheltered last winter, a Jewish family from Stuttgart we hid for a few months, but they had to leave when the local police said they'd had reports of Jews hiding in the area. There was a man from Munich, a socialist. We kept him in here but he was very ill and died. You don't need to tell me your story but—'

'Is it safe here?'

She shrugged. 'There are fifteen priests living in the house. Three of them are very sympathetic to the Nazis, but they're quite infirm and live in the nursing wing, which is on the other side of the house. Most of the others just turn a blind eye but two of the priests are committed anti-Nazis: they believe it is our duty as Christians to do all we can to help their victims. You're in trouble, aren't you?'

Jack nodded.

'Stay here. Father Albrecht will come to see you.'

—

It was dusk when Jack heard the door unlock. He watched as the dark shape of a tall man moved slowly into the room and coughed gently.

'My name is Father Albrecht: Frau Haussmann told me you were here.'

Jack came out from the shadows. Enough light penetrated the room for him to make out the distinguished face of a man in his seventies. The priest guided him to a sofa wedged into the corner and they sat next to each other.

'Frau Haussmann says you're in trouble, in which case it may help if you tell me what kind of trouble you're in and where you wish to go.'

Jack Miller had spent much of his childhood in Philadelphia in the company of Roman Catholic priests. Until the age of seventeen he'd seriously thought about becoming a priest himself, that was until he fell in love with an older woman and assumed he'd made himself ineligible to serve God in the way he'd planned. It was not something he regretted. But by then he'd developed an instinct for understanding the clergy: there were some he trusted and others he didn't. Father Albrecht was one he immediately trusted. He told him he was a Catholic and when Father Albrecht asked where he was from Jack said he'd recently been living in Switzerland.

166

The priest leaned back and folded his arms. 'Switzerland, I see, I see... in which case I understand your situation. Please say no more. I take it you wish to return there?'

'As soon as possible, please, Father.' He was aware of the catch in his voice and the priest noticed it too, a hand holding his shoulder.

'Don't despair, my son. Even at the darkest moments in the night we are assured another day approaches: one should always be sustained by hope. I think I have a solution but will need some time, and of course tomorrow is Sunday, which is a busy day. In the meantime, you'll be safe here.'

Early on the Monday morning Frau Haussmann hurried Jack into the main house and to a book-lined study behind the chapel. Father Albrecht beckoned Jack over to his desk.

'I'm proposing you use this Swiss passport, which belongs to Father Johannes. But it's not nearly as straightforward as it may seem. Father Johannes was born in 1862, making him eighty-one years of age, considerably older than you. This means the passport is useless for you as it stands. But my colleague Father August is a very skilled scribe and he has managed to alter it. Have a look.'

It was a Swiss passport issued at the German consulate in Munich in March 1930. It showed that Johannes Küng – occupation: priest – was born in Langenthal, Canton of Berne on 20 September 1899.

'You'd need a strong magnifying glass to suspect anything. It means you are forty-four years of age: unfortunately, it would be too hard to alter the eight, but this is an excellent effort. The passport was actually issued in 1920 when Father Johannes was fifty-eight, but fortunately the photograph makes him look younger. Here's a pair of spectacles almost identical to the ones he's wearing in the photo. Try them on.'

The priest nodded admiringly at Jack, as if he were a much-loved nephew displaying his new school uniform.

'We'll give you some white hair dye to help make you look more like Father Johannes. I would suggest you travel tomorrow:

it's the twentieth of April – Hitler's birthday, a day for parades and celebrations. Hopefully people may be distracted.'

–

Early on the Tuesday morning Father Albrecht drove Jack to the railway station in nearby Tübingen. Over a black suit and dog collar Jack wore a large black cassock smelling strongly of mothballs. Frau Haussman had cut his hair and dyed it a whitish-grey and he'd also been given a black felt hat with a wide brim. Attired as a priest he'd begun to feel like one.

He carried a small, battered suitcase containing a few clothes, a spare pair of shoes and a leather-bound Bible.

Father Albrecht parked in a narrow road behind the station.

'You have the money?'

'Yes, Father, thank you. I can't thank you enough and I—'

'Don't thank me: I should thank you for giving us an opportunity to do some good when everywhere around us we see evil. All I ask is that one day, when, please God, this nightmare is over, you come back and see us. Hurry now!'

Jack Miller spent much of the journey from Tübingen to Singen appearing to doze by the window, the railway policeman apologising profusely when he tapped him on the shoulder for his papers and ticket.

He knew the most difficult point in the journey would come at Singen, where he'd buy the ticket for the short journey to Schaffhausen, in Switzerland. He'd be attempting to leave the Reich without an exit visa. The clerk at the ticket kiosk shook his head and sent him to the police office in the station.

The officer on duty checked the passport – he didn't appear to have any problem with it – and asked the purpose of his visit to Switzerland.

'It is some years since I have been back, but my sister recently informed me that my dear mother is very unwell in a hospital in Berne.'

The officer nodded and asked the priest where his parish was.

'My parish is in Cologne, but I'm afraid the church and much of the surrounding area was destroyed in an air raid by the British at the end of May last year.' He shook his head, hoping to indicate his disapproval. 'Now I am based at the cathedral.'

'Do you intend to return to the Reich?'

'Of course! Hopefully in a week or so.'

'But you have no exit visa.'

'The letter from my sister arrived only two days ago and I'm afraid in the circumstances I failed to prepare for this journey as I should have done. I recall the last time I visited Switzerland I didn't need such papers as I am a Swiss citizen.'

'That was the case, Father, but not since 1940, I'm afraid. Please wait here.'

He waited for an hour, doing his best to remain calm despite a growing sense that his story would not withstand too much scrutiny. A phone call to their colleagues in Cologne could soon expose him. He was on his own in the office, and looking out onto the concourse he realised he could slip away. But he also realised he couldn't be more inconspicuous.

'I've spoken to the Gestapo officer on duty.' The policeman had bustled back into the room and sat behind his desk. Jack felt a cold wave of nausea sweep through him. 'Not meaning any offence, Father, but I take it you said your prayers this morning?'

'Of course, I—'

'Well, they've been answered: you're lucky on two counts. Firstly, it's the Führer's birthday and the Gestapo officer is required at a celebratory lunch. And secondly—' he opened a drawer and removed a document which he filled in as he spoke – 'he's a good Catholic from Bavaria: he said I should fill in a form allowing you to travel. Here.'

And with that he stamped the document and pushed it towards the American, shaking his head to indicate this was against his better judgement.

The train arrived in Schaffhausen just half an hour after leaving Singen.

He'd last been in the town when he'd escaped from Germany in December 1941. The Swiss police checked his papers once the train crossed the border and the younger of the two who questioned him appeared bothered by the passport.

'This passport looks like one issued earlier than 1930.'

'That's when I got it at the consulate in Munich.'

'Yes, I can see that, but I'm saying it looks like an early version: I'm sure they stopped issuing these about five years before.'

'I seem to recall them saying something at the time about having to use up these copies. I don't know, maybe check with the consulate?'

He shook his head. He clearly wasn't going to bother with that.

The train was slowing down as it approached Schaffhausen. The older policeman tapped the younger on the shoulder.

'Come on, Suter, there are other passengers to check. The father is hardly going to mislead us, is he?'

Chapter 18

Switzerland
April 1943

Afterwards, Basil Remington Barber had remarked to Noel Moore that the reunion between Jack Miller and Sophia von Naundorf had been surprisingly low key

'I thought it would be like… you know, Noel, like it is in those romantic films my wife is so keen on: falling into each other's arms, lots of tears and hugging – perhaps a few bars of romantic music. But it was all rather… well… restrained, if you know what I mean.'

Noel replied that he did know what he meant but maybe the pair had been inhibited by their presence.

'Some things are best done in private, sir.'

It had all happened so fast.

On the Saturday there'd been what Basil acknowledged had been a most unpleasant confrontation with Sophia at the safe house they'd taken her to on the southern outskirts of Berne after rescuing her from the Russians the previous day. He'd expected her to be grateful, but she'd made a terrible fuss about wanting to see Jack again and making it clear her co-operation was dependant on that. She'd spent the next few days sulking in her room and there'd been a very tense exchange of coded telegrams with London. Barney Allen had insisted on knowing where the hell Jack was and when was he due back and Basil wondered how much longer he could pretend that he had everything in hand.

Somehow, he'd had it in his mind that the American would be back in Switzerland on the Monday. He'd made this assumption for no other reason than he'd told Miller to head back that weekend – meaning he'd have had just over a week in Germany. Noel had insisted it may take longer and they shouldn't be unduly worried yet, but Monday came and went, as did Tuesday, and then the ambassador called him in and said he'd started getting pointed messages from London which he could really do without and perhaps Basil could expedite matters.

'Expedite' was a word frequently used by the ambassador these days and it always manage to rankle Basil. He asked the ambassador – sarcastically, he'd thought – whether it would help 'expedite matters' if he himself went into Germany and the ambassador replied that actually maybe that was something they could give consideration to. In due course, naturally.

Basil Remington-Barber drank far too much on the Tuesday night, and as a consequence arrived late at Thunstrasse on the Wednesday and then spent most of the morning drinking black coffee in his office while Noel Moore stared at a large map of Germany.

The call came in the middle of the afternoon. The duty officer said someone was on the line from a telephone box in Schaff-hausen and at first Basil didn't put two and two together, but Noel did and he hurried down and by the time Basil joined him Noel had already arranged for a car and driver to take him to Schaffhausen to collect Jack Miller.

They arrived back at the embassy later that night and the three of them gathered in the secure room on the ambassador's floor.

Jack seemed very calm and said he quite understood when they said they'd need to do the first debrief straight away and that took them past midnight. Basil and Noel had agreed they'd say nothing to Jack about Sophia until they'd completed the second debrief, which was late on the Thursday morning.

They were satisfied with what he'd told them, satisfied enough for Basil to confidently tell Barney Allen in London that he'd re-established a network in the Ruhr. Yet again Jack Miller had proved his mettle and Basil would write the report to ensure he'd be able to share a good deal of the credit.

He'd also be able to tell the ambassador that he'd managed to expedite matters and there'd be no need for him to go into Germany, though of course he'd have been more than willing.

Around three o'clock they'd casually mentioned to Jack that they were taking him to the safe house he'd originally been taken to when he first escaped to Switzerland back in December 1941.

You look like you could do with a few days rest: good food, fresh air, then back to work.

As the car pulled up outside the house, Basil turned to him. 'Sophia's here, Jack.'

The American had looked at them in utter shock, as if he'd not heard what they were saying, and then reacted as if they'd given him some bad news.

'What do you mean… is she alive, what's happened to her?'

Noel helped him out of the car and put his arm round Jack's shoulder. 'It's nothing to be upset about: she's absolutely fine, Jack. Managed to get herself tangled up with the Soviets – we're still not sure how and why – but we were tipped off about her whereabouts last Friday and managed to rescue her. She's been here since then.'

Jack was already bounding up the stone steps of the house and followed Noel into a sitting room at the rear. Sophia was sitting in an armchair in the bay window and stood up when they entered.

For what seemed like an eternity the two lovers looked at each other in silence. They moved closer and then stopped, each looking at the other in disbelief and in a manner suggesting they thought this may be a trap. Eventually they moved closer and each held the other's hands, as if they were about to start a dance.

'Well, all's well that ends well, eh?' Basil had positioned himself next to the pair like a priest officiating at their wedding, smiling at them in an avuncular manner.

'I'd say this calls for a drink, wouldn't you? Not yet four o'clock but never too early on an occasion like this!'

Noel coughed and said actually he thought the occasion called for Sophia and Jack to be left alone. Basil got the hint, saying he and Noel had some catching up to do – as he imagined they did too – and maybe they'd have that drink a bit later on.

–

Noel had mentioned to Basil that he was slightly concerned that this could all end in tears.

'Not sure what you mean, Noel.'

'What I mean, Basil, is what if it turns out that one of them is not as keen as the other is? Maybe they were more concerned for their safety than anything else. If that's the case then we could be in danger of losing an excellent agent, possibly two.'

But Noel Moore needn't have worried.

The pair asked to be left alone for the rest of the day and when Basil and Noel returned on the Friday morning, a shocked house-keeper took them aside before they'd even entered the house and told them that the lady and the gentleman had shared a room that night.

'And they were still in it this morning!'

Basil seemed unsure what to say, but Noel said she really wasn't to worry and in fact everything was in order and she ought to remember that one of the conditions of her very generous employment here was that whatever went on in this house was to be treated in the utmost confidence.

They couldn't get much sense out of either Sophia or Jack that day or indeed the following one and in Basil's opinion they were unlikely to do so for quite a while. The pair only had eyes for each other, although he did manage to extract from them an assurance that now they knew each other was safe they were more than happy to resume their service as British agents.

In due course.

On that basis Basil did a deal with London: give them a week off and then it would be back to work. Basil decided to send them to Lausanne, in his opinion the most quintessentially French city in Switzerland. He booked them into the Hôtel de la Paix on Avenue Benjamin-Constant, close to the north shore of Lake Léman.

He himself drove them down there on the Sunday and said he'd collect them the following Saturday. 'First of May: new start.'

He left them with strict instructions to keep themselves to themselves and to be as discreet as possible. They weren't to mix with other people.

They didn't look as if they had any intention of doing so.

But as so often happened in Basil's experience, circumstances soon changed. On the Thursday there was a series of urgent telegrams from London, culminating with a coded radio transmission, which was only used as a last resort. Matters were pretty clear. Barney Allen wanted Sophia and Jack back in Berne immediately.

Their holiday was over.

There was a new mission and they were the ideal people for it.

Part Two

Chapter 19

England
April 1943

'I don't imagine I'm allowed to ask how your war's going, Barney, eh?'

Barney Allen raised his eyebrows in a manner to suggest this was indeed so.

'Quite understand... must be awfully difficult to keep matters to oneself.'

Barney Allen muttered something about it not being a problem so long as people didn't ask questions he was unable to answer and his cousin Andrew – A. A. – blushed and said he was sorry and Barney said not to worry, really...

'And how are Christine and the children?'

Barney said they were fine, thank you very much, and if the war went on much longer James would soon be getting his call-up papers!

'And... Patricia – how is she, and the children of course?'

A. A. said Patricia was well and then went into some detail about her mother's unsuccessful knee operation and said his eldest, Andrew, wouldn't be far behind James, though his mother did wonder if his asthma would exempt him from National Service.

They exchanged some pleasantries about their fathers, and reminisced about childhood holidays but it was obvious A. A. wanted to say something but was unsure how to broach it.

'And the RAF, how are you finding it, A. A.?'

His cousin said he was... well 'enjoying' would be the wrong word of course, but it was certainly busier and far more interesting than the City and he wasn't sure if Barney was aware but soon after his promotion to wing commander, he'd been transferred to Fighter Command HQ at Bentley Priory and even though the Battle of Britain was over it still felt like one was at the heart of...

His voice trailed away and he turned round to check no one was listening, even though they were sitting in a near-deserted lounge in A. A.'s club.

'It's what I wanted to talk to you about, actually, Barney, confidentially of course.'

'Of course. Is it connected with my line of work?'

'Possibly, Barney, and if not, you may know who'd be interested.'

'Go on.'

'Through my work I've had occasion to visit RAF Northolt a few times. 303 Squadron is based there, one of the Polish Squadrons in the RAF, and bloody marvellous chaps they are too. They all managed to escape from Poland before the Nazis could get them. 303 flew Hurricanes in the Battle of Britain: absolute heroes.

'I've become rather pally with an officer called Stanisław Makowski. Stan's a flight lieutenant in the RAF but his Polish rank is captain. The other week Stan confided in me: he was very nervous, insisted he didn't want to go through official channels.

'He said Polish politics in London are very complicated with lots of different factions and just because they were all opposed to the Nazis, it didn't mean that there weren't tensions between the different groups and a good deal of distrust too.

'Evidently he's involved in one of the smaller resistance groups and they have access to some intelligence that may be of considerable interest to Great Britain. The reason he was approaching me informally was that he felt he could trust me and didn't want anyone in the Polish Government in Exile to find out about it. If he went through the RAF then there's a danger it may get back to the Polish Government here, because most things do.'

'Did he give any hint what it was about?'

'No, though he did say it was something of enormous importance and Stan's not a chap normally given to hyperbole: pilots rarely are, in my experience. He said if I thought I could help then he'd arrange for me to meet a more senior member of his group in London — I think Stan's more of a messenger.'

'And you said?'

'I told Stan I'd come back to him — my intention was to discuss it with you first, Barney, and decide the best course of action. But I'm afraid he seems to have taken that as a "yes": he rang me at Bentley Priory this afternoon to say he's set up the meeting and how grateful he is and what an enormous contribution I'll be making to the war effort, et cetera. I ought to tell you, Barney, that I rather jumped the gun and asked him if I could bring someone with me — two of them, two of me, so to speak.'

'And who did you say this someone would be, A. A.?'

A. A. smiled awkwardly. 'I told them it would be my cousin: the Poles take family awfully seriously. I didn't say what you did, of course. I just said you could be trusted as much as me.'

Barney Allen waved away the steward who was hovering in the doorway. Going along would be a breach of various protocols: he ought to clear it first with Piers Devereaux and there was the issue of whether this was actually a matter for MI5 and then it involved a government in exile so the Foreign Office ought to be involved… it was all so complicated. He'd send a note to Piers in the morning, that ought to cover him if anything went wrong.

'I hope you don't mind, Barney, but it may well turn out to be useful for you, who knows?'

'And when will this jolly family outing be taking place, A. A.?'

'He's rather sprung it on me, I fear, Barney.' A. A. glanced anxiously at his wristwatch. 'It's in an hour's time and it all seems to be rather cloak and dagger, though I imagine you're quite used to that.'

—

Barney Allen soon realised that whoever they were going to meet knew exactly what they were doing. He'd thought about getting in touch with Hugh Harper at MI5 – they knew each other from school – to see if he could arrange for one or two of Bartholomew's Disciples to follow them. The Disciples was the name given to an elite team based in London, skilled at following people and watching what they were up to.

But there was no time for that.

It was all very quick.

A. A.'s instructions were to go to a call box and telephone a number Stan had given him. Barney was with him in the call box.

'Where are you?'

'Pall Mall.'

A slight pause. 'Very well: walk please to Piccadilly Circus and catch the number 88 bus heading west. Stay on the bus until the last stop, which is Acton Green, by the Duke of Sussex public house. Enter it and order a drink and after five minutes use the call box inside the pub to ring this number again.'

A. A. had made the phone call as instructed.

Stay where you are: a woman will find you soon. Do what she says.

For the next half hour, they sat quietly in the pub, impatiently toying with their half pints of warm bitter, the blackout blinds helping to cast the Victorian interior in a gloomy light, as if it were still lit by gaslight. Barney spotted the woman entering the pub, an attractive woman in her thirties, blonde hair falling from under a dark beret. When she'd bought her drink, she moved to the table next to them, everything about her relaxed. Barney was impressed, so much so that he wondered whether he'd been wrong in assuming she was their contact.

She waited five minutes before turning round, an unlit cigarette in her hand. Did they have a light, she asked in a foreign accent. She leaned closer to the flame and spoke very quietly.

I'll leave in a few minutes: please follow me.

They did so as she headed north up Beaconsfield Road and soon after it became Acton Lane, she turned into Somerset Road.

She opened the gate of a bay-windowed terraced house, a slight nod of her head indicating they should follow her.

Stanisław Makowski was waiting in the back room in his RAF flight lieutenant's uniform. Standing alongside him, with his back to the curtains, was a taller man in a dark suit and with a scowl on his face. He indicated they should sit down, and for a while he studied Barney Allen, trying to weigh up his unexpected visitor before a smile briefly crossed his face and he nodded.

'Very well: if Stanisław trusts Andrew and Andrew assures us you are most trustworthy then… then perhaps I will take that view too. When I explain the situation, you will appreciate the risk I'm taking. Pull your chairs closer together, please, and I ask you to listen carefully.'

The man ran his long fingers through a head of thick hair and then pressed the tips of the fingers of both hands together as he gathered his thoughts.

'I obviously hope that you will be in a position to act upon the information that I am about to share with you. However, for reasons that will become obvious, I don't want you to divulge the identities of Stanisław or myself.'

He coughed and then drew himself up. 'My name is Piotr Drobiński: prior to the Nazi invasion of Poland, I was a diplomat in our embassy in The Hague. I managed to escape and am now an official with the Polish Government in Exile here in London. I work out of our headquarters in Portland Place.

'Before becoming a diplomat I was a lecturer in Polish History at the University of Poznań and while I was there, I became part of what is known as the Poznań Group. Have either of you heard of it?'

Both shook their heads.

'Few people have, thankfully. Life really is too short for me to go into detail now about the complexities of Polish politics and the various factions within it, but for the purposes of this conversation let me just say that the Poznań Group was a collection of like-minded individuals in the city: it was initially based around the university, which is how I became involved, but also included some professionals in the city and a number of Polish air force officers at Ławica airport: hence Stanisław's involvement. If we had one common denominator it was that we were democrats – centrists if you like: not right wing, but not communists either. Poznań has a high proportion of ethnic Germans, but our group comprised Poles and a few Jews, which was unusual too. One has to acknowledge there's a very strong strain of anti-Semitism in Polish society.

'Very few members of the Poznań Group remain in Poland. Some have been killed, others have fled or been captured, some have disappeared. The few who remain have to be very careful, but they are hoping to keep the group going: with the way the war is turning against the Nazis we want to have some influence when the war ends. Recently I received a message from a close friend at the university, Bolesław Piotrowski. Bolesław was also a member of the Poznań Group and has remained in the city, though I understand he's now working in a factory. According to this message, in February Bolesław was approached by an emissary from the Jewish ghetto in Warsaw. At one stage half a million Jews were crammed into it, but last summer the Nazis deported hundreds of thousands of them to a death camp called Treblinka. Now only fifty thousand remain.

'According to this emissary, one of those remaining in the ghetto is a man called Roman Loszynski. Before the Nazi invasion, Loszynski was a very brilliant professor in the Department of Advanced and Applied Electronics at the university. He was also at the centre of the development of a secret device for the Polish air force to use in their new PZL bomber. This device would improve the capabilities of the plane's bombing function. It would make it more accurate. As I understand it, the device came in two parts: a transmitter and a receiver. The receiving device would be on the bomber and signal the optimum time to release their bomb.'

'If I may interject.' Stanisław Makowski looked apologetic but keen to speak. 'From the point of view of the air force, I can assure you this device could totally transform aerial bombing. Even though I'm a fighter pilot, I was aware of this project. General Brygady Wiśniewski, Air Vice Marshal of the Polish Air Force, was in charge of the project and thought very highly of it.'

Piotr Drobiński continued. 'Apparently, they were terrified the device would fall into German hands, so everything to do with it at the university was destroyed. However, Roman Loszynski had already gone into hiding and no more was heard of him. It was assumed he'd been murdered along with his family and most of the other Jews in Poland.

'This emissary told us Roman and his family had in fact escaped to Warsaw and were in the ghetto using the name Fiszer. And not only that, somehow Roman had managed to take with him the prototypes of the devices and many of the plans and his notes.

'Another member of the group – Henryk Kamiński – has gone to Warsaw to try and rescue Roman and his family and the devices. This happened in February, but it has taken all this time for the message to reach us in London.'

'And... you want... what precisely?'

Drobiński waited as he lit a cigarette and looked round for an ashtray. 'We want the British to have the devices. We don't doubt they will be of inestimable benefit. We will undertake to get Roman and the machines to the Polish border and hand them over to you. In return, the Poznań Group wants an assurance you will look after Roman and ensure he's able to complete the development of the device in safety. We want the device to be given to the RAF. We also want recognition for the Poznań Group, that we have been responsible for this, and we need money and arms smuggled in to us – we know the British supply the Armia Krajowa and the Soviets arm the Gwardia Ludowa. If we have more weapons, then we will have more influence. That's how Polish politics works these days.'

Drobiński leaned back to indicate he'd finished. He must have sensed that Barney Allen was the more important of the two cousins because he'd addressed all of his remarks to him and now looked directly at him, waiting for a response.

'I can promise you I will raise this as a matter of importance first thing tomorrow morning. I happen to know something about the RAF's bombing campaigns and I have no doubt this matter will be of interest to the people involved. But may I ask, Piotr, do you have any proof of this?'

The Polish diplomat shook his head. 'No, you'll have to take my word for it. Just as I'm taking a risk now, so you'll be taking a risk too. All contact should be through Stanisław or myself. You have our number.'

—

Barney Allen found it difficult to believe the speed of the reaction the following morning. He made sure he was in Head Office by seven, hoping to catch Piers Devereaux before he became too tied up.

'Can I just run something by you, Piers? It's a contact of a source of mine, appears genuine enough, but who knows… and there are undoubted complications…'

Piers appeared to be in one of his less disobliging moods and said no intelligence worth its salt was not without its complications and he was all ears.

Barney Allen carefully recounted what he'd been told, leaving out the names of the two Poles he'd met the previous night and only referring to the Poznań Group as 'a group of anti-Nazi Poles'. Roman Loszynski became a 'Jewish scientist'.

When he finished there was no obvious reaction from Piers Devereaux at first. He'd spent much of the time drumming a pencil on his blotting pad and making the occasional note.

'No proof, Barney?'

'Not as such, no.'

'And this scientist, do we know where he is in Warsaw?'

'No.'

A few more questions. Barney got the impression his answers were less than satisfactory.

'And your source, Barney, the one with the contact with this chap you won't name... reliable?'

Barney assured him he was.

'And you said this business – if true – had undoubted complications. Those were your words, I believe.'

Barney said they were indeed. The complications were twofold as he saw them. 'Getting this chap to safety and then making sure the Polish Government in Exile don't catch wind of what's going on. My contact doesn't trust them: they're dominated by the Armia Krajowa – the Home Army – apparently and he doesn't want them muscling in.'

Piers Devereaux pursed his lips and looked as if he'd reverted to his disobliging self, as if he was about to dismiss the whole matter.

'This is remarkable, Barney; you do appreciate that? If this is true then it could change the course of the war. You recall that meeting with Frank Hamilton and his bright young chap from Bomber Command back in February? Well, they were saying how much the accuracy of our bombing – or lack of – was a real problem and they wanted our help with eyes on the ground, as they termed it.'

'Of course, which is why I'd hoped this would be interesting. What was it they said, that only one in three of our bombs got within five miles of their target?'

'Something like that, yes: this device your chap is talking about could totally transform the effectiveness of our bombing campaign. You're around all day I hope, Barney?'

He said he was.

'Let me make a few calls.'

–

187

They met in Downing Street early that afternoon, in a secure room in the basement, its damp atmosphere not helped by cigarette smoke, which had nowhere to go with the sealed doors shut.

Air Vice-Marshal Frank Hamilton, the Head of RAF Intelligence Branch, was there along with Group Captain Martin Marlow from Bomber Command who they'd met at the country house in February. At either end of the table sat two of the prime minister's advisers: Roly Pearson who was his intelligence man, Lord Swalcliffe who advised on all matters scientific. The two men were known to share a mutual distrust and glared at each other like two elderly lions, past their most dangerous days but still capable of the odd roar.

Piers Devereux had arranged the meeting through Roly Pearson and made sure he was aware it was conditional on one thing, which he asked him to clarify at the start. Pearson delivered his lines as per his script.

Potentially outstanding intelligence... source is most secret... sensitive... under no circumstances is anyone to question the source or ask further details... matter to be kept very much under our hat... Winston very much on board with this...

Barney then took over, carefully explaining the situation, and noticed how interested the two RAF men were from the outset. When he finished, he paused, closed his notebook and took a sip of water.

'And there we are,' said Piers Devereaux, 'assuming you're interested, we then have the small matter of getting this scientist over here and getting him to work.'

'With no idea who the hell he is?'

'I do know who he is, Lord Swalcliffe, and of course when he's here his identity will be more widely known, but I'm sure you'll appreciate that until then security and secrecy must be paramount.'

'But we're being asked to believe something told to you by a contact of a contact, with no proof? This could be an example of Nazi disinformation or it could just be some fanciful notion that a half-baked idea is more important than it actually is. This is, of course, very much my area.' Lord Swalcliffe paused to look round the room in an apparent attempt to assert his authority. 'I've been intimately involved in matters relating to our bombing campaign and the technology associated with it. We have the Oboe and Gee-H navigation systems which of course depend on the ground equipment being based in England. The idea there's a device that can be placed near the target and is small enough to remain undetected but powerful enough to send a signal to a receiver on board a bomber twenty thousand feet above it, travelling at a speed of around two hundred and eighty miles an hour... I'm sorry, Devereux, this all feel very tenuous and the risk —'

'If I may?' It was Martin Marlow, the young group captain from Bomber Command. 'I'm sorry to interrupt but I feel I ought to point out that this is also my area of interest and I became aware in 1939 — before the war — of rumours that the Poles were developing such a device. It would be unusual if they weren't, all air forces including our own are constantly seeking to improve their technology and the accuracy of aerial bombing has always been a priority. We know that the PZL 37 was a very highly regarded aircraft and the gossip was that the Poles were working on a portable device to maximise the accuracy of its precision bombing. I would say this sounds credible.'

'At the very least,' said Frank Hamilton, 'it's something we'd want to look at.'

A silence fell over the room before Lord Swalcliffe muttered, 'Very well then.'

Roly Pearson clapped his hands. 'Winston will be delighted. He has a soft spot for the Poles, you know, feels they've been rather hard done by.'

—

Piers Devereux and Barney Allen remained in the fetid basement room with Roly Pearson after the others had left.

'What was it your contact said about handing the scientist over, Barney?'

'They'd get him to the Polish border and then hand him over to us.'

All three men shook their heads before turning their attention to a large map on the wall.

'Christ, which border does he mean? Half of Poland's now been swallowed up into Germany, the Nazis control Ukraine to the east, in fact they control all of Poland's borders. How the hell are we going to get him here?'

Piers Devereux turned away from the map. 'We'll find a way, Roly, won't we, Barney?'

Chapter 20

Austria and Poland
April, May 1943

It was a few minutes after six-thirty on the first day of May and the sun had already begun to rise in a clear sky, the surface of the Danube now picked out by a light becoming brighter by the minute. In the space of a quarter of an hour it had transformed from a dark void to a river bustling into life.

Sophia von Naundorf stood three feet behind the window on the second floor above the bar on Seitenhafenstrasse, just across the road from the entrance to the dock. She'd been in the bleak, chilly room since the previous afternoon: the woman she knew as Hilde had hurried her there and told her to wait. When the bar closed at night, she said, the landlord would bring her some food and allow her to use the toilet.

'Is he with us?'

'Who?'

'The landlord.'

Hilde shrugged as if she'd not really thought about it. 'He's broke: the Nazis keep imposing new curfews so he loses business. He's got bribes to pay to keep the place going as it is, so I guess the answer to your question is that he's doing this for money.'

'But can we trust him?'

Hilde looked annoyed. 'It's a bit late to ask that now: you're in Vienna. There's a surprising shortage of people willing to help!'

She'd remained in the room all night. When the landlord did come up, he seemed anxious to stay: perhaps she'd like to share a drink with him, or maybe she'd find his room more comfortable?

She tried to be polite. She was very grateful, she assured him, but she needed to remain in this room and she had to be alert. The landlord moved closer to her, his face and head covered by a sheen of perspiration, near enough for her to smell the tobacco and alcohol on his breath.

He looked defeated: he didn't believe her but knew there was not much he could do about it.

'You understand what you have to do in the morning?'

He nodded, but slightly uncertainly, as if he wasn't that sure.

'He'll arrive sometime around seven o'clock. Be ready to let him in. Then bring him up here.'

The landlord nodded. 'He's your man, isn't he?' He gave her a knowing smile, his broad grin revealing a mouth full of yellow teeth and plenty of gaps. He winked and nodded at the camp bed against a wall.

'You're being paid well to do what we say, not to ask questions. Understand?'

He stepped back, defeated once again.

She slept fitfully that night, a quarter of an hour here, twenty minutes there. When she woke at five-thirty, she moved towards the window, waiting for the sun to rise over the docks around at the southern end of Leopoldstadt, Vienna's Second District.

–

It was exactly seven o'clock when she first spotted him. Two barges arrived from the east and as far as she could tell one of them flew the Slovakian flag.

He was walking between two other members of the crew as they approached the exit and the police checkpoint. He looked just as he'd been described to her: short, with a black scarf wrapped round his neck, a light grey cloth cap and a large green rucksack held over one shoulder.

It was all fine so far, but there was still the checkpoint to get through and then the landlord had to do what he'd been told to do. Sophia realised she'd moved too close to the window and stepped back. She could hear voices below her and what she thought was shouting, so she moved to the side of the window to steal a glimpse. Fortunately, it seemed another crew must have arrived at the checkpoint at the same time and they appeared to be joking with the two policemen.

It's the end of their shift. They'll be tired. Hopefully they'll just want to go home.

She only realised he must have already passed through the checkpoint when she heard a door open and close downstairs and voices, one of which was that of the landlord, speaking too loudly.

Moments later there were footsteps and then the door unlocked and the landlord entered, followed by the man with the black scarf and the green rucksack. He was holding his cap and smiling in the awkward manner of someone meeting another for the first time.

The landlord stood between them, beaming and apparently proud of himself for having opened a door and brought someone up the stairs without a hitch. He hovered like a waiter expecting a tip.

Sophia thanked him very much and said they'd be leaving soon, but she'd be grateful if he could leave them for a few minutes.

They waited in silence as they listened to the landlord slowly descend the stairs, and then shook hands formally.

'I'm very pleased to meet you, I'm Sophia von Naundorf.'

He nodded his head, still shaking her hand. 'Roman Loszynski.'

–

It had never occurred to him that life outside the ghetto would be so perilous.

The conditions there were beyond appalling; disease was rife, there was little food and they lived in derelict buildings waiting for the Germans to come for them and take them to the death camps, as they'd already done for hundreds of thousands of others in the ghetto.

And then their escape route opened up.

Henryk Kamiński had arrived from Poznań and a deal had been done with the Jewish Fighting Organisation who ran the resistance in the ghetto. The Poznań Group would supply the Jewish resistance with half a dozen Błyskawica sub-machine guns, fifteen Vis semi-automatic pistols and three and half dozen Sidolówka hand grenades.

In return, the Resistance would smuggle Roman Loszynski out of the ghetto, along with his wife, Lea, and their children, Max and Raisa. Roman Loszynski would bring with him the two devices and the blueprints and notes that went with them. The Poznań Group would then take them to safety.

This had been agreed in the middle of February and Roman had the impression everything was very amicable and he assumed that by the beginning of March they'd be living somewhere where they'd no longer be under threat, no longer existing in a condemned cell. Somewhere they'd be safe and able to lead a normal life.

He imagined this would be in England: he had no idea how they'd get there, but he knew the Poznań Group was well connected and with the prospect of getting hold of the devices he was confident the British would pull out all the stops to get them to safety.

But the beginning of March came and went and Roman was becoming increasingly anxious. Everyone in the ghetto knew it was just a matter of time before the Germans came to finish the job they'd tried to start in January. He'd been to see Marek Weiss to ask when he and his family would be able to escape, but got the impression this was the least of his problems.

'As soon as we get the weapons, we'll get you out of the ghetto.'

'And my family.'

'Yes – and your family.'

'But why the delay?'

'Ask your friends in Poznań that. This is all their idea: they're the ones who promised us these weapons. It's up to them to make the delivery.'

Henryk Kamiński arrived back in the ghetto on the last day of March. By then Roman Loszynski and his family had been moved to the basement of a building next door to the Jewish Fighting Organisation headquarters on Zamenhofa. If they ignored the complete lack of daylight, it was more comfortable – if that was the right word – than the tenement house on Nowolipie. It was warmer – sometimes too warm – and they usually got one meal a day.

Kamiński could not have been more apologetic. After they'd last met in February, he'd planned to return to Poznań to organise the weapons. He'd sent a message to Bolesław Piotrowski but he received an urgent reply: the Gestapo were looking for him. He was to stay in Warsaw.

And it wasn't just that it was much harder to organise the weapons from there, he told Roman. Somehow the Home Army appeared to have caught wind of what was going on. So Kamiński had gone into hiding for a month. When he felt it was safe to emerge, he realised he wasn't going to be able to organise the weapons and the escape of Roman and his family on his own.

So, he made a decision. The one other resistance organisation the Poznań Group trusted was Żegota. This group had been formed by the Polish Secret State, which represented most of the resistance groups in Poland and came under the Polish Government in Exile in London. Żegota had been formed for a very specific purpose: to save as many Jews in Poland as possible.

Henryk Kamiński had one contact in Żegota, a man called Julius, with an address on Agrykola Street, close to Łazienki Park and Ujazdów Castle. Julius asked him a lot of questions and told him to return three days later and when he did so he was given instructions to go to 24 Żurawia Street first thing the following morning and ask for Zofia.

The address on Żurawia Street turned out to be the headquarters of Żegota and Zofia turned out to be very senior in the organisation. She wanted Mr Kamiński to be very clear, she said, pausing to draw on the cigarette that never left her lips.

'The primary purpose of Żegota is to rescue Jews. We don't get involved in armed resistance as such. But we recognise that helping you obtain these weapons could be a means to an end. If we help you with these weapons, will you be able to help our funds? Our work is very costly.'

Henryk Kamiński said he was sure they'd be able to help.

'And we will undertake to get the Jewish family out of Warsaw. With the situation in the ghetto, it's not safe to hide them there. Do you have any thoughts about where you'd like them to go?'

–

Roman and Lea Loszynski were woken in the early hours of the morning of Friday 16 April. Marek Weiss explained that they'd finally received the weapons promised to them back in February. Now they were ready to fulfil their side of the deal and smuggle the family out of the ghetto. The plan was for the boxes of equipment to be taken by one route and Roman and his family by another.

'I'd rather keep everything with me.'

'It's too risky. Your journey will be dangerous enough as it is. I've chosen four fighters to escort you: two of them will carry the children, Zhenia will be in charge. You'll leave tonight. Try and get as much rest as you can before then.'

The journey through the sewers took six hours. Max and Raisa had been drugged before they set off and then strapped to the backs of the young fighters carrying them. It was still pitch dark when they emerged on the other side of the wall on Świętojerska, not far from the river. They hid in the cellar of an abandoned house until noon on the Saturday when a battered van arrived to take them to the safe house near Wschodnia station on the other side of the Vistula, where they were reunited with Henryk Kamiński. The devices had arrived safely before them.

They remained in the concealed cellar under the house through that weekend. The children were too exhausted to move and Żegota needed a few days to sort out their false papers. A woman called Zofia had arrived at the house on the Sunday with a man who took their photographs. Zofia was a Żegota agent and before she left, she took Roman and Lea aside.

'How much do the children know?'

'Know about what?'

'Do they realise they'll have to pretend to be someone else? That's not easy for anyone and especially for children. We'll make sure their papers have their own dates of birth, but even then, remembering a false identity when you're under pressure is very difficult.'

Lea said they'd explain it to them carefully.

'Of course you will, but don't underestimate the Germans. If they stop a family, they'll question the children first. At least you all speak good Polish. So many of the Jewish families we rescue have Polish as their second language and they speak it with a Yiddish accent and that gives them away. We'll have the papers ready by the middle of the week and hopefully by then we'll have worked out a route.'

'Where are we going?'

Zofia looked at Henryk Kamiński who answered. 'South, close to the Slovakian border. That's what we've been told.'

'Slovakia? That's hardly—'

'That's all we know at the moment, Roman, but these instructions are coming from London. Our people there are working with the British. They'll know what they're doing. They'll get you to safety through Slovakia.'

They were reconciled to waiting a few days at the safe house. Being outside the ghetto for the first time in more than three years seemed to have a calming effect, at least on the children. Both Max and Raisa slept better than they had done for a long time. Roman was beginning to feel optimistic: Henryk had assured him the British were now involved. They would know what they were doing. They could be out of Poland within a day or two.

At six-thirty on the Monday morning – it was April 19 – Lea woke Roman.

Can you hear that?

He'd heard nothing, having been fast asleep, but the two of them crept out of their room in the cellar and halfway up the stairs where they could hear the undoubted sound of explosions. Henryk soon joined them and together they climbed to the top floor of the house. From a bedroom window they could see smoke rising from the ghetto across the river to the west and the sounds of repeated gunfire and artillery.

The three of them hurried back to the cellar.

It was much later that evening when Zofia arrived. She was normally very calm, not given to showing any emotion. Now she couldn't hide her feelings, a combination of excitement and concern.

'The Germans went into the ghetto at six o'clock this morning. This is their big move to clear it out.' She had to hold a match with two hands as she attempted to light her cigarette. 'They entered the central ghetto and advanced towards Nalewki Street but the Jewish Fighting Organisation was waiting for them there. The battle lasted for two hours and then the Germans retreated. Another German column got to the Gesia-Zamenhof junction and advanced up Zamenhof. There was a fierce battle at the junction with Mila and that German column retreated. Since then, the Germans have been shelling the ghetto. Our information is that the Jewish resistance are now in their bunkers. The Germans will return at first light.'

She paused and slowly shook her head. 'They have some weapons, more than we thought they'd have, but how long can they resist the Nazis – two, three more days?'

Roman said he wouldn't be surprised if it lasted longer. 'The ghetto is a warren of bunkers and cellars and underground passages. The sewer system is far more elaborate than the Germans realise, apparently.'

'Nonetheless, I think we need to hurry with your journey. We've noticed today that there are fewer German patrols and checkpoints around the city: they're throwing everything they have at the ghetto. We need to take advantage of this while the fighting is still going on. I'll be back tomorrow night: be ready to leave first thing on Wednesday morning.'

Zofia slipped into the cellar late on the Tuesday night. The uprising in the ghetto was remarkable, she told the three adults, gathered around her, desperate for any information. 'The resistance is well prepared and the Germans weren't expecting street-fighting like this. Here, these are your new papers.'

She spread them out on the small table.

The Loszynski family were now the Wójciks. Roman was Tadeusz Wójcik, his wife was Klara, and Max and Raisa were Mieczysław and Janina. There was no question the documents were excellent. Żegota had a reputation for producing first-class forgeries.

'We've given you an address in Krakow.' Zofia was talking softly, pointing to one of the cards. 'The railway stations are closed in Warsaw because of the uprising, so we'll go to Lublin by bus and then you take the train to Krakow where you'll stay one night and then head south. Wake the children up now and make sure they memorise their new names. Keep them awake until we leave: with some luck they'll then sleep during the journey. In my experience, sleeping children look more credible. Your boxes will travel separately.'

—

Zofia stayed that night in the cellar of the safe house. The following morning, they left the house at seven and walked to the bus stop, Zofia standing ahead of them in the queue and sitting apart when they boarded. The journey to Lublin took three and a half hours, meaning they arrived in the city just after eleven. Roman noticed a steady stream of German convoys heading towards Warsaw. No Germans checked their papers once they'd got on the bus. He found it hard to believe the rest of the journey would be so straightforward.

Zofia spoke to them briefly once they'd got off at Lublin. They were to follow her to the railway station and then she'd leave them.

'Here's your money: purchase the tickets to Krakow, via Kielce. There's a train due to depart at eleven-thirty: if you catch that one it's due in Kielce at a quarter to three. There's a train from Kielce to Krakow at a quarter past three. If you catch that one, then you'll be in Krakow by six.'

The worst part of the journey was at Kielce railway station. It was a short walk from the platform they arrived on across the concourse to the platform for the Krakow train. As they approached the ticket barrier a checkpoint formed, a Gestapo officer between two Polish police. The Gestapo officer waved the Wójcik family forwards.

'Papers!'

He seemed out of breath as he studied the papers, glancing at the photographs and then at each member of the family.

'Your name?' He was looking directly at Raisa.

'Janina.' She replied very clearly, almost too clearly and looked pleased with herself for remembering correctly.

He handed the papers to a policeman who spoke to Tadeusz Wójcik.

'Purpose of your journey?'

'To return home: we live in Krakow.'

'I can see that: where have you been?'

There was a commotion behind them and he turned round: dozens of German troops were entering the station and were forming up.

'I said, where have you been?'

'Lublin – here's our tickets, we've just come from there.'

'And what were you doing in Lublin?'

'Visiting my uncle,' said Klara Wójcik. Roman was surprised how his wife managed to sound mildly annoyed as she moved in front of the children. 'He's not been at all well and we wanted to make sure he's looked after, and also let him see the children.'

'Do you have his address?'

'Of course I have his address!'

'Wait a minute.'

The Gestapo officer was craning his neck to look beyond them at the troops: they now filled the concourse and more of them were coming in. It was becoming chaotic as other passengers were pushed out of the way. Another Gestapo officer approached him.

'They've commandeered the Częstochowa train to get them to Warsaw but passengers are refusing to leave the train. We'd better go and try and persuade them nicely, eh?'

The crowd of passengers was now pushing forward for the Krakow train.

Five minutes later the Wójciks were on it, the children looking excitedly through the window at the sights around them.

It was six-thirty when they left Krakow station. Zofia's instructions had been for them to leave the station and head towards the Old Town.

Someone will find you.

They'd hardly walked a hundred yards when a young man approached them from behind.

Uncle Tadeusz, Aunt Klara! How are you? Come with me, I have Father's car.

Once they were in the car, he said to call him Andrzej. 'I'm taking you to a house in Dębniki, in the south west of the city. The housekeeper's one of us: you'll stay there overnight.'

Andrzej appeared the next Thursday morning to tell them they'd be leaving within the hour. A lorry would take them to their destination: the driver was someone they trusted.

It was an uncomfortable journey of two and a half hours. They felt the lorry pull off a main road and bounce along a rough track before it turned round and came to a stop. The driver knocked on the partition and told them it was clear, but they needed to hurry.

They followed Andrzej across a farmyard into a building between the barn and the farmhouse. They went down a set of steps into a large, low-ceilinged room. In one corner four beds were arranged against the wall. In the centre of the room was a table, on the top of which was a suitcase, which Andrzej proudly pointed out to Roman.

Open it!

Neatly wedged between tightly packed clothes were the Tatra boxes and underneath them a folder containing the blueprints and Roman's notebooks.

—

'That's out of the question. I refuse to go along with it.'

It was later that night: the children were asleep on their beds and Roman and Lea were sitting round the table with Andrzej and an older man who'd arrived a few minutes earlier. They'd not yet been introduced.

'You know where we are, Roman?'

'You've told me already, Andrzej: we're just outside Zakopane.'

'Exactly: close to the border with Slovakia. It's five, six miles away over the Tatra Mountains. You can see Slovakia from here. Pavol here is the most reliable guide we have: he knows routes over the mountains no one else knows. He's also a member of the Slovak resistance. He can get you and your equipment into Slovakia tomorrow night. But that journey would be impossible with Lea and the children.'

Pavol nodded in agreement. He had the tanned and lined face of someone who spent his life outdoors. His enormous hands were folded in front of him on the table.

'Lea and the children will be safe here. This is an isolated farm: the Germans hardly ever come here so they can stay for as long as they need to. You're still a long way from safety, Roman, you must know that. When it's the right time, we'll bring them to you.'

Roman shook his head again but Lea placed a hand on his arm. 'I think he's right, Roman. We're exhausted and I can't believe we can go any further with the children. You're still a fit man. You can go over the mountains, and remember, you speak excellent

German. I speak very little and the children, not a word. We'll be safer here.'

Roman shook his head once more, but this time in a resigned manner.

'Was this the plan all along, Andrzej? I'd have never left Warsaw if I realised I'd have to leave my wife and children behind.'

'And you think you'd have all been safe in Warsaw, Roman? Come on, the Jews are holding out against the Germans, but for how much longer? You've saved their lives. They'll be safe here. They'll be looked after.'

Chapter 21

Slovakia, Austria and Switzerland
April, May 1943

They crossed the Tatra Mountains into Slovakia on the night of Friday 23 April.

Pavol effortlessly carried a large rucksack containing the devices, sprinting up ridges, hopping from rock to rock, pausing only to turn round every so often to check that Roman was still there, a smile on his leathered face indicating he was taking some pleasure from his charge observing the ease with which he managed the mountains.

He was a man of very few words, occasionally announcing how long he thought they had left or checking whether Roman wanted a break. Soon after the sun began to rise, Pavol pointed into the distance to a tiny hut, tucked between a turn in the rocks.

They stayed in the hut all that Saturday and continued their descent at nightfall. The journey through the mountains, and then through the less demanding but still rough terrain below them – the Lower Tatras – continued for days. During the day they would sleep in huts or the outhouses of isolated farms.

On the Wednesday they reached a town called Brezno and Pavol left him there, in the house of a schoolteacher and his wife, both of whom spoke good Polish and assured him he'd be well looked after. The following morning, they took him to the bus stop, from where he'd travel to Banská Bystrica and then to Bratislava. He'd be using his Tadeusz Wójcik papers and if questioned would explain he'd been ordered to report to the Employment Office in Bratislava.

The station in Bratislava is outside the city centre: walk down the hill to the second bus stop. A tall woman in a blue coat will approach you and ask if this is the right bus stop for the castle. You're to go with her.

'And if she doesn't approach me?'

The schoolteacher and his wife both shrugged. They had no idea.

It was beginning to get dark when the train arrived at Bratislava. The German sentry who checked his papers looked little more than eighteen, his helmet too big for him, and he found it difficult to hide his exhaustion as he indicated Roman should show him his papers.

He checked them and then said something Roman couldn't make out. A lady behind him said he was asking for his Work Transfer Document.

'I'm terribly sorry but I don't have it.' Tadeusz Wójcik addressed the young soldier in German, smiling as he did so. The other man seemed grateful he was being spoken to in his own language.

'You're meant to have that document if you're travelling for work.'

'I know – thank you! That is exactly what I was telling my boss in Krakow when the authorities told him to send his best engineers here. The man should have waited a day to get the right paperwork, but he didn't want to displease the authorities… and now…' He gestured towards his papers. And now he was in trouble.

Roman asked the soldier where he was from and he replied Koblenz and he looked momentarily forlorn as he said that, as if his thoughts were of his hometown. Roman said it was the most wonderful part of Germany and the Mosel wines – unquestionably the best!

The queue was growing behind him and the soldier said very well, he'd stamp the papers as long as Herr Wójcik reported to the Employment Office first thing in the morning.

The woman in the blue coat – she wasn't that tall, as it happened – spoke with him in German after they'd identified each other. They were on a trolleybus to the city centre. She handed him a black scarf and a light grey cloth cap and told him to put them on. She gave him a large green rucksack too.

'When we get off, I'll take you to the tram to the port area and tell you when to get off, but I'll stay on the tram: I'd be too conspicuous there. Walk in the direction of the river and when you see three tall cranes alongside each other go towards the quay. The *Jelka* is moored there. The skipper is Ján Kuchár: he'll be the only person board.'

When he took Roman below deck, Ján Kuchár explained that the *Jelka* was a large steam tugboat whose job was to tow barges on the Danube. 'Tomorrow night we're pulling five barges laden with coal to Vienna. We depart sometime after eleven – it's safer that way, slower, of course, but less chance of being bombed in the dark. You'll remain in my cabin until we dock in Vienna. When you leave the port there's a bar across the road. You're to go to the rear entrance and someone will let you in.'

–

The man who let him in asked what he wanted. Roman explained he'd been told to come here to meet someone – a lady – and the man wiped his nose with the back of his arm and gestured that Roman should follow him.

Sophia von Naundorf could not have been more charming. Once they were satisfied the bar owner had gone downstairs, she said she hoped he'd had a good journey and he said it was fine apart from the constant smell of coal dust. She pointed to a suitcase.

'Your clothes are in there: a suit, shirt, tie, an overcoat – everything to make you look like a proper German gentleman. I understand you're carrying some equipment with you? You're to put that in the case and cover it with the clothes you're wearing. Get changed now, please.'

She'd turned to face the wall as he changed into his new clothes and then she showed him their papers.

'We will be husband and wife, Gerhard and Johanna Krüger. You were an officer in the Wehrmacht: a major in the 29th Motorized Infantry Division, which is also known as the Falcon Division. You were wounded in the Battle of Smolensk in September 1941 and invalided out of the army. This bandage here – you're to strap it round your knee. It will cause you to limp, there's a walking stick for you to use too. Your story will also be that you had a breakdown after your injury, that will explain why I will do most of the talking.'

The bar owner had agreed to drive them in his van on his way to collect his supplies. He seemed glad to be getting rid of them. They crossed the Danube Canal on Stadionbrücke into the Third District and he then dropped them by the side of the Botanical Gardens. She checked with him the quickest way to get to Fleischmarkt in the First District and he said it was quite a walk, he'd be happy to take them, for a fee of course. Sophia said she was very grateful, but they preferred to walk, the man they were due to meet wouldn't be there for a while.

She paused by the side of the road watching the bar owner's van disappear into the distance.

'We're meeting someone at Fleischmarkt?'

She shook her head. 'That's what I want him to think. I'm not sure how much I trust him. We needed to be in the van to get away from the port, but now he's served his purpose. Come, we head this way. It's not too far. I hope that case isn't too heavy. And remember to limp.'

It was a few minutes before nine on the morning of Saturday May 1 when they arrived at Südbahnhof. Sophia had already bought first-class tickets for her and Roman to travel to Innsbruck. The train was scheduled to leave at nine-thirty, giving Sophia just enough time to brief Roman.

'Our destination is Feldkirch – west of Innsbruck. It's close to the Swiss border, which is where we're heading. There's a psychiatric clinic, which has a reputation for being very good – and you have a reservation there. The plan is to get close to the clinic and then cross the border. Our story will be that we've been in Vienna for you to see a psychiatrist and get a referral. I have all the papers. But please try and speak as little as possible: your German is good, but the Polish accent is detectable.'

The first-class ticket helped. They travelled in a comfortable compartment with one other passenger, an elderly lady. The first inspection was soon after they'd left Vienna, Roman dozing as Sophia explained to the guard and the policeman that her husband was a sick man.

'He served the Reich and look at him now – a shadow of himself. He is desperate to fight again, but he's in no fit state. We travelled all the way to Vienna to see a specialist in that field and he has referred us to the clinic – you can see everything there in the letters.'

Roman opened his eyes just wide enough to see Sophia weeping so convincingly that both the uniformed men in the doorway looked embarrassed and said they quite understood and all the paperwork appeared to be in order so if they could just check their cases, they'd leave them alone.

'That won't be necessary, officer.'

'I beg your pardon?'

It was the elderly lady, a fur stole round her shoulders and an elaborate hat on her head. Her manner was of someone who expected to be listened to.

'Didn't you hear what the lady said? Look at the poor man! He's a wreck, all in the service of the Reich. Where were you injured?'

Roman stirred and said at the Battle of Smolensk. In 1941.

'You hear him? On the Russian front – while you were no doubt bothering passengers travelling first class!'

The two men disappeared into the corridor and Sophia thanked the woman very much, but avoided the latter's efforts to engage in conversation. The woman left the train at Salzburg and was replaced by a man in his sixties who was determined to travel in silence.

The train arrived in Innsbruck just before five o'clock. They were staying at The Grand on Südtiroler Platz, just across the road from the station.

They remained in Innsbruck until the Monday morning. Sophia was worried that travelling west on a Sunday could be difficult: there were few trains and she knew Roman needed to be as fit as possible. When the elderly woman on the train had described him as a wreck, she wasn't far wrong: he looked exhausted. He slept for most of the Sunday.

The following morning, they left Innsbruck for Feldkirch, arriving there just before midday. 'This is where we're at our most vulnerable,' Sophia confided on the train. 'We're close to the border and we have no reason not to be heading for the clinic. At least we ought to head in that direction.'

'Which direction?'

'The direction of the clinic: it's in the south of the town. Very close to the border with Liechtenstein, as it happens.'

Roman nodded as he looked out of the window, the glorious scenery now caught by a bright sunlight. 'Excuse my ignorance,' he said, 'but Liechtenstein – it's part of Austria, I thought – is that correct?'

She shook her head. 'They'd put you in prison if they heard you say that in Liechtenstein! It's an independent country, run by some kind of duke, I think.'

'And it's an ally of Germany?'

'No, it's neutral. Like Switzerland.'

–

They checked into a *pension* close to the station in Feldkirch, telling the owner they were there for a walking holiday for a day or two and perhaps if he could recommend a shop to buy suitable clothing?

When they returned from the shop, they asked the *pension* owner for suggestions of where to walk. The prettiest routes were to the north, he said. To the east was the most demanding, to the south was the least interesting but the easiest and to the west was very pretty too but being by the Swiss border full of security.

They told him they were really novices so south seemed the best idea and he said in that case he'd recommend the woods to the south-east of the town, but they'd need to be careful. 'If you take the wrong path you could end up in Liechtenstein: it's a surprisingly easy place to get into but a devil of one to get out of, and you'll die of boredom while waiting. They're building proper fences soon: they should have done so years ago!'

They left their cases in the *pension* along with the clothes they'd changed out of. They just carried their rucksacks, managing to get the Tatra boxes in them. They booked and paid for dinner at the *pension* that night and when they asked the owner – who was falling over himself to please them – how to get to the woods, he offered to drive them.

There was one checkpoint just as the town began to fade into countryside and the owner talked them through it. Ten minutes after they'd been dropped off, they were in the wood, crouching in the bracken and staring at what they took to be the border, a series of ten-foot-high white posts spaced five yards apart. They waited for another quarter of an hour, during which time they didn't hear or see a soul. Moments later they were in Liechtenstein.

–

Noel Moore had taken the call that Monday evening. The call came through to the telephone line in the embassy that was reserved for Sophia von Naundorf. She'd been promised someone would answer it at any time of the day or night.

The line was normally in the duty office but by the Monday they were expecting to hear from Sophia any day now as they knew Roman and his devices had arrived in Vienna on the Saturday, so Noel had had the line switched through to his office.

The sun was setting over Berne and Noel was contemplating switching the line back to the duty office and leaving for the night when it rang.

It was unquestionably the Sophia Line, as Basil called it. He looked at the phone for a moment or two before picking it up.

'Berne Furniture Supplies, this is Karl speaking.' They'd joked about that. Basil insisted he sounded like a furniture salesman and Sophia said he sounded like a Karl.

A slight pause. 'I am enquiring if the French sofa has arrived yet.' She sounded very calm. The reference to the French sofa and the use of the word 'arrived' meant it was unequivocal good news. He just hoped she wasn't confused, though that would be most unlikely.

'It has – and when would you like me to deliver it?'

If she replied 'as soon as possible' that would mean they'd been caught.

'Whenever suits you: tomorrow would be convenient.'

Noel Moore almost wept with relief and heard himself say 'thank heavens' and then he asked her if she was able to say where she was.

'Vaduz.'

'I beg your pardon, my dear? The line isn't as clear as one would like.'

'Vaduz. It's a town in Liechtenstein. In fact, I think it may be the only town in Liechtenstein.'

The ambassador was changing for a diplomatic dinner when he was persuaded to return to his office in the embassy.

'But Liechtenstein is neutral, Basil. Can't they just stroll across the border into Switzerland?'

'I'm not sure we can take that risk, Sir Christopher. Inevitably they have links with the Austrians – well, the Germans, they're one and the same these days. There's always a chance someone could decide to hand them over. Especially if they realise they aren't who they say they are.'

'And this Roman – he's the Jew, eh?'

'Exactly, sir.'

'So, what is it you'd like me to do?'

'I understand the head of the Federal Political Department will be at the dinner tonight.'

'Charles, yes...'

'Call in a favour and ask him to issue papers permitting Gerhard and Johanna Krüger to cross the border under Swiss protection. There's a border post on the Sevelen Bridge in Vaduz. We'll be waiting on the other side.'

'Very well. And what happens then?'

'I imagine,' said Basil, 'that London will want to get their hands on Roman Loszynski and his boxes pretty damn quick. We'll need to organise something clever, through France I'd have thought.'

–

Basil Remington-Barber never did have to organise something clever through France, though it certainly wasn't for the want of trying.

The Polish chap had been very amenable when he arrived in Berne. It had all been rather jolly, in fact: Sophia and Jack were of course delighted to be reunited once more and Roman seemed very relieved to be there.

But the next day he was in a bit of a state, fretting and then demanding to know when his wife and children would be joining him in Switzerland.

It all seemed to be a bit of a pattern, Basil had remarked to Noel. *We get them out of danger and then they get all... worked up, wanting this and that.* Noel said it was understandable and he'd have a word with Roman.

He explained to Roman he wouldn't be staying in Switzerland for very long: arrangements were being made for him and his machines – which Roman wouldn't let out of his sight – to be smuggled into France where an RAF plane would fly him back to England. There he'd have access to the finest workshop the RAF had. Everything he needed to work on the machines would be at his disposal.

This was when Roman said he wasn't going anywhere and sat back in his chair with his arms folded tightly high across his chest.

Petulant was the word that came to Basil's mind.

'When we were in Zakopane I was told very clearly by the people rescuing us that Lea and the children would stay there for a while and then be brought to me when it was safe. That's more likely to happen if I'm in Switzerland. I'm not going to England: not without my family.'

Basil said the problem was they were in Switzerland and were rather caught in the middle between London and Poland and it was very difficult to know who said what and when and certainly while they'd do their best, it would be rash to think that Roman's family would be able to leave Poland in the near future and if they were somewhere safe in Poland then maybe that was for the best.

'I tell you what,' said Basil. 'I'll have a word with London. It's their game after all.'

–

They were surprised – very pleasantly surprised – quite how well Barney Allen had taken it.

Leave it with me for a day or two, Basil.

And a day or two later he'd come back to him and said to ask Roman what equipment he needed to develop his machinery beyond the prototype stage and Roman supplied a list, which surprised Basil because it wasn't very long at all and some of it was rather basic, the kind of things his brother-in-law – a dab hand at fixing cars and the like – kept in his garage at home.

Barney Allen replied the very next day.

'The French Section at the SOE has a jolly good man in Geneva: Jewish chap from Strasbourg, brilliant engineer, escaped from the Nazis, now he makes and services radio equipment for the SOE from a very well-equipped workshop in Geneva. Send Roman there and give the French chap whatever funds he needs.'

'Are you sure, Barney? You're being awfully understanding.'

'I already had my concerns about getting Roman into France and safely onto a Lysander and back here. We've had a few nasty experiences recently. The Nazis are infiltrating too many resistance groups. This way we keep Roman happy and safe and there's another consideration – when the devices are ready to test, we don't need to worry about how to get them into Germany, do we?'

Basil said he wasn't quite sure what Barney meant.

'Think about it, Basil: they'll be with you in Switzerland, won't they? You just need to get someone to pop over the border with them, eh?'

Chapter 22

England
May 1943

'Well, we meet again. Just like a school reunion!'

They were meeting in the same stuffy room in the basement of Downing Street, the participants the same as the previous month: Piers Devereux and Barney Allen from MI6, Frank Hamilton and Martin Marlow from the RAF, Sir Roland Pearson and Lord Swalcliffe from Downing Street.

Roly Pearson was treating it with the jollity of a school reunion, acting very much as the host and said Winston was *delighted*, though of course he hadn't gone into too much detail with him and he understood that Air Marshal Harris was also *delighted*, and Frank Hamilton said that was indeed the case, not least because Bomber Command was coming under a good deal of criticism over the effectiveness of the Ruhr bombing campaign.

Roly Pearson continued in this vein for a while until he was interrupted by Piers Devereux who suggested that perhaps they could now turn to the purpose of the meeting and get an update from Barney?

Barney Allen removed a folder from his briefcase, which he placed on the table in front of him. 'You all received your copies yesterday afternoon, I trust? My apologies for not allowing longer to digest this report, but you'll appreciate that time is of the essence.'

'Perhaps if you were able to summarise it, Barney?'

'Of course: the report details how, thanks to the efforts of the Polish and Slovakian resistance, Roman Loszynski escaped from Warsaw on the twenty-first of April and arrived in Vienna on the first of May, which was a Saturday: he was met there by Sophia von Naundorf and they entered Switzerland on Tuesday the fourth, via Liechtenstein.

'I remain of the view that bringing his wife and two young children is out of the question, so they remain in Poland where they're being hidden by the resistance. I think it is fair to say that Mr Loszynski is extremely unhappy with this, so much so that he refused to leave Switzerland: he feels he is nearer to them there than he would be in this country. As it so happens, I believe this is no bad thing. I had concerns about getting him and his equipment from Switzerland to England. I understand we've had some bad experiences recently getting people out through France and I felt there was too much risk. This was your view too, Piers?'

'It was indeed: SOE say too many resistance circuits in central France have been infiltrated recently. I agreed with Barney that we'd best keep Loszynski in Switzerland. SOE are being very helpful: they've given us access to a workshop in Geneva and we've moved him there and Sophia and Jack Miller are keeping an eye on him.'

'What we're interested in is these machines he's brought with him. When can we test the damn things?'

'Very soon, I'm told, Lord Swalcliffe. Loszynski regards the version he brought with him as Mark One. He's currently developing a Mark Two and says when a Mark Three is completed it will be ready to be tested.'

'Which will be when, Barney?'

'I'm told within a week to ten days, Roly. There was one particular part that Loszynski needed, some complicated little electronic unit which we managed to borrow, for want of a better word, from the University of Geneva.'

'Bomber Command are extremely keen to test it as soon as possible,' said Group Captain Marlow.

'And how do you propose to do that?' Lord Swalcliffe leaned back, as if he'd asked a pupil a difficult question for which he didn't expect Barney to have an answer.

'We'll fly an agent into France where he'll be looked after by the Cathedral Circuit, one of the few resistance groups we can still trust. They'll get the agent into Switzerland and he'll meet the team in Geneva, pick up the transmitter part of the device and then take it into Germany, where it will be tested at a time and location to be co-ordinated with Bomber Command.'

'And the receiver unit, the one which goes on the plane?'

'That will come out in the diplomatic bag via Lisbon.'

'And where in Germany do you propose he takes the transmitter?'

'There's an agent in Düsseldorf called Felix who Miller says is very much on board.'

The room fell quiet, everyone in it having the same thought, which was eventually expressed by Roly Pearson, no longer sounding as upbeat as he normally did.

'We're expecting an awful lot, aren't we? Agent flies to France, resistance gets him in and out of Switzerland, to Germany and back to Switzerland, then France and Germany again. How big did you say this device is, Barney?'

'The size of a biscuit tin, though Loszynski hopes the Mark Three will be far more compact.'

'How much more compact?'

'The size of a small biscuit tin, I understand.'

'Rather like the ones we get toffees in at Christmas?'

'Hopefully, Roly, yes.'

'Well, it's going to require an enormous amount of luck.'

'I know, sir.'

'And this agent you're sending in: I hope it's someone bloody good?'

There was a pause: Barney looked at Piers Devereux who coughed before replying. 'He's the ideal agent, Roly.'

'I doubt he's the ideal agent, Piers: the reports on him are mixed at best.'

'I doubt the reports on anyone are universally positive, Barney. I've told you many times, secret agents are by their nature flawed in some way: they're not ordinary people because ordinary, normal people aren't suited to or attracted to a clandestine life. We have to accept that a good secret agent is in many ways a rough diamond. You have his file there, don't you?'

Barney Allen opened the file on his lap and sipped from a cup of tea, which had turned cold.

'Philippe Moreau, born Auxerre, France, in October 1912 to a French father and an English mother. Family moved to England in 1926 when Philippe was fourteen. They settled in London and he left school at fifteen and joined the Wireless Telegraph and Signal Company, eventually becoming an electronics engineer at their factory in Chelmsford in Essex. He's described as physically very fit. He was conscripted in 1940 and when the army realised he was fluent in French he was recommended to the SOE, who initially rejected him.'

'I think that's an unfair interpretation, Barney. The way I read it, he was deferred by the SOE. They felt he had an excitable personality and wasn't good at taking instructions.'

'The report says he was disruptive on his assessment course.'

'Well, I probably would be too. Doesn't make him bad agent material. But you've met him, Barney – do you think he's up to it?'

'I accept he's probably the best we have at the moment. His French is mother-tongue standard and he also has excellent German. The Wireless Telegraph and Signal Company sent him to work in Hamburg for a couple of years.'

'So we have a chap here who speaks both French and German and understands electronics. With the greatest respect, Barney, I think we need to stop worrying about him and get him over there. You say Frank has sorted out the transport?'

–

'I had to get Arthur Harris to intervene on this, you know, Barney.'

It was the afternoon of Friday 21 May and Air Vice-Marshal Frank Hamilton and Barney Allen were in the back of an RAF staff car on the way from London to Kent. Barney Allen said how grateful he was and said Downing Street would be very appreciative, but the RAF man was keen to make his point, again.

'161 squadron had to be prevailed upon, I can tell you that. Even taking off from Hawkinge is still two hundred and seventy miles from the landing point. The range of the Lysander is six hundred miles, Barney: that's a round trip of five hundred and forty miles, which leaves very little margin for error. All you need is a nasty cross wind or a strong headwind and you're in trouble. The Lysander will be flying at its limits.'

'It will be empty on the way back.'

'That helps, of course, but even so...'

They arrived at RAF Hawkinge just north of Folkestone at three o'clock. Philippe Moreau was already there with his SOE dispatcher in a Nissen hut close to the apron. Moreau was considerably more nervous than when they'd previously met: less cocky, no wisecracks and constantly drawing on a cigarette. Barney said perhaps now would be a good time to run through everything once more.

'I've just had a word with the station commander who says the optimum time for take-off will be a quarter to one in the morning. There's a nasty easterly blowing over the Channel and northern France, but that should have gone by then. Come over here, Philippe, and we'll look at the map.'

Barney traced the route with his forefinger. 'We're here, near Folkestone. You'll cross into France just south of Calais and then head south-east over Arras and Saint-Quentin, keeping north of Reims before heading due south and landing here, just north of the town of Saint-Dizier. The woods are quite dense in the area, but the resistance has chosen the landing site carefully. You're in their hands then. I imagine they'll have somewhere for you to hide until later on the Saturday and then you'll head off for Switzerland. With any luck you'll be in Geneva on the Monday.'

Philippe Moreau looked at the map for a bit longer, all the time holding a cigarette to his mouth. 'And then I go to Germany?'

'The resistance chaps who're taking you into Switzerland will look after that. It's quite a way to Düsseldorf but…'

Barney Allen's voice trailed off.

'But what?'

'But I'm sure they'll get you there in one piece. You have all your paperwork?'

Moreau nodded. He'd be Benoît Morel, a factory worker from Auxerre, which was his hometown and hopefully he would be confident answering any questions about it.

In the intervening hours Philippe Moreau changed into his French clothes and the SOE dispatcher carried out a thorough inspection of his belongings to ensure nothing could be linked to England. They sat quietly in the Nissen hut. A roast dinner was brought for Philippe Moreau, but he just picked at it. At midnight the station commander came in: the weather had lifted considerably and they were bringing the take-off forward to a quarter past midnight.

The Frenchman picked up a bit after that. Barney had brought a hip flask with him and poured a small Cognac for Moreau who drank it in one go and said it was very good, please could he have some more. He was holding the small glass out, waiting for it to be refilled.

Barney Allen thought of Oliver Twist and Philippe Moreau did indeed have something of a Dickensian air about him as he sat expectantly across the table, smaller than he'd seemed before, a bit too eager to please, clearly very nervous. Barney gave him another measure, worried it may be too much. Moreau started talking about his family, a rambling monologue about his mother and then an account of the various women in his life, many of whom seemed to overlap, which included two current ones – a married woman considerably older than him and the other significantly younger.

In normal circumstances that would have set one or two alarm bells ringing, complicated love lives were never a good thing for an agent to carry with them into the field, but Barney decided now wasn't the time for all that.

He realised he was shivering, despite the Nissen hut being very warm. The young Frenchman was now talking about his landlady's cat and how he'd always wanted a dog and Barney said maybe he could get one when he got back to England and Moreau gave him a knowing look followed by a shrug and then a muttered, 'If I get back.'

A friend of Barney Allen's was a barrister who'd represented a man sentenced to death and had been present for the execution. He'd told of how it was only a short walk from the man's cell, along the landing and into the execution chamber. It was, he told Barney, quite the longest and most harrowing experience of his life.

Barney Allen felt very much like that as he accompanied Philippe Moreau the short distance from the hut to the Lysander waiting on the apron.

That was what he'd become now: someone making decisions that determined the fate of other people, dispatching young men to an uncertain fate, though as he watched the plane hurry down the runway, he wondered quite how uncertain it really was.

Chapter 23

France
May 1943

The landing field just north of Saint-Dizier had been well chosen: forests to the north, east and west ensuring it was secluded and protected from the wind. The final part of the descent was a bit tight as the pilot gave himself just enough clearance of the trees but the beacons were well placed and the field itself not too rough.

The pilot taxied to the far end and told his passenger to get a move on. The man clambered out and was hurried away by two dark figures. Moments later the Lysander was airborne and heading home.

Philippe Moreau – now Benoît Morel – was hustled into the woods and with a man on either side of him ran for what seemed like an eternity. When they came to a road, they waited in the undergrowth until they heard an owl-like sound and then crept across it. A woman was waiting for him in a ditch on the other side and she whispered the plan: they would walk for another two hours to a farmhouse where they'd stay for a few hours.

'And then?'

'And then you'll go to Switzerland. For now, though, it's best we don't talk.'

–

It wasn't that Philippe thought he knew better than the woman – Barney Allen had given him a bit of a stern talking to before he left about doing what he was told and not questioning orders

– but he did wonder about her. In his training they'd been taught the importance of avoiding being caught out in the open. Now, instead of using the cover of the hedgerow, they were crossing open fields and he couldn't help thinking how visible they were under the full moon.

By four o'clock he began to form the view that they were lost. They'd been walking for far longer than two hours. He tried to talk to her: he said there was no shame in admitting they were lost; it was easily done and maybe it would be better if they started to look for somewhere to hide because before they knew it would be sunrise and then they'd be in trouble.

She shook her head and said it wasn't much further. They crossed another two fields and were now alongside a road and he worried that any German driving down it would easily spot them.

'We'll wait by the crossroads there: one of our comrades will collect us in his van.'

'I thought you said we were going to a farmhouse?'

She hesitated before saying he'd be driving them to the farmhouse. At the crossroads there was a sign for Nancy and now he began to get very worried because he knew they ought to be much further south of Nancy than the sign indicated. Just as he was wondering how much he trusted her, a car pulled up followed by a van and the woman walked to the car and spoke to the driver.

Philippe Moreau edged back into the field.

Nothing felt right. He crouched down and hoped no one had seen him. He'd run back across the field and into a deep ditch they passed a few minutes earlier.

But when he turned round two men were walking towards him, almost casually and when he turned again, he saw the woman standing by the car and heard a man ask whether this was him and she nodded.

–

They kept him in the cell for a few hours.

He'd been roughed up when he arrived at the Gestapo headquarters in Nancy and although it hadn't felt too brutal at the time, he'd been kneed in the groin and as he lay on the floor in his cell it was clear that pain wasn't going away.

He tried to remember everything he'd been told about what to do if he was captured.

Hold out for as long as possible.

Stick to your cover story for as long as you can: it ought to be good enough to satisfy them for a while.

Give them bits and pieces of information: start with what you think they know already.

All of which seemed fine in a classroom but the way he felt now was very different. He was in pain, cold and wet, absolutely terrified, convinced they were going to torture him and he'd happily tell them whatever they wanted to know to stop them doing that.

The only problem was, he didn't know very much.

He just knew he was being taken to Geneva but he had no idea who he'd meet there. All he knew was he'd get his instructions and then take a box containing some equipment to Düsseldorf.

A man called Felix. He remembered that. Maybe they'd know of a man called Felix in Düsseldorf and be satisfied with that.

He had no idea what time it was when the interrogation began. Despite everything, he was starving and eagerly ate the stew they gave him in the interrogation room and gratefully covered himself with the blanket.

The Gestapo officer who eventually interrogated him was a very large man with a disconcertingly high-pitched voice, almost as if he was imitating someone. He spoke good French and wasn't unpleasant at first.

Please could you tell me who you are and the purpose of your mission?

He explained that his name was Benoît Morel and he was from Auxerre and he was in the area because he'd previously met a woman who he was ashamed to say was married and he'd come to this area to look for her but got lost and he'd asked another

224

woman the way and now... well, he didn't understand, but here he was.

The German shook his head and said he was shocked that the British had sent him over with such a poor cover story and Philippe Moreau realised he was nodding in agreement.

'This is your last opportunity to tell me the whole story: I need everything – the purpose of your mission, who your contacts are, who your contacts were in England – everything.'

He was about to ask how he knew about England but realised that was a trap so decided to say nothing. The German looked annoyed.

'*Sprechen Sie Deutsch?*'

Do you speak German?

They'd warned him about this. *They always ask that early on: don't let on you understand the language.*

He stared blankly at the German who then said in German that if he was lying then he'd die a horrible death, but Philip managed to give nothing away and even allowed a faint smile.

'The woman who led you to us – she's seen sense and is working for us. She told us you were arriving this evening from England. Unfortunately, she'd not been told where you were landing, otherwise we'd have captured the plane too! So, you see, we know you've arrived from England.'

Philippe Moreau decided that before they started to torture him, he'd give them something at this point – his trainer called it a titbit. He said he'd been forced to come over and he was to go to Auxerre where he was to meet a man in the cloisters of the Abbey of Saint-Germain and he'd receive his instructions from him. He then went into some detail about Auxerre, which seemed to satisfy the German for a while, the various places he was to visit, where he'd go if the man he was meant to meet in the cloisters at the Abbey wasn't there, where he was to leave messages...

The German was taking quite extensive notes and Philip felt that at the very least he'd want to check everything out with his colleagues in Auxerre and that would give him another day to get his thoughts together and maybe…

'Nonsense.' The German pushed the table at him so hard it smashed into his ribs and his chair toppled over, sending him sprawling over the floor. He was about to haul himself up when he felt a kick in his back and a pair of hands drag him across the room by his collar.

He feigned unconsciousness, during which time he heard the Gestapo officer speak – in his high-pitched voice – to someone else in German.

'Hang him up, leave him there for a while.'

Startled, he looked up, convinced they were about to hang him. Instead, he was strung up against the wall in an X shape, his hands and feet shackled by chains to bolts set in the brickwork.

The Gestapo officer watched as two other men drenched him in bucket after bucket of cold water. He felt as if he was drowning and when he tried to shout out that he'd tell them whatever they wanted to know, no words would come out. He must have blacked out because he heard the high-pitched voice in the distance say something about leaving him there to think about it.

–

He had no idea how long they left him there. It was certainly many hours, and by the time they returned – and drenched him again in water – he'd lost all feeling in his arms and his legs were agony.

As soon as the Gestapo officer entered the room he began to speak, as if pleading for his life.

'Switzerland…'

'What about Switzerland?'

'I was being taken there to meet a man who was going to explain to me how a piece of machinery worked and then I was to take it into Germany.'

'What machinery?'

'I have no idea, other than it was something to do with bombs.'

'So, you were going to take a bomb into Germany?'

'It's not a bomb, I don't think so at any rate…'

'How were you going to get to Germany?'

'Back through France: the people who met me yesterday or whenever it was… they were going to help me. I was told very little, they said I'd be given my instructions at each stage. I don't have the names of anyone other than the man I was to meet in Düsseldorf.'

'You never said anything about Düsseldorf.'

'I was going to tell you. I was to meet a man there called Felix.'

'And how were you going to find him?'

'I was going to be told that in Switzerland.'

'Do you at least know where in Switzerland?'

'Geneva, I think.'

The Gestapo officer paced around the room and then called in another man. They spoke in German and clearly had no idea the man hanging from the wall understood every word.

'You've fouled up here, Klaus: you should have followed them further. That bloody woman now admits her instructions were that he'd be collected by others who were going to take him to his next place. We could have seen what he was meant to be up to in Switzerland. Christ, if they hear about this upstairs. You go to work on him, see what else he can tell us.'

Klaus was a man of few words, delivered in a deep voice and a heavy accent. He used a knife to remove the clothes of the man who wasn't Benoît Morel and the same knife to cut him. Every so often he'd stop and ask him if he'd remembered anything and Moreau would blurt out a word here and a phrase there, which another man in the room would write down.

He told them his real name was Philippe Moreau and he was indeed from Auxerre and they'd moved to England in 1926 and he'd become a *very* senior electronics engineer at the Wireless Telegraph and Signal Company and there was so much he could help them with.

He then went into some detail about the projects he was aware of, talked about his time in Hamburg, how by the time he left there in 1937 he'd become sympathetic to the Nazi cause and had been blackmailed into working for the British because of a misunderstanding over some money and...

He paused. The German had made a deep horizontal cut across his torso, at the bottom of the ribs and it was now bleeding quite profusely and this and the pain was making him feel very light-headed.

He blacked out again and when he came round the other German was in the room and he was being drenched with cold water. He began to cough violently and realised he was coughing up a lot of blood and that seemed to worry them because he heard someone shout in German to cut him down and to go and get a medic.

They lay him on the floor and covered him in a blanket and the medic looked so concerned that Philippe Moreau found himself thinking more clearly than he had done and he remembered the Englishman had told him a German woman and an American man would meet him in Geneva and that they'd be the ones briefing him and there was something about a transmitter and...

He tried to speak but now he was beginning to find it impossible: every time he opened his mouth it was blood rather than words which came out and he was colder than he'd ever felt in his life.

Chapter 24

England, Switzerland, France and Germany
June 1943

'You're certain, are you?'

'Yes, I'm afraid so, sir.'

Barney Allen couldn't stop himself thinking that the woman the SOE had sent over to give him the shocking news that Wednesday morning was really most attractive. He knew it was inappropriate to have such thoughts as she was informing him of the death of Philippe Moreau, but he couldn't help himself.

'Contrary to what we understood, sir, it seems that Cathedral Circuit had been compromised. We think it was just one person who betrayed it: the woman who was meant to escort Moreau from the landing area to a farmhouse led him into a trap. She also betrayed another half dozen members of the circuit and they've all been arrested by the Gestapo. The other members of the circuit have gone into hiding.'

She spoke excellent English with just a hint of a French accent, enough to sound most alluring, as dreadful as the news she was giving was. 'We have a contact in the Gestapo headquarters in Nancy and according to them Philippe Moreau was brought in on the Saturday and tortured. It seems he died on the Sunday. He wasn't executed, he bled to death.'

Barney Allen shifted uncomfortably in his chair and muttered, 'Oh God,' and thought of that short walk from the Nissen hut to the waiting Lysander at RAF Hawkinge. It was less than a week ago.

'And does your contact in Nancy know whether poor Philippe revealed anything?'

'We have no idea, sir, though it would appear the interrogation was by no means over when he died. The fact that he wasn't executed would indicate that at the very least he'd not told them everything.'

They talked a bit more. As the sun fell on her face and her hair loosened, he realised once more what an attractive woman she was: the kind who might fit in well here at Head Office. He liked the way she looked at him and he liked the way French women managed to wear their make-up in such a sophisticated manner, certainly compared to their English counterparts. He thanked her very much and said he hoped they'd meet again and then rang Piers Devereux and said he needed to see him and, yes, he was afraid it was urgent.

Piers Devereux took the news surprisingly calmly. 'I'm afraid it happens, Barney: an occupational hazard, you might say.'

Barney felt that was a bit cold. 'Thank Christ he knew so little about his mission.'

'Yes – and at least we now have the receiver. And the RAF chaps are pleased with it, you say?'

'Apparently very much so, yes: they're just itching to try it out.'

'But with our French friend out of the game... we still need to find a way to get the Tatra box or whatever it's called into Germany, don't we?'

'Indeed, Piers.'

Both men looked at each other, as if they knew what the other was thinking but were waiting to see who'd say it first.

'Do you think she's up to it?'

–

'And how's he getting on?'

Basil Remington-Barber and Noel Moore had driven down from Berne apparently to see how Roman Loszynski was. He'd been in Geneva for nearly three weeks now and had made substantial progress in that time.

Sophia von Naundorf and Jack Miller were with him the whole time, the three of them sharing an apartment on Rue d'Italie with views over the Jardin Anglais and the Promenade du Lac beyond it.

One of them always accompanied Roman to and from the workshop in the basement on Rue Kléberg and one of the embassy security officers was always there with him.

The meeting felt like a parents' evening, with Roman the pupil in question.

'He's delighted with how it's going. He says he spent so much time over the past few years making notes and planning that as soon as he got back in a workshop again, he was able to make good progress. He had the Mark Two version completed in a week and the Mark Three was completed two days ago. It's ready to be tested. Shouldn't the man who's taking it into Germany be here by now?'

Basil ignored Sophia's question and asked instead how Roman was in himself. Jack answered.

'When he's in the workshop he's fine, it's like he's in another world – completely immersed in what he's doing and nothing distracts him. He's usually in there by half seven or eight and we have to drag him away twelve hours later otherwise he'd never sleep or eat.'

'There's another reason, too.' Sophia moved closer to Basil and Noel, about to share a confidence. 'When he's not in the workshop, not absorbed by his work, then all he thinks about is his wife and children. He feels terribly guilty that he had to leave them in Poland, he's full of remorse about that. I'd say more than that, actually, I'd say he's haunted by their absence. I'm concerned that unless we can give him an assurance that they'll be brought to Switzerland soon then he may give up. Is there anything you can tell him?'

'Come on, Sophia, you saw what it was like getting him out of Austria into Switzerland. I can't see how we're going to manage it with the rest of his family, none of whom speak German. I think the best plan is to let him think there's a plan and just hope they can remain hidden in Poland. The Nazis destroyed the ghetto in Warsaw, you know? The Jews held out for nearly a month, imagine that, less than a thousand men and woman resisting the German Army for that long.'

'And the man who's coming to collect the transmitter, Basil: where is he?'

Basil told Jack there'd been a hiccup on that score and Jack said he'd prefer it if Basil came to the point and as was so often the case when Basil failed to come to the point it was Noel who had to do so.

'The agent they'd recruited was a Frenchman who spoke fluent German and was an electronics engineer. He was in almost every respect ideal.'

'But?'

'But he got caught, I'm afraid – soon after he was dropped off in France. As far as London can gather, the resistance group looking after him was betrayed. He ended up as a prisoner of the Gestapo in Nancy and died under interrogation.'

'What did he know about us?'

'Nothing, thankfully, other than that he was being escorted to Switzerland and would then be taking a piece of unspecified equipment to Düsseldorf and that his contact there was code-named Felix, but that's all.'

'London's view—' Basil stood up and moved to the window '—is that this operation has been slightly dented but certainly not compromised. We share London's view that it would be prudent not to do the test in Düsseldorf, but other than that the operation is still very much on.'

Jack Miller leaned back and closed his eyes in resignation.

He knew the question Sophia was about to ask.

And he also knew the answer.

'Who will take the machine into Germany then?'

'That, Sophia, is what we need to discuss with you.'

'Your name is Irmgard von Strobl. Your husband is Major Erich von Strobl, a Wehrmacht officer based in Lyon. You currently live with him in the married officer's quarters close to the main German garrison in the city. Your marital home in is Frankfurt. You are returning there for a visit.'

Noel Moore paused as he moved his ashtray from the table and opened up a map and angled it so Sophia von Naundorf could see better.

'You'll be catching a train at Mulhouse.' The Englishman's finger tapped on the French city. 'Mulhouse is just under twenty miles from the Swiss border. The Gare de Mulhouse-Ville railway station is perfect: trains travel from Lyon in the south and from Mulhouse you can take a train to Frankfurt.'

He placed a folder on the map and began to remove documents from it. 'All your papers are here, including a travel permit. This is your ticket from Lyon to Mulhouse and here is the ticket… this one, here… from Mulhouse to Frankfurt. The train will stop at Strasbourg, Karlsruhe, Mannheim and Darmstadt before it reaches Frankfurt. You get off at this station, here, before you get to Frankfurt.'

Sophia moved the tickets from the map and studied it carefully. 'And if I'm asked why I got off at Mulhouse and then again before the train reached Frankfurt?'

'I doubt you will be, but say you felt unwell and needed some fresh air.'

'You're assuming they buy that, Noel.' Jack Miller had his arm round Sophia's shoulder and squeezed it.

'She's the wife of a German officer, Jack, that role should come naturally. On the list of suspicious train passengers, wives of German officers come fairly low down.'

'But she'll be carrying that device, for Christ's sake, Noel. It's a—'

'Relax, Jack: it will be very well concealed. The whole point of creating a convincing cover like this is that Frau von Strobl will be so above suspicion that they won't see the need to search her luggage.'

–

She'd left Basel in the early hours of the Tuesday morning, the first day of June. She'd slipped across the border by foot under the cover of darkness and into a waiting van where she hid in the back until daylight. The van arrived in Mulhouse by eight-thirty but waited close to the station until eleven o'clock. Noel had taken the view it would make more sense for her journey from Mulhouse to start around then.

No one searched her luggage, but a young SS officer had insisted on carrying her case onto the train at Mulhouse. He couldn't have been more polite and as he lifted it onto the luggage rack, he did remark how heavy it was and she replied her husband always said the same.

He turned out to be a very useful travelling companion, waving away the Gestapo inspection just before they arrived in Strasbourg. He left the train at Karlsruhe, meaning she didn't have to explain to anyone why she was getting off early. It was close to four o'clock that afternoon when she left the train at Mannheim, checking in at the Bahnhof-Hotel National close to the station and across the road from the Reichsbank. She paid thirty-four Reichsmarks for an en-suite room for two nights, explaining to the obliging man at reception that she needed to rest and would appreciate a quiet room on the top floor and if there was a view of the River Neckar that would be much appreciated. She slipped him two Reichsmarks for his understanding.

She would remain in her room for the remainder of that day, she decided. Tomorrow was Wednesday, the day it had been decided by London that she needed to get to work.

–

Irmgard von Strobl woke early on the morning of Wednesday 2 June. It was in her nature to write lists and now she had learnt to create mental lists. There was plenty to do that day.

Mannheim turned out to be a surprisingly easy city to get around: it was known as the Quadratestadt because of the way the centre of the city was laid in a grid design. After breakfast in the hotel, she went for a long walk, crossing the River Neckar on Adolf Hitler Brücke and into the area known as Neckarstadt. She strolled to the end of Kronprinzen Strasse. The furniture factory was set back from the street, with scrubland on three of its four sides. She was a bit disconcerted by the proximity of the housing and thought some of them were bound to be hit, but her mind soon turned to more important matters as she remembered Noel Moore's instructions.

They've chosen this place for two reasons, Sophia: one, it must look like a random target, one of no strategic value whatsoever. And two, because of that there'll be little if no security around it, which will make it easier for you to set the trap.

She spotted the ideal point, not overlooked by any houses or other buildings and with a high wall between the road and the factory. She then found a residential street a block north of the factory. If stopped she'd say that was where she was heading.

She walked back into the centre of Mannheim, this time crossing on the Friedrichs Brücke. She checked everything in the Tatra box was in order and unscrewed the tip of her umbrella and checked the telescopic antenna was in one piece. She screwed the tip of the umbrella back on. She'd wait until four-thirty: the factory closed at five and she wanted to be away from the area by six o'clock.

She was at the river end of Kronprinzen Strasse when the policeman walked towards her. In Berlin she'd noticed how much older policemen were getting these days. The younger ones were all being conscripted. This one appeared to be well into his fifties, perhaps even older, and he was definitely heading towards her, so she called out and asked for his help.

235

She was heading for this address she said, showing him the name of the road just north of the factory. It was the address of an old lady, a friend of the family who she'd not seen in years, and as she was in Mannheim, she'd felt she had to look her up. She'd even bought her a box of biscuits!

The policeman showed her where to go: carry on up Kronprinzen Strasse, past the furniture factory and you'll find it soon after that.

She thanked him very much and said he looked tired and he seemed happy of the excuse to talk. He was tired, he said. These days their shifts were two hours longer and they only got one day off a week and each month there were fewer of them and then he stopped, suddenly realising he may have said too much, and she said she quite understood and how grateful she was for men like Officer...? She apologised for not having caught his name.

Müller – Alois Müller, he told her. She headed up to the factory. If she was stopped, she'd be able to mention Officer Müller: a name always made an explanation that much more plausible. The last of the workers were leaving when she came to the factory. She waited in a small park nearby and when she returned the site was deserted. She found the spot she'd identified earlier – not overlooked, protected by a high wall. She removed the biscuit tin from the bag and the telescopic antenna from inside the umbrella. She connected one end of the wire to the antenna, the other through the hole she'd made in the tin to the small socket. Everything seemed fine. She turned on the battery and the little green light glowed.

Average battery life is eight hours: don't panic and turn it on too early. Certainly not before five in the evening.

She looked at her watch. It was twenty to six. She covered the biscuit tin with rubble and then ran the wire along the side of the wall and began to fix the antenna to it. She was almost done.

'Come here!'

The voice came from the other side of the wall, just a few feet from her. She froze in terror. She'd been caught red-handed. The antenna was still in her hand, it couldn't be more incriminating. She looked at where the biscuit tin was and noticed a mound of rubble over it. It was all too obvious. Mentioning Officer Müller's name was hardly likely to save her now. She felt sick and thought about Jack and how he'd take the news and wondered how brave she'd be and doubted she'd be very brave at all.

'I said, come here: now!'

A man's menacing voice. She saw his faint shadow fall beyond the wall.

She imagined the stomach-churning fear her husband must have felt in his final moments, but that was of little consolation. She leaned on the wall for support. Her heart was beating so fast she felt she was about to collapse.

'One more time: come here!'

She held up her hands, surprised she'd not actually seen him yet.

Chapter 25

England and Germany
June 1943

They left London on the Wednesday morning, Barney Allen and Piers Devereux sitting apart in the back of the Service car, hardly exchanging a word as they headed out of London and up the Great North Road.

It had been a fraught few days: Barney had slept little since the decision had been made the previous week. He'd gone home to Oxfordshire that weekend unsure what, if anything, he should tell his wife.

He'd broached the subject tentatively: he told her he was likely to be out of contact for a while during the following week and she said wasn't that always the case and what was he trying to say? He realised he couldn't actually say very much so he muttered something about possibly having to going away for a day or two – more likely two – and she really wasn't to worry.

She looked up from her embroidery, peering at him over the top of her spectacles. 'Putting it like that, Barnaby, does give me cause to worry!'

Calling him Barnaby was always a bad sign. She sounded like his mother.

'When you say you're going away, is this the Service sending you somewhere?'

'I've told you, my dear I'm unable to talk about my work with the Service.'

'So they are sending you away. Good heavens, Barney, you're being sent into Europe as an agent! Could they really not find someone more suitable?'

He tried hard not to look as annoyed as he felt and he told her he'd said enough but he wanted her to know that while she had no reason whatsoever to worry, just in case anything ever happened to him he wanted her to know... to know that, that he...

'To know what, Barney?'

'That I'm terribly fond of you, Margaret, and very grateful for everything you've—'

'You're having an affair, aren't you, Barnaby? Who is it, some young girl in a uniform? French, no doubt, Alice said Ronald told her that half of the men he works with in Whitehall are having affairs with French women.'

He managed to persuade her that he most certainly wasn't having an affair. He was simply going to be away for a day or two and he just wanted her... not to worry.

If she'd known even half of it, she'd certainly have had every reason to worry, he reflected. He was worried sick, though reluctant to admit it to anyone, especially Devereux who kept looking at him and asking if he was all right.

The driver told them they were approaching Newark and it wouldn't be too long now and Barney Allen felt his throat tighten. Piers glanced over at him and his sympathetic smile made him feel even worse.

It had been Frank Hamilton's idea. He and Piers had met with the RAF Intelligence chief the previous Thursday, the day after they'd heard about Philippe Moreau's death and had decided to send Sophia into Germany with the transmitting device, the biscuit tin. 'So, Düsseldorf is now out of the question.'

'Of course.'

'I've spoken to Bomber Command: they're most keen for the test to go ahead, as you can imagine. We've put our heads together and come up with a new target.'

239

The air vice-marshal pointed to the map on the wall in Piers Devereux's office. 'Mannheim: about forty-five miles south, south-west of Frankfurt. Frankfurt's a regular target of ours these days. Bomber Command are suggesting mounting a major air raid on Frankfurt with one of the planes having the receiver device in it. That aircraft can peel away from the main raid, as if it's veered off course: happens all the time and usually the German fighters don't go after lone planes, not while there's still an air raid on. Plan is for that aircraft to head south, drop its bombs when it picks up the signal from the transmitter and then head home. It will just seem like an aircraft is ditching its load: not uncommon.'

'Isn't it rather risky, Frank?'

'It's bloody risky, Barney, but what on earth did you imagine it would be?'

Piers said this sounded like a very good idea and when did Frank think this could happen?

'Bomber Command have been looking at the weather and other operational factors. They feel this ought to happen as far as possible from a full moon. The next full moon in that area is on the eighteenth of June, so they're suggesting going for next Wednesday night, the second of June.'

Piers and Barney said the sooner the better so that sounded like a decent plan.

'617 Squadron up at RAF Scampton in Lincolnshire has been selected for this: their Lancasters are ideal. Squadron Leader Harry Wright is the man they're suggesting is in charge and I've heard he's jolly good.'

'Very good, Frank, thank you and…'

'There is one other thing: a suggestion of Harry Wright's and I think there's some merit in it.'

'Go on, Frank.'

'He suggested one of you may like to go along for the trip? See how it works and all that?'

Barney had almost admired the smooth way in which Piers had volunteered him for the mission. *This was Barney's mission, and he really didn't think it would be right for him to muscle in and spoil the fun and of course Barney must be the one to go on the flight.*

Which was why they were now turning off the Great North Way and heading towards Lincoln and as the sun spread over the long landscape of fields Barney Allen wondered whether these would be his final views of the English countryside.

–

'Five hundred and fifty-five miles.' Squadron Leader Harry Wright puffed on his pipe in the briefing room at RAF Scampton. It was seven o'clock in the evening and Piers Devereux had just asked how far it was to Mannheim.

'But of course, that is if we fly from A to B without any deviation, which won't be the case. The plan is to fly out due east over the North Sea and then turn south, crossing the Dutch coast just south of Rotterdam and then to head south-east with the rest of the chaps until we're over Frankfurt, before pulling away and heading down to Mannheim. I would estimate three hours until we're over Mannheim.'

'And that's within the range of the plane?'

Barney Allen must have looked as worried as he felt because the squadron leader told him not to worry. 'Comfortably within range: the Lancaster can do two and a half thousand miles easily, and that's with a full bombload of fourteen thousand pounds. We'll be carrying half that.'

Air Vice Marshal Frank Hamilton said he'd had another word with the station commander and with Bomber Command and they'd agreed 617 Squadron would take off at nine-thirty. 'In two and a half hours,' he added helpfully.

'Over target around midnight-thirty, ten minutes at the most to do the business and, depending on the wind and whatever the enemy chuck at us, home by four o'clock. If you really enjoy it, sir, you can join us for the same tomorrow night.'

They boarded the Lancaster at a quarter to nine. Barney would be sitting in the cramped area behind the cockpit, in between the wireless operator and the navigator. The wireless operator was Flight Sergeant Graham Crown, a thin, chatty man, and together with Squadron Leader Wright he explained how they'd decided to place the receiver device next to the wireless operator.

'The bomb aimers' position is in the nose of the plane, underneath and ahead of the cockpit, and it's too noisy there for them to concentrate on the signal. Plan is when I hear it, I tell them over comms.'

'And then he presses the button.'

'We're told that if the system works as it should do then we ought to start picking up the signal about six miles out. Given the speed we're travelling out, that means if we release the bombs straight away then they ought to land on the target.' Squadron Leader Wright nodded approvingly as he spoke. 'If it works then it's a bloody marvellous system. Now then, sir, make sure you wrap up nice and warm: it can get slightly chilly at twenty thousand feet!'

–

From her room on the top floor of the hotel Sophia had a good view of Neckarstadt.

She'd returned to the Bahnhof-Hotel National at seven o'clock that evening. Her experience at the furniture factory had shredded her nerves. Convinced she'd been caught, she'd decided she would seem less threatening if she dropped to her knees and raised her hands and waited for them to come for her.

It was then she heard the man's voice – the one who'd been shouting 'come here' sound more friendly.

'There you are! Where have you been?' And this was following by excited barking as man and dog were reunited. She was just able to see them as they walked past the wall.

From half past eleven that night she'd waited by the window of her room, kneeling on the floor so the curtains remained closed, with just her head above the windowsill. Around twelve fifteen she heard faint *crump* sounds to the north and thought she saw flashes of light, but it was hard to tell.

A quarter of an hour later the air raid sirens disturbed the peace of Mannheim. There was some anti-aircraft fire from the east and then the sound of an aircraft approaching from the north. She put her head between the curtain and the window in time to see the explosions: bright flashes, two then three more, white at first and then yellow, followed by the red of the flames. There was no doubt it was somewhere in Neckarstadt.

She'd have to wait until the morning to find out where.

–

For most of the flight Barney Allen had gripped the narrow bench he was perched on, his stomach churning every time the Lancaster lurched up or down, which seemed to be most of the time.

Flight Sergeant Crown frequently checked Barney was all right and reassured him he'd soon get used to the feeling of flying in a bomber at two hundred and eighty miles an hour.

'How soon?'

'Ten flights, I'd say!'

Squadron Leader Wright was sitting a couple of feet in front of him and turned round every so often to shout out their progress.

That's Rotterdam down there… Over Frankfurt soon… Nice night for it…

They were over Frankfurt at midnight: their Lancaster held a few miles back from the main attack and then headed east before looping round towards Mannheim.

The navigator, another flight sergeant – first name Jack – called out the distance as they approached Mannheim.

'Eighteen miles… sixteen… twelve… nine… seven… six… five…'

Barney glanced anxiously at Crown. The young wireless operator was holding his hand over an earphone and fiddling with the dial on the receiving device.

'Got it! A bit faint but it's there! Release!'

Barney was surprised at how the Lancaster lurched as the bombs were released, the plane pitching and appearing to climb suddenly.

'That's it, sir: we're heading home.' The squadron leader appeared to be smiling.

'Did we hit our target?'

'I don't have the foggiest idea, sir.'

–

She checked out of the hotel at ten o'clock the following morning. At one point before she'd left Switzerland there had been some talk of her visiting the factory the following morning to assess the extent of the damage, but then it was decided that was too risky. Instead, the RAF would take reconnaissance photographs.

Her main fear was that the bombs would miss their target altogether and the biscuit tin and antenna would be found and, somehow, she'd be linked with it.

The man at reception who she'd tipped generously when she arrived on the Tuesday asked her how her stay had been, and she said it had been a most pleasant rest.

'And where are you heading now, if I may ask?'

'Home, to Frankfurt.'

He nodded kindly.

'I heard an air raid last night: I hope there wasn't much damage?'

He looked around to make sure they weren't overheard. One didn't talk publicly about air raids these days.

'We've experienced far worse, I can tell you. The main raid last night was over Frankfurt, I'm afraid. This was just one or two stray bombers I'm told. Apparently, it destroyed a furniture factory in Neckarstadt though. What has a furniture factory got to do with the war?'

As he handed her the invoice his voice dropped to a whisper. 'And the concierge says he heard a dozen houses were hit too: women and children killed.'

He shook his head and Sophia did too as she thanked him very much and said she'd very much enjoyed her stay.

—

She made sure she also told the concierge and the security officer at the hotel she was on her way to Frankfurt. At the station she waited at the back of the overheated café and watched as the ten-thirty train to Frankfurt departed.

There were three direct trains a day to Lörrach and the next one was due to depart at eleven o'clock.

She was still Irmgard von Strobl, wife of Major Erich von Strobl, a Wehrmacht officer based in Lyon. Her cover story was not as credible as it had been for her journey to Mannheim. Then, she was heading in the direction of her hometown.

Now, she was heading away from it, but at least her suitcase no longer had the transmitting device in it and her umbrella no longer concealed an antenna. If pressed she'd say was visiting friends in Lörrach.

But she was never pressed: one Gestapo check during the journey, the officer seemingly more concerned with checking all the passengers' bags and only glancing at their *kennkarten*.

She arrived at Lörrach Hauptbahnhof at a quarter past two: the rendezvous still an hour away. She decided to stay in the station, sitting in the shadow of an already gloomy cafeteria. At a quarter past three she left the station by the smaller exit next to the luggage depot and then down a small alley with three black-painted huts at the end. She knocked on the door of the middle one.

It was quickly opened by a thickset man with a large moustache who was looking beyond her, checking she'd not been followed. He looked so hostile she wondered whether she had picked the right hut.

'What do you want?'

'I'm terribly sorry, I appear to be lost: I was looking for the way to shops.'

He nodded and now looked more relaxed.

'Come in, quick: my name's Christoph.'

He locked the door behind her and gestured for her to sit down.

'The train to Basel leaves in an hour: we'll be in Reichs Bahnhof by five o'clock. There are two Englishmen and a very anxious American waiting for you there!'

Chapter 26

London and Geneva
June 1943

'It's my understanding, Barney, that you're unlikely to be resigning from the Service and volunteering for the RAF?'

Roly Pearson guffawed loudly at his own joke, his laughter eventually dissolving into a bout of noisy coughing and Piers Devereux had to pour a glass of water for him.

Barney Allen said there was indeed no cause to worry. He'd had his fill of flying and, in any case, it would be unfair to deny Roly a turn.

'I doubt I'd fit in terribly well, in more ways than one!' The Downing Street intelligence chief was now mopping his face with an enormous handkerchief and occasionally spluttering into it.

'I was there to greet Barney when he landed back at RAF Scampton,' said Piers Devereux. 'I think it's fair to say you were rather green around the edges, eh, Barney? But jolly well done, took guts to go on that flight.'

There was a muttering of 'hear, hear' around the table, even Lord Swalcliffe joining in.

'Those bomber chaps are bloody heroes: I was just a passenger. The death rate is appalling, isn't it, Frank?'

'Bomber Command estimate that new crew last on average just two weeks. Since the current bombing of the Ruhr began, we're losing half of our aircraft.' Air Vice-Marshal Frank Hamilton shook his head and the room fell into a sombre silence. Roly Pearson suggested perhaps Frank brought everyone up to date.

The air vice-marshal reached down into his briefcase and handed a pile of folders to Group Captain Marlow who then distributed them around the room.

'The Mannheim raid that Barney was on took place on the night of Wednesday the second and the very early morning of Thursday the third. Today's Tuesday, so it was almost one week ago. So as not to alert the Germans any more than was necessary, we decided to delay the aerial photographic reconnaissance until the Friday, rather than the day after the raid. It's taken until now for the photographs to be processed and analysed. Martin, perhaps you'd be able to talk us through them?'

Group Captain Martin Marlow checked his photographs were in the correct order. 'You have some fourteen photographs taken before the raid – all marked "A" and fourteen taken after the rad, all marked "B": the before and after, if you like.

'The analysts have been studying them very closely. Their conclusion is that a considerable amount of damage was caused to the factory. According to their assessment, around twenty per cent of the factory was seriously damaged with a further twenty per cent suffering moderate damage. The analysts also use what they call the disruption factor to estimate the extent to which the factory's production capability is affected by the raid, which is an important consideration in assessing the effectiveness of a raid. The analysts are of the view that in this case the disruption factor – which we express in terms of the period of time a factory is out of action – is between three and five weeks. If this were an armaments factory, that would be very disruptive.'

'That sounds like the raid was a success then, Marlow?'

'Yes, Mr Devereux, to an extent. There are some reservations though. If you could look at the map you have in your packs…'

He waited as everyone looked for the maps and unfolded the large A3 sheets.

'The map shows the factory and the surrounding area. The factory has been highlighted in green crayon and you'll see it is a rectangular plot, running north to south. The twenty per cent area that we assess as having been seriously damaged is at the southernmost end of the site. The twenty per cent which we assess as having been moderately damaged is just above it. The sixty per cent of the factory which was undamaged is to the north.

'If you look at the sections highlighted in blue crayon – these are residential streets to the south-west of the factory. Two roads in particular were pretty much destroyed by our bombs: Uhland-strasse and Eichendorff Strasse. You can see the damage on the marked photographs. The analysts say there would have been what they describe as "substantial" casualties in those streets.'

'Civilian casualties are unfortunate, of course, but they're an inevitable consequence of bombing an urban area, are they not? God knows we've had enough of our own: London, Coventry, Liverpool…'

Group Captain Marlow began to answer but was stopped by Frank Hamilton.

'They are indeed, Piers, but the point we are making is not to do with the civilian casualties per se, but rather to do with their location. It was the southern end of the factory which was hit and then two residential streets further to the south. According to the wireless operator, the Lancaster was five miles north of the target when he heard a faint signal from the ground. He estimates that the instruction to release the bombs was given when the aircraft was four miles from the target. The Lancaster was flying at over two hundred miles an hour with an altitude of nineteen thousand feet, so the mathematics are somewhat complicated and certainly above my head but clearly had the signal been stronger and picked up at around seven miles from target then it is possible that the whole of the factory would have been hit and not just the southern part of it.'

'That is indeed my recollection,' said Barney Allen. 'We were almost over the target when Crown picked up the signal. It sounds as if we need to feed this back to Switzerland.'

'Indeed, this was the Mark Three version we were using. Loszynski now needs to be told to come up with a Mark Four with a stronger signal.'

'And then what, Frank?'

'Then we need someone to take it back into Germany, Roly. And this time, I think we need to go for key targets in the Ruhr.'

–

They met in the workshop in the basement on Rue Kléberg, where Roman Loszynski was enthusiastically demonstrating the machinery to Basil Remington-Barber and Noel Moore. Noel suggested they have a chat, about the purpose of their trip down to Geneva. They joined Sophia and Jack at a table at the back of the workshop.

'Today is Thursday, isn't it? One week since Sophia returned from her trip to Germany. Two days ago, there was a meeting in London to assess the damage caused by the bombing of the factory in Mannheim. They are of the view that the bombing was broadly a success, in that part of the factory was hit: they say that… where are we?' He'd paused to look at a sheet of paper and tutted as he put on his reading glasses. 'Here we are… twenty per cent of the factory seriously damaged, a further twenty per cent moderately damaged. The damage was to the southern end of the site. There was also substantial damage to two residential streets south of the factory. There's a lot of technical stuff here for you to look at, Roman, mathematical formulae and the like, but what they seem to be saying is that the Lancaster bomber picked up a faint signal when they were around five miles north of the target. Lots of calculations follow, but in essence they seem to be saying that if a Mark Four could be produced with attention being given to making the signal stronger then they think that will work?'

'Does it say what altitude the aircraft was when it received the signal?'

'Nineteen thousand feet, it says here, Roman.'

'Well, that's too high: I have said that the aircraft needs to be no higher than fifteen thousand feet. The speed is crucial too. Do you know what speed it was travelling at?'

'It's all here. Perhaps you have a good look at it and then work on a Mark Four. How does that sound?'

'It sounds very much as I expected. In my field, getting a complicated device like this to work is very much a matter of trial and error. I think with the refinements I'll make and your air force understanding the need to fly lower and slower, then the results could be even better. I'm confident of that.'

'And how long do you think it will take you?'

Roman Loszynski shrugged. 'Today is the tenth: perhaps by the end of next week?'

'So, by the eighteenth of June?'

'Possibly. May I ask a question while you're all here? It's about my family. It is unspeakably difficult for me to concentrate on my work when I know my family are still in Poland. I'd understood they would follow me here, but I hear nothing. I feel beyond despair. I don't know how much longer I can cope with this situation.'

'We do understand, Roman, we really do.' Noel was looking him in the eye and patting his arm. 'I can assure you we have a plan and we're working to bring your wife and children to Switzerland. But you did the journey yourself, Roman, you know how perilous it is and I'm sure you'll understand it will be even more so for a woman and two children who speak no German.'

'When will they be here?'

'In July, Roman, I very much hope in July.'

–

The two British diplomats walked back across the Pont du Mont-Blanc with Sophia and Jack. They strolled along the Promenade du Lac until they came to Quai Gustave Ador where they stood watching the *jet d'eau*, the enormous water fountain on Lac Léman.

'When you said his family would be here in July, Basil: did you mean that?'

'I think I said I *hope* they'd be here in July, Sophia. I hope they'll be here by then, but I very much doubt it. But so long as Roman believes it while he continues to work on his device…'

'So, we're tricking him?'

'We're trying to defeat the Nazis, Sophia. On which subject, who would you say are your most reliable agents in the Ruhr, Jack?'

'Lotte in Gelsenkirchen, unquestionably… and then I'd say Felix in in Düsseldorf.'

'Düsseldorf is out of the question, the agent who was captured in France knew about it, though why they'd told him that is beyond me. What about that chap in Duisburg?'

'Rainer? I'd say he's less willing and more nervous than Felix.'

'They want to try the Mark Four device out in the Ruhr. Gelsenkirchen and Duisburg will be ideal.'

Basil turned to face the fountain, wiping the water from its fine spray from his face. 'All you'll need to do is deliver the device to the two agents, Sophia. You'll be miles away once the raids take place.'

Chapter 27

Roman Loszynski had been as good as his word – a point not lost on him as he reminded Basil about *his* promise to bring his family to Switzerland in July. Basil muttered something about 'July' and said he was very grateful Roman had completed the Mark Four version of the Tatra boxes.

They were gathered round the table in the workshop in the basement on Rue Kléberg in Geneva. Roman turned on an angle poise lamp so they could see it even better and looked at it admiringly, an artist proud of his creation.

'I've made a number of modifications, which I'm confident will significantly enhance the performance of the transmitter. I think this is as close as we'll get to it being an operational version. Briefly, I've adjusted both the oscillator and modulator, which ought make the signal stronger. I've also rectified a fault on the battery.'

He reached under the table and produced an umbrella. 'The same one as you used before to conceal the antenna: there are two in here now.'

They all nodded admiringly and Noel asked when it would be ready and Roman said it was ready now, as he'd promised.

'I always keep my word,' he said, looking directly at Basil. 'And I expect you to do the same.'

They travelled from Geneva to Basel the following morning, the Saturday, going straight to a safe house on Maien Gasse, close to the Women's Hospital, and when they gathered in the lounge later that afternoon the shutters had been closed and Noel said this would be a good time to start the briefing.

'We have decided that it would be safer for you to travel to the two target cities on your own, Sophia.' He spoke very deliberately, as if he'd rehearsed what he was saying. 'You are, after all, German and, as fluent as Jack is, you are inevitably more... credible, that's the right word. Plus of course you're a woman, which always give less rise to suspicion: with Jack there's always a question mark as to why he's not in the forces.'

Jack started to speak, but Noel told him to wait. 'I'm about to explain everything to you: the idea, Jack, is that you will be back-up for Sophia. You will travel with her as far as Düsseldorf and wait for her there.'

'What's the point of that?'

'As a military man I can tell you that the strength of an army is in the way it deploys its forces. A rash senior officer will commit all his forces to an attack, a wise one holds some back, placing them in the most effective strategic positions. You'll be Sophia's back-up, Jack.'

'Thank you for your seminar on military strategy, Basil, but with respect, as you English say, this is a clandestine operation in Nazi Germany, not the trenches on the Somme.'

'Exactly: all the more reason to exercise caution. Now let me go through the journey with you. Gather round.'

–

Sophia and Jack were left alone on the Saturday evening at the safe house on Maien Gasse. There'd been the briefing soon after they'd arrived, but it had been shorter than they were expecting.

Basil fussed around for a while and then left – they were given to understand he was staying at a hotel – but Noel remained in the house along with two of the security officers. They ate a largely silent dinner with Noel who said he was having an early night and suggested they did the same: there'd be more briefings the next morning and then they'd be heading off. Good night.

Their room was the only one on the top floor and there was a door at the top of the stairs, giving them more privacy than they'd expected in a safe house the day before a mission into Germany. Sophia was noticably more relaxed than Jack.

'No one can hear us up here, Jack.' She'd checked their bedroom door was shut and had led Jack over to the bed.

'I think we should do what Noel suggests and get an early night.'

'Really, Jack? That's not like you!' She'd slipped off her dress and was running her fingers through his hair. He moved away from her.

'What's up, Jack?'

He shook his head and walked over to the window. 'Aren't you nervous, Sophia? We're going into Germany tomorrow. I can't believe you can think about anything else.'

'It would take your mind off it, Jack.'

'I doubt it. Remember, I was a prisoner of the Gestapo just two months ago. I was lucky: I escaped. There's only so much luck someone can have. In English there's a saying about a cat having nine lives. I feel like I've used all of mine up.'

'But you're not a cat!'

'Come on, Sophia.' He moved over to the bed and sat next to her, taking her hand in his, his thumb stroking her wrist. 'I never imagined I'd be going back there so soon. It's all very well sitting in these briefings, isn't it? Basil and Noel being terribly polite and reassuring and telling us we'll be fine as long as we're careful, but – it's not really like that, is it? Sitting here in Basel, waiting to leave it feels like we're standing on the edge of a cliff in the dark, about to step into the void…'

'And you think this will be a holiday for me in my homeland? I'm as scared as you are, Jack, but we have to do this. We have an obligation. We should see this as a religious mission. But we must be positive in the way we approach it. We must conquer our nerves. Come now.'

She placed her hand behind his head and pulled him towards her and this time there was no resistance from Jack.

–

Late on the Sunday evening – 20 June – the city was silent as they headed north along St Johanns Vorstadt, the car eventually stopping by a park.

Noel said it shouldn't be too long and maybe it would be a good idea for them to run through their identities just once more, dates of birth et cetera.

Erich and Alma Walter… from Cologne… Erich a teacher and Alma a leading light in the Frauenschaft, *hence her visits to Duisburg and Gelsenkirchen to help other German women and…*

A torchlight blinked a few yards ahead of them and Noel told them to wait. He left the car and walked towards the figure behind the torch. Moments later he returned.

'Follow him, keep at a distance and don't talk, not even to each other. Hurry up now, take care.'

Basil turned round in the passenger seat and started to wish them the *very* best of luck and said he'd see them *very* soon, but by then they were on the pavement and the figure ahead of them had started to walk, so they followed him.

Ten minutes later they were on the banks of the Rhine, the river silent apart from a chopping sound as the water lapped the side. The man slowed down, allowing them to come closer. They were just a couple of yards behind him when he turned round and gestured towards a barge docked at a small quay. He nodded and said they should get on board quickly and go straight below deck.

As Sophia climbed on board, she spotted the name on the side.

They could just make out a man in the small wheelhouse: he smiled as they walked past and politely doffed his cap. At the bottom of the ladder another man was waiting: he appeared to be in his late sixties and behind him was a woman, wiping her hands on a towel and smiling at them as if they were entering her café. They were shown into a tiny cabin, which was taken up almost entirely by one narrow bed. On top of the bed were two sets of oil-stained working clothes.

The man they'd followed appeared in the doorway and told them to get changed quickly and then come out. 'We set sail in half an hour: I'll call you out when we're ready.'

When he returned, he introduced the old man as Paul. 'You—' he pointed at Jack '—you go with Paul into the engine room and make yourself look busy. You, go with Dora here and make sure you're busy too. Your hair looks far too neat: Dora, do something about that, maybe give her an old scarf. And just remember, both of you, you're my crew, understand? The man in the wheelhouse is Emil, he's my cousin.'

The German police came aboard as the barge crossed the Swiss border, just minutes after leaving the port. Jack heard little in the engine room and hardly looked up when someone opened the hatch and noted there were two of them there and said good before shutting the hatch. Sophia heard a bit more as she was squeezed next to Dora in the tiny galley. The policeman said something about Bruno having plenty of crew and Dora said it still wasn't enough and turned round and handed a cake to him.

An hour later they were gathered round a table secured to the floor in the small area alongside the galley, off which were the cabins.

'I'm Bruno, this is my wife, Dora. Paul came out of retirement a year into the war, he's never happier than when he's down there: he even sleeps alongside his wretched engines. Paul is totally trustworthy: I usually have one other crew member, Hans, but he's remained in Düsseldorf and you have his papers and those of his wife. These identities are only to be used while you're on the river, understand?'

Bruno was a large man, but as so often the case with men who spent their lives on boats, moved with a grace which belied his size. He had a thick mop of jet-black hair, flecked with grey. Dora looked nervous; a permanent smile set on her face.

Bruno said that as their cabin was so small, they should take it in turns to use the bed. Sophia said she wasn't tired, and Jack should go ahead.

Dora went to their cabin and soon Sophia and Bruno were alone at the table. He said nothing as he busied himself with his pipe. Basil had spoken very highly of him.

If he survives the war, Bruno will be one of the richest men in Germany. The barge is his own and before the war he was struggling. Now he makes a fortune: he sails coal down from the Ruhr to Basel and then ships machinery back to Germany. His wealth comes from the extras he gets on board: he's smuggled Jews out of Germany and God knows what else back into the country. He's trustworthy and pays his crew well and, somehow, he doesn't have a problem with the German authorities: he bribes them and is an expert at concealing things on his barge.

'You're from Berlin, yes?'

'Pardon?'

'I like to guess where people are from and I think you're from Berlin.'

Bruno leant forward, looking for confirmation. Sophia shrugged in a manner she hoped he'd understand, that she wasn't going to answer.

'It's not your accent, though there are traces of it – you don't pronounce the letter "g", that's a giveaway. It's more the way you hold yourself, you have a Berliner's attitude. Do you know what I mean?'

'I'm not sure I do, to be frank.'

'An air of arrogance, without necessarily being arrogant, if that makes sense.'

'But I'm not arrogant!'

'Ah ha! So, you *are* from Berlin. Don't worry, I don't care where you're from. My job is where you're going to. Your friend though, I don't think he's German, is he?'

Sophia smiled – as if she was going to tell him anything! – and Bruno smiled too, to show he understood.

'Tell me, are you doing this for the money?'

She shook her head.

'Shame: those of us who do it for the money, we're far more trustworthy. It's a commercial decision with us, like signing a contract and then honouring it, though it helps that I hate the Nazis. Paul and Emil, I've known them both all my life and they also like money and dislike Nazis. Dora, she dislikes the Nazis more than I do, and the money – she has plenty of plans for it once this damned war is over.'

'I'm surprised that women are allowed on board?'

'Before the war, it was rare to see a woman on board the Rhine barges. But now, so many of the crew who were on the boats before the war have been conscripted into the Kriegsmarine. That's why we have retired crew like Paul and women like Dora on board. And you.'

He looked at her through the smoke from his pipe and then glanced at his watch. Soon it would be his turn in the wheelhouse he said.

'When will we arrive in Duisburg?'

'It's three hundred and seventy nautical miles from Basel and I'll try and keep to six knots, so allowing for stops, probably sometime Thursday morning. Fortunately, we're now allowed to sail at night: at the start of the war, they didn't want us to, but now with all the bombing they reckon its safer. I know this river like the back of my hand, it's not a problem.'

'And the authorities won't cause any problems?'

Bruno shrugged. 'I wouldn't go as far as that but, look, we're travelling in Germany, they're not bothered so much. When we travel towards Switzerland or up to Rotterdam, it's a very different story. Also, the wooden crates in the hold, I don't know what's in them – just machinery I'm told, but I know it's to do with armaments. That's why they checked it when we crossed the border. They'll know the *Elfriede* is carrying important cargo for the war and they won't want to delay us.'

–

The *Elfriede* arrived in Düsseldorf on the Wednesday afternoon, docking just south of the Skagerrak Brücke to refuel and for Bruno to visit the port office to be given details of his next journey once he'd finished in Duisburg.

Sophia and Jack knew he'd be staying in Düsseldorf but they assumed he'd remain on the barge until dark. But soon after Bruno left, Dora told Jack to get ready. They'd be leaving in five minutes.

It was a hurried farewell, as tense and as fleeting as when they'd parted in Berlin more than two years before. They kissed briefly and held each other tight and Jack said it would be just a few days and he'd find a good restaurant in Düsseldorf, but he was too emotional for it to sound light-hearted in the way he'd intended and Sophia said that was the last thing on her mind and as Jack began to explain it had been intended as a joke, Dora took him by the elbow and said they really must get going.

She took him by tram to the place he'd be staying, Basil's idea of being held behind the front line. In this case it was Dora's sister's house in Oberbilk, to the south-east of the city centre. She'd already explained that her sister lived on her own: her husband was guarding beaches in France, both her sons were somewhere on the eastern front.

The *Elfriede* set sail just before sunset that Wednesday evening. It was still dark when Dora woke Sophia on the Thursday morning: they were about to dock in Duisburg, she should get changed. She could hear shouting from the deck and wondered if there was a problem, but Dora said they'd been told they had to unload their cargo as soon as it was light.

Bruno joined them below deck. 'They don't know what they're doing these days. They wanted me to unload immediately but I told them they were mad to ask me to do it in the dark. It's a problem for you though: once I start to unload, port security will come onboard, and when I've finished, I'll be expected to head back to Düsseldorf straight away. You'll need to be off the barge before then.'

'What time will that be?'

'Sunrise is around twenty past five, in half an hour's time. You'll need to leave by five, while it's still dark. I'm not sure what you'll do at that time of the morning: it's too early for you to be wandering around.'

'What about Axel's?'

'That's a good idea, Dora. You take her there.'

Axel's turned out to be a small ship's chandlers on Hafen Strasse, close to where the *Elfriede* was docked. It was a small place, dwarfed by larger chandlers in the same area. Dora explained that Axel was an old friend of Bruno's and a terrible businessman, but Bruno was one of his best customers.

Axel himself let them in at the back: a short, taciturn man, unnaturally pale and with a nervous twitch. Dora asked if her friend could stay here for a few hours: she'd sit quietly upstairs and then disappear.

'How many hours, Dora?'

Dora looked at her watched and said until eleven o'clock. Axel twitched and said how about ten and Dora said this wasn't a negotiation: her friend would wait where no one would see her and then leave at eleven.

Sophia sat in Axel's untidy room upstairs: a bed that looked as if the sheets hadn't been changed in months, dirty clothes strewn around the room. Axel came up once or twice, each time looking at his watch and at her and on the last occasion he sat on the filthy bed and said she may be more comfortable sitting there too, with him, if she liked.

She thanked him very much but said she was fine where she was. At eleven o'clock, Axel came up once more. It was quiet downstairs. Now she should leave.

It was a warm summer's day as she crossed the Hafen Kanal, then the Ruhr and walked across Kassler Feld and a footbridge over the Innenhafen into the centre of Duisburg, all the time the map of the city displayed in her mind as she carefully followed her instructions. She walked past a bakery, which smelled and looked like the bakeries she remembered before the war. Through the windows she spotted empty tables at the back so she went in. For the next half hour it was as if the war was over or indeed had never begun. The cakes – she had three – were wonderful and the coffee even tasted like coffee, at least for the first few sips. She was tempted to ask the owner how she managed to make such wonderful cakes: how did she get hold of so much butter and sugar – and real flour? But she decided that would only draw attention to herself.

It was noon when she arrived at the station. She walked in through the Saar Strasse entrance, hung around for a while looking at the timetables and then left through a side door. Five minutes later she was on Universitäts Strasse, booking herself a room with a bath for two nights at the Prinzregent.

–

Rainer Kühn was very much as Jack had described him: a large man wearing a well-cut pin-striped suit and the confidence and authority that evidently came with being the manager of the best hotel in the city.

Jack had explained how she was to approach him, how Rainer would know who she was and, if she was honest, Sophia was of the view it all felt rather contrived: what guest would seek out the manager of the hotel about towels?

Nonetheless she asked the concierge if she could see the manager who she understood was called Herr Kühn and the concierge said by all means, but perhaps he could help? Sophia said that was very kind but Herr Kühn was actually a friend of friend and she would like to say hello in person, so the concierge said to follow him, which was how Sophia – Alma Walter – was in the office of the manager who said of course, please do come in and please sit down and how could he help?

'I arrived this morning from Cologne and checked in to your fine hotel.'

Rainer nodded a bit too appreciatively and stared at Sophia in what she recognised as that familiar leering manner; confident she'd soon fall for his charms. He said how honoured he was she'd chosen to stay there and if she'd care to join him for an aperitif later then—

'I'm afraid I'm disappointed with the quality of the towels.'

Rainer looked surprised for the few moments until what she was saying sunk in. Then he looked shocked. The colour drained from his red face and he muttered that he was very sorry and he said he'd arrange for them to be changed.

'That is very kind of you: and perhaps I could have an extra bath towel too?'

For a moment Rainer looked as if he was about to cry and she remembered how Jack had described him as scared. He straightened himself up and reached for an unlit cigar and said yes, he understood but—

'But?'

'But I wasn't expecting a woman.'

'Is that a problem?'

'Not at all, Frau Walter, not at all – in fact it's a pleasure. And how can I help?'

Jack had advised her that Rainer was the kind of person she needed to come straight to the point with. Unless she was clear and direct he'd probably choose to not understand.

'You know the Vereinigte steelworks in Ruhrort?'

'Of course. I pass it on my way home.'

'And what time is that?'

'Usually around eight o'clock, once I've checked all is well in the dining room.'

'Excellent: tonight, on your way home, you will stop at the steelworks and find a concealed spot as near to the building as possible. There you will hide a small box I will give you and attach an aerial to it. There are more instructions, but it's not too complicated – it can't be if I can manage it.'

She gave him a soft smile and ran her fingers across her lips and blinked a few times, but he now seemed immune to this. He looked horrified.

'Are you mad? That's sabotage!'

'I promise you, it isn't: it's not a bomb or anything like that. It's simply to help with photography. As soon as you've placed it there you leave. It will take no more than five minutes. You can pretend you stopped to relieve yourself.'

'It's five minutes' drive from my home.'

'You have a very weak bladder.'

'Why can't I drop you near there and you can do it? You seem to know how it works. I can then pick you up and bring you back here. I'm hopeless with technical things.'

'You'll have a good reason for being in the area. I don't. Look, it's nearly one o'clock. Maybe after lunch I can show you exactly what you need to do? Then we could have that aperitif.'

–

The hotel manager spent much of the afternoon in the room of the guest he knew as Alma Walter. Sophia had her reservations about him from the outset, but couldn't decide whether this was down to the fact that she just disliked him personally or because she wondered if he was up to the job.

She feared it was the latter, not least because Jack – whose judgement she trusted – clearly had his doubts about Rainer. He said all the right things though: the sooner the war ended the better, and if whatever he was being asked to do helped bring that about then that was no bad thing.

She showed him how the transmitting device worked: how to set it, how to start the battery – that button there, that's right

– how to attach the lead from the antenna through the hole she'd already made on the side of the tin.

'And you understand about where to attach the antenna?'

'As high as possible, you said.'

'That's right. You should be able to conceal the transmitter and antenna under your coat.'

'I wouldn't normally wear a coat in June.'

'I suggest you do tonight.'

She was sitting on the bed, Rainer alongside her on a chair and she kept moving as he contrived to get closer to her, his hand frequently brushing her knee. Once he'd kept it there and told her how astonished he was someone as pretty her was doing a job like this and she'd just smiled, gently moving his hand as it crept up her thigh, and said they really ought to concentrate.

'And after I've left the device?'

'You go home. Tomorrow morning you come into work.'

'And you?'

'I'll be here, Rainer. Maybe if all goes well you could come up and tell me all about it?' She smoothed the top of the bed and worried she'd gone too far but there was no doubt that Rainer's nervous, edgy mood had changed over the past hour.

'And how long will you stay?'

'I leave tomorrow afternoon, after you've told me how everything went.'

'Where will you be going, Frau Walter?'

'Back home to Cologne.'

–

The steelworks couldn't have been more than two miles to the north of the hotel and Sophia watched in awe as a series of explosions turned the night into day. She knew that the raid in Mannheim had been carried out by just one aircraft, but it was clear this was a full-scale raid.

The air raid siren had sounded around one o'clock on the Friday morning and as in Mannheim, Sophia had peeked through the curtains. But this raid was longer and five minutes after the alarm sounded there was an urgent knock at her door to tell her to come down to the air raid shelter in the basement of the hotel.

The all-clear didn't sound until two o'clock, after which she lay in bed for an hour, unable to sleep, so she checked her case was properly packed and at six o'clock was down at reception.

She told the duty manager that the previous night's raid had shaken her so badly that she'd decided to return home without delay and he said he quite understood.

'Could you tell me the time of the first train to Cologne?'

'Assuming the railway lines are still functioning after last night's activities then I'd suggest taking the quarter to seven service to Düsseldorf and change there for the Cologne train.'

She thanked him very much and asked if she could purchase a ticket at the hotel and he said of course, leave it to me. She asked him what time the manager would be in and he said not before nine and she asked him to pass on her regards.

'He's been so helpful.'

She crossed the road to the station, aware there was more security than there'd been the previous day. She slipped into the ladies' cloakroom and removed the trilby-style hat with a large feather she'd made a point of wearing at the hotel. She replaced it with a fawn-coloured beret and took of her raincoat.

She left the station and walked up the road to the bus station. By twenty to seven she was on a crowded bus to Essen, happily seated behind two women who traded detailed descriptions of the previous night's raid.

The Vereinigte steelworks in Ruhrort… a direct hit, my neighbour said… could be months before it's working again…

The bus arrived in Essen at five to eight. She found a telephone box and called the Gelsenkirchen number she'd memorised. The person who answered did so in a very calm manner and gave all the correct responses.

Sophia bought a copy of the *Völkischer Beobachter* at a kiosk and found a cafeteria near the station where she was able to spend an hour, leaving it in time to catch the nine-twenty train to Gelsenkirchen.

–

Rainer Kühn arrived at the hotel at half past nine.

The duty manager remarked that he looked unwell and he replied he'd not slept well because of the raid. The duty manager said of course and was about to say that the charming Frau Walter had checked out and had asked to pass on her good wishes and thanks to him, but the manager looked distracted and said he'd be in his office and he didn't want to be disturbed.

Kühn sat at his desk for a good hour, doing little more than staring at the wall and reflecting what a fool he'd been. He bitterly regretted ever helping the American and. once he'd returned, he'd been naïve that was putting it mildly – in agreeing to help. There was no doubt he'd been charmed by the woman and he wondered if she wasn't actually as attracted to him as he'd thought she may have been.

He had thought about throwing the box and the antenna away and then telling Frau Walter that he had followed her instructions, but he'd been worried she may find out the truth and what worried him most was the American's threat that he had evidence that he'd worked for the British.

That threat had made up his mind and he'd followed her instructions, parking his Daimler close to the steelworks in Ruhrort and then finding a secluded spot close to the factory, following her instructions and then relieving himself against the wall.

No one had seen him and he'd driven home. He neither ate nor slept that night and when the air raid started, he'd felt a strange sense of relief and then realised that he may be responsible for it in some way and if it helped end the war – who knows? – then that was no bad thing.

He'd driven in this morning as close to Ruhrort as he could get and there was no doubt the damage was extensive.

He was startled by the hotel security officer knocking on the door.

'We've had a telephone call from the Gestapo, sir.'

Rainer gripped the side of the desk and felt bile rising in him.

'It seems they're investigating last night's raid in Ruhrort because there are reports that trespassers may have been seen in the factory.'

'What kind of trespassers?'

'Teenagers, sir, possibly a boy and a girl.'

'Well then, what on earth does this have to do with us?'

'Because they're also checking out all the private cars seen in the area. Apparently, a police officer had noted your car parked near the factory.'

He gripped the desk so hard his hand caught a splinter and he winced in pain. 'It's on my way home, for heaven's sake.'

'Yes, sir, but your car was parked, apparently.'

Rainer let go of the desk and leaned back, closing his eyes to recall what could possibly account for that.

'Ah yes, I stopped to relieve myself.'

'Well, there we are, sir, that would explain it. They want to come in anyway to have a word with you: who knows, you may have seen the trespassers?'

Rainer said of course, he was always happy to help the Gestapo.

When his security officer left, he opened his safe and took out his bottle of Scotch and poured himself a large measure.

When the security officer brought the man from the Gestapo in it was all very amiable at first but then another man from the Gestapo came in and within moments the atmosphere had turned hostile.

His Daimler had been spotted near the factory and was parked there for ten minutes and how long does it take a man to have a piss?

Rainer explained as best he could that he had felt unwell, which would account for the length of time there, and come to think of it maybe he had seen a boy and a girl climb over a gate and—

They replied that was nonsense and they'd actually had a report from a woman who lived in an apartment that overlooked where he'd stopped and she'd seen him position something on the ground and something else on a wall – she'd mentioned a wire – and what could he say to that?

He said nothing for a moment or two as he did his best to compose himself. He realised he was trapped and decided to tell them about Frau Walter. He told them how the guest in room 346: an odd sort who'd asked him to leave a tin or something near the factory as it was a gift for a friend to collect and, foolishly, he'd been rather taken by her – they'd see she is a most attractive woman – and he'd agreed and it was now something he bitterly regretted but she'd shown him another of those tins in her room and if they went up there now – she'd still be there – then she was the person they needed to speak to.

The two Gestapo men looked at him incredulously and Rainer had to admit to himself that it all sounded rather far-fetched but then he had nothing incriminating on him or elsewhere and she was bound to be caught red-handed when they went up to her room. He may lose his job, but she'd surely take all the blame.

They told the security officer to go and find the woman.

He returned five minutes later with the duty manager.

'Frau Walter checked out just after six o'clock this morning, sir.'

'Did she say why?'

'Something about last night's bombing, sir: she wanted to go home.'

'And where is home?'

'Cologne: I have her address here. If it helps, she purchased a ticket for the quarter to seven train to Düsseldorf.'

One of the Gestapo officers hurried out of the room and the other stared at Rainer, trying to work out whether he was a fool or a traitor.

The duty manager coughed and said there was one more thing. 'She asked me to pass on her regards to you, sir: said you'd been so helpful.'

Chapter 28

Poland
June 1943

Lea Loszynski and her two children had remained in hiding at the farmhouse near Zakopane after Roman had left on 23 April, nearly two months, just.

Lea Loszynski was confused about a lot of things these days. For a start, she had to remember her name was now Klara Wójcik, from Krakow – she seemed to have more trouble remembering that than Max and Raisa, who'd adapted surprisingly easily to their new names: Mieczysław and Janina.

She was also confused about dates: not just when they'd arrived at the farm but even what day it was now. Sometimes the farmer or his wife would bring an old copy of *Nowy Kurier Warszawski*, the Nazi occupation newspaper. It was full of propaganda and nonsense, of course, but with little else to do, she devoured every word before tearing the pages up to use as toilet paper. The newspaper didn't help much with what day it was, it only confused her more.

The irony was that she used to have such a good memory. She attributed her current confusion to her physical state. The farmer's wife brought them food every two or three days and it was barely enough for one day, so she gave most of her share to the children and subsisted mostly on water and stale rye bread.

As a result, she had a constant sense of feeling light-headed and confused, a state compounded by a permanent feeling of fear that they'd be arrested at any time, alert to every sound, unable to sleep for more than an hour at a time, trying desperately hard to persuade the children that everything was fine and they weren't to worry, but, please... remember to keep quiet.

Andrzej, the young man from Żegota who'd brought them there from Krakow, visited the farm every couple of weeks. In the middle of May he told Lea that Roman had made it safely to Switzerland. She asked about their own journey to Switzerland and he said they were working on it. It wasn't easy though: they needed to get the money together and that was proving to be a problem.

'Have they said anything to you?'

'Who?'

'The farmer and his wife: they now say it's getting too dangerous for them and keep asking for more money. Our funds are very low.'

'I thought you said it was safe here and we could stay as long as we need to?'

Andrzej looked slightly embarrassed and said something about circumstances changing, but he was working on it. 'I've just paid them for the next two weeks, so you're fine until the beginning of June.'

'And what happens then?'

'I'll be back by the end of May. I'll pay them then.'

But Andrzej didn't return at the end of May and one afternoon the farmer took Klara aside.

'Andrzej isn't coming back,' he said, looking at her as if it was her fault.

'I'm sure he'll be here any day now, he promised—'

'You don't understand: he's not coming back here, he's dead.'

'Are you sure?'

'Of course I'm sure! He was arrested by the Gestapo in Krakow a week ago, a whole group of them were. He was killed trying to escape. It's too dangerous for you to remain here: you'll need to leave – now.'

She began to weep. Could they not stay for another week then maybe someone else would turn up and pay them?

'There is no one else: what do you imagine, that Poland is full of people lining up to help you Jews? You're lucky we didn't turn you in weeks ago, we'd have got a reward. All of that lot from Krakow who were helping you, they're either dead or in prison. Since the Nazis crushed the Uprising in the ghetto, there's no one in Warsaw who can help you either. Unless you've been hiding money and can pay us, you're going to have to leave.'

Lea was unable to speak.

'I'll tell you what: you remember Pavol, the man who took your husband into Slovakia?'

Lea nodded.

'I can get a message to him. He and his people over the Tatra Mountains may be able to help you: but whatever happens, I want you away from here within two days.'

–

Pavol arrived the following night. He came into the bunker and told her to wake the children. Max and Raisa sat up confused in their beds, blinking at the light. He studied them carefully as a doctor would observe his patients and talked with them for a while and asked their names and without hesitation, they both gave their new names, Mieczysław and Janina Wójcik, from Krakow.

'Go back to sleep, I'll have a word with your mother.'

She placed herself opposite him at the table in the middle of the room. Pavol sat expressionless, saying nothing as he slowly prepared a cigarette. Then he shook his head.

'I can't do it.'

'What do you mean?'

'It would be impossible to get you over the mountains – your husband just about managed it and he's quite strong. But for you and the children... no.'

His cigarette was ready now and he took a moment to light it, concentrating on it for another moment or two.

'And in any case, Slovakia's too hostile. There's a possibility we could try and get you into the Protectorate – it's what the Nazis call Bohemia and Moravia now. The population there's less hostile, the resistance groups are better established. But it would still be a difficult journey. We'd have to travel through Upper Silesia, which is now part of Germany. If we could get to the border near Ostrava, but...'

He stopped and looked directly at Lea, for the first time his face showing some expression. It was a look of regret.

'But your son's the problem, I'm afraid. You all speak good Polish, no trace of a Jewish accent, and you and your daughter – you're both fair-haired: neither of you look obviously Jewish. But your son does, there's no escaping it. I—'

'But when we travelled here from Warsaw, no one suspected him.'

'Maybe, but you must have been lucky. You were travelling through cities for how long – two days? This is very different: the journey will take weeks and we'll be relying on the goodwill of local people, dozens of them. Someone's bound to suspect Mieczysław and then inform on you all. It's a risk I can't take. I'm sorry.'

'Is there any way you could help us?'

'I can take you and the girl.'

'What about my son?'

'Send him into the countryside: if he heads east and hides then sooner or later the Red Army will arrive.'

'I can't possibly abandon him – he's my son!'

'I understand, but I was just thinking of a solution. Otherwise, my advice is to get out of here as soon as possible. I don't trust Tadeusz one bit. Promise him you'll leave Thursday night but go tomorrow night instead, without him knowing, obviously. If he's going to betray you, he'd want you arrested as you leave the farm, not before. Only travel at night, keep away from roads and don't trust anyone.'

They left the farm near Zakopane at midnight on Wednesday, which according to Pavol was 9 June. That morning she'd taken Pavol's advice and begged the farmer to let them stay for another week. He was having none of it. They had to go. Very reluctantly she said they'd do so on Thursday night.

She let the children go to sleep normally on the Wednesday night, knowing it would be the last time they'd sleep in a bed for a while. When she woke them at midnight, she told them they were going on an adventure: they must dress warmly and were to take the blankets too – and the most important part of the adventure was to be as quiet as possible! They crept away from the farm, cutting across the fields and heading west. Lea had decided to head into Upper Silesia, as Pavol had mentioned, and then into Moravia. Once they arrived there, she'd work out what to do next. Moravia sounded like the promised land; the name almost had a biblical ring to it.

It didn't take the children too long to realise that this wasn't an adventure after all and they began to complain at the pace their mother was making them go at. Eventually she stopped and knelt down beside them.

This is very dangerous – but if you're very good, at the end of the journey we'll get to see Daddy.

They asked how soon that would be and she said a few days and the faster they walked, the sooner they'd see him. She doubted they'd manage no more than two miles an hour, possibly getting as far as ten miles away from the farm by the time it became light. She wondered whether the farmer would report them: after all, how would he look if he told the Germans he'd been hiding Jews but now they'd escaped?

By the time it was light they came across a dense wood and walked through it for another hour, by which time the children were clearly exhausted and she was too. They came to a small glade with a brook running through it and decided this was a good place as any to stop.

The children soon fell asleep, but the thoughts chasing around Lea's mind wouldn't allow her any rest. Their situation was hopeless: their chances of getting anywhere near Switzerland were so remote as to be impossible. They were exposed enough while they were in Poland and even if they managed to get into Moravia, they wouldn't speak the language. And if they made it through the Protectorate then they'd have to travel through either Bavaria or Austria and that didn't bear thinking about.

Max woke up and asked her why she was crying and she said she wasn't, she was just tired. He turned over and went back to sleep and by the afternoon Lea had dozed for a while and come up with a plan. It was now Thursday: they'd walk for the next three nights. That would be when she'd find someone to shelter them.

They'd rely on the kindness of strangers.

–

By the time they stopped early on the Sunday morning she had no idea where they were: she wasn't even sure it was Sunday and she certainly wasn't sure they'd been heading in the right direction. For all Lea knew, they could have headed north or even gone round in circles. They'd arrived in a small forest half an hour before sunrise and found somewhere to bed down. Not long before they'd reached the forest, they'd passed by what at first appeared to be a cowshed: a low, single-storey building isolated in the middle of a cornfield, with just a small track leading to it.

They were almost upon the building when Lea spotted a light on in a window. They crouched down and after a few minutes the rear door opened and an old woman stood in the doorway, looking around her before picking up a bucket and taking it to a ditch and emptying the contents. Lea watched for a few more minutes. As far as she could tell, the old lady was on her own.

There were no obvious signs around the building that people worked there: no farm equipment, no animals.

This, she decided, was where she'd seek help. She'd concocted a story of sorts over the past few days. From the brief glimpse Lea had had of her and her surroundings she decided she was a kindly soul, someone living on her own in the middle of nowhere, isolated and possibly abandoned, rather like them.

She rested until noon and with the children asleep crept out of the forest to spend another hour watching the building. It was as silent as the fields around it, the sun bouncing off the corrugated iron roof. She spotted the old woman open a window and shake something but there was no sign or sound of anyone else.

She returned to the forest. She decided to make her move around seven o'clock, before the old woman turned in for the night. Lea told the children she was going to find somewhere safe for them to stay for a few days – maybe even longer than that. Somewhere they could sleep in a bed and eat proper meals. She may be away for an hour, perhaps a bit longer, but under no circumstances were they to leave where they were. Even when it got dark, they weren't to move.

Did they understand?

Max nodded, but Raisa said if they were going to stay somewhere for a few days or even longer then what about Daddy – weren't they meant to be seeing him in a few days too? Lea bit her lip and waited a moment before replying. Yes, she assured Raisa, of course they'd see Daddy soon too, but only if they did exactly what they were told.

–

There was something disarmingly bucolic about the house as Lea got to within a few yards of it, hiding behind a large shrub to assure herself for one last time that the old woman was indeed on her own.

Birds were chirping and a large black cat strolled out of the open door and flopped down on the ground, lifting its head high to catch a scent. A light wind caused the field of corn to rustle and she could feel the warmth of the evening sun. She walked confidently to the door and knocked on it. The old woman appeared in the hallway, watching from the dark interior, more of a shadow than anything else. She said nothing as she wiped her hands on a large apron. Lea wished her a good evening and said she was sorry to disturb her but she was from Krakow and she was looking for work: she didn't want money, just food and somewhere to sleep.

She tried to sound confident and friendly. She'd decided not to mention the children just yet. The old woman said nothing, watching her carefully as she continued to rhythmically wipe her hands on her apron. Then she turned round and said something into a doorway behind her. Lea watched in horror as two men appeared out of the doorway and approached her. Both were in their thirties – they looked like brothers, well-built and with a menacing look about them. She instinctively backed away and looked round, as if to leave. One of them told her to stay where she was and asked her name.

'Klara Wójcik.'

'You don't look like a Klara Wójcik.'

'I'm from Krakow, my husband was sent away and I've come to the countryside for work and...'

'There's plenty of work in Krakow.'

'I bet she's a Jew,' said the other man. 'Remember the ones who turned up at Nowak's farm last month: what was the reward they got?'

'Enough for them to afford to buy two pigs at the market.'

'No, three pigs,' said the old woman. 'But that was for five Jews. This one's on her own. Maybe we'll just get the one pig.'

'I assure you I'm not a Jew, I—'

'Go on then, recite the Lord's Prayer!'

Lea started to recite what little she could remember of it: 'Our Father, who art in heaven, hallowed be—'

'Everyone knows that: what about the Apostle's Creed, eh? Come on then!'

Lea started to cry. She knew her journey had come to an end. She'd hoped to find someone kind, someone who'd help – but now her situation was hopeless. At least they knew nothing about the children. She knew she'd never see them again and that realisation broke her: she sunk to her knees and heard herself pleading.

Please let me go... I don't want to cause any trouble... I'm all on my own... I'll work hard...

But by then the two men had grabbed her by the arms and dragged her into a filthy scullery where they bound her legs and tied her arms to a pipe running down a wall. There was a brief discussion between the two: one said they should hand her over to the Germans now. The other said they should wait until the morning.

'We'll still get our reward but, in the meantime, we can have a bit of fun!'

Chapter 29

Gelsenkirchen, Germany
June 1943

Sophia spent most of the short train journey from Duisburg to Gelsenkirchen staring through the grime-streaked windows. It seemed that every inch of the landscape was crammed with industry: the smoking chimneys of huge factory complexes, coal mine after coal mine, railway sidings the width of three football pitches, dozens of wagons tethered together, beasts of burden standing forlornly as they waited for a locomotive to take them on their way.

The smell was overpowering, too. The elderly railway policeman who checked her papers closed a window across the aisle from her and had to support himself against a seat to catch his breath against the acrid air.

She spotted some signs of bomb damage, but it was very sporadic, more inconveniences than anything else. Just before they crossed the Rhine–Herne Canal at Altenessen she did spot one factory that appeared to have been levelled to the ground, but that was the heaviest evidence of bombing she saw.

She knew that Gelsenkirchen had been little more than a pit village a century ago and was now a major industrial centre and there was ample evidence of that as the train entered the town. The ingredients that make up a town appeared to have been dropped in as an afterthought after the railway lines and sidings, the coal mines and the factories had been put in place.

From the station she headed into the Altstadt, which in truth didn't seem very old at all. It was all rather bleak, lacking in charm and every surface coated in a fine layer of coal dust. The sky was streaked with plumes of smokes, most of them a dirty brown colour, and the omnipresent smell made Berlin seem like a spring meadow by comparison.

She checked into the Hans Sachs on Bahnhofstrasse. It was earlier than she'd have liked, but she was exhausted and needed to rest before her meeting. The receptionist seemed to have been up all night and looked equally exhausted, so much so that Sophia took the opportunity to slightly alter her name when she filled in the registration card: Frau Alma Walter became Frl. A. Valte. If challenged she could always blame her bad handwriting.

At a quarter past twelve she left the hotel through a side entrance, taking her room key, ignoring the strict instructions she'd received to the contrary when checking in. She crossed over to Augusta Strasse and entered the Sinn department store through a rear entrance.

The arrangements for the rendezvous Jack had made with Lotte already felt far more credible than those with Rainer. She felt more confident about this mission.

Basil had told her too how much he liked department stores. *They must have been designed with agents in mind! All those different areas and corridors… internal staircases, multiple entrances and exits – you can't go wrong!*

It was twelve-twenty when she entered the store: the meeting was taking place on the third floor, so she took the stairs to the second floor and looked at the shoes for a while: she thought the selection in Berlin had been bad, but here it was far worse, just two or three styles, dour and overpriced, seemingly designed for women involved in manual work.

She arrived in the glove and scarf section on the third floor at exactly twelve-thirty. She assured the assistant who quickly approached her that she was just looking around and spent five minutes looking at the scarves: the selection not as depressing as with the shoes downstairs, but compared to Wertheim's in Berlin, this place was a struggling corner store.

She became aware of a woman close to her and waited a minute before allowing herself to glance in that direction.

She's a good ten years older than you, Sophia, mid-forties I'd say and not as slim as you — she's shorter too. Her hair is quite short and is going grey and I told her to wear her dark brown coat with a blue scarf.

As far as she could tell the woman matched Jack's description of Lotte so Sophia backed slowly away from the scarves and walked towards the gloves where the woman was now. She didn't seem to have so much as glanced at her, but gradually the two of them edged closer. The woman was holding a pair of dark blue felt gloves.

'Do you think these match my scarf?'

Sophia was about to say it was the wrong blue, but kept to the script.

'I would say so, they're very pretty.' They looked like the kind of gloves her maid used to wear.

'I was wondering about buying some brown ones.'

'No, I'd say those are just right for you.'

They both turned and smiled at each other and the woman said very quietly that she was Lotte and was delighted to meet her and Sophia said likewise and maybe they could go somewhere quiet?

She followed Lotte out of the store, through a rear entrance and eventually onto Kirch Strasse, which turned out to bisect two large cemeteries, Catholics to the south, Protestants to the north — one of them closer to heaven, Sophia wasn't sure which. Lotte entered the Protestant cemetery, eventually coming to a secluded area. They were all alone.

'Did you have a good journey here?'

Sophia said she did, thank you, and asked how safe they were here.

'I wouldn't bring you somewhere I didn't think was safe, would I? From here I can see the path we came down. It's very quiet at this time of day. You have something for me?'

Sophia removed the Tatra box from her large handbag and placed it on the bench between them. She explained patiently how it worked – where to attach the lead to the antenna, turning on the battery et cetera – and Lotte took it all in, occasionally checking a detail and not looking confused or panicked as Rainer had done in Duisburg the previous day.

When Sophia had finished, she handed the tin and the umbrella to Lotte. 'The location is the marshalling yard at Gelsenkirchen-Bismarck, I presume you know it?'

'Of course. Whereabouts shall I place it?'

'Somewhere as concealed as possible and ideally where the antenna can be put on a wall or a fence.'

'It's very well guarded, you know.'

Sophia shrugged. Those were her orders. 'It must be in place by midnight, at the latest. Place it as close as possible to the marshalling yard. Will you be able to get there?'

Lotte said she'd find a way.

Sophia asked if she had any more questions and they ran through what she needed to do one more time and then Lotte said she really had to get back to work and suggested Sophia remained here for another ten minutes so they weren't seen leaving together. They both stood up and Lotte hesitated for a moment and then shook Sophia's hand, uncertainly at first and then with a much firmer grip.

'I promise you I will do my very best.'

'Thank you very much, Lotte.'

They stood in silence, each still holding the hand they'd been shaking, a long conversation that would never be started hanging over them.

'I don't know if you ever see the American – Jack. I imagine you can't say one way or the other but if you ever see him or can get a message to him, please tell him I've always done my best.'

–

Sophia managed to get back into the hotel through the side door and back to her room without anyone noticing. She remained in her room until seven o'clock and then went down to reception where the man behind the desk told her there was a café opposite the post office where a respectable woman could eat alone.

She was back in her room by half eight, anxious whether Lotte would be able to place the device and what would happen if she was caught. The railway marshalling yard at Gelsenkirchen-Bismarck was at least two miles to the north and it was a large open area with no housing around it. When Basil and Noel had briefed her they'd said the target was surrounded by coal mines and factories and if any of the bombs missed their target then they wouldn't go to waste.

She remained dressed. Her room was on the first floor and on the wrong side of the building and she doubted she'd see very much. She'd best be ready for a few hours in an air raid shelter.

—

Lotte arrived home early at the apartment she shared with her mother in Wanne on the east of Gelsenkirchen. It wasn't too far from the marshalling yard but getting there would be very difficult.

She knew it wasn't her place to argue or discuss the matter with the elegant woman who she thought could be from Berlin. She'd have preferred somewhere less remote, but long ago she'd realised what her place in society was and it wasn't one where you argued with people. One did as one was told.

She made supper for her mother and ate very little herself as she listened to her mother tell her that she'd heard Goebbels on the radio giving a speech in Dresden and assuring people the war would be won by the end of the year and what did Lotte think?

'I beg your pardon, Mother?'

'You weren't listening, were you? I asked if you think this war will be won by the end of the year?'

It had been some time since Lotte had argued with her mother. She nodded and said she certainly hoped so and they'd better get a move on because she needed to get her ready for bed.

Lotte had devised her plan on the way home from work. It wasn't foolproof by any means, but it was the best she could come up with. She prepared her mother's usual sleeping draught, but tonight doubled the dose. She'd done it before and it had had the desired effect. She would sleep soundly for the next twelve hours and certainly wouldn't hear her daughter leave.

By nine-thirty Lotte had changed, the tin and the antenna concealed in a rucksack she wore under her jacket. She paused in the hallway, the apartment, which had been her home all her life, now silent apart from the constant rhythm of her mother's gentle snores. She stepped into the small lounge, a room that could have been cosy but had a formal feel to it thanks to her mother's menagerie of precisely placed pottery animals and her obsession with religious paintings, now joined by a large one of Hitler.

She looked at the photograph of her father in its silver frame, a handsome man, aged forty-three – a year younger than she was now – looking slightly awkward in his infantry uniform, taken just a few weeks before he was killed at Passchendaele in October 1917.

She opened her handbag and took out the small, slightly creased photograph of Georg, the only man she'd ever loved. He was just eighteen when he died, less than a year after her father, this time in the Battle of Amiens. For a while she'd had the photograph framed by her bedside, but her mother had made her remove it. She'd never approved of Georg, a man who believed in socialism rather than religion. Instead, Lotte carried Georg around with her, but to her eternal regret had glued the photograph to a piece of card to protect it, meaning his final message to her was lost forever.

She slipped out of the flat and headed west back into Gelsenkirchen, past the entrance to the Pluto mine and through Haverkamp. If she was stopped, she had her work identity card with her: the Buer synthetic oil plant was just north of the marshalling yard, on the other side of the canal. She'd also brought a file with her and her excuse would be that she'd forgotten to leave it with a manager for an early morning meeting.

At the end of Braubauerschaft she reached her second Protestant cemetery of the day. She entered it through a gap in the railings where it backed on to the railway line, just a hundred yards or so from the marshalling yard. The tracks seemed to be busy, workmen moving around and some soldiers too. This cemetery was smaller than the one she'd met the woman in earlier in the day. It was older too and more overgrown, which meant she could find somewhere to hide.

She could still hear noise from the railway so she waited until ten-thirty before heading back to the fence adjoining Gelsenkirchen-Bismarck passenger station, just east of the marshalling yard.

To her horror, the whole area was now teeming with soldiers, dozens of them patrolling the tracks, walking up and down, no more than three yards apart. She watched for a few more minutes but the patrols continued.

She'd warned the woman from Berlin that security was tight round here, but this was as intense as she'd ever seen it. There could be any number of reasons: reports of sabotage, an escaped prisoner or slave labourer, a tip-off maybe, or just routine security.

Whatever the reason, she realised she couldn't get any closer to the marshalling yard. On the other hand, the elegant woman had said she should place it as close as possible to the yard and arguably the cemetery was close enough, so she set about rigging it up, her mouth moving silently as she repeated the instructions to herself: priming the device, attaching the lead to the socket in the box, turning on the battery...

She placed the box under a tree and managed to wedge the antenna over a bough which she just managed to reach standing on a broken gravestone.

She paused for a while, worried someone may have heard her but it was silent in the graveyard, apart from the rustling of the trees and shrubs around her and the noise from the railway in the near distance.

It was eleven o'clock when she decided to head home. She walked slowly in a crouching position, squeezing through the gap in the fence and round to the main road and her route home. But at the end of the narrow alley, she came to a halt. At least a dozen military trucks were parked just where she'd emerge, with soldiers milling around them, joking and smoking.

As she watched them, a train pulled into the station, its brakes squealing and piercing the still of the night. An officer had stopped just a few yards from her and was talking to someone else – it would be another hour before they could board, he said: he was tired of his men being kept waiting.

There was no question that they'd see her, so she crawled back into the cemetery and made her way cautiously to the main entrance, but as she approached Goethe Strasse there were more military vehicles parked up and dozens of soldiers hanging around the entrance, some sitting on the benches.

She'd prepared a story of sorts in case she was stopped on her way back: this time she'd say that she'd had to return to her office to collect the document. She was aware it sounded less than plausible but given there was nothing incriminating on her she may just get away with it.

But being stopped on the street was one thing, being seen coming out of the cemetery quite another. There was no question they'd search the cemetery and they'd be bound to discover the device and the antenna hanging from the tree. She couldn't risk leaving the cemetery.

She must remain there, regardless of the consequences.

She felt a strange calm as she retreated back into the heart of the graveyard. She'd had a premonition it would end like this: that this was one task that was too fraught with danger, where she had little control over the risks she was taking.

She sat on the grass next to the tomb of a boy called Erich who'd died at the age of twelve in the last century. She thought of her father for a while, a gentle and very liberal man, and she wondered how he'd ended up with her mother and then thought that maybe her mother was as she was because she'd been widowed so young.

She removed the photograph of Georg from the handbag and could just make out some of his features in the little light there was: his shy grin, the beautiful sweep of his hair, the firm jaw – and so young, always so young. She thought as she so often did of the life they'd have had together, away from this town – he'd always promised that – maybe they'd even have travelled outside of Germany. Her dream had been to visit Italy. To her surprise she felt warms tears tickle down her face and soon she was sobbing and as hard as she tried, she couldn't stop herself. She buried her face in her scarf, scared the noise of her crying may alert the troops.

She wiped the tears away with her scarf and now a shaft of moonlight caught Georg's picture and she noticed that it was coming unstuck in one corner. She took out a hairpin and managed to wedge it into the gap, enabling her to peel the photograph away from the cardboard backing. And now for the first time in more than twenty years she saw his faded handwriting and his message.

You'll always be in my heart
I'll always be by your side
We'll never be apart

She'd gasped when she read the message, which had somehow drifted from her memory years ago. She was still reading it when she heard the distant drone of aircraft. As they came closer, she realised they were approaching from the north and flying low. She felt the ground rumble under her, the vibrations becoming violent as the first bombs landed and she wondered what would happen to the bodies in the graves.

There was a blinding flash behind her and a series of enormous explosions and splinters from falling trees struck her like arrows. She clasped the photograph of Georg closer to her heart.

–

Sophia had worried people may think she looked too prepared for the rush to the bomb shelter after the air raid siren sounded.

The fact that one of the guests was dressed and even wearing a beret was the least of people's concerns though. It was a major air raid, even by Gelsenkirchen's standards. As they crowded into the shelter someone remarked that this was the worst raid he'd seen and another asked him sarcastically how he could see anything and the other man replied that he knew full what he meant: the British were flying so low and the bombs were actually hitting the town this time and not the fields around it.

When Sophia looked up a woman was staring at her and Sophia realised, she may have been smiling, so she smiled again at the woman and offered her a biscuit and the woman thanked her and said she was too worried to eat. Her Hans was out there, she said. Sophia didn't ask where 'there' was.

Sophia closed her eyes and rehearsed her journey tomorrow. It would be the Saturday and she knew trains were less frequent but she planned to catch an early one to Essen and from there to Düsseldorf, where Jack would be waiting for her because before leaving the hotel, she'd ring the number she'd memorised and leave a message about a niece coming to visit her uncle later that day.

She smiled once more as she thought of Jack. They may have to wait in Düsseldorf for a day or two until the *Elfriede* was heading south, but soon they'd be back in Switzerland, together again. The all-clear sounded around two-thirty and to her surprise she quickly fell asleep.

–

It was Sophia's utter misfortune that the investigation in Duisburg into the bombing of the steelworks and the suspicious role the manager of the Prinzregent may or may not have had in it was passed by the Gestapo to the Kripo, the criminal police.

They had a reputation for being particularly sharp and methodical and it was a further misfortune that the investigation was led by Kriminaldirektor Klaus Braun, an experienced detective who'd been forced to retire in 1938 after being overheard telling colleagues he didn't think politics and policing mixed well together. Now, needs must, and with so many detectives being conscripted, he was back.

At first Braun wondered quite what this was all about: it was odd that the hotel manager's Daimler had been parked near the factory but nothing more than that and it was certainly odd that he'd then told the Gestapo an unlikely tale about one of his guests asking him to leave a metal box on some wasteland near the steelworks.

But Kriminaldirektor Klaus Braun, being Kriminaldirektor Klaus Braun, set about matters methodically. First, they'd find Frau Alma Walter and take it from there. Except there was no trace of Frau Alma Walter from Cologne and the address near the Volksgarten was one of a number of tenement blocks in Cologne destroyed the previous year. His colleagues at the Kripo in Cologne confirmed that according to their records and those in the Rathaus, there'd never been a Frau Alma Walter in the city.

Now Braun decided this was indeed suspicious. The Gestapo had insisted on interrogating the hotel manager themselves, which was something he didn't like to think about too much, not so much because he was appalled at their methods – though he was, but he had learnt to keep quiet about that. It was more that he never quite trusted information gathered as a result of torture.

But the Gestapo assured him Rainer Kühn wouldn't stop talking. He'd told them Frau Alma Walter was a British spy, although as far as he could tell, she was a Berliner. And he said he'd been recruited before the war by an American, who'd been back to visit him much to his surprise – well shock, actually – back in April. He'd been recruited against his will, of course; he'd made

289

the most dreadful misjudgement, which he bitterly regretted, but now he was very happy to co-operate.

Kriminaldirektor Klaus Braun ordered that the search for this woman must be made a priority. He said that wherever she'd gone when she'd left Duisburg on the Friday morning, it wasn't going to be Cologne. They spoke to the staff at the station and then to all the bus drivers and one of them remembered a woman matching her description who he'd taken to Essen that morning. An elderly railway policeman was sure he'd seen her on the train from Essen to Gelsenkirchen on the Friday morning.

It was late on the Saturday morning when they heard back from their colleagues in Gelsenkirchen. A guest at the Hans Sachs on Bahnhofstrasse had signed herself in as Fraulein A. Valte but her *kennkarte* details matched those of the Frau Alma Walter who'd been a guest at the Prinzregent: the same letter followed by the same sequence of six digits on the card. They established she'd checked out at seven-thirty that morning and caught a train to Essen, though it had been delayed and hadn't left until nearer nine o'clock.

For once, Kriminaldirektor Klaus Braun was grateful for the disruption caused by the British bombing. The train had also been delayed en route, meaning she'd not arrived in Essen until ten-thirty where she'd bought a ticket – first class, believe it or not – for the eleven-thirty train to Düsseldorf.

'It was delayed, I'm afraid, Klaus,' his colleague in Essen informed him on the phone from the station manager's office in Essen.

'Don't be afraid, I'm delighted. What time did it leave?'

'At a quarter to one, but it will be delayed because they've closed the line at Ratingen.'

'What time do they think it will arrive in Düsseldorf?'

'Not before two-thirty, I'm afraid, Klaus.'

Kriminaldirektor Klaus Braun glanced at his watch: it was twenty past two. He reminded his colleague in Essen not to be afraid and then asked the operator to connect him to the police at Düsseldorf station and, yes, it was urgent.

Chapter 30

Düsseldorf, Germany
June 1943

The few days they'd spent apart had been unbearable for Jack Miller. The message that morning to say she was on her way had come as an almighty relief.

Jack felt he and Sophia no longer needed to be together to communicate. He could feel her presence close to him and intuitively knew how she'd be feeling now: nervous and alert, of course – but also excited that they'd be together soon. Their relationship had reached the point where words were not the most important part of it, because they understood how each other felt.

And that Saturday afternoon he waited impatiently at the back of Düsseldorf station, his neck craning to spot her train, excited and quite unaware of the drama about to unfold in front of him.

–

It had been a particularly trying journey from Gelsenkirchen. Sophia von Naundorf checked out of the Hans Sachs Hotel at half past seven and found a telephone box next to the station: the Düsseldorf number was answered almost immediately.

'Please tell Hans that his niece Maria will be arriving today, from Essen.'

A slight pause before a woman's voice said, 'Very well,' and then put down the phone.

At the station the passengers were told there were delays to all destinations. Someone said it was to do with the bombing last night – apparently the marshalling yard at Gelsenkirchen-Bismarck had been destroyed. Another person said it was routine maintenance and someone else said what do you expect, it's always like this on a Saturday.

She was sure she'd heard another passenger say 'yes and on Mondays and the rest of the week too', which was so subversive they'd have been arrested had the wrong person overheard them.

The Essen train finally left Gelsenkirchen at nine o'clock, but there were more delays en route, meaning they didn't arrive until ten-thirty. She bought a first-class ticket to Düsseldorf, reserving a seat for the eleven-thirty train.

She sat at the back of the first-class lounge, not exactly relaxed, but pleased to be away from Gelsenkirchen and more than anything else, excited that within a couple of hours she'd be with Jack. There was no better way to test a relationship than when you were apart. When Karl-Heinrich was away from Berlin she felt relief and was able to relax, but when she was apart from Jack it was the opposite. She'd never had a moment's doubt how much she missed him and loved him. Düsseldorf would still be fraught with danger and they still had to make their way back to Switzerland, but at least they'd be together.

And hopefully, never apart again.

In the event, the eleven-thirty from Essen to Düsseldorf became the quarter to one, a weary ticket clerk explaining that this was due to routine maintenance at Ratingen.

It was ten to three when the train pulled into Düsseldorf after being held for another ten minutes just short of the platform. As she left the train she peered through the crowds and the rising steam and caught sight of Jack as she approached the ticket barrier: the tall, handsome figure standing back from the crowd and looking urgently for her.

But something was wrong.

Then she remembered.

If I'm holding my jacket over my shoulder, everything's fine.
If I'm wearing my jacket, there's a problem.

Jack was wearing his jacket, a worried expression on his face as he seemed to stand on his toes to spot her.

She stopped and opened her handbag as if looking for her ticket before turning round, hoping she could get back on the train on the pretext of searching for something she may have left there.

That would be her escape route.

Jack would spot that.

But the moment she turned round she spotted three policemen closing in on her, one of them shouting for her to stop.

She turned round again, now facing the ticket barrier, where two more policemen and three men in plainclothes were hurrying towards her.

Beyond them was Jack, a look of sheer horror on his face as he stepped back, before becoming lost in the shadows.

—

He'd been at Düsseldorf station since eleven o'clock, which he realised wasn't too smart, but there was no other way if he wasn't to miss Sophia whenever she arrived.

They really ought to have made better arrangements, like a fall-back rendezvous point. He'd mention that to Basil and Noel in the debrief. Sometimes they could be sloppy, to use one of their own favoured words.

He positioned himself at the back of the concourse with a good view of the Essen platform. A group of policemen pushed past him as they rushed towards the ticket barrier, followed by three or four plainclothes officers. He watched as they spoke with what appeared to be the stationmaster and there was much gesticulating and pointing at the arrivals board. Jack Miller strolled forward as nonchalantly as he could manage, standing just behind the stationmaster and two of the plainclothes officers.

'…well in that case hold the train now, I need to get my men in position!'

The stationmaster said this was most inconvenient and the taller of the two plainclothes officers said his attitude was most inconvenient and had been noted.

'You'll do as I say: hold the Essen train for another few minutes. You're then to let the passengers disembark normally and leave her to us: you understand?'

The stationmaster assured him he did indeed understand and hurried off. Jack walked slowly to the back of the concourse, desperately thinking if he could cause some kind of diversion, though for the life of him he couldn't think what. He felt himself beginning to panic and wasn't sure if he should remain in the station. At that moment the Essen train appeared like a lumbering iron beast and it was only then that Jack remembered he was holding his jacket over his shoulder.

He hurriedly put it on and just moments later he spotted her, her elegant, effortless walk as if she were floating an inch or so above the ground, the trace of a smile on her beautiful face and her fawn-coloured trilby-style hat with a large bow at the front placed at a jaunty angle.

–

Kriminaldirektor Klaus Braun arrived in Düsseldorf from Duisburg later that Saturday afternoon. A colleague from the local Kripo met him at the station and briefed him as they drove the short distance across town to the Polizeipräsidium, the police headquarters on Fürstenwall.

'The Gestapo are itching to get their hands on your prisoner, sir.'

'I'm not surprised: I hope you're managing to hold them off?'

'As it happens, you're in luck. Do you know Oberregierungsrat Walter Albath?'

'I know the name.'

'Albath runs the Gestapo here with a rod of iron, literally and metaphorically. But recently he's taken to disappearing at weekends: the rumour is he keeps a mistress in Cologne and he's there from late Friday to early Monday. They say even the Führer himself would have a hard job finding him on a weekend.'

'So who's in charge of the Gestapo here while he's away?'

'Kriminalinspektor Franz Lindner is the duty officer this weekend, sir.'

'Good job I outrank him, isn't it?'

Kriminaldirektor Klaus Braun was not a naïve man. He was fully aware that in the hierarchy of the Reich, the Gestapo was positioned well above the Kripo. In theory, the Gestapo could elbow the criminal police out of any investigation without needing an excuse to do so.

But recently life had become more complicated. As the war had gone on it had become evident that the Gestapo's expertise was as a political police force, enforcing the excesses of the regime. When it came to criminal investigations there was a grudging acceptance that notwithstanding everything, the professional detectives of the Kripo may not be that bad after all. Braun knew it was down to his skills as a detective that he'd tracked Alma Walter to Gelsenkirchen and had her arrested when she arrived in Düsseldorf.

This was his case. Breaking up an enemy spy ring would be an enormous achievement and he was damned if he was going to let the Gestapo take it from him. As long as he outranked this Franz Lindner, he'd be able to keep the case, at least until Walter Albath arrived back in the city on Monday.

As soon as they arrived at the Polizeipräsidium he asked to be taken to see the woman arrested at the station. He was on his way to the interrogation room when a heavily built man hurried after him, moving in front to block his progress along the corridor.

'Kriminalinspektor Franz Lindner,' he said, breathing heavily and wiping the sweat from his brow. He held up his metal Gestapo identity tag. 'Gestapo.'

'Kriminaldirektor Klaus Braun,' he replied, putting a hand on the other man's shoulder to gently move him out of the way. The manner in which he'd said 'Kriminaldirektor' made it clear he was pulling rank.

'I understand, Herr Braun, that you've been most helpful in the early stages of this case but that was in Duisburg and this is Düsseldorf and from now on I will take charge.'

Braun carried on walking. Even though he was quite a few years older than the Gestapo man, he was clearly fitter and speeded up. He said he was very grateful of the offer to help but the protocol was that as this was an active investigation the officer who'd started it was expected to continue with it, until someone more senior said otherwise.

He turned round and smiled at Lindner who looked furious. Braun knew this was a temporary victory. He probably had little more than twenty-four hours to get something out of this woman.

–

Jack Miller had moved into the shadows at the back of the station as he watched the nightmare unfold ahead of him.

He'd watched as Sophia was surrounded by police and led through the ticket barrier and across the concourse. He wasn't sure whether she'd seen him, but she appeared to be calm, saying little and not looking around. They took her to a side exit, with a large sign saying 'Paketpost' over it. He knew this led to Vulkan Strasse. It was a restricted area. He wouldn't be able to follow so he relied on his instincts.

If she'd been arrested by the Gestapo, they'd almost certainly take her to the notorious Gefängnis, the prison on Metzer Strasse in the north of the city, next to the enormous Rheinmetall armaments factory. But given the involvement of uniformed officers he suspected she'd been taken by the regular police and their destination was likely to be the Polizeipräsidium on the banks of the Rhine.

His hunch was correct. He caught a taxi from the rank on Wilhelm Platz and as it turned into Mackensen Platz he spotted three police cars pull up in front of the building and Sophia being bundled out. He told the taxi to drop him outside the main post office on Adolf Hitler Platz. He queued for a telephone box to come free and then dialled the number of Dora's sister's house in Oberbilk.

I'm afraid I was unable to collect my niece at the station: I'm going to look for her. Perhaps you'd be so good as to mention this to your brother-in-law?

From there he walked quickly to Königs Allee and the Cornelius bar, which was just opening. He couldn't see Felix behind the counter, in fact none of the bar staff looked familiar. He asked the man behind the bar if Felix was on duty tonight and the man looked as if he'd seen a ghost.

He shook his head and said he'd never heard of any Felix and Jack said he must have because Felix had been here for years, he *was* the Cornelius. The man looked round and leaned towards Jack.

'Felix was arrested weeks ago and no one's heard of him since. You'd best leave now.'

Jack walked along the banks of the Rhine, an otherwise calm and pleasant early summer's afternoon doing nothing to lift the utter despair he felt. He needed help and had nowhere to turn. Bruno wasn't going to be back for a day or two and Jack couldn't wait that long.

The he remembered Siegfried.

'Next time you find yourself in Düsseldorf, Jack, do me a favour and look this chap up: see what you make of him.'

It was November 1938, exactly a year after Jack Miller had been recruited as an MI6 agent and Barney Allen had joined him Berlin for what he called a 'catch-up'. Barney felt they needed more agents in the big Ruhr cities and he had a suggestion, although he wasn't exactly effusive as he handed Jack a photograph with some details typed on the back.

'Chap's name is Schroth, Siegfried Schroth.'

Jack Miller looked at the photograph of Siegfried Schroth: it was a professionally-taken portrait, well-lit with the subject slightly leaning towards camera, wearing a dark bow-tie against a crisp white shirt and what looked very much like an excess of make-up.

'He's an actor.' Barney Allen pronounced 'actor' with a hint of distaste. 'You can probably tell from his photograph. He was part of a troupe which toured England in July. They were from the Stadt-Theater in Düsseldorf and had come over to England to sing operettas at various provincial towns, sounds dreadful: I can't stand anyone singing on a stage.

'You can probably imagine how it was, one night in Leicester, two in Birmingham, another in Norwich... sounds ghastly, being dragged round the country singing to unappreciative audiences, staying in those appalling guesthouses. Nonetheless, our colleagues in MI5 were watching them because there was a concern one or two of them may be Nazi agents operating under theatrical cover. Christ: Nazis and operetta, what an awful thought...'

Barney Allen paused for a while and shook his head.

'However, the MI5 chap did overhear Siegfried Schroth being remarkably indiscreet, describing the Nazis as being a disgrace to German culture. They passed this on to us in case we were interested, and we arranged for someone to bump into him, if you understand.'

Jack said he did, wondering quite where this was going.

'Our man took the view that Schroth wasn't for us. He couldn't rule out the possibility of him having sounded off like that for our benefit when in fact he was a Nazi all the time. But more to the point, he thought he was too extrovert and exuberant, liked to gossip and drink too much, not what we expect to see in an agent.'

'But what we do expect to see in an actor. Did he know we were interested in him?'

'Of course not, Jack, it was my colleague Tom Gilbey who was handling him and I'm not totally convinced that Tom called that one right. You never know... there's a school of thought which says people from the world of show business make damn good spies, being used to playing parts et cetera. So I ran it past Tom and he agreed maybe it was worth checking on Schroth again – if you'd be so good, next time you're in Düsseldorf.'

The next time Jack was there was in the February of 1939. He contacted Siegfried Schroth at the Stadt Theater on Wetekam Strasse, telling him he'd seen him perform in England the previous summer and thought he was wonderful and now he was here and, blow me, if he hadn't walked past the theatre and seen his picture!

Siegfried Schroth was flattered of course and allowed Jack to buy him a very expensive dinner at Bettermanns on Josephinen Strasse. He was marvellous company, but Jack concluded that Tom Gilbey had probably been correct: Siegfried Schroth was too verbose, too much of a gossip to be a reliable secret agent.

Notwithstanding this, Jack looked Siegfried up the next time he was in Düsseldorf, if only to enjoy his gossip and have a good meal. He became convinced the actor was no Nazi, though by the time the war began he'd clearly learnt to be more careful in expressing any political views.

–

Siegfried had a small apartment on Jahn Strasse, at the end furthest from the city centre and Jack decided to head there. Siegfried opened the door and the actor stepped back in shock and blinked, before peering into the corridor to check no one was around and gesturing for Jack to hurry in.

Jack had decided to take the enormous risk of telling Siegfried everything. Yes, he had indeed been an American journalist when they met previously but he also worked for the British and desperately needed help. He had no one else to turn to.

Siegfried had said nothing in the twenty minutes it took Jack to explain himself. Once Jack finished, he reached over to the sideboard and poured them both a very generous measure of German brandy.

'But I'm a performer, Jack... not that I get to perform much these days. I've learnt to keep my head down and avoid anything political.'

'This isn't anything political, Siegfried, it's rescuing a woman.'

'From the Gestapo!'

'No, from the Polizeipräsidium.'

'Exactly... I know the place, Jack, it's like a fortress.'

'What do you mean you know the place?'

'I work there, Jack.'

The American stared at him in disbelief.

'Don't look so worried, Jack, I'm not a policeman. There's so little work at the Stadt-Theater these days we've all had to get other jobs. I found one as a clerk in the records department at the Polizeipräsidium: at least it's nearby and it's warm and I've even been promoted to senior clerk, would you believe. Some of my colleagues from the theatre have ended up working in factories and others have been conscripted.'

Siegfried explained how he helped to organise the records: archiving those of cases that were finished with and creating new records for current investigations.

'Do you wear a uniform?'

'Don't be ridiculous, Jack. I wear a suit.'

Jack stood up and asked Siegfried to give him a minute or two to think. He paced around the small apartment; its walls adorned with photographs of its owner in various theatrical roles. He stopped by one: a younger Siegfried dressed as a cavalry officer.

'You look quite the part there.'

'I should certainly hope so: the magic of the theatre is that one can get the audience to believe that you're someone else, even though they can see you on stage. Once you put on the costume and the lights go on, you become that character.'

Jack sat down and carefully explained to Siegfried what he had in mind. Siegfried was dismissive at first, unwilling to entertain Jack's idea and calling it an act of madness. But then Jack asked him when he'd last been on stage and he admitted it was over a year ago and after that he became less reluctant and started asking Jack questions and making helpful suggestions.

Gradually, his mood changed from hostile to almost enthusiastic. He said he'd go along with it, but on one condition. When Siegfried explained what that condition was Jack hesitated briefly before replying, saying that sounded fair enough.

–

Kriminaldirektor Klaus Braun interrogated Sophia until nine o'clock on the Saturday night. He'd soon realised she was going to be no pushover. She was of an altogether different calibre to the hotel manager in Duisburg.

Whereas Rainer Kühn had been nervous and confused, this woman was calm and collected. She wasn't rushed with her answers, but nor was she hesitant. She managed to convey very persuasively that she was perplexed as to why she'd been arrested. And she stuck to her story: she was Frau Alma Walter from Cologne, on her way back to her home city, and had decided to travel via Düsseldorf. She explained how she was active in the Frauenschaft and had taken it on herself – as an act of patriotic duty – to visit Duisburg and Gelsenkirchen, but had begun to feel unwell and had decided to return home.

When Braun informed her there were no records of a Frau Alma Walter from an address near the Volksgarten in Cologne she shrugged and said she wasn't surprised. There'd been a lot of bombing, she explained. As far as she was aware, almost all the records had been destroyed! That wasn't her fault, was it?

Braun said of course not and found himself smiling at her and then reassuring her that... please, there's no reason to cry, would you like a drink...? He realised he was being charmed by her, a quite beautiful woman, with the most extraordinary eyes and a refined air about her and all in all it was quite disconcerting.

He decided to leave the questioning until the morning. When he returned to the office one of his Kripo colleagues took him aside.

'Lindner's still around, he's desperate to question the woman. He wants her transferred to the Gefängnis. He's been trying to get hold of Oberregierungsrat Albath, but without any luck. So far.'

—

At a quarter past seven on the Sunday morning Kriminaldirektor Klaus Braun arrived back the Polizeipräsidium to resume his questioning of the woman who insisted she was Alma Walter from Cologne.

Braun entered the police headquarters through the main entrance on Mackensen Platz. At almost exactly the same time, Siegfried Schroth entered the building through the less imposing entrance on Fürstenwall. While Braun headed to an upper floor to prepare for a long day of questioning, Schroth's destination was the records department on the lower ground floor at the rear of the building. He knew the duty clerk would have gone off duty at seven o'clock and he also knew – because it was custom and practice on Sunday mornings and he did it himself – that the day duty clerk wouldn't come in until nearer nine o'clock.

That gave him just under two hours. He found the previous days' booking records with the details of the prisoner who'd been arrested at the station. With her custody number he was able to fill in a new custody form, which would be identical to the one being used upstairs. From the safe in the office of the head of criminal records he removed a blank Prisoner Transfer Form. These were tedious documents which took some time to fill in and were considered an encumbrance by most officers. As a result, it was often left to the clerks to complete them and, to make matters easier – especially at night or over the weekend – there were even a few blank copies already stamped and signed by Oberst der Polizei Weber, the most senior police officer in the district: the man in a position to authorise the transfer of prisoners.

It was just after half past eight when he'd filled in all the forms. He put them in an envelope which he taped to the inside of the back of his jacket. But he had one more place to visit in the Polizeipräsidium. If it was locked or busy or someone spotted him, then their plan would stand no chance.

It was located at the other end of the lower ground floor, a stuffy and dimly lit, windowless area at the end of a long, sloping corridor that smelled of disinfectant. The door was open and it was silent, apart from the noisy snoring of the duty officer, fast asleep in a small cubicle. It took Siegfried Schroth just five minutes to find what he wanted.

He left the Polizeipräsidium well before nine o'clock, slipping out of the building with the familiar sensation of excitement and trepidation he used to experience when he was about to go on the stage.

Chapter 31

Poland
June 1943

Max and Raisa started to argue soon after darkness fell over the forest that Sunday night.

They had no way of knowing the exact time, but they'd developed a sense of gauging approximately at what point in the day or night they were at. They knew their mother had left at around seven o'clock, telling them she may be away for an hour, perhaps a bit longer. When night wrapped itself around the forest and the air somehow felt rarer and the temperature dropped and with the heavy canopy above them blocking out what little light there was, they both realised she was long overdue.

Raisa said they should go and look for her but Max reminded her of what their mother had said: they weren't to leave where they were under any circumstances. She'd come back for them.

They stopped their whispered bickering and drifted off to sleep. When they woke at dawn, they drank some water and chewed on raw turnip and then decided maybe their mother was waiting until it was light before making her way back.

When she'd still not returned an hour later they decided they could go in search of her. What if she'd fallen and didn't want to call out for them?

They discussed where to go and Raisa reminded Max that their mother had said she was going to look for somewhere safe for them to hide.

'Do you remember that strange house we passed yesterday: the one in the middle of a field that looked like a cowshed? Maybe that's where she's gone.'

'What makes you think that?'

'Because she was so interested in the place: we spent ages watching it, didn't we?'

They agreed that's where they would go. But they'd be careful: they'd remain hidden the whole time.

—

Lea was aware of her fate the moment the two brothers dragged her into the scullery and said they were going to have some fun with her.

They didn't return for the best part of an hour but in that time Lea had found a surprising inner calm. She knew Roman was safe in Switzerland and the children had not been discovered and she'd avoided mentioning them. They'd be safe in the forest, she decided. But she was in no doubt that a dreadful fate awaited her: she just hoped it would be quick.

The brothers returned to the scullery dragging a heavily stained mattress, which they threw her onto. They tied a filthy cloth which tasted of oil round her mouth and told her to keep quiet: they didn't want their mother to be disturbed.

They finished with her an hour later, both men exhausted and affected by the bottle of vodka they'd drunk their way through as they took turns raping her. She was bleeding and in pain and totally humiliated of course, but she concentrated her thoughts on the rest of the family.

They were safe.

Roman would soon be reunited with Max and Raisa.

She was sacrificing herself for them.

—

Nothing prepared the children for what they saw when they emerged from the forest and crawled through the undergrowth to the edge of the cornfield. The cowshed was ahead of them and in the patch of wasteland behind it lay the naked and bloody body of a woman they realised was their mother.

At first, they thought she was dead, and Raisa had to hold Max down, but then they saw two men pouring buckets of cold water over her and soon after that their mother stirred and sat up and then the old woman came out of the house and handed her some clothes. Within minutes their mother had been dragged away and, in the distance, they heard a scream and some shouting, after which there was the noise of an engine starting followed by silence.

The wind rustled through the field in their direction, the heads of corn pointing towards the forest, as if instructing them to return there.

They found their hiding place and for the next two or three days they sat in a state of shock, first one weeping, then the other. They tried to console each other, but they knew they'd never see their mother again. All they could do was what she'd told them to do and stay where they were.

–

Lea Loszynski arrived at the Gestapo headquarters in Pomorska Street in Krakow later that day. The two brothers carried her into Pomorska Street and told the officer on duty they'd found this Jew trying to break into their house and here she was.

The Gestapo officer hardly looked up: he said they could go now and when they asked about their reward, he told them to get lost, the only reward they were getting was that they weren't being arrested too!

She told them her real name and that she'd been in Warsaw during the ghetto Uprising and had escaped and was trying to get to Slovakia. All her family had been killed in Warsaw, she said. She admitted the identity she was carrying – Klara Wójcik – was a false one. She suspected they'd have found that out anyway and thought it would help to admit it and hopefully stop them interrogating her.

But they were barely interested in her. They took a note of her name and put her into a cell to await the next transport. When her eyes adjusted to the gloomy interior, she realised she wasn't alone: half a dozen adults and maybe ten children, slumped on the floor or sharing a small bench.

No one said a word, though a woman who looked her age nodded.

'They said I'd be on the next transport,' she asked. 'Do you know where that's to?'

'You mean you don't know?' It was an older man, his arm in a sling.

Lea said she didn't. She wasn't from round here.

'Auschwitz,' said the woman. 'They're taking us to Auschwitz.'

'And then we die,' said the man with his arm in a sling.

—

Raisa recalled an argument her parents once had in front of them. She'd asked her mother what a miracle was and her father said there was no such thing: everything had a scientific explanation. Their mother had told him it was important to believe in miracles: you never know when you'll need them!

A few days after they'd seen their mother taken away Max and Raisa experienced a miracle.

They hadn't eaten for two days and felt too lethargic to do anything, even to go to the stream. They'd taken to sleeping a lot and felt very light-headed. Raisa was asleep, the warmth of the afternoon sun on her face, when Max prodded her in the ribs and told her to wake up. When she did, he pointed ahead of them.

Fifty yards away, clearly visible through a gap in the trees stood an old man. He raised his hands in greeting and smiled in their direction before moving closer to them, slowly and in a manner designed to reassure them. When he was no more than twenty yards away, he stopped and put the big knapsack he was carrying on the ground and then knelt down and pulled out a large flask, some bread, cheese and sausages and a bag of apples. He pointed at the food and then at them, at which point Max started to say something, but the man shook his head and put a finger to his lips.

Moments later he waved goodbye and disappeared into the forest.

The man returned every three or four days. He brought enough food to last them until his next visit and Raisa decided that they should store some of it, in case something happened to the man.

At first, they tried to speak with him. They told him their names were Mieczysław and Janina Wójcik, from Krakow but he'd shake his head and put a finger to his lips and eventually they realised they weren't to say a word.

One day he brought blankets with him, then a large tarpaulin and after a few weeks he brought a bag of clothes, including shoes that were too big but still very welcome.

When the summer began to fade and the nights became bitterly cold and the forest was painted with frost, they began to worry. They both knew they wouldn't survive a winter in the forest. They debated whether to say anything to the man but one afternoon he indicated they should follow him and bring everything they had with them. He carried the blankets and the tarpaulins and marched ahead, always keeping twenty yards in front.

They must have walked for three hours, possibly longer. At one stage they climbed up a steep slope and then down the other side into a particularly dense area of forest, before following the course of a fast-running stream, the stones around it green with moss, the air fresh and full of the noise of birds.

The man then disappeared. One moment he was ahead of them, walking through some trees, the next he was gone. Max and Raisa stood close together, neither saying a word but both thinking the same: they'd been abandoned again.

But then the man appeared, waving at them and giving a low whistle, which sounded like that of an animal.

He was in the doorway of a wooden hut that was so well camouflaged by the forest that they'd not spotted it. He beckoned to them to join him.

It was evident he'd prepared the hut for them. It was small and sparse, with two narrow beds along each side wall and a table in the middle. Around the walls were shelves, with food and plates on them. There was a small stove with a pile of wood next to it and an axe on top of the wood. He showed them how to use the stove and pointed to the hook on the inside of the door, making it clear they should keep it locked.

And then he was gone.

The hut saw them through that winter and that of 1944 too. His visits became less frequent in the depths of winter, but that mattered less as Max and Raisa became stronger and more confident. They learned to forage in the forest, which was the best part of the stream to catch fish, which mushrooms and berries were edible, the patches where vegetables grew.

When he brought them food the bread was usually wrapped in newspaper and they'd read the crumpled sheets and it was clear there was a lot of fighting going on.

As the winter of 1944 turned into 1945 – they knew that because they had a copy of a newspaper dated 14 January – they heard the rumble of artillery fire around them, at one stage sounding as if it was in the forest itself.

They never saw the man after that. Since moving to the hut they'd made notches on the door to mark the number of days between his visits and by the time the winter of 1945 turned into spring and the number of notches reached one hundred, they decided to venture out.

The forest was once again silent, no more sounds of artillery.

It was, they decided, time to try and get to Switzerland.

Chapter 32

'It's absolutely appalling news, there's no pretending otherwise. It was so promising… and now it's all gone…'

'Up in smoke?'

'I'm afraid so, Roly, literally… Basil's absolutely devastated. Never known him to be so down: blames himself and one does have to wonder whether he perhaps took his eye off the ball.' Piers Devereux spread his hands in a forlorn gesture that emphasised the helplessness of the situation. For someone usually so considered in his choice of words he now appeared to be lost for them.

They were meeting in a secure room in the War Office, the enormous building on the corner of Whitehall and Horse Guards Avenue. Air Vice-Marshal Frank Hamilton had an office here and as their normal meeting room in Downing Street was being refurbished, this was deemed to be a suitable venue.

It was a more comfortable room than the one in Downing Street: spacious and well lit, no unpleasant smells and a trolley with both tea and coffee along with a large plate of biscuits, which Sir Roly Pearson had requisitioned and placed close to him.

It was late on a Friday afternoon, 2 July, and normally at this time the participants would be thinking about their weekend. That was now the last thing on their minds. Air Vice-Marshal Frank Hamilton was accompanied by Group Captain Martin Marlow, Piers Devereux by Barney Allen and Tom Gilbey from MI6. The two great beasts of Downing Street were there, sitting at opposite ends of the table, a palpable air of distrust and dislike hanging between them, barely acknowledging each other's presence: Sir Roly Pearson who co-ordinated intelligence for the prime minister, Lord Swalcliffe who did the same for science.

But it was those not present who were to dominate the meeting, along with the truly appalling events of that week.

The awkward silence that was the tradition of such occasions descended on the room – a reluctance to be the first to speak, a preference for someone else to place their cards on the table. There was a good deal of coughing and rearranging of papers until Roly Pearson said it was all such a terrible shame and a chorus of muttered agreement echoed around the room.

'Before we consider Basil's report, perhaps we could review the bombing campaign: Martin?'

Group Captain Martin Marlow from Bomber Command picked up two very large cards, each with a series of photographs on them. 'Apologies for the delay, but the aerial reconnaissance had to be repeated a few days after the raids because of poor weather conditions.

'This board shows the Vereinigte steelworks and the area surrounding it in the Ruhrort part of Duisburg. The raid took place in the very early hours of Friday twenty-fifth June, which is exactly three weeks ago. According to our analysts the damage to the site was considerable, as you can see from the before and after photographs here.

'The disruption factor – in other words the length of time which the factory is out of action for – is likely to be at least one month, which is very good. According to the wireless operator on the Lancaster with the receiver on board, they picked up the signal eight miles from target, which is a considerable improvement on the first raid on Mannheim at the beginning of June, when I understand the signal was not received until four miles from target.'

'So, a big success then?'

'Very much so, Frank, yes. A much stronger signal and no doubt helped by flying at fifteen thousand feet this time. One could of course attribute this to luck but then we had very similar results the following night.'

Group Captain Marlow put the Duisburg board behind him and picked up another. 'Gelsenkirchen, twenty-four hours later, early hours of the morning of Saturday twenty-sixth of June. The target was a much larger one, the marshalling yard at Gelsenkirchen–Bismarck. The signal was picked up at six miles, but the target covered a much larger area and you can see from the before and after photographs here that there is significant damage. In addition, the Graf Bismarck Colliery here – just north of the target, sustained enough damage to bring the mine to a halt for at least a week. Just south of that, on the other side of the canal, is a power station which appears to have taken at least one direct hit. Out analyst's assessment is that the disruption factor for the marshalling yard and the power station is in the region of two to three weeks. Perhaps if I pass these around?'

It took a while for everyone to finish studying the photographs. Piers Devereux was the next to speak.

'Would I be right in thinking that the view of the RAF is that Tatra has been a success?'

'The Mark Four version of it? Unquestionably so.'

'Therefore, all the more reason to regard what happened in Geneva as such a dreadful disappointment.' It was Lord Swalcliffe who'd spoken, for the first time that afternoon.

No one responded for a while and then Barney Allen did so, with a bitter edge to his voice. 'Disappointment? I'd say it was a good deal more than. It was a disaster!'

–

'It's on Elfenstrasse in Berne and you're to ask to see Ładoś or Kühl: can you remember that?'

Roman Loszynski nodded at Andrzej. It was May and they were at the farm just outside Zakopane, the night Andrzej had brought Pavol to meet them and the young man from Żegota had taken him outside. He was telling him who he should contact in Switzerland – in an emergency.

'Tell them you have come from Częstochowa and have a message from Paweł's mother. They'll ask you her name and where she lives and you're to reply...'

'Magdalena from Bydgoszcz, yes you've told me twice.'

'I'm just checking you remember. Then they'll know to trust you.'

—

Now it was a Tuesday – 22 June – and Roman Loszynski was standing outside number twenty Elfenstrasse. Two Swiss police officers were standing in front of the iron-barred gate, behind it an imposing three-storey building, not unlike a fine French château, surrounded by an immaculate garden. A large brass plaque announced this was the Polish Legation to Switzerland.

A tall man in dark suit appeared on the other side of the gates and called Roman over and asked how he could help. Roman replied in Polish. He needed to see Aleksander Ładoś or Juliusz Kühl.

'Do you have an appointment?'

'No, but... I have come from Częstochowa and have a message from Paweł's mother.'

The man nodded. 'And can you please tell me her name and where she lives?'

'Her name is Magdalena and she's from Bydgoszcz.'

The man nodded and said to follow him. When they entered the building, he paused and said he hoped he understood, but he'd need to search him.

Ten minutes later Roman Loszynski was in an elegant upper-floor office in a world that didn't officially exist. The building at 20 Elfenstrasse was the legation of a country occupied by the Germans, the two diplomats sitting opposite him not officially recognised by the Swiss authorities.

Aleksander Ładoś was the chargé d'Affaires, Juliusz Kühl his deputy. Along with other unofficial diplomats in the unofficial embassy and members of the local Jewish community, they were busy issuing thousands of passports apparently from South American countries in an effort to save as many Jews as possible. They had close links with the Żegota in Poland and the coded phrase the man opposite them had given indicated he was very important. They asked him to tell his story.

It took the best part of an hour, with frequent interruptions from the two diplomats to ask questions.

'And you say you're working on these devices in Geneva?'

Loszynski nodded.

'With the British?'

He nodded again.

'How were you able to get away today?'

Loszynski explained how the American and the German woman had left at the weekend to take the Tatra into Germany for testing. He'd been left on his own, with two men from the British embassy guarding him.

'Not very well, by the looks of it?'

'They've let me go for short walks on my own. At first they followed me, but I think they decided I could be trusted and no longer follow me. This morning I woke up early, dressed before they did and said I was going out for five minutes to get some fresh air. I caught a taxi to the station and a train here.'

Aleksander Ładoś asked him what he wanted.

'I'm desperate for information on my family. I've reached the point where I don't feel I can go on much longer, certainly without knowing if they're safe or even just what's happened to them.'

'The work you've told us you're doing for the British – for the Allied cause, against the Nazis – is clearly of vital importance. If Poland is to be free then work like yours is essential, it's—'

'Of course, I understand that, but I feel everything that's happened to me... the Nazi invasion, living in the ghetto, escaping Poland, leaving my family behind... has become too much: life feels unbearable. If I could get some news of my family, maybe I could concentrate properly on my work and get on with my life.'

'There is a tragic story behind all of us,' said Juliusz. 'As hard as that is we have to try and put it to one side and understand that the greater cause is defeating the Nazis and freeing Poland. When that happens, we can look for our families and...'

Loszynski said of course he understood that, otherwise he wouldn't have escaped from Poland on his own, but he owed it to himself to do everything he could to find out if there was any news on his family.

Aleksander Łados said very well and took something from a drawer. Moments later an opened street map of Geneva was spread out on the desk. 'Show us where you live and where the workshop is.'

'The apartment is just here, on Rue d'Italie. The workshop is on Rue Kléberg – which is... here.'

'How do you get there?'

'This, across this bridge.' He traced the route with his fore-finger, tapping it on the bridge.

'The Pont du Mont-Blanc? Good, I know it.' Juliusz was studying the map as he spoke. 'It's Tuesday today: it will take a few days for us to find anything out; you must be patient. I can't promise we'll be successful, but I promise we'll do our best. When we have information, I'll come to Geneva. Either on your way to work or from it, I'll pass you on the bridge, from the opposite direction. You mustn't show any sign of recognising me, but when you see me you'll know you're to find a way of meeting me as soon as you can in the Jardin Anglais. Do you know it?'

He said he did.

'There's a large statue there,' said Juliusz, 'of a man and a woman, I think. It's called the National Monument. Once we've crossed on the bridge I'll head there and wait for you.'

'There's something else, Roman,' said Aleksander Ładoś. 'You must realise the chances of us getting any information out of Poland are remote and even if we do, the likelihood is it will not be good news. You know what the situation is like there. For the civilian population it is terrible, undoubtedly the worse occupation in Europe. But for Jews, it is so much worse.'

Roman said he knew that, but not knowing anything was proving unbearable. He was prepared to take the risk.

–

On the Tuesday after his visit to Berne, Roman Loszynski decided it would take weeks rather than days for them to get news from Poland, if they were going to get anything out at all, which he was beginning to doubt and he was also beginning to wonder if that may be for the best, or at least, if not for the best, then better than knowing bad news, or no news, which was pretty much the same.

As he and Bert crossed the Pont du Mont-Blanc on the way back to the apartment that evening he was amazed to see Juliusz ambling towards them, slightly overdressed for the warm weather but other than that looking every bit the Swiss gentleman, nothing about him would cause anyone else to so much as glance in his direction.

Back in the apartment Reg said he'd prepare supper and Bert was fiddling with his pipe and Roman announced he was going for a walk and Bert said they'd only just got back but Roman replied that he wanted to go to the lake and would be back in no more than ten minutes, and at least it would get him away from the smell of the pipe. The misunderstanding of the previous Tuesday – that was how Roman had described it when he returned from Berne – was in the past. He'd been very apologetic: he'd just needed time on his own, he'd told them. They promised to say nothing to Mr Remington-Barber or to Mr Moore, just so long as it didn't happen again.

They all laughed and Roman said he'd see them soon.

There was no sign of Juliusz by the statue, which turned out to be of two women and according to a sign on the plinth commemorated the unification of the Republic of Geneva and Switzerland in eighteen something and Roman was thinking about how he'd had no idea there'd ever been a Republic of Geneva when Juliusz tapped him on the elbow and said they needed to talk.

–

'We finally heard back from Poland late last night.'

Juliusz said nothing for a moment and when Roman looked at him he could see his face was grey and his eyes were red. Juliusz paused again and shook his head.

'Are you sure that you want to hear all this?'

Roman didn't reply.

'Remember, it's hard enough to get any news out of Poland,' said Juliusz, 'and even then one has to be most circumspect, it's not always reliable. We don't know for sure which of our contacts have been compromised and which haven't.'

Roman said he was sure, though given Juliusz's behaviour he wasn't actually so sure. But it was too late now. He felt light-headed and suggested they sit but Juliusz said it was best to keep moving.

It was a while before he resumed speaking and coughed awkwardly before he did. Roman noticed that Juliusz was now addressing him in informal speech. 'The Żegota cell in Krakow was broken by the Gestapo at the end of May: nearly all of them were either killed or arrested. The man who was in contact with your family – Andrzej – was one of those killed. However, the woman who helped you escape from Warsaw, Zofia, managed to escape from Warsaw after the Uprising and now she's in Krakow. According to her, on Monday the fourteenth of June a woman called Klara Wójcik was brought to the Gestapo headquarters in Krakow, at Pomorska Street. From what Zofia was told, she admitted to the Gestapo that her real name was Lea Loszynski and she told them she was originally from Poznań but had escaped from the Warsaw ghetto.'

He turned to look at Roman who took a while to realise Juliusz was seeking confirmation. He said it was the identity Żegota had given them when they fled Warsaw.

'Your wife was kept at the Gestapo headquarters in Pomorska Street until the Thursday and I'm terribly sorry to tell you...'

Juliusz made a gesture with his hands, as if trying to help himself form the words. 'I'm so sorry to inform you that Lea was one of a group of fifty Jews transported from Krakow to Auschwitz.'

They carried on walking, in step, both men's heads lowered, the park, which had been noisy, now eerily quiet as if people were listening in. Roman moved forward as if by instinct: his hearing now felt as if there'd been an enormous explosion and he felt dizzy.

'And the children?'

Juliusz hesitated and coughed a few times.

'You have to tell me. I wasn't expecting good news.'

'I'm afraid that Zofia believes they were with her. There is no record of their names but half of those on the transport were children and her contact says Lea was certainly with a boy and a girl when she left the building. She was holding their hands.'

Juliusz said nothing as they walked on for a while, quite a long while, onto the Promenade du Lac, neither saying a word as the spray caught them and the sun bounced off the surface of the lake.

Eventually Juliusz said something about everyone suffering the most terrible tragedies and if Roman ever needed help he knew where they were but in the meantime the work he was doing was of such incalculable importance that he must take strength from that, it was very much the view of the Polish Government in Exile that he should continue this work and... he shrugged, unable to think of anything else to say and Roman Loszynski said yes of course and he was most grateful to Juliusz for bringing him the news, as dreadful as it was, and please send his regards to Mr Ładoś.

'You have a report from Basil, I understand?'

Barney Allen said yes, Roly, he did indeed and if he could hang on for a moment, he'd find it. In the corridor outside the meeting room in the War Office there was laughter and two men loudly wished each other a good weekend and there was some reference to golf and Barney then announced he'd found it.

'Perhaps if I read Basil's report out in full? It came through this morning and was decoded just before this meeting. It's quite thorough.'

There was a muttering of assent around the table. Barney Allen coughed as he put on his reading glasses and reminded the others these were Basil's words.

'Roman Loszynski remained in Geneva to continue working on the Tatra devices while our two principal agents were in Germany. Loszynski stayed in the apartment in Rue d'Italie along with two security officers from the British Embassy in Berne: Corporal Bert Wood and Corporal Reg Garston. During the day he was at the workshop on Rue Kléberg. My instructions were that at all times Loszynski should be accompanied by at least one of the security officers.

'Corporals Wood and Garston say that they returned to the apartment at approximately six on Tuesday evening.'

Piers Devereux interrupted and said to be clear, that was this Tuesday, wasn't it? And Barney said yes, the twenty-ninth of June. He continued reading.

'They admit that contrary to their orders, they were regretfully in the habit of allowing Loszynski to go for short walks, which he did that evening. They say he was in the habit of doing this and they felt it was not unreasonable to cut him some slack given the pressure he was under.

'They report that Loszynski did not return to the apartment until a quarter to eleven on Tuesday night. They now say they very much regret having allowed him to leave the apartment unaccompanied and had determined that had he not returned by eleven they were going to call either Noel or myself. Loszynski explained that he'd lost track of time and that he was fine but wanted to go straight to bed.

'The following morning – so, Wednesday – he was accompanied to the workshop by Corporal Garston, who says there was nothing in Loszynski's behaviour to give any cause for concern or suspicion. They stopped on the way for Loszynski to purchase some cigarettes and matches but he was acting normally. The following is Corporal Garston's own account of what happened when they arrived at the workshop on Rue Kléberg.

'I unlocked the door, which is a bit of an effort, as you know, after we had that metal door fitted and all those locks. As soon as it opened, Roman pushed past me and before I knew it, he'd slammed the door shut with me on the wrong side of it. I know I'm a strong man, but I didn't stand a chance. I could hear him closing the bolts and I shouted at him to open it and then I heard a noise inside – it was a whooshing noise, like fireworks, and that was followed by the crackling sound of flames and then smoke started to seep out from under the door and I had to go up to the street because it was hard to breathe down there. Someone said they'd called the fire brigade, but it took them ten minutes to get there and then it was another, I don't know, five minutes before they could break in and they had to put the fire out and the workshop was completely destroyed – I've never seen anything like it, it was all charred, like cinder. Even Roman's body. The way he closed that door on me, it must have been deliberate. Why on earth would he go and do something like that?'

There was a stunned silence. Eventually Tom Gilbey said it was a good question, why indeed would he do something like that?

Frank Hamilton muttered something about the two corporals needing to be disciplined and another person said Basil didn't come out of the whole business exactly smelling of roses either, but Roly Pearson raised his voice and said this all sounded rather like shutting the stable door after the horse had bolted.

'It's a dreadful business, too dreadful. I don't imagine there's any way of saving Tatra, is there, Frank?'

Frank Hamilton said there wasn't, though he did feel it was right to point out that the Ruhr bombing campaign was coming to an end anyway.

'Of course, had Loszynski and the devices been brought back to this country it would have been an altogether different matter, but then with the benefit of hindsight...'

'With the benefit of hindsight,' said Piers Devereux, 'perhaps one ought to have realised the effect on Loszynski of not knowing about his family. It must have driven the poor chap mad. One can only assume that this led to him blowing everything up.'

The long silence was punctuated by a slamming of doors in the corridor and laughter further down it.

'Unless he somehow found out about his family?'

Everything looked at Barney as if he knew something, but he shook his head. 'I'm just guessing. We'll never know, will we?'

Acting on a silent cue the participants in the meeting began to gather their papers and prepare to leave. Sir Roly Pearson had remained seated, turning his chair to face the window, glimpses of the River Thames just visible through it. When he spoke it was in a louder voice than usual, like a preacher trying to gain the congregation's attention in a noisy church.

'One does sometimes so despair when one is confronted by bad news.'

There was a muttering of agreement, the congregation dutifully concurring with the preacher, who wasn't finished yet.

'And, Tom – I hear Lyon is a disaster too?'

'I'm afraid it is, Roly. We need to find out what the hell's going on there.'

Roly Pearson grunted. 'And the German woman and the American: I don't suppose you have any idea as to where they are, do you, Barney?'

'Sadly not, Roly: all I know is that they're overdue. One's keeping one's fingers crossed.'

Chapter 33

Germany and Switzerland
June and July 1943

Sophia von Naundorf was interrogated for most of the Sunday by the Kripo detective from Duisburg. Kriminaldirektor Klaus Braun was not an unpleasant man in many respects: he was polite, referring to her as Frau Walter, even though the crux of his case against her was that no such person existed.

He insisted her story didn't stand up: not only was there no trace of her in Cologne but her explanation about visiting Duisburg and Gelsenkirchen on behalf of the Frauenschaft was paper thin. And the hotel in Gelsenkirchen, filling in her details incorrectly, and then of course the hotel manager in Duisburg who insisted that she was a British agent.

She said she was surprised Herr Kriminaldirektor had fallen for such nonsense. The hotel manager had behaved most improperly towards her and she'd rejected his advances. This was clearly his way of getting his own back.

Late on the Sunday night he told her the investigation would probably be taken away from him very soon.

'So far I've resisted the efforts of the Gestapo to take this case over. But I fear unless I've got somewhere with you by the morning the matter will be taken out of my hands and you'll then be a prisoner of the Gestapo. You're clearly a very smart woman: I think you know what that entails.'

She'd been taken down to the cells after that: it was damp and the mattress on the narrow bed was so filthy that she covered it with the single threadbare blanket she'd been given.

She lay there unable to sleep, cold and with the deep silence occasionally broken by cries or screams from distant parts. She decided she'd give him something in the morning, though she wasn't sure what.

She did allow herself a few minutes to imagine that Jack may try to rescue her, but realised such thoughts were so Quixotic as to be an indulgence.

–

They left Siegfried's apartment on apartment on Jahn Strasse at one o'clock on the Monday morning, taking the back stairs to the basement garage and not putting their boots on until they got there.

Siegfried kept an eye on an elderly neighbour, running the odd errand for him, and this neighbour had a Volkswagen which he kept parked in the garage but never used. Occasionally he'd ask Siegfried to take the car out for a short drive: he didn't want its engine to seize up.

Siegfried had taken the key when he checked on the neighbour that afternoon and now, they were settling themselves into the car. It was a short drive from the apartment to the Polizeipräsidium. When they arrived, they parked the car outside the side entrance on Fürstenwall.

'Remember to let me do most of the talking.'

'Yes, Siegfried, but remember also we don't actually want much talking, do we? Keep it quick and to the point, act like we're in a hurry.'

They exchanged salutes with the policeman on duty at the entrance and headed down to the cells. Jack was amazed at Siegfried: over the course of an hour that afternoon he'd transformed himself with the help of the uniform and make-up into a police officer. He looked totally different and quite authoritative too. He'd also applied make-up to Jack, somehow making him appear far more Teutonic.

And now both men were marching down the corridor in the uniforms Siegfried had removed from the police station earlier that day. They were Orpo officers, Siegfried a *Hauptwachtmeister*, a senior sergeant which he knew would outrank the sergeant in charge of the cells that night. Jack was a *Rottmeister*, a mere corporal.

The sergeant on duty said nothing as Siegfried placed the papers in front of him. He frowned and put on his reading glasses and then studied the papers, nodding as he carefully read them.

The prisoner's correct custody number was there.

The Prisoner Transfer Approval Form was correctly signed by Oberst der Polizei Weber.

The Custody Request document from the Orpo in Duisburg seemed to be in order.

'Very well then, very well: I'm just surprised Kriminaldirektor Klaus Braun didn't mention anything about this when he finished with the prisoner this evening.'

'What time was that?'

'Ten o'clock: the last thing he said was to have her ready for seven-thirty in the morning.'

'What is your name?'

'I beg your pardon?'

'I want your name.'

'*Wachtmeister* Franks, sir: Karl Franks.'

'Well then, Franks, that was three and a half hours ago: the situation has clearly changed, hasn't it? You've taken long enough over this as it is. Bring the prisoner here and look smart about it!'

Franks looked up, clearly unsure what to do. Jack Miller – Police Corporal Jack Miller – smiled at him but the good cop, bad cop routine didn't seem to work on another police officer.

'This doesn't feel right to me, *Hauptwachtmeister*.'

'What doesn't feel right?' Siegfried impatiently drummed his fingers on the desk and sighed. It was an impressive performance, though Jack resisted the urge to applaud.

'This…' The sergeant pointed at the papers Siegfried had presented him with. 'According to the timestamps, the Custody

Request from the Orpo in Duisburg was issued *after* the Prisoner Transfer Approval Form. Surely it should be the other way round? The request is made for a transfer and then it is approved. That's the way it's always worked.'

Siegfried glared at the custody sergeant. It was all they needed, someone who was a bit too clever by half.

'Tell me, Franks, are you suggesting that Oberst der Polizei Weber has made an error? Not everything happens in the order that penpushers like you want it to!'

'Of course not, but I'm simply pointing out that there appears to be a discrepancy and I—'

'And I'll tell you what!' Siegfried was shouting so loud that the custody sergeant jumped back in shock. 'How about I call Oberst der Polizei Weber and apologise for waking him up at two o'clock in the morning but the custody sergeant here at the Polizeipräsidium – name of Franks – is in a particularly officious mood and is questioning the form you signed and...'

There was a pause as Franks looked at the forms and then at Siegfried before evidently deciding that it wasn't worth making a fuss. His voice had a resigned air to it when he replied.

'Of course – I was simply pointing out an apparent inconsistency. When I do the handover in the morning everything has to be in order. But I'm sure it will be fine.'

'Of course it will. Now then, we've wasted enough time already. Have the prisoner brought up here now!'

–

Five minutes later Sophia was brought to them. In the narrow corridor it took her a moment or two to realise that the man in the police corporal's uniform was Jack. He grabbed her arm and pulled her towards him, catching the smell of fear on her, shocked at how pale and sick she looked, her eyes red.

She gasped very briefly as she recognised Jack and gave him an incredulous look, but that lasted no more than a second before she composed herself and asked where she was going, and Siegfried told her to shut up and get a move on.

She said nothing as she was marched down the corridor, Jack gripping her upper arm tightly. At one point he leant towards and said she was not to worry, but to play along.

You're a terrified prisoner. Act like one!

When they reached the guard at the door on Fürstenwall he pushed her roughly past him and down the steps towards the Volkswagen.

Once in Siegfried's apartment Sophia sat in a state of shock as Jack explained what had happened. She kept shaking her head and said there must be a catch and Jack said not at all, it was all down to Siegfried being so resourceful and creative.

'Dora's sister told me yesterday that the *Elfriede* arrives in Düsseldorf on Wednesday night from Rotterdam. The plan is for it to load at first light Thursday and then head for Berne. They'll be at the same quay just south of the Skagerrak Brücke that they used when we arrived here. We'll need to stay here until then.'

–

'Totally out of the question: you must think I'm mad!'

'You don't understand, Bruno: without Siegfried, Sophia would have become a prisoner of the Gestapo and who knows what she'd have said under torture? There's a chance you and Dora may have been implicated. You ought to be thanking Siegfried rather than—'

'Rather than what?'

'Rather than being so hostile to him. We owe our lives to him. All of us do.'

'Well, I'll tell you what, I'll go and thank him and shake his hand and then he can go home. He's not coming with us. What the hell do you think this is – a bloody pleasure cruise?'

They were in the small warehouse alongside the quay where the *Elfriede* was docked and Wednesday night had only just become Thursday morning. The three of them – Jack, Sophia and

Siegfried – had been hiding there since the Monday afternoon. Bruno was not taking the news of an extra passenger very well.

'I'm sorry, Bruno, but bringing him along with us was a condition he insisted on if he was going to help us.'

There was an awkward silence. Sophia and Siegfried had been at the other end of the warehouse with Dora, but it was hard to imagine they'd not overheard Bruno. Siegfried walked over and shook Bruno's hand, which was accepted reluctantly.

Then he spoke with Bruno. Except it wasn't Siegfried who spoke, just as it hadn't been Siegfried who'd spoken with the custody sergeant the previous night. This was a man with a rasping voice, hoarse from years of smoking, the voice of an older man and in an accent Jack could recognise as working class but speaking in a dialect he could barely follow.

Bruno listened to him with his mouth open in astonishment. When Siegfried finished, Bruno's broke into peals of laughter and hugged the other man.

'What was all that about?'

'That…' Bruno paused to catch his breath and pointed at Siegfried, 'that was the best Rhenish dialect I've ever heard. If you hadn't told me who he was, I'd have sworn he'd been a Rhine boatman since he left school. Once we've got him in some dirty dungarees, I promise you there won't be a soul on the river who'll doubt him.'

–

They hid in the warehouse until the *Elfriede* had been loaded and searched on the Thursday morning. At eight o'clock the barge slipped its moorings and turned purposefully into the grey Rhine, the river choppy and seemingly resentful of its peace being disturbed again.

It was 1 July and Bruno reckoned they'd be in Basel late on the Saturday. 'But we're leaving the Reich: the security will be much tighter. I've known boats to be held for two, three days while they wait to be searched. And I warn you, the searches can be very thorough. You won't be able to sit in your cabins and pretend to be crew for this one, I can assure you.'

They were sat round the table: Bruno and Dora, with Jack, Sophia and Siegfried. Sophia asked what they'd do, and Bruno told them not to worry. He had a plan.

–

Early on the Saturday afternoon Bruno told them it was time.

'In about two hours we'll arrive at Weil am Rhein: that's the last port on the Rhine that's still in the Reich and it's where the barges get pulled in and searched. You two need to go to your hiding places now. Siegfried, you'll stay up here as a deckhand.'

Bruno led them to the cargo area of the barge, where the huge pile of coal was covered by a massive tarpaulin. One end of it was open and a large pile of coal had been shovelled to expose two barrels, buried under the coal. Each barrel was just big enough to take an adult. Sophia and Jack squeezed in feet first. Bruno passed them bottles of water and the rubber hosepipes which would run from an opening in the barrel's lids to the deck. These should stop you suffocating, he'd assured them.

He fixed the lids into position and once Bruno had checked they were safe, began to shovel the coal back over the barrels. Once they were totally covered, they pulled the tarpaulin back over the coal, checking that the hosepipes weren't obstructed.

The *Elfriede* arrived at Weil am Rhein at four-thirty. Siegfried was next to Bruno in the wheelhouse as the barge's skipper scanned the river bank through his binoculars.

'It looks good.'

'What do you mean, Bruno?'

'I can only see the *Wasserschutzpolizei* there, the river police. Sometimes the Gestapo decide to search the barges and they're much more thorough and on the rare occasions the SS are there then we know we're in trouble: they're usually there because they've been tipped off and they search every inch of the boat.

There are five barges ahead of us. With some luck they'll be in a hurry.'

It was six o'clock by the time the *Elfriede* came to be searched and the barge was cleared within twenty minutes. A *Wasserschutzpolizei* search dog ran over the barge but seemed to be in as much of a hurry as his handler. The officer in charge of the search greeted Dora like an old friend and shared a raucous joke with Siegfried as he ate the cake Dora gave him.

The *Elfriede* docked in Basel just after eight o'clock that Saturday night, but it was nine o'clock before the Swiss police had completed their check. During that time Bruno had made a telephone call.

At ten-thirty a van pulled alongside the quay and by midnight they were in a safe house in Berne, where Noel Moore took one look at the state of the three of them and agreed they needed to get cleaned up.

'We'll have a good chat in the morning. Basil's rather tied up with something, but he should be with us by then.'

—

In the event it was late on the Sunday morning before Sophia and Jack met with Basil Remington-Barber and Noel Moore. Siegfried, they were told, had been taken to another safe house.

There was no explanation for the delay and there was a tense atmosphere in the room, which neither Sophia nor Jack could put their finger on. Noel wasn't quite as impassive as usual and was smoking continuously. But there was unquestionably something up with Basil: none of his upper-class charm, no twinkle in his eye. Instead, he looked pale and edgy, as if he'd been crying, or drinking. Or both.

Jack asked him if he was all right and he waved away the question and said they really needed to get down to business. He was looking at his notes rather than at either of them, frequently pausing and running his fingers through his hair.

'The bombing of the Vereinigte steelworks in Ruhrort in Duisburg was just over a week ago: the railway marshalling yard in Gelsenkirchen a day later. As far as I can gather from what London tells us, the preliminary reports from the subsequent aerial reconnaissance suggest the attacks on both targets were most successful. Barney Allen says the RAF are delighted. They're giving it a nine out of ten, whatever that means.'

'I would imagine it means it's very good, Basil: you ought to look happier than you do!'

'Yes, I do realise that, Jack, but nevertheless one is waiting for more intelligence... and it's a shame you weren't able to get on-the-ground photographs after the raids, Sophia.'

'Are you serious. Basil? Couldn't you show a small amount of appreciation? Sophia put her life on the line, for Christ's sake, and—'

Sophia put a hand on Jack's and said she could speak for herself. 'I took the view my priority was to escape. It was too risky to go anywhere near the bombsites. Surely it would have alerted the Germans to what we were up to if I was caught.'

Basil said that was all very well and *of course* he was most appreciative, but she was caught, wasn't she?

Sophia explained calmly that from what she could gather from her interrogation in Düsseldorf the hotel manager in Duisburg had been arrested and told them she was a British agent. 'I was about to be handed over to the Gestapo on Monday morning, Basil. Jack's rescue was... miraculous. The fact that he rescued me and we were able to escape back to Switzerland...'

She looked at Basil, who for the first time looked directly back at her and muttered, 'Of course, of course... well done, Jack, eh?'

Jack said Siegfried had been marvellous: he couldn't commend him highly enough and... Jack paused, aware of an awkward atmosphere.

'And while we're on the subject of Siegfried, may I just say that in terms of protocol, one should have been told you wanted to bring a friend along with you: at that point I would still have considered him a security risk.'

Jack slammed the table and said that was complete nonsense and so began a shouting match, which only ended when Noel calmed everyone down and said there had, perhaps, been a misunderstanding.

'The very fact that you were able to escape back to Switzerland shows that Siegfried is to be trusted. I cannot tell you how pleased London are: I understand Tom Gilbey and Barney Allen are fighting over who should take credit for his recruitment.'

'It should be Jack?'

'Of course, Sophia, of course.'

'I cannot tell you how remarkable he is, Basil: as a policeman and a barge deckhand, he wasn't just playing those parts – he actually *became* those people! He was utterly persuasive.'

Basil nodded, as if he was persuaded too. 'When I was number two in Bucharest, many years ago, I became quite pally with my French opposite number from the Deuxième Bureau and he had quite a thing about using actors and actresses as espionage agents. He always said a convincing disguise is one quarter in how you look and three quarters in the mind, and actors tend to be jolly good at that. London are rather keen for us to sign Siegfried up.'

There was a long silence: Noel said there'd need to be a much longer debrief and perhaps tomorrow they could start writing a detailed report and then the long silence returned, punctuated only by the sound of a dog barking in the far distance along with the slow ticking of a clock on the mantelpiece.

Basil cleared his throat and when he looked up at them his eyes seemed to have filled with tears and he was gripping a pencil tightly between his two hands.

'I'm afraid…' He stopped and coughed again. 'I'm afraid that I have to give you some most appalling news.'

Epilogue

Poland
May 1945

It took Max and Raisa three days to leave the forest.

They eventually found their way to the edge of it, from where they could see the house that looked like a cowshed in the middle of a cornfield. They watched it for a while from a safe distance, not because they believed their mother would still be there, but more because it was where they'd last seen her and although neither said as much to the other, it was somehow their last ever memory of her.

They carried on from there, uncertain of where they were heading. They travelled at night, keeping to the hedgerow and forests, only occasionally venturing out to walk along a country lane and then only when the night was at its darkest.

They'd been walking for two nights when they came to a small village with steep slopes on either side and as far as they could tell there was no way round it so they started down the dirt track running through it. Within seconds they were surrounded by a group of half a dozen men who couldn't have been more menacing.

Who were they, the men demanded to know? And what were they doing here – why were they trying to break into their homes?

Gripping each other's hand, the children told them they were Mieczysław and Janina Wójcik from Krakow and they were heading home.

From where?

The children hesitated and the men began to rough Max up. It was at that point that Raisa called out 'Max' and one of the men spotted her using a different name and announced they'd caught two Jewish children and they knew what to do with them.

They dragged the children along the dirt track, punching them as they did so and just as someone said they should take them into the forest, there was the low rumble of a heavy vehicle approaching. The dirt track vibrated and then the bright head-lights illuminated a large truck pulling up in front of them, with shouting coming from it. The group of men disappeared into the shadows, leaving Max and Raisa standing on their own, terrified and blinded by the headlights, clutching on to each other.

The men who climbed out of the truck were dressed in a uniform the children hadn't seen before and the man who told them to come over spoke in Polish but with a foreign accent.

It was the same questions as before – who were they, what were they doing here – but this time less menacing, and when they both started crying the soldiers told them not to worry and said to come and sit down in the cab of the truck, where they gave them biscuits and water.

'You mustn't worry: the Germans are gone, finished! The Red Army is in charge now!'

Raisa explained how they'd been hiding in a forest for nearly two years and had started to run out of food so had decided to leave and these men had stopped them and thought they were Jews and…

Max told Raisa to stop, but by now an officer had come over and was listening intently along with the other men and the soldier who spoke good Polish said, 'Ah, Leytenant Marshak… looks like we've found two more of your lot here.'

The young officer smiled and in halting Yiddish told them to tell him their story.

–

The Red Army unit that had saved them was from the 110th Rifle
Division based in Krakow. They took them back to the city and
Leytenant Marshak – they were to call him Mikhail Danielovich –
assumed personal responsibility for them: they were given clothes
and their own room in the barracks and a Red Army doctor
checked them over.

No sooner had they arrived in Krakow than the children
insisted they had to get to Switzerland. Their father was there,
they said: he'd be waiting for them. Leytenant Marshak told them
he couldn't look after them for ever: soon his unit would be
moving on. But as for going to Switzerland – that would
be impossible: he explained how it was so far away and very
difficult to get into and the war was still going on. They should
stay in Krakow, he said, there were people coming back to the
city who could look after them. Or there were refugee camps for
Jewish children in Italy… maybe…

But Max and Raisa were having none of it. They had to go:
their father would be waiting for them. If the Russians couldn't
help them, they'd walk to Switzerland. Leytenant Marshak told
them he understood, but they were to wait.

They waited until the middle of May. A week before, there'd
been much celebration in the city as the war in Europe ended.
The following week Leytenant Marshak brought a man to see
Max and Raisa. He'd already told them about him: Polkovnik
Krupkin was a very important man, a Polkovnik was senior
colonel in the NKGB, no less. His family knew Polkovnik
Krupkin's family from Minsk. He was a distant cousin. He was
risking his job helping them.

Polkovnik Krupkin turned out to be much older than the
Leytenant. His uniform was of a better quality than the ones
they'd seen around the barracks and on his shoulder were three
stars and two stripes, which they realised made him important. He
spoke quietly, his Yiddish more fluent than the young Leytenant's.

He listened in silence to their story, sitting very still and
occasionally looking down at the ground and then smoothing his
steel grey hair and fiddling with his collar. When they'd finished

talking, he held their hands and talked quietly: he could arrange for them to live in the Soviet Union. Maybe Minsk, where he was from. They'd be looked after, he said: after all that had happened, children like them should grow up under socialism. In due course they could try and contact their father, but they must understand that was so complicated and...

But they both shook their heads and said they'd only go to Switzerland, where their father would be waiting for them. If he couldn't help they'd walk there, even if it took a week. Polkovnik Krupkin nodded as if he was expecting that response and said it would take far longer than a week and it was still dangerous. But he'd do his best to help, though they weren't to tell anyone of his involvement. *Not a word!*

'I'll arrange all the paperwork: Mikhail Danielovich will be authorised to escort you to the Soviet Legation in Berne, which is the capital of Switzerland. I have a colleague there, Commissar Stepanov.'

'And will he know where our father is?'

Polkovnik Krupkin shrugged and smiled.

'If anyone can find your father, it will be Arkady.'

Author's Note

Agent in Peril is a work of fiction, so any similarities between characters in the book and real people are unintended and should be regarded as purely coincidental.

Inevitably there are a few exceptions to this, which will be obvious in most cases, though I've also featured some lesser-known real people either as characters in the book or by referring to them. An example of this is Walter Albath, the head of the Gestapo in Düsseldorf.

To ensure my books feel as accurate and as authentic as possible I do try, where possible, to use real locations and buildings which existed in that period – for example towns, government buildings and embassies, hotels and railway stations. By and large, if I name the location of somewhere in the book then it is more likely than not to correspond to the actual location during the war. The same applies to military units.

The plot of *Agent in Peril* is similarly substantially based on real events and I hope it is useful if I refer to some of those now.

The PZL.37 – the Polish bomber also known as the *Łoś* and first referred to in the prologue – was developed in Poland and began service with the Polish Air Force in 1938 and was a very highly regarded medium bomber. It ceased production once the war began, but a number of the aircraft were captured by the Romanians, with Germany and the Soviet Union also getting hold of some.

The transmitting and receiving devices – the Tatra box – used in the plot in connection with the PZL.37 and subsequently by the RAF is entirely fictional.

The Ruhr bombing campaign was indeed carried out between March and July 1943. Also based on fact are the issues raised in the book around accuracy – along with the dreadful toll on RAF aircrew – and the debate between the RAF's preference for strategic bombing as opposed to the precision bombing strategy preferred by the United States.

The references in Chapter 6 to the August 1941 Bomber Command report on the effectiveness of raids on Europe and the 1943 Area Bombing Directive and the authorisation for a Combined Bombing Offensive in the Ruhr valley are also historically accurate.

The general references to which German cities were bombed along with the targets within them is broadly accurate, although the raids described in the book are mostly fictional. Every town or city in the Ruhr mentioned in *Agent in Peril* was bombed at some stage in 1943 by the RAF. I decided not to refer to the bombing of the Möhne, Edersee and Sorpe dams – better known as the Dam Buster raid – because even though they were carried out in mid May 1943 I felt they'd be a diversion from the plot. However, in Chapter 25 Barney Allen is an observer on an RAF Lancaster from 617 Squadron – the Dam Busters squadron – on a bombing mission over Mannheim. That squadron was indeed based at RAF Scampton in Lincolnshire (where the Dam Busters raid was launched from) and although Barney's mission was a fictious one, Mannheim was a target of the RAF during the war.

I'd like to express my gratitude to Osprey Publishing for providing me with an early proof of *The Ruhr 1943: The RAF's Brutal Fight for Germany's Industrial Heartland*, which was most useful in my research and is a book I'd recommend to anyone wanting to know more about that campaign.

It's important to mention the role Polish pilots played in the RAF during the war. Nearly a hundred and fifty Polish pilots escaped the Nazi invasion and made their way to the United Kingdom and are recognised as some of its most effective pilots, not least during the Battle of Britain when the Polish 302 and 303 squadrons were particularly highly regarded.

Even today – perhaps even more so today – discussions of events in Poland during the war and different allegiances are mired in controversy. Nonetheless I thought it would be helpful if I briefly outlined the role of the different organisations referred to in *Agent in Peril*.

At the outset I should say that there's no question that full responsibility for the atrocities and brutality of the Nazis in Poland and the murder of six million of its citizens – three million of them Jewish – is that of the Germans. But having said that, there was some collaboration and, more to the point, some organisations and individuals opposed to the Nazis that were also extremely anti Semitic. It is important to understand this in the context of the plot.

The Armia Krajowa, or Home Army, was the main resistance organisation Poland and owed its allegiance to the Polish Underground State, and through it to the Polish Government in Exile based in London. The AK was the largest resistance organisation in Nazi Europe with nearly half a million members and it covered a wide range of political views. Some elements were left-wing, centrists and liberals and committed to democracy, others were on the far-right and were known for betraying Jews, which explains the distrust many Jews had of the AK.

There were other resistance groups too, separate from the AK, such as the socialist People's Guard and the People's Army, which owed their allegiance to the Soviet Union.

Żegota was an organisation established by the Polish Underground State with the specific purpose of helping Jews in Poland. The courage of the people involved in Żegota cannot be overstated. It's believed that around one hundred and twenty thousand Polish Jews survived the war in Poland outside of the German camps (with a further two hundred thousand surviving by fleeing east) and Żegota is thought to be responsible for saving around half of them.

The Poznań Group, which is at the heart of the plot, is entirely fictional.

The details of the Warsaw ghetto used throughout *Agent in Peril* correspond very closely to actual events. The Nazis established some twelve hundred ghettos in occupied eastern Europe. They were primarily a place to confine and hold Jews prior to transporting them to extermination camps and also as places of forced labour. The Warsaw ghetto, set up at the end of 1940, was by far the largest of the ghettos. At its height, around four hundred and fifty thousand Jews were crammed into an area of around three and half square kilometres. Many of the ghetto's inhabitants were Jews deported to it from other parts of Poland, such as the Loszynskis from Poznań. At the end of July 1942, a two-month programme of mass deportations began, at the end of which 265,000 people had been deported to the Nazi death camp of Treblinka. Virtually all were murdered within hours of their arrival.

The fifty thousand Jews remaining in the ghetto knew it was only a matter of time before the Nazis returned, but when they did, they were prepared. Two resistance organisations had been established within the ghetto: the largest was the ZOB, the one featured in the book. The other resistance group was a smaller right-wing one, the ZZW. The ZOB comprised two main groupings, the left-wing Zionists and the secular, socialist Bund. A cousin of mine, Yitzhak Sukniek, was a leading fighter in the ZOB and is credited with a number of 'kills' of Nazi troops during the Uprising. He was killed trying to escape from the ghetto at the end of Uprising. He was twenty-three.

In Chapter 2, Sophia visits the headquarters of the International Committee of the Red Cross on Avenue de la Paix in Geneva. She fails to persuade them to investigate the war crimes of her husband. Sadly, this was not atypical: the ICRC was quite selective in what war crimes it chose to investigate during the Second World War and they had a particularly poor record in monitoring the Nazi's treatment of Jews.

Earlier in Chapter 2 Sophia visits Bank Leu on Paradeplatz in Geneva. This bank existed until 2007 and during the Second

World War was one of many Swiss banks used by Nazis to deposit money or other valuables they'd stolen.

Chapter 20 is set primarily in Austria and I refer to it as such. In fact, once the Nazis took over Austria in 1938 it was subsumed into the Third Reich and ceased to exist as an independent country, being known as 'Ostmark' until 1942 and after that as the Alpine and Danube Region.

The British Embassy in Berne was based on Thunstrasse during the war and that is still its location.

In Chapter 32 we meet the Chargé d'Affaires at the then unofficial Polish Legation in Berne, Aleksander Ładoś and his deputy, Juliusz Kühl. Both men existed in real life and the legation was based at 20 Elfenstrasse and did owe its allegiance to the Polish Government in Exile in London. Along with other staff at the Legation and members of the Swiss Jewish community, Ładoś and Kühl were instrumental in saving hundreds of Jews by issuing passports, some from other countries.

Currencies and their relative value are tricky to get across in a novel. Broadly, I've based £1 in 1938 on being the equivalent of (just under) £69 in 2021 and $1 being worth $18.55 today. I also work on the basis of £1 (during the war) being worth around 12 Reichsmarks.

I'd like to express my sincere thanks and appreciation to the many people who've helped bring about the publication of this book. First and foremost, my agent, Gordon Wise, and his colleagues at Curtis Brown. Gordon has been enormously supportive over a number of years and continues to be an enormous help. My publishers, Canelo, couldn't have been more impressive with the manner in which they've handled the first of the Wolf Pack novels and before that the Prince series and the re-issuing of the Spy Masters novels. As ever, Michael Bhaskar and Kit Nevile and indeed the whole team at Canelo have been thoroughly professional, supportive and encouraging throughout the writing and publication process. My thanks too to Jo Gledhill for her skilful copy-edit, and to everyone who helped me with aspects of the book and answered seemingly odd questions as I was writing it.

And finally, to my family – especially my wife, Sonia, my daughters and their partners and my grandsons – for their encouragement, understanding and love.

Alex Gerlis
London
January 2022